Praise for th

Awful Intent

"Grabs you by the throat until the thrilling ending. All too true of what can happen in rural law enforcement."

—Deputy Sheriff Jared Johnson

"An engaging story about law and order in the west, complete with gun battles, aerial stunts and a hero just out for a hike."

—Police Sergeant Louise Speth

"WOW! Brown has outdone himself on this one. His books are always interesting and entertaining, but this one added a current twist to a captivating plot."

—Sheriff Gary Ogilvie, Ret.

Bad Penny

"A non-stop page turner . . . there's nothing quite like finding redemption through taking on a gang of scumbags. Bad Penny is intense."

—Larry Correia
New York Times Bestselling Author

"John Brown understands trouble makers and misfits. A Green Beret against a drug cartel, hardly a fair fight. Bad Penny will keep your attention and raise your pulse rate."

—Lieutenant Colonel Marcus Custer
U.S. Army Special Forces, Ret.

"An excellent attempt-at-redemption story set in a hard land with a cast of characters from all along the good-guy bad-guy continuum."

—Deputy Sheriff Mark Lee

JOHN D. BROWN

AWFUL INTENT

A THRILLER

AWFUL INTENT

Published by Blacksword Enterprises, LLC

ISBN 13: 978-1-940427-13-3

ISBN 10: 1-940427-13-4

First edition: March, 2016

For Eric Allen,
keeper of skins and bones

Contents

1

Runner

FRANK WAS SITTING in the shade and scent of a pine atop a knoll in the desert wilderness of Southern Utah when the man crested the hill on the far side of the dry creek bed. The man was medium height, medium build; he had dark hair, brown skin, and a little goatee. He was probably in his late twenties, early thirties. He glanced back, fearful and wide-eyed, then rushed down through the sparse pinyon pines and junipers on the steep, sunbaked slope.

The man had no smart phone for tunes, no fanny pack, no water. No jogging shoes or shorts. He wore no sunglasses. These were all things you'd want if you were out on a jaunt, enjoying the desert wilds. Instead, he was in long pants and a red-checkered, short-sleeved shirt that was ripped up one side. He was taking desperate strides. He glanced back again, up at the crest of the hill.

Frank's binoculars rested on top of his pack. A few feet beyond that lay a large collared lizard that had either taken Frank for a rock or assumed it was safe to come join the man party. The lizard was a fabulous specimen with a foot-long turquoise body, a black and white collar, and a sand-colored head.

Frank grabbed his binoculars and glassed the man. He had scrapes and blood on his arm. Scrapes and blood on his face. At least, it looked like blood.

The main predators down in this area were mountain lions. Could have been a lion that had slashed him up. Or maybe the man and a few others had been back in the canyons of the White Cliffs which towered to the north and east of Frank. Maybe they'd had an accident. Maybe someone had fallen from some height. Except the man wasn't wearing climbing gear either. So maybe there'd been some other kind of accident.

Frank gathered himself to stand and call out when the woman topped the rise. She was medium height, slender, with dark hair pulled into one long braid down her back and brown skin. She too was in her late twenties or early thirties. She was in a short-sleeved shirt, long pants, and sturdy shoes.

Unlike the man, she did not glance back. She marked the man's path and took off after him. Frank glassed her. She had a face like an angry storm. A face hell-bent on violence.

Something a few hundred feet above the knoll flashed in the sun. Frank looked up. It took him a moment, but then he spotted, of all things, a four-rotor drone, and he realized he'd heard its soft whine earlier, but the breeze through the pine needles had masked it. He squinted and saw a black thing mounted on the bottom, which was probably some type of camera. Frank looked back at the two individuals running down the slope.

The woman ran on a line that would take her a bit to the side of the man, like she was expecting him to turn upstream, and her course would allow her to intercept him at the bottom of the hill.

Then a white pickup rounded the corner of the hill a few hundred yards downstream of the man and woman. It was driving on a scratch of dirt road that sometimes merged with the streambed and sometimes ran to the side. There were two men in the cab, and Frank realized the woman wasn't trying to cut the running man off—she was trying to herd him, drive him like a deer into those two.

The man didn't see the pickup. He couldn't down in the snaky dry river bed because a bend stood between him and the truck. He probably couldn't hear the truck either over his own labored breath. And he wouldn't see them. Fear didn't bring you nuance. Fear brought you only the facts in front of your face. And sometimes not even that.

The woman and man reached the dry, sandy streambed at about the same time, she about ten yards upstream.

The man looked at her, then ran the other way, downstream, toward the white pickup.

He ran ten, twenty, thirty yards, and then he must have finally heard the pickup over his labored breath, heard it coming up the draw, because he stopped, then tried to turn back up the hill. But the woman was there. She was fast and strong and caught up to him before he was three strides up the slope. She launched herself onto his back like a cougar. But instead of biting down on his neck, she took him in a vicious one-armed choke.

Her weight pulled the man up and back. 120 or 130 extra pounds clinging to one's back tended to do that. The man lost his balance and fell.

She fell with him, but didn't let go. Her arm was like iron around his neck, strangling him.

The man struggled to rise, but the woman yanked him down. He tried to pull her arm away, failed, then punched his fist up, past his ear, and into her face.

Her head rocked back.

He struck again, and a third time. Three solid blows that dazed her and loosened her grip.

The man struggled free, but before he could take two steps, the woman rolled up and sprang at him again, entangling his legs and causing him to stumble to the ground.

Then the pickup came flying around the bend, a cloud of desert dust billowing up behind it. The truck roared up to the spot of the scuffle. The driver slammed on the brakes, and the truck came to a skidding halt. The doors to the cab flew open, and the two men jumped out. The passenger, a skinny whip of a man, grabbed a shovel from the pickup bed.

The running man kicked free of the woman and began to scramble away. He got to his feet, but he wasn't fast enough. The passenger flew at him. The shovel's steel flashed in the sun. Then the passenger struck the running man in the head from behind with the flat of the blade.

The running man stumbled into some loose rock and went down with a heavy crash.

Then the two men from the truck fell on him, punching, then restraining him, but the blow had knocked him unconscious. Or something worse.

Frank's skin prickled. His heartbeat picked up a notch. He was now on full alert.

The driver, a big guy with a caterpillar brow, hefted the running man over his shoulders, then carried him to the bed of the pickup. In the bed of the truck, the woman laid out a tarp that was silver on one side, blue on the other. The big guy thumped the running man into the middle of it. Then the three of them wrapped him in the tarp and fastened it with bungees.

The running man wasn't moving.

The woman and shovel man got in the cab on the passenger's side. The driver slipped his muscular body and caterpillar brow behind the wheel on the other. Then they turned the truck around and gunned it back down the dry draw. When they got to the mouth of the streambed, they headed south.

Frank blew out a tense breath and collected his thoughts. He knew there were a number of troubled-youth rehabilitation programs that operated in the area. But he was pretty sure none of them employed the shovel technique as a means of correction. And the running man hadn't been exactly a youth.

The spectacular cliffs and canyons in this area would make it a dandy place for an executive team building weekend. But it wasn't the weekend. And, again, Frank didn't know of any bonding exercises that included being knocked in the head with tempered steel.

Predator, accident, and wilderness program went off the list. That didn't leave too many options. None of them were good. And he didn't think that mob would be all that happy to find out there'd been a witness to their desert crime.

The whine above became louder, and Frank remembered the drone. He slowly looked up. The drone, still high above the knoll, had moved closer to Frank's position. It was almost directly above him now, hovering, the camera pointing straight down.

2
Call

FRANK DIDN'T MOVE. His shorts and brown Cowboy Donut tee-shirt weren't exactly camo, but the mind saw what it expected to see. And if Frank didn't move, whoever was on the other end of that video feed could easily see nothing but desert rock in the shade of the pine.

A breeze gusted, and the drone slid a few yards to the side.

Frank held motionless, hoping that camera didn't zoom in, letting the operator see his red day pack, or the white sock tops coming out of his boots, or the fact that Frank generally didn't look like a rock or a stick.

The breeze gusted again through the pine. The whine of the drone's rotors climbed in pitch, and the little machine took off almost straight north to the White Cliffs, the opposite direction the pickup had gone.

Frank watched it, knowing some cameras had great range, and kept still.

He had been on his way to Los Angeles to hook up with his sister Kim and nephew Tony. He thought he'd be able to just drive through this area, taking the sights in from his car. About sixty miles north, he'd stopped in Circleville, the town where the Old West train robber Butch Cassidy had grown up. He figured he'd continue on without stopping, but the majesty of the staircase cliffs of Southern Utah had stopped him dead in his tracks, forcing him out of the Nova again and again to stand and let the power of the views roll over him. Purple and white thunderheads far to the south had only made it more spectacular.

The views had awoken a desire in him that he could not resist. Not after spending six years in a cement box. If he'd learned one thing during his years in the fine penal establishment in Coalinga, California, it was that you appreciated every day you spent outside the box.

Frank had enjoyed a great career in the U.S. Army's Special Forces as an 18B, a weapon's sergeant. He'd decided not to re-up so he could come home and save his marriage, but he'd been too late, and Blanca had left him anyway. And then he'd made the dumb decision to fall in with a piece of work called Simon Haas, which had led him to prison. And prison had led him to insight.

And so Frank had found a dirt road leading into the wilderness. He'd found a little trailhead, and after driving a bit, he set out on foot, exploring the desert hills, a slot canyon, and finally this knoll with its stunning view.

The Grand Staircase was a series of cliffs and mesas about ninety miles wide and sixty long. It started just over the Arizona border, miles north of the Grand Canyon, with the Chocolate Cliffs. They were followed by a relatively flat area a few miles wide. Next came the Vermillion Cliffs, followed by another few miles of desert hills dotted with juniper and pinyon and scrub. Then came the White Cliffs follow by another flat piece, which was followed by the steps for the Grays, Pinks, and Blues. It was a multi-colored stairway for giants, with ragged lines of cliffs rising hundreds of feet into the air.

Frank expected the White Cliffs, the ones to the north and east of his current position, would be spectacular in the slant light of sunset and the distant storm. And so he'd settled down with his pack a few hours early to watch the show. He'd seen a huge golden eagle. Watched two crows harry a hawk. He thought he'd seen some big horn sheep in the distance, but they'd moved too fast, and he couldn't tell if they'd just been mule deer. A pink paraglider in a trike had flown by. The trike looked like a three-wheeled go-kart with a big fan on the back, hanging from a thin parachute. Happily, the trike soon buzzed away, leaving Frank alone again.

As the time passed, the blue sky, the heat and red rock, and the whisperings of the breeze in the juniper and pine had washed over him, filling him with a quiet glory. But all that was broken now by the man in the tarp.

The drone continued north at a brisk pace, dwindling to nothing more than a speck.

Frank scanned the skies for other vehicles, but saw none, and figured he was safe. He let out a sigh.

The large collared lizard cocked its head, listening.

Frank said to his companion, "Could be that man had it coming."

The lizard cocked its head farther.

"Maybe he was a fugitive from the law. Maybe those were correctional officers."

They *had* used a drone.

Frank said, "Or maybe that was some poor sap that ran across some marijuana grow."

Frank had come out to commune with his maker and enjoy the show, but that wasn't going to happen now. Murder kind of messed up the effect. He thought about his options. He could get out on the road and then call 911. But there were a lot of roads out here, and who knew which one the pickup would take? If he really wanted to make sure the authorities hooked up with the Shovel Gang, he'd need to keep them in his sights, which would bring its own dangers. But Frank didn't see any other way.

He stood with his pack and turned to the lizard. "You with me? Or are you all show?"

The lizard froze. And then it must have finally realized Frank wasn't a tree because it suddenly shot out down the hill, kicking up bits of leaves and sand. Frank watched it streak its turquoise self down the slope and disappear under some rocks.

"Typical pretty boy," Frank said and scanned the north sky. The drone was almost to the face of the White Cliffs, but it was so tiny now, Frank lost it as soon as he found it.

He thought about that guy in his blue-tarp shroud. If those three had been correctional officers, he'd soon see a chopper and lots of vehicles with flashing lights. And then he wouldn't have to call, even though he sure as heck wouldn't be coming back to this spot.

But the law enforcement angle was a very long bet, and so Frank hustled around the crown of the knoll to the other side. He found no choppers in the distance, no sirens in the desert or flashing lights. There was only the pickup's dust trail, heading south. And he was fairly sure those three weren't zooming the guy off to the hospital.

From what Frank could see, that road would lead them past the foothills, then cut west, taking them not too far from where he'd parked his Nova and where his cell phone lay.

They had a more circuitous route. Frank, on the other hand, had a straight line to his car. He drained his water bottle, then began to run down the side of the knoll with big loping strides that took him through a scattering of desert cedar trees and past an outcropping of rock that looked like a rabbit's head. He loped his way down to the valley floor, then set out in a fast jog.

Highway 89 lay a few miles away. In one direction, it led to the border town of Kanab. In the other direction, it led deeper into Utah. Frank needed to see which way the pickup would go, but it was going to be mighty hard if he was way out here.

He lengthened his stride, ran up and down two more hills, and reached the flat. The southern Utah desert in this area was a world of sandy, pale orange dirt dotted with scrub. He imagined when the wind blew, residents would find the sand drifted on their porches like snow.

He ran over the orange dirt, passing a thorny greasewood, a swath of salt brush, and green rabbit brush with small yellow flowers. The sand kicked up onto his legs and fell into his shoes. He followed an opening through a thirty-yard patch of sparse prickly pear, then crossed a section of bare sandstone as wide as a parking lot.

Frank could do a six minute mile on hard pavement without much trouble at all, but this sandy dirt was slowing him down. In the distance, he could see the dust trail of the pickup. It still hadn't made its turn. So maybe he'd beat it. Then the direction of the pickup changed. It was now heading toward the Nova.

Frank kept running. He was going all out, streaking through salt brush and juniper, knowing that even though it was sparse, there was enough of it between him and the pickup to keep him hidden. Then he topped a little rise and saw the gray ribbon of Highway 89 in the distance, a little green car motoring along. He saw the pickup and its smoking dust trail.

If he struck out now, they would probably see him hoofing it through the brush. They would see his direction and draw a mental line right back to the knoll. And if that happened, he didn't think things would turn out well. So he took up a position in the shade of a desert cedar, his lungs working, and watched as the pickup blew past the Nova in a cloud of dust, followed the dirt road to the highway. It slowed, its brake lights illuminating.

From this height he could see into the pickup bed. The man in the tarp was still there.

Then the truck pulled onto the asphalt, turned north, and accelerated.

Frank sprinted for his car, his pack smacking his back, the sand flying, the scrub scratching at his bare legs below his shorts.

A minute or so later, he broke out onto the dirt road and hoofed it to the Nova, which, thanks to the pickup, had a fine coating of dust on it. He pulled his keys out, wishing the doors had remote entry, but he hadn't installed it on the old gal, and remote entry was nothing more than a Star Trek dream back in the '70s.

He inserted the key, unlocked the door, and threw himself and his pack in. He closed the door, turned her over, and the Nova roared to life. It roared extra loud because the muffler was shot. He'd been hoping to get a quick repair in Kanab. No time for repairs now.

Frank threw her into gear, cranked the wheel, and floored it. The Nova made a nice spinning U-turn in a cloud of dust and noise, then shot out along the dirt road. He shifted up and said to her, "You're doing great."

He'd been working on her. Frank and this car were on a journey together. And her new 350 aluminum LS horses that he'd pulled out of a wrecked Corvette were performing just fine.

The car rumbled along the dirt road, dust billowing behind it. Then Frank came to the highway. He slowed, looked left and right, geared down, turned the direction the pickup had gone, then punched it.

The Nova accelerated, the rpms climbing high. He shifted again, and the Nova roared up the road, shedding dust.

The white pickup was nowhere to be seen.

Frank pushed his speed higher, far above the legal limit, and cranked his window down, letting the wind rush in to cool off the hot interior.

He followed the highway along a straight stretch for about two miles, and then it began to curve and bend through and over a number of rocky hills. He passed three vehicles coming the other direction, skirted some guy pedaling along with his bicycle fitted with saddlebags on the front and back for long-distance trekking, then roared around a bend and saw the pickup far ahead. It disappeared over a rise.

Frank pulled out his cell phone, glanced down, dialed 911, then looked up again. He gave the Nova more gas.

The dispatcher answered.

Frank said, "I need to report an aggravated assault. Maybe murder. I don't know the victim's condition. He was hit in the head with a shovel."

Frank topped the rise, saw the pickup go around a bend.

"Where are you, sir?"

"I'm on Highway 89, going north. I just passed milepost number seventy-five. The victim is wrapped in a blue tarp in the bed of a white Ford F-series pickup, which I am following and have in my visual."

Frank raced around the bend and saw the pickup a short distance ahead, cruising at good-citizen speed, just three folks out on a pleasure drive, keeping the laws of the land and transporting a corpse in the back.

Frank slowed to match their speed.

The dispatcher said, "Are you hurt?"

"I am fine," Frank said.

"Is the victim hurt?"

"He's wrapped in a tarp. He might be dead."

"The closest hospital is in Kanab. You need to turn around."

"I am not in the pickup carrying the man in the tarp. There are two men and a woman in the pickup. They are the ones that assaulted the victim. I don't know where they are taking him. That's why I'm following."

"Hold on," the dispatcher said. There was a pause, in which he assumed she was putting out a call on the police radio.

She came back on. “Sir, where are you now?”

“I just passed milepost seventy-six.”

“What is your name?”

He hesitated a moment. This was it. A name would lead to an address, and that would lead to his stellar record, and there would be all sorts of questions about what relationship an ex-con would have with the folks in the white pickup.

“Frank Shaw,” he said.

“Mr. Shaw, you said you witnessed the assault?”

“Yes, I did.” And with those words he knew he was going to be asked to give a statement, in person, and that the officer would take one look at him and his tattoos and figure he was part of the murder club.

If it came to court, those three in the pickup could feed their defense lawyer a line of bull claiming Frank had done the deed. That they were actually fleeing him. Storms had been washing over the area. More summer rain was forecast, which meant all of the nice footprints that told the story clearly could easily be washed away. And that would leave one of him against three of them. Frank had no motive to brain that man, but with Frank’s history and the six degrees of Kevin Bacon crap, who knew what kind of connection a prosecuting attorney might devise?

He could hang up right now. He could say it was all a big mistake. He could turn off his cell phone and turn around and drive, without a care, to L.A.

“Mr. Shaw, can you see the license plate number?”

Frank could turn a blind eye to lots of things. Jaywalking, running stop signs, wearing socks with Crocs. But some things you just couldn’t let slide.

“Mr. Shaw?”

“Not yet,” he said. “But I soon will.”

3

Driver

FRANK EASED ONTO the accelerator, hoping that what the three in the cab would see was a motorist on a two-lane highway in a hurry. Unless they recognized the Nova. And that was a problem because a '71 Nova tended to stick out on today's roads.

He closed the distance to a few car lengths. He could see the heads of the two men and the woman up in the cab.

He read off the Utah plate number, then looked up.

The man on the passenger's side was watching him in the side mirror.

"We just passed milepost seventy-seven," Frank said.

The woman in the cab pulled out her cell phone and began to talk.

Frank said, "I'm going to ease back and follow from a safer distance."

"Mr. Shaw, can you give us a description of the people involved?"

The driver now glanced in his rearview mirror.

"Yeah," Frank said. "You got someone coming out?"

"Yes, we do."

Which meant Frank only had to keep them in his sights, and keep far enough away that if they decided he needed to be dissuaded, he had plenty of room to maneuver.

The woman in the cab now turned around and looked at Frank, talking on her cell phone like maybe she was giving a description, and Frank wondered. These folks had hunted a man down with boots on the ground and a drone to guide them. That meant they were organized, so how many were in on this? Was she now calling in reinforcements to help deal with Frank or just freaking out?

Maybe he could give her something to calm her nerves and make them conclude he wasn't a threat.

"Hang on," he said and slid his thumb over his phone's microphone.

He smiled big enough for the people in the cab to see, then began to laugh like the dispatcher had told him the funniest joke in the world. "You're kidding me," he said and let off the gas. "No way!" he said and laughed some more.

The Nova began to drop back.

"Hilarious," he said. He shook his head and did a big Santa ho-ho-ho.

The Nova dropped back more. The woman turned back around, then hung up her phone. The three in the cab had some kind of discussion, but the result of it didn't change anything. They didn't speed up, didn't slow down, didn't make any kind of move. They just kept cruising along, the driver and skinny shovel man checking their mirrors every so often to make sure he was still there.

A lot of discipline was being demonstrated up in that cab, which meant they either had decided he wasn't a threat, or they had a plan.

Frank played his comedy routine a few seconds more, then moved his thumb back off the microphone.

"Sorry," he said. "They were getting suspicious."

"Can you give me their descriptions, Mr. Shaw?"

Frank described the three people in the cab and the one in the bed of the pickup. He described the location of the incident, the events, the timing, and what they'd find there. He gave the details in good military fashion. He'd done plenty of surveillance and recon in his day. In fact, the solitude of sitting up on that knoll with his binoculars had brought back memories of the many missions he'd conducted in Afghanistan as a Green Beret. The only things he'd needed to be completely transported were a few folks wearing keffiyehs, the Middle Eastern head scarves, and a couple of decorative goats.

Frank shook his head. Those years in the service had been bright ones. And then he'd made a number of stupid decisions that had taken him out of the service of Uncle Sam and into the employment of someone who didn't have Sam's scruples. Frank let himself take a gig protecting the wrong kind of noun for the wrong kind of people, and that had landed him in prison. But that was all behind him now. Frank had a five-, ten-, and fifteen-year plan. This time he was going to do life right.

He passed mile eighty, crossed over the Virgin River, and soon after that saw signs announcing Mt. Carmel Junction, which wasn't really a town, but a couple of tourist stops around a turnoff. However, the turnoff was an important one, taking people to and from Zion's National Park. And because it was important, Frank figured a cop would be here, and he could hand all this over.

A few moments later, a gas station came into view. Then the little Best Western motel and a place called the Thunderbird Restaurant and Gift Shop. On the other side of the road was an RV park with lots of nice shade trees.

The pickup slowed, but it did not take the turnoff to Zion's. It rode straight through, past another little motel and gas station, and then was accelerating out of Mt. Carmel Junction on the other side. Frank followed, twenty seconds behind, passing the motel and gas station, then exiting and traveling along the farms running by the river and the cedar-dotted hills on either side.

There had been no law enforcement in Mt. Carmel Junction, nor anyone from the sheriff's, nor the Highway Patrol.

He picked up the phone and said to the dispatcher, "How far out are your people?"

"They're coming, Mr. Shaw. They should meet you in Orderville, just a few miles ahead."

Keeping one hand on the wheel, Frank pulled out the map he'd purchased at a gas station when he'd decided to stop and hike around a bit and found his position. The map had the outline of the county on it. There was one main road leading through the county. There was a lot of backcountry. Maybe that's where the law was.

He put the map on the passenger's seat and followed the pickup another five minutes to Orderville, a larger town, which took a whopping whole minute to breeze through. And still no cops.

He said to the dispatcher, "I just went through Orderville."

She said, "The sheriff is coming. Keep going on to Glendale."

It was possible that all law enforcement in the county had been called to some other big event, but he began to wonder.

The valley narrowed as he left Orderville, cutting out the view of the cliffs. He followed the pickup, which was still going an even three miles an hour under the speed limit. A blue minivan, a brown sedan, and a big yellow pickup all bunched up behind Frank, then moved out into the other lane and passed him. When they came to the pickup, they passed it too. As he drove, the dispatcher asked him where he was from, his destination, and confirmed his cell number. A few minutes later Frank was in Glendale, and there was still no cop.

"I don't see anyone," Frank said.

"Sheriff Hood is almost there," the dispatcher said.

Frank expected the pickup to blow through this tiny town as well, but it didn't. At the last cross-street, it slowed, then turned and headed up Glendale Bench Rd., which climbed out of the canyon Highway 89 followed.

About a minute later, Frank came to the cross-street and remembered seeing this place coming down. On the corner stood a house on a four-acre lot. And on that lot were rows and rows of old cars and trucks from what looked like the '40's and on. Not a junkyard, more like a memorial.

"I'm heading up the road," Frank said and turned.

"You're going to get into dirt road fairly quickly," the dispatcher said. "Are you in a four-wheel drive?"

"I'm in a '71 Nova."

"Storms are forecast. You don't want to be out there when it rains, Mr. Shaw."

"Flash floods?"

"Those can be a problem if you're down in a streambed, but the bigger issue is the clay in the road itself. When it gets wet, it makes the surface impossibly slick. Impassable. You will get stuck. Many four-wheelers can't even make it."

Frank said, "Where does this road lead?"

She said, "Into the wilderness area. There's a network of dirt roads out there that can take you all the way north and east into Garfield County. It's fairly remote. If you don't have a map, it's easy to get lost."

Frank thought remote was where he'd want to go if he had a dead man in the back. He also thought he didn't like how this was shaping up. Law enforcement wasn't anywhere to be seen, and now this little hit squad was leading him out into the backcountry.

"How good's the cell service out there?" he asked.

"It runs out real quick," she said.

The three in the pickup gunned it up the road that wound its way up and out of the valley. Frank followed, his Nova handling the climb and turns nicely. By now, they had to be thinking that Frank wasn't just another motorist.

He thought about what he would do if he had someone on his tail. Option one: try to lose them. Option two: make it so they can't follow. Option three: let them catch you at a place of your choosing, and then bury them. Frank wondered which it was.

He also wondered where in the Sam Hill the sheriff was.

He took a curve and then another, and then he crested the top of the climb. Up ahead, the asphalt ended, and a dirt road led into hills of juniper and pine that stretched out as far as he could see.

The pickup was way ahead, racing over the dirt road. Racing into an area where he wouldn't have cell coverage, where it would be really easy to set up and take out the lone driver in the car behind you without a soul being the wiser.

"I'm going to give it just a few more minutes," he said to the dispatcher. "See how it goes." Then the Nova thumped off the asphalt and onto the rumble of the dirt.

4

Off-Road

THE PICKUP HAD big tires with fat treads made for loose dirt. It had high suspension. And the driver was making the most of it, racing ahead of Frank. If Frank didn't keep up, he was going to lose them.

The Nova wasn't built for dirt, but Frank pushed it, winding up and down a section of cedar and sage hills. He came to a relatively straight stretch and saw the pickup at the far end going all out. Frank punched it and didn't start keeping pace until he was close to eighty. The pickup flew to the end of the stretch and cornered. Frank slowed, but misjudged how much the road bent, and he had to slam on the brakes and turn, slewing the back end of the car around. He straightened her out, geared down, gave her the gas, and accelerated.

He gunned it up and around another set of turns and across another straight stretch, but the pickup was outpacing him. He poured on the speed as much as he could, but gravel and dirt were tricky. Take a corner too fast, brake too hard, and the car would slide. Then it would catch on something, and flip, and he'd find himself meeting Jesus in a bunch of cedars.

He raced up the road, topped a hill, and saw them probably half a mile ahead, then he rumbled down the hill and lost them again. He thought that if they got too far ahead, he might be able to get some elevation to watch them and point the sheriff in the general direction, but the cedars and pine grew right up to the side of the road and cut visibility down to just a few dozen feet. Unless he got up on the slopes, he wasn't going to see much of anything.

Frank looked at his phone and saw he'd lost his cell signal, and he told himself he was going to stop on the next rise. He'd climb a tree if he had to. Except when he got to the next rise, he saw a side road shooting off the one he was on.

Frank slowed, then stopped a few yards before the fork in the road. Then he got out of his car and studied the dirt. Someone with truck-sized tires had skidded to a halt and turned onto the side road. The scraping on the surface of the dirt road was clear.

It could have been someone earlier today. But it looked like there was just a little more dust hanging in the air on the side road than one he was now on.

Frank was no Dudley Do-Right. Number one, he didn't have a horse. Number two, that man's voice was too high. But he could save the cops having to split up into two directions if he just verified the direction of the pickup at this fork.

So Frank got back into the Nova and followed the side road. A hundred yards later, the cedars gave way to a large open meadow of sage and grass. On the other side of the meadow, maybe a quarter mile away, was a barbed-wire fence. A little behind it were more trees. And in those trees stood a ranch house, a barn, and some other buildings.

Frank got out of the Nova with his binoculars and looked for his friends. He spotted a white pickup, but white pickups were about as common as grass in these parts. There was a chance he'd taken the wrong fork.

The road led across the meadow to a gate in the barbed-wire fence. The gate had a stone and mortar base built up on either side. From each of those bases rose a thick pine pole that had been oiled a fine yellow. Another pole lay across the top. There was a sign there. Frank glassed it.

The sign said Elkhorn Ranch. Above the lettering was mounted a large rack of elk antlers. Below it was the ranch's brand, something that looked like a mixture of a J and a P. Behind the gate were more cedar and pine followed by a canyon running between cliffs of orange and white.

Frank was thinking he might need to go back out to the main road to verify he'd made the right decision when a drone rose from the trees and began to fly in his direction. It rose to maybe two hundred feet, then hovered over the meadow, watching.

It was possible another group of people out here had both a white pickup and a drone. If Frank were a rancher, he supposed a drone would be a handy thing to search for cattle and coyotes. It would be a handy thing to search for big game. But another rancher wouldn't have sent the thing up to watch Frank. Another rancher wouldn't even be aware that Frank was around.

He suddenly became very wary. Put a drone up, and you could direct your people precisely to where they needed to go to circle round and sneak up behind your target. Maybe that's what they'd done with the man in the tarp.

Frank turned and scanned the cedars and pine. He listened. They had been far enough ahead of him to stop and drop two of their members off. Two against one would be a great ratio, especially if they had guns. On the other hand, if they thought they could take him out with a shovel, they were in for a surprise.

But they'd only drop a hit squad off if they thought he was some random citizen. How did they know he wasn't some off-duty deputy?

Frank decided they probably hadn't dropped anyone off because if he were in their shoes, he'd be far more worried about disposing of the body. It was a big if, but Frank decided not to withdraw. However, he wouldn't stay here forever. Sooner or later, they'd send out a crew.

He looked at the time on his cell phone and decided to give the sheriff seven minutes. Frank wasn't a Green Beret anymore. He wasn't the law. He was an employee of Walmart during graveyards and a cruller boy at Cowboy Donut in the wee hours of the morning after that. Which meant that in seven minutes, Doughnut Man Frank was going to pull back from his forward operating position.

While he waited, Frank glassed the ranch and drone and did periodic checks for the unlikely event that Caterpillar Brow and Shovel Man were indeed circling round.

He caught flashes of two other males at the ranch as well as the vague shadow of someone at a window, but nothing else. He walked a slow little patrol of his area, stopping and listening, and heard nothing but the whine of another paraglider far in the distance, one with a rainbow parachute.

By this time, six minutes and forty-five seconds had passed, and so he fetched the car keys out of his pocket and headed for the Nova. Just before he got to the driver's door, he heard the rumble of a vehicle. It was the deep rumble of a truck, and he wondered if the pickup had circled around, but then he saw the flashing police lights through the trees.

5
Sheriff

FRANK WATCHED THE white Ford Explorer turn into the dirt lane. The vehicle had Sheriff written in big letters on the side. A woman was driving it. She rolled up and parked a couple of car lengths behind the Nova, then killed the lights on top and got out.

She wore boots, dark pants with cargo pockets, a tan shirt, an ear piece for her mobile radio, and a dark baseball cap with "Sheriff" written large above "Kane County" across the front. She had a black ballistic vest underneath the shirt, giving her top a bulky look. Her duty belt held the normal gear—firearm, radio, pepper spray, a primary set of cuffs, and the rest.

She said, "Are you Mr. Shaw?"

Frank nodded. "Yes, I am. I think the pickup is in there."

"I'm Sheriff Hood," she said.

Sheriff Hood had some good height, probably around 5'10", and was in her early thirties. She had well-muscled arms and fine cheekbones and auburn hair that was tucked up under her cap. She was an attractive woman that didn't need much makeup and apparently didn't care to wear it here. He noticed she wasn't wearing any rings either. Maybe that was pure practicality. Or maybe Sheriff Hood was single.

Frank's lizard brain, the brain at the back, the powerful one which experts had said evolved first and took care of primal functions like food and sex and fighting off saber-tooth tigers, perked up at the possibility. But Frank's frontal brain, the neo-cortex, told the other guy to sit down.

The sheriff walked a few steps in front of her vehicle and motioned at his Nova. "Is this your vehicle?"

"Yes, ma'am," Frank said.

She looked at his license plate. "Wyoming," she said.

"Yes, ma'am."

"We ran a search but couldn't find you in Rock Springs."

Why had they run a search? He said, "I'm unlisted."

She nodded.

And Frank figured if they'd run a search on that bit of data, they'd tried to pull up more.

"Mr. Shaw, you want to tell me what's going on?"

Frank pushed off the Nova, but didn't approach her. He knew what he looked like. And if they were running searches, they might have a number of his key facts already—ex-con, ex-military, someone who had been trained to kill and had proven he was willing to break the law. He didn't want to alarm her. And the best way to do that was to keep a safe distance.

He said, "I don't know these people from Adam. As I told the dispatcher, I was just passing through to visit relatives in L.A. I set up on a knoll to watch the sunset."

She held up a finger for him to hold and said, "Roger that." She waited and said, "Ten twenty-five." Waited some more and said, "Thanks, Cathy."

Frank noticed she was wearing an ear piece. She must have received some communication through her radio.

A moment later, she turned back to him and said, "You can continue."

He said, "I can repeat everything I told the dispatcher, but I think the key thing you've got to know is that there's a man who's in pretty bad shape. If he's not dead, I guarantee he's going to need medical help."

"We've got EMTs coming," she said, then looked up. "Is that a drone?"

"Yes, ma'am," Frank said. "They used a drone to hunt their man down."

She said, "I got the report from dispatch, but I want to hear it from the source."

So Frank gave her the abbreviated version. She nodded, listened, and asked questions, and then someone on her radio must have called again because she held up another finger.

When she finished, Frank said, "So are you going to go talk to them?"

"We're going to wait," she said.

"A man might die."

"A man might," she replied.

And she was just going to let him?

She saw his expression. "Mr. Shaw, if you interpreted what you saw correctly, at the very least we've got aggravated assault, aggravated kidnapping, maybe murder."

He nodded.

"As good as I am, we've only got one of me. And there are at least three of them."

That wasn't true: there was also Frank. In the right circumstances, he might count for two. But she wouldn't see it that way. Nor would he if he were in her shoes. He'd see a tattooed ex-con and wonder why such a fine upstanding citizen would be way out here in the middle of nowhere with a threesome who assaulted people with shovels. He'd be trying to make a connection between Frank's past and the current situation. It would be almost impossible not to.

He motioned at the ranch and said, "It looks like a big spread."

"Elkhorn is probably close to 4,000 acres."

"Hoo," Frank said. "That's a lot of land. Is this the only way in?"

"No," she said. "That canyon is long and has a number of trails heading out of it. You get up on the flat, and there are a number of roads there too."

"So if they were wanting to hide something . . ." Frank said and trailed off.

"If they are wanting to hide something, they're going to have a really good head start."

She smiled, and Frank couldn't tell what that meant. Was she blatantly giving Caterpillar Brow and his gang time? She'd taken her own sweet time to join in on the fun. Or was she truly playing it safe and waiting for backup, and her calm, friendly behavior was her way of putting him at ease?

Frank looked up at the drone. He looked back down at the sheriff.

"Your department have any drones?"

"Nope," she said. "Not yet."

"You want me to hang around?"

"I think you'd better," she said. "We'll want a full report."

He didn't respond. He'd already given two reports.

Then a guy with big blond hair down to his shoulders came bicycling around the side of the ranch house. He was on a woman's bike, maybe a three-speeder, with a basket on the front. He pedaled down through the trees to the gate with the elk horns on it, bounced across the cattle guard, then began to follow the road which ran through the meadow towards Frank and the sheriff.

Sheriff Hood asked, "Is that one of the people you saw?"

Frank said, "I've never seen him before in my life."

The long-hair on the woman's bike waved at them and continued on like he was coming over for a happy visit with the neighbors, except there weren't any neighbors out here. Not unless you counted lizards and snakes.

"Seems friendly enough," said Sheriff Hood.

Frank said, "I wonder if that's what the guy in the tarp said."

6

Long-Hair

SHERIFF HOOD PULLED a little notebook out of her pants pocket and said, "You want to give me the description of the people involved again?"

Frank told her about Caterpillar Brow, Shovel Man, and the woman. He described the victim's red-checkered shirt, his height and build. The sheriff nodded and wrote it all down. Then she clicked her pen and put it and her notebook back.

She pointed at the shark tattoo on Frank's calf and said, "What's that one for?"

Frank looked down. "It's from an earlier time, back when I worked for Uncle Sam."

"Special Forces, right?"

Was she guessing? Or had they indeed run his information, and then run the results of that search in another government database? A nice big one.

"Yeah," he said.

"I thought the Army frowned on tattoos."

"They do. Then they don't. Then they do."

The sheriff nodded. "So shark, water. Were you a SEAL?"

"Oh, Lord, no," he said. "SEALs are part of the Navy. Special Forces, which are also known as Green Berets, are part of the Army. They're the folks that get the work done."

"SEALs aren't special forces?"

"Both groups fall under the umbrella of special *operations* forces."

"But you do the same thing?"

"I don't do anything anymore," he said. "But no. SEALs are primarily a direct action force. They show up. They kill the carbon-based life form that's the target of the mission. Or rescue it. Or blow something up. Then they get out.

"Green Berets, on the other hand, are more long-term. They focus on unconventional warfare and foreign internal defense, supporting and training a local resistance force, or the government troops, whichever ones are the good guys. Sometimes the types of missions overlap. For example, both groups do special reconnaissance, sneaking in behind enemy lines and seeing things they shouldn't. But SEALs are killing machines. There's nobody like them in the world, unless you're talking about Delta and the CIA black ops.

"Green Berets need to be killing machines, but they also need to be teachers, and medics, and engineers, and stick around for a while. Here's another way to think about it. Green Berets are required to learn a foreign language. SEALs, well, speaking to indigenous folk is not in the job description. Not unless you're speaking with the language of the bullet."

"So why the shark?"

"Some of the teams specialize in different methods of getting to their area of operation. I was on a scuba team."

She nodded and said, "What made you leave?"

Frank paused. Little Sheriff Sweetness was collecting intel on him. She was good, but he wasn't going to be collected. "It's a long story," he said. "We probably don't have the time now. Our tree-hugging biker with his basket will be here before I even start. But maybe I can take you out for lunch, and we can discuss this matter in greater detail."

"Unlikely," she said. "I don't go on lunch dates with men who have a history of showing they can't be trusted."

"Ouch," he said.

"I'm sure you'll get over it."

"A person can change."

"Can they?" she asked.

Sheriff Hood was a tough cookie. He said, "I can see you're a no frou-frou kind of gal. Given your druthers, you're burgers and fries, aren't you? No, wait. I retract that assessment. It's steak. Right? Medium rare, maybe with a little bit of moo still kicking about."

"Steak is too often nothing more than overrated shoe leather."

"You've got to select the right cut. You've got to look for high quality."

"It's too inconsistent."

Frank rubbed his chin and considered her. Athletic, strong, healthy. "Salmon?" he guessed.

"Darn," she said in mock sympathy. "That's strike three. You're out."

"Baseball is a game of many innings," he said.

"Mr. Shaw, you're on the wrong field. Where I come from, when you're out, you don't play."

Definitely a tough cookie. Frank thought of all the games where being out met her definition. "So it's cage fighting," he said. "Or is it death ball?"

"It's off limits," she said.

She meant she was off limits. "You're mixing a lot of metaphors," he said and grinned.

She gave him a look.

He put his hands up, indicating he wouldn't press it. But he knew she was not seeing the facts. He was a reformed guy. A doughnut man and an upstanding employee of Walmart. And he was proud of that. He was proud of where he was going. And she was missing out on a free lunch with a man who still opened a woman's door. But he wouldn't press it now.

So they stood there in silence for a bit, watching the long-hair approach on his three-speed bicycle, and then something on the shoulder of the road caught her attention. She walked over and scuffed a rock out of the dirt with her boot and picked it up. She brushed it off, then began to toss it like someone might toss a baseball before hucking it.

Was this some psychological thing? Some new cop intimidation technique?

Frank said, "What you got there?"

"A rock."

He said, "You're not planning on using that, are you?"

"What?"

"The rock. I'm on your side."

She caught the rock, then cocked her head, a bit confused.

He said, "Besides, I'm thinking a felon's probably going to require, at the very least, a taser."

She still looked confused, then comprehension lit up her face, and she laughed. It was a contagious laugh that made him smile.

"Mr. Shaw," she said and held the rock up for him to see. "This rock is not to bean someone in the head with. At least, I don't have any reason to bean anyone yet. It's for my resident entrepreneur."

Frank looked at it. It was a black rock with a white vein running through it. No gold. No emerald. It didn't look like any semi-precious gem he knew.

"You come out here, pick up rocks, and sell them to the tourists? That's your gig?"

She smiled. It was a nice smile.

"My daughter makes pet rocks."

"Like a rock with eyes glued onto it?"

"Yes, there are those. You can put a little series of them on a flat piece of walnut and call it a family. Or two together as man and wife. But she's gone way beyond that."

"Oh?" Frank asked. "She does rock towns?"

"She glues rocks together, does a little bit of painting, makes figurines."

Frank couldn't picture what she was talking about.

"Little people," she said. "She's ramping up for Halloween. She's got Rockula, Frankenstone, Darth Igneous. You've got to have obsidian to make that one."

"Ah," Frank said. "A little Michaelangela."

"People love them. There's a place in St. George that buys a dozen at a time. A friend told her about Etsy, and she's started now to sell online."

"I'm impressed," Frank said.

"I think she came from another planet," said Sheriff Hood.

Frank smiled and motioned at the rock in her hand. "So what is that one going to be?"

"Turn it so the white vein runs up and down, and I think we have ourselves a sharp dresser. She'll glue on rock feet, legs, and a head. Maybe we'll have a stud in a tux."

"Your daughter's creating studs?"

"It was just an example."

"You sure you're not into baseball?" Frank asked.

She lifted an eyebrow and gave him a look that said he was treading the line.

"She make much selling rocks?" Frank asked.

"You'd be surprised. Last month she cleared two hundred bucks."

"That's good money for a kid." It would also be a nice little chunk of change for an ex-con who sometimes ran out of dough before the month's end.

"She financed her own scooter."

Frank was liking this little girl. He was also letting the entrepreneurial gears in his mind turn. He had a five year plan that required a sizeable amount of cash. Maybe, in addition to the jobs at Walmart and Cowboy Donut, he should add a side gig of selling studs on the internet to people in New York City who'd forgotten there were such things as rocks. But there was no time to explore the idea because the long-hair on the bicycle began to bike up the slight incline just below Frank and the sheriff.

A slight breeze picked up. High above, the pitch of the drone's motors increased as they tried to keep it positioned where the operator might watch them. Over at the ranch, the bed of a white pickup backed up into view through the trees.

Frank peered closer and realized that was the vehicle. Heck, the shovel was still sticking up on the rack.

"There's your pickup," he said. "And the murder weapon."

Sheriff Hood put the rock in her pant's cargo pocket and followed Frank's gaze. "We don't know yet if it's murder."

"If it isn't murder, it's something pretty close."

"We shall see. Our friend is almost here. I'm sure he'll have plenty of information."

The guy on the three-speeder bike was pedaling up the hill, laboring for breath. It wasn't a big hill, which meant he was either in terrible shape, or he'd been exerting himself quite a bit before he got on the bicycle.

He pedaled up, all smiles and big white corn teeth, and stopped a dozen yards away.

He said, "Officer, I can't tell you how happy we are to see you."

"Oh?"

"That fellow," he said and pointed an accusatory finger at Frank, "has wigged out a couple of my associates."

Frank narrowed his eyes.

"And what's your name?" the sheriff asked politely.

"Bill," he said.

"Bill, are you the owner of the ranch?"

"No," he said.

The sheriff said, "It's a beautiful spot, isn't it?"

"Gorgeous."

"What's your last name, Bill?"

"Peterson," he said.

"How many are in your group?"

"Oh, they come and go. Friends, family."

She nodded. "I know how that is. I just had family visit myself. You've been here a while?"

"Yeah."

She waited.

He shrugged. "A couple of weeks."

She smiled her friendly smile. "How many are there now?"

"Oh, six or eight of us."

"Which is it?" she asked and smiled again, just a sweet little lady cop with a gun and a taser and mace and an expandable baton on her duty belt.

"Well," Bill said and brought up his fingers to count, "let's see. Right now, there's Marko and Ralph. Grace, Hannah. Carl, Big Z, and myself. So seven."

"We had a report that a man was hit in the head with a shovel and transported to this ranch. What do you know about that?"

Bill blinked then looked at the sheriff like he hadn't heard her, like this was crazy news. "What?"

Sheriff Hood said ever so sweetly. "Is the owner there?"

"No."

Frank thought, cops have rules. The Fourth Amendment says she can't just do a search. Without an owner, nobody could give her consent. But she didn't need a warrant to prevent serious injury, like leaving a guy to die in a tarp.

"Do you mind if I just look around on the property for a second? Just a routine check?"

Bill hesitated. "Aren't you going to do something about him?"

Frank thought, if she goes in alone, she won't know who was involved. But Frank would. He'd have no problem picking the perpetrators out of a lineup. Frank said, "Bill, do you mind if I come with the sheriff? Maybe I got mixed up."

Bill looked at the sheriff. "Is he an officer?"

"No," she said.

Back at the ranch, the driver of the pickup put it in gear, then accelerated in the opposite direction of where Frank, Bill, and the sheriff stood. He passed by the ranch house and barn, then drove up through the trees, following the road into the canyon.

Bill watched the pickup go. When it had disappeared, he turned around, looked at Frank, then the sheriff. He was probably weighing the options: make a stink and act like he was hiding something or let them in. He finally came to some conclusion. "We don't want any problems, but this man here, well, he threatened my friends."

"Let me come get a report from them," she said. "There won't be any problems. We'll only take just a minute." Her tone made it seem like they were only going in to check the gas meter.

A brief look flashed across Bill's face. Frank had seen that look before in the eyes of men at the Coalinga prison, but Bill put it away quickly.

"Well, okay," he said. "Follow me." Then he grinned. It was a grin with a bit of crocodile in it, like if they'd just come down to the water's edge, he'd show them a neat surprise.

7

Ranch

BILL TURNED HIS BICYCLE around and began to roll back down the hill.

Frank and the sheriff watched him go.

Frank said, "When was the last time any kind of self-respecting villain got around on a three-speeder?"

"I'm sure a self-respecting villain takes whatever ride is most appropriate."

Frank knew there had been some big time criminal who had ridden a bicycle once, and then it came to him. "Ha!" Frank said, "Miss Almira Gulch."

"What?" the sheriff asked.

"It's a who," Frank said. "It's the name of the gal who stole Toto and rode off with him stuffed in her basket."

"You're talking about *The Wizard of Oz*?"

"Do you think Bill is her brother? Maybe the bicycle thing runs in the family."

"Right," she said, clearly unconvinced. "Maybe they'll next send out the flying monkeys."

Frank pointed up at the drone. "I think they already have."

The sheriff looked at the drone, looked back down at Frank and narrowed her eyes like maybe he'd actually made a connection.

He said, "I'm telling you. That boy's got a pointy black hat somewhere in his closet."

"We'll see."

"I thought you were waiting for backup."

"Backup will arrive soon enough. I'd like you to stay here."

"You're going need me to identify the three who mobbed the guy."

"I don't want any trouble from you."

"Sheriff," he said, "I don't cause trouble. I bake doughnuts. Some of them have pretty sprinkles."

"Your record says otherwise."

Yeah, he thought, that record. "People make mistakes sometimes. And the record isn't all there is to a man."

"Uh-huh. I'm still wondering what your connection is to this crew."

"This is my connection. My only connection. I saw them take the guy down, saw them beat him, saw them put him in the truck. And now with you, I saw them take that truck and head off when law enforcement came."

She nodded, thinking.

He said, "I'm not going to do anything. I'll just stand there and look around and make them wonder what the ugly tattooed guy is doing with Jenny Law. My presence will also probably make them think twice about getting any ideas about there being seven of them and only one of you."

She said, "Doughnuts, eh?"

He pointed at the Cowboy Donut emblazoned on his tee-shirt. "Doughnuts," he confirmed.

"You ever had Dunford's?"

"You're talking about those chocolate doughnuts."

"My aunt up by Salt Lake loves them."

Frank said, "Dunford is like a Ford. At the Cowboy, we sell Cadillacs."

She nodded, assessing his offer to come with her.

He decided he needed to back off and said, "Look, I can stay here. Whatever you want."

She said, "Mr. Shaw. I'm going to go up and get a closer look. You can follow me in your car. When we get in, you point them out to me."

"Whatever I can do to help," Frank said.

The sheriff pushed a button on the radio on her duty belt and said, "Cathy, ten thirty-two three."

Frank didn't hear Cathy's response, but the sheriff said, "Mr. Shaw will be following me to the ranch."

Cathy probably replied, but Frank didn't hear it. And he realized an earpiece for her mobile radio was actually a smart idea. If something came in from another officer, it wasn't going to alert the folks she was talking with. Nor would it distract from any conversations.

She said, "You were once in Special Forces. I assume you know how to be discrete."

"Yes, ma'am," he replied.

Then the sheriff walked back and got into her Explorer, and Frank got into the Nova. Frank started his engine, let the sheriff pass, then pulled in behind her, and they made their way down the slope, but they didn't get too far too fast because Bill was riding down the middle of the road, stuck in turtle speed, acting like he was on a joy ride while giving the folks in the pickup all the time they might need to find one of those back roads.

For the next few minutes the bicycle, police SUV, and Nova caravanned along at about three miles per hour, and then Bill took the wide way around a mud hole clinging to its last bit of moisture, and the sheriff took her chance and gunned it past him. Frank followed in the Nova. He waved at Bill as he drove by. When they were past, Frank glanced in his rearview mirror. Interestingly enough, Bill was suddenly pedaling a lot harder.

Frank looked at the ranch ahead. A short road ran up from the fat lodge pole arch with the elk horns to a cluster of buildings standing amidst pines and aspen. In the middle of the buildings was a large, graveled roundabout so someone could drive to each place in turn. On one side was the big ranch house. It was an expensive-looking unit with vaulted two-story windows, rock and corrugated metal siding, and nice pieces of exposed timber. On the other side was a barn with a matching finish. There was a covered parking area and corrals. Farther back was a bunk house and another building. The whole place had been xeriscaped with drought-resistant grasses and artistic rocks. There were stands of yellow wildflowers under some of the dark pines. It didn't smell like a working man's ranch. It smelled of money.

Then Frank noticed the security camera at the peak of an eave of the house. There was another on the barn. There were two others on poles pointed out. One was watching the drive.

That was a lot of security for a ranch house. So maybe this was some muckity-muck millionaire retreat. A place for politicians to gather for dinners that set each attendee back 10,000 bucks.

They rumbled over the cattle guard beneath the lodge pole entrance, then up the road to the ranch house. Behind them, Bill was now standing up on the pedals, really working his three-speeder, trying to keep up.

The sheriff drove to the front of the ranch house, turned so her Explorer was facing mostly away from the house, and stopped. It was a smart move to turn her vehicle that way. It prevented her from having to back out.

Two men and a woman were standing out on the porch, waiting. The woman Frank recognized. She was the one that had sprung onto the running man like a wildcat. But the two men with her were all wrong—one had a decent beard, the other was wearing a purple polo shirt and didn't look like he knew how to even handle a shovel. Neither of them had been in the truck earlier.

Frank looked around. There was a white pickup parked around the side of the house, but it had different plates than the one he'd followed. Next to it was a nice big brown Lincoln. There were some ATVs over by the covered parking. A big guy stood down there. He wasn't big as in fat. He was big as in tall, big-boned, big hands. He was wearing sunglasses, standing, not at attention, but ready for action. There was a rifle lying on one of the ATVs. A nice AR-15.

The sheriff called something in on her radio. He hoped her rear camera was recording the folks on the porch and her front camera the guy by the ATVs.

Frank stopped a few car lengths behind, wanting to give her plenty of room and to get a clear view of Bill's family and friends.

The three on the porch, Mr. Sunglasses over by the ATVs, and Bill made five. There had been two in the truck. That was seven, unless Bill wasn't counting them, which meant there were at least two others unaccounted for.

Frank turned off the Nova and stepped onto the asphalt.

All eyes focused on him, and Frank waved hello and smiled.

Bill's friends and family did not wave back.

Frank scanned the place again. He didn't see anyone else, just an empty corral and another security camera. But the windows of the big house were open, and a burst of radio came through. Frank turned to the sound, and then one of the men on the porch whistled, and the radio went off.

The sound that had come through the windows had not been music or advertising or any other kind of programming. It had been the sound of Sheriff Hood speaking in ten-code, which meant these folks had a scanner. Unless law enforcement here had upgraded to 800 megahertz, which meant a scanner was not required, and then these folks could have been on a website that allowed them to listen in.

Learn the ten-codes and any local variations, and anyone could become a citizen of Scanner Land. Even way out here on the Elkhorn.

Frank looked at the trio on the porch. He looked at the guy standing ready by his rifle. He wondered how much they knew about him from the conversations over the police radio.

The sheriff got out of her Explorer just in time for Bill to come huffing up on his bike.

"It's all right," Bill called to the three on the porch. "The sheriff just wants to talk."

Frank wondered what Bill would have said if the sheriff had wanted to do more, like look around. Would that have not been all right?

The three on the porch relaxed a little. Mr. Sunglasses with his rifle did not. Bill skirted round Frank to the steps of the porch.

Sheriff closed the door to her SUV, walked to the back end, then stopped. She was on this side of the vehicle, away from Mr. Sunglasses and his rifle. She was also a respectable distance away from the folks on the porch. She had at least ten yards plus a row of bushes and the porch rail between her and them. It was enough room to pull a taser or gun should someone on the porch decide to charge. Although Frank highly doubted any of them would do that, not with him standing there as back up. Alone, the sheriff would have seemed more vulnerable. But add another big body, and that changed the equation in many people's minds entirely.

The sheriff smiled and said, "How you folks doing?"

The woman said, "We are fine, but that man has been following us."

She wasn't American, but Frank couldn't place the accent.

The sheriff said, "Dispatch relayed your message to me."

Dispatch? These folks had called dispatch? About him?

Frank suddenly got a bad feeling.

The sheriff said, "So I'm here to find out what's going on."

The woman said, "It's like I said. We were out, enjoying a ride, when we saw him watching us. We got scared. And he chased us."

They were out on a joy ride, and he'd just up and chased them?

Frank's mind began to whir. When had they called this fiction in? And he realized they could have called it in when he was out on the road. They would have heard his call, maybe heard about his background, and gotten a very sly idea.

Which meant the sheriff had been weighing two stories. On the one hand, she had some out-of-town vacation renters, in an expensive place, claiming to have been threatened by a scary man. On the other hand, she had that scary man, who happened to be an ex-con, claiming these vacationers were running men down in the wilderness and throwing them in the backs of pickups.

Which one would she believe? Which would he believe? Which one would anyone believe?

The answer was obvious.

Now he knew why she hadn't waited for backup to enter the ranch. She wasn't worried about any killers in a pickup.

The sheriff took out her notebook and said, "I understand there were four of you?"

The three on the porch hesitated.

"Yeah," Bill cut in.

"Were you with them?" Sheriff Hood asked Bill.

"No," Bill said. "It was Marko, Hannah, Ralph, and Carl."

"Is Carl the fellow by the ATVs?"

"That's Ezekiel," Bill said. "Let me get Carl." He walked toward the house. "Carl," he yelled. "Carl, the sheriff needs to talk to you."

"So?" the sheriff said quietly to Frank.

Was she playing him, or did she really think he might be telling the truth? "I recognize the woman, but these aren't the men."

Frank looked over at Sunglasses. He'd taken up position behind his ATV, like maybe he could drop to a knee and use the vehicle not only as a shield, but to steady his hand should he need to aim that rifle. Frank noticed Bill had stepped out of the line of fire.

There was movement upstairs by an open window. Frank looked up, but didn't see anyone. However, if a shooter was up there, then he or she and Sunglasses had set up a pretty good crossfire.

Did the sheriff even see it?

But who in their right mind was going to shoot down a sheriff who had just called in her position on the radio?

The answer was that nobody would do that, not unless they had a way to cover their tracks. And one good way to do that would be to kill them both and pin the shooting on the ex-con.

Frank's bad feeling suddenly got a lot worse.

A man appeared in the hallway. He opened the screen door and walked out of the house onto the porch.

He was medium height, medium build, dark hair. He was wearing the red-checkered shirt, complete with the dark stain and tear up the side.

"Is that him?" the sheriff asked.

It was his shirt, the exact shirt with the tear. Those were his pants, his skin, his hair. But it was not the man in the tarp.

8

Lies

FRANK GLANCED OVER at Sunglasses with his rifle, then at Bill with his grinning anticipation, like he was waiting for his opponent to stupidly make the move that would remove his queen or rook from the board.

They were all positioned, waiting. He could see it in their eyes, in the way they held themselves. They were all waiting for the signal.

He'd seen this before in the prison yard. Dirk, a skinny, nobody meth user, had been hanging out with his so-called buddy by the fence. But he'd been oblivious to the men around them who were acting so hard like it was just another day in the yard that you knew it was anything but. And then Dirk had said something, and suddenly the men turned into a mob. One second they were standing there. The next they came at him. But they'd never just been standing there. They'd been waiting, primed to jump.

"Mr. Shaw," the sheriff said.

The difference between then and now was that this mob had at least one rifle. So Frank turned to the sheriff and said, "Son of a gun, that's him."

"That's the man you thought was injured?"

"Yes," Frank said and knew he'd just torpedoed his story.

"Carl," she called out. "Can you come here for a moment?"

Carl shrugged. "Sure," he said and walked off the porch to the asphalt. He gave Frank an irritated look, then turned back to the sheriff. "Do you need us to make an official statement?"

She pointed at a spot next to a tall yucca and said, "Can you stand there and show me your head."

Carl walked over to the yucca, a few paces away from her, and modeled his head. He gave her the full 360 view.

There was no blood. No dirt. Frank could see it from where he was standing. Carl also had no bruises, scrapes, or blood anywhere visible to the naked eye.

At about that time, flickering police lights appeared through the trees in front of the ranch. It was another Ford Explorer. Another vehicle soon appeared behind that one.

"Carl, my deputies are coming, and they'll get your statement. If I could get you to go back up to the porch, that would be best."

Carl went.

The sheriff motioned at Frank, "Do any of you know this man?"

The three men shook their heads. The woman said, "The first time I saw him was today."

There was that accent again. She had nice toffee skin, but that wasn't Spanish he was hearing. It wasn't Portuguese.

The sheriff turned to Frank and looked at him. "Mr. Shaw, let's go over to your car and talk."

Frank walked with the sheriff back to his car.

She said, "Mr. Shaw, you know, it's a pretty big deal calling 911. Are you taking any medications?"

"No," Frank said.

"Maybe you've got a little heat exhaustion. A day out hiking in the sun can do that to you."

"Yeah," Frank said.

She said, "Can I see your license and confirm our information?"

Frank opened his wallet, removed his Wyoming driver's license, and held it out. She took it and wrote down his information.

When she handed it back, she said, "Where are you headed?"

"L.A." he explained again.

"Can I just look in your car a bit?" she asked.

It was probably the most pleasant request he'd ever received to do a drug check.

"Sure," Frank said.

But she didn't move. She waited for her deputies to drive up. And while one had him stand spread eagle against the car and patted him down, the other helped the sheriff search his car. They looked under his seats, in the glove box, in the doors, in the engine compartment. They popped the trunk and rifled through the clothes in his duffle bag. They found his bottle of chocolate whey protein, opened it and shook the contents around to make sure nothing illegal was inside.

"It whips up really good with bananas," Frank offered. "Perfect for after a workout."

"We're good," the deputy said. His name plate said Johnson. He was bald with a goatee. He look liked he could have been a bouncer but had chosen the path of righteousness instead.

"I'm clean," Frank said.

"It appears you are," the sheriff said and put his clothes back into his bag.

She said, "Mr. Shaw, I tell you what I'm going to do. Do you know the legal definition of assault?"

"Yeah," Frank said.

"It's the threat of and the ability to cause someone imminent harm. These people might argue your behavior on the road constitutes assault."

He glanced at the folks on the porch and Mr. Sunglasses. Their bodies were relaxed. They were looking at him with knowing expressions. He said, "I did not assault them."

She said, "Somebody with your background, you don't need to get into any more trouble. Are you hearing me?"

"Loud and clear," Frank said.

She said, "I don't think these folks are going to want us to take it to the next level. They're just here for the sights."

Yes, Frank thought, with security cameras and shovels, that's how everyone saw the sights.

"So I'm going to give you a warning. Because you don't want any trouble. Right?"

"Right," he said.

"I'm going to go talk to these people. I want you to head out and continue safely to L.A. You shouldn't be on these back roads. Not with your car. Not with the storms we've been having. Should I have one of the deputies escort you?"

"I'm good," Frank said.

He considered telling her the truth. But that would only earn him a trip to the station. And if these renters, who didn't seem to be here for vacation fun, were actually willing to take down one law enforcement officer, who was to say they weren't willing to take down three? Go big or go home, and "Ex-con Kills Three Officers" was a fine big headline.

Mr. Sunglasses was still by the ATVs with his assault rifle. And someone else was still upstairs by the window.

Frank said, "Did you see the guy with the rifle over there?"

"Mr. Shaw," she warned.

He nodded. He didn't want a headline. "I'll leave it in your capable hands."

"That's right. Go get yourself hydrated. There's a store in Glendale. Better yet, there's an artisan bakery in Orderville. That's right up your baking alley. They've got sandwiches and some killer pastries. Can I count on you?"

"Yes, sheriff," he said.

A dark-haired woman in her thirties suddenly threw open the door to the front of the house and crossed over to Bill. She had short hair and had dyed part of it Kool-aide pink. She whispered something in his ear.

Bill sighed in frustration. "Sheriff," he called. "We have some goats loose. Can I send a couple of these guys out?"

Frank wondered: since when did million-dollar vacation home rentals include taking care of goats?

"Have we got your statements?" the sheriff asked.

"Yes," her deputy replied.

"Then go get your goats," the sheriff said.

"Zeke," Bill called. "The goats are out."

Mr. Sunglasses turned, but did nothing, like he didn't know what Bill was talking about.

"Marko, Ralph," Bill said and motioned at the two men on the porch. "You two go with Zeke." He raised his voice. "We've got to get them in."

Goats, security cameras, police scanners, and a man in a checkered shirt who'd disappeared. Frank hoped the sheriff was picking this up.

Bill and his two buddies hustled over to the ATVs. The three of them talked to Zeke briefly, then Bill turned around and came back all smiles.

Behind him Zeke, the guy with the beard, and the man in the purple shirt got on their ATVs, started them, then punched it up the road. The road where the pickup had gone.

Frank heard the whine of rotors up above, then saw the drone streaking above the trees in the direction Zeke and the others were heading.

"Mr. Shaw," the sheriff said.

"Right," Frank said.

"Have a nice day, Mr. Shaw," the sheriff said.

"Are you sure you don't want to do lunch?" Frank asked.

"Mr. Shaw, it's time to make your way to Los Angeles."

"Okay," Frank said. "I'll catch you next time." And he got into his car. He started up the Nova, then pulled away from the fine ranch house and drove back towards the meadow.

Frank didn't think Zeke and company were heading up the canyon to take care of any goats.

He rolled under the horned lodge pole entrance, back over the cattle guard, and across the meadow. He told himself he should visit that artisan bakery. Told himself people died at the hands of bad men all the time. Told himself the running man probably had it coming. In fact, the running man was probably some seedy low-life that was part of their muckity-muck operation.

Then again, that might not be the situation at all.

The other minor point was all of this was going to become part of his record, and Frank didn't need anything else attached to his name in a government database.

Frank came to the turnoff. One direction led back to Glendale. The other probably led to some of those roads the sheriff had said connected up on top at the back of the Elkhorn property.

He stopped. There was something about the woman's accent. Something tickling his mind.

If he turned right, he could find that artisan bakery and eat the lies that had been told about him and the situation. If he turned left, he was likely to earn the ire of Sheriff Hood. But he might also find something worth her attention.

Frank decided he wasn't particularly hungry for lies at the moment. He didn't think the man in the tarp was either, so he turned left and headed away from Glendale. Maybe he could find one of those roads. The crew back at the ranch was full of such swell guys, there was no way he wanted to miss their goat party.

9

Goats

FRANK WAS HAPPY there was a hill and a lot of cedar and pinyon between him and the ranch to cover his wrong turn. There was no way anyone there could see him directly, but he kept it slow for a quarter mile anyway so he didn't kick up any dust.

He examined his map, but it wasn't detailed enough in this area, which meant he'd have to find a road the old-fashioned way. He continued up and down the hills, the ragged slopes and sheer faces of the cliffs rising to his left. He drove for a few minutes, but didn't see any road leading up to the mesa above. However, that didn't mean he couldn't get on top. The range wasn't miles and miles of sheer cliff. There were sections of cliffs, but there were also sections of steep slope and rock. There were also draws and small canyons. From above, the mesa probably looked like a fat turkey foot with many long and crooked toes.

All Frank had to do was find one with a way to the top. The road bent close to the foot of one toe, and Frank saw his opportunity. The slope was steep, but it was dirt and scrub all the way up.

He drove the Nova off the road and parked between two cedars. He downed the last of a plastic bottle of water, then got his binoculars. He put them in his slim pack along with his cell phone. He had two other items already in the bag. A Leatherman multi-tool and a little baggie of crackers he'd been planning on enjoying with the sunset. Then he got out of the car, locked it, and headed off at a jog through the desert trees for the slope at the back of this toe. A couple of minutes later, he passed by some red boulders the size of trucks, then found himself at the base of the slope. It was a bit steeper than it had seemed from the road, but it was still passable, and Frank began what looked like a couple hundred foot climb.

Frank ran the hills around his home in Rock Springs, Wyoming. He ran in the summer sun and through winter snow. He hoofed it up this hill, pausing only twice to catch his breath, knowing it had definitely been harder in the glory days with a seventy-pound ruck sack and a rifle. He reached the crest, sweating, his breath deep and quick.

There was an old barbed-wire fence just under the crest of the hill, probably erected decades ago to keep cattle off the slopes. It was sagging a bit now. In one section, it was completely gone, which meant the Elkhorn wasn't working the range as it once had been.

Frank moved over the fence and to the relatively flat tabletop of land up above and found he could see for miles around. It was spectacular. To the north rose the Pink Cliffs. To the east were miles and miles of wilderness. Down below the slope lay the undulating table of cedar and pine. And there was the Nova, just visible if you knew where to look.

He turned back to the mesa which was dotted with sagebrush and low grass. The remnants of a dirt road ran through the sparse scrub.

Frank followed it at a jog. The top of this toe of the mesa widened out and met up with the top of a toe that connected to the Elkhorn. Frank continued to run, then heard the whine of a motorcycle in the canyon next to the tabletop, the canyon that led back down to the Elkhorn. Ahead, a little rise of rock that included a cluster of short junipers stood at the edge of the mesa. Frank ran for it, then kept low as he approached the crest of the slope. It wouldn't do for anyone to spot him.

Down below, the sound of the motorcycle grew louder.

Frank slowed, crouched lower, then slipped in between the junipers and rocks. He ran into a few thin strands of spiderweb with his face, brushed them away, then moved forward until he could see down into the canyon.

Below was a juncture with another canyon that led into the mesa on the other side. A little father up was yet another juncture. It was a convocation of toes. It was also a convocation of men.

In the center was a white pickup. Coming up from the ranch was the motorcyclist, a rifle slung across his back. Coming down from farther up the canyon on an ATV was Mr. Sunglasses, the one with the AR-15, the one Bill had called Zeke.

Two rifles was a lot of firepower for goats. Most goatherds Frank had seen didn't need to do anything more than wave their arms to urge the goats in the right direction.

Frank took out his binoculars and looked at the pickup. It was the one he'd seen earlier sans the body in the back. And that was Caterpillar Brow and Shovel Man in the cab.

Frank glassed the ground all around the truck, looking for the grave. If you had a body you wanted hidden, you needed to bury it deep. Otherwise the skunks and other animals would dig it out. The methane would also call to the buzzards, and they'd begin swooping over the area, and then swooping lower and lower until they'd swoop only inches above the sagebrush. Frank had witnessed this on a number of his hike-runs. It was an awesome sight to be close to such a large wingspan as it rushed past, so close you heard the wind over the large brown feathers.

Frank looked in a wider circle. He wasn't seeing any sign of digging. So maybe they had dug the grave somewhere else, or maybe there was some deep crevice or slot they'd thrown him into.

Frank took out his cell phone and took a picture.

Then Frank heard another, smaller whine. A moment later, a drone sped out of the canyon across from Frank, then turned back toward the Elkhorn. This was a slightly different model than the one Frank had seen before. He put his glasses down, looked around. There was another drone farther up the canyon. Then a louder whine rose from the direction of the ranch. Frank turned and saw a third drone come up from the Elkhorn. It was followed by yet another.

What was it with all these drones?

Frank thought that if he'd just hid a body, or was in the process of doing so, he'd want an eye in the sky to give a warning as well. But who kept, not one, but a small squadron of them?

One of the drones went up the canyon where the first had come from. The other headed farther up the main thoroughfare. Drones didn't have an unlimited range. Those powered by battery often had a twenty- or thirty-minute max, and that was if you weren't pushing them hard. If you wanted to go longer, you needed a gas-powered motor. Get a big enough tank, and you might go an hour. You might go more, but very few hobbyists needed that kind of range.

These last two drones were loud, definitely running on gas, with a longer range and flight time.

Frank brought the binocular up and searched as much of the canyon as he could see, taking his time, working in a grid pattern, but he didn't find a grave.

He looked at the men—Caterpillar Brow, Shovel Man, Zeke, and the motorcyclists. Where were the other two that had left with Zeke? Perhaps they'd been given the grunt duty to finish the digging while these four stood watch. Or to misdirect the police at the ranch, just a little over a mile farther down the canyon.

And here was another thing. Back at the ranch there had been two women, two men on the porch, Carl who'd come up in the red-checkered shirt, Zeke, and Bill. That made seven. But the guy on the dirt bike was someone new, which meant Bill had lied. There were more than seven at the ranch.

Frank took pictures of the men below. Took a picture of the last drone before it disappeared around a bend farther up the canyon.

The man in the tarp could be in the canyon across from Frank, but he didn't think so. All the drones were now north of this location. The first drone he saw had probably just been scouting the canyon to see if anyone was there. Those other drones were now probably watching the area around the digging, which meant Frank had an opportunity to document the two men in the act of burying the dead man and clear his name. He needed to move.

He kept low and backed out of the juniper and rocks, picking up some prickles and juniper rash as he did. Frank looked above the mesa to see if any drones were about. If it were him, he'd have one high, looking at the big picture. But he didn't see one and figured their mistake was his good fortune.

He crawled a good twenty-five yards away from the edge of the mesa, then stood and ran north through the sparse sage and prickly pear and salt brush. He heard the motorcyclist pass him in the canyon below. Frank kept running. A few minutes later, he spotted some cedars at the edge of the mesa a hundred yards or so ahead. He ran until he was almost even with them, then carefully approached, took up position, and looked down into the canyon below.

The man on the motorcycle had already passed this spot, but Frank didn't need to go any farther. The bottom of the canyon here widened enough to accommodate a strip of fields. To the side of one field lay a thin stack of aluminum irrigation pipe—thirty-foot sections of three-inch diameter pipe that farmers strung out and moved by hand. But it was clear they hadn't been moving it this year because the grass in the fields was sparse and brown. There'd been no first or second crop cut here. Farther down, there were some large corrals that were past their prime. There was a shed. And there was also a backhoe.

And that backhoe had been busy. It was standing next to a long trench that was big enough to bury two cars end to end. There were things inside that trench, but Frank couldn't make them out.

He brought out his binoculars, and still couldn't make it out. It looked like large white bags partially covered with dirt. Then he saw a head and the picture shifted. Those weren't bags. They were goats. He saw legs and more heads. The trench was piled with dead goats. A lot of dead goats.

It looked like someone had started to use the backhoe to cover them over and stopped in the middle of the job.

It appeared Bill did indeed have a goat problem.

A mass burial. And what better place to hide the man in the tarp? Put him below the goats, and anyone digging down in the goat graveyard would stop before they ever got to him.

But if that were the case, why would they have stopped? Why not cover the whole thing? Why wasn't somebody in that backhoe right now?

Frank scanned the canyon, but couldn't see anyone. He wanted to go down and uncover what they'd already buried. There was another bit of rocky cover a few dozen yards north of his position. Frank carefully moved out of his current hide, and made his way there. When he was satisfied he couldn't be seen by anyone in the canyon, he took out his phone and snapped shots of the trench, backhoe, and graves.

Then he noticed three temporary pens had been erected in this last field. The fencing was made of white netting, probably three-and-a-half feet tall. There were little posts every twelve feet or so. Frank knew a rancher who used such fences. They were electric, made for goats or sheep. You had to check those fences often. Nobody would just put them up here and leave them long-term. So they would have been recently erected. But the grass in those pens had all been burned. They were nothing but black and gray ash.

So they'd had the goats. And now they were all dead. And the area where they'd been kept had been burned.

Frank knew the bodies of cattle with mad cow disease were often burned. Maybe the goats got mad goat disease. But, then, the bodies in the graves were not burned. Just the grass in the pens.

Frank saw plastic watering troughs stacked up by the shed and figured that was the final confirmation that the goats had been kept in those pens.

Maybe the man in the tarp had uncovered the fact that they were selling bad meat.

Frank listened, trying to see if he could hear someone digging a grave somewhere else. But the only thing he could hear was the motorcycle and the drones in the distance.

He should go down and take a closer look. He identified the most inconspicuous route, but before he could move, the whine of a drone rose to the north of Frank's position.

Frank looked up the canyon, but couldn't see anything. He listened again and realized the sound wasn't coming from the canyon, but above the mesa. From a position that would probably give the operator a good view of everything up here, including Frank.

He scanned the skies north and found the drone a couple hundred feet above the mesa tabletop. It flew to the far side of the mesa, turned, then moved back toward the Elkhorn canyon side. When it reached the canyon, it turned again and started to fly back to the far side.

It was searching the mesa tabletop in a methodical pattern, back and forth. A few more passes, and it would fly over Frank's position, and if the operator wasn't a blind man, he'd see Frank crouching by the rocks.

Frank looked around. Maybe he could go back to his previous hide in the cedars where there was more cover, but then he watched the drone come low and circle a scrubby group of trees in its path. The operator wasn't just flying over, he or she was looking hard. Frank's little cedar hide would only attract extra attention. And the trees weren't all that big anyway.

A few dozen yards down the rock and dirt slope into the canyon was some sagebrush. They weren't very big bushes, but if Frank could get under some of those branches, it would break up his outline. They might miss him. Might overlook the man hiding in plain sight.

He prepared to move, and then caught movement up on the mesa tabletop on the other side of the canyon. Frank turned and saw the guy with the beard that had originally gone with Zeke to take care of Bill's goat problem. He had a rifle and was walking up to the edge of the slope.

There was more movement down below. The second man who'd gone with Zeke, the man in the purple polo shirt, was coming out of a little turkey-toe draw, carrying a dark handgun.

This firepower was not for the goats. Something else was going on.

Up top, Beard Man began to survey the canyon.

Frank abandoned his idea of hiding in the sage and slowly sank back down behind his rocks.

Beard Man had a scope on his rifle. Frank was confident that if he were seen, Beard Man would scope him, and then Frank would be well on his way to joining the man in the tarp.

To the north, the drone reached the far end of the mesa and turned.

Frank wondered if the man in the tarp was up the turkey toe that Purple Polo had come out of, but there was no time to wait for Purple Polo and Beard Man to leave so he could investigate. His best bet was to take pictures and hand them over to the sheriff.

Frank quickly captured what he could on his cell.

Polo and Beard Man talked on their hand-held radios, then Beard

Man started to descend to join his friend. Frank figured now was his chance. He waited for Beard Man to get a little lower, but Beard Man didn't continue descending to the bottom. He stopped, picked something up, then began to hike back up to his previous position.

Maybe he'd seen an Indian arrow head. Or a lizard skull. Or maybe he, like Sheriff Hood, had a corner on selling rocks to tourists.

Frank didn't think he'd get this chance again. He scrambled a few feet away from the edge of the tabletop on his hands and knees, rose to a crouch, and a few yards later began to run. It appeared to Frank that his side of the canyon was just a little higher than the one Beard Man was on, which meant if he just got farther in, he could remove himself from Beard Man's line of sight.

Frank moved in a south-easterly direction. He glanced back, saw the top half of Beard Man who was looking up the canyon, his rifle slung over his shoulder. He was looking north toward the drone that had just finished its last pass and was now turning around over the canyon.

Frank kept low and slow and then moved behind some scrubby junipers that hid him from Beard Man's line of sight. The drone continued its search, moving closer.

It would have been best to take it slow, but Frank didn't have the time. So he ran for all he was worth away from the canyon and back toward where he'd come up to the mesa. The cedar hide slid by him on his right. He pounded over the orange dirt, trying not to step in the middle of any prickly pear. He ran up one side of the slightest of swells and back down the other side again. He stopped and turned. He could not see Beard Man, which meant the man couldn't see him.

Frank looked north. The drone was still there, but it wasn't scanning. It was holding its position, pointing its camera, it seemed, right at him.

"Hell," Frank said, and then he turned and ran.

In the distance, the whine of the motorcycle seemed to change direction and get louder. Even though it wasn't on the mesa yet, it soon would be, and then the mystery man Bill had failed to note wouldn't need the drone to keep him apprised of Frank's position.

Frank wiped his brow and kept moving. For some odd reason, he just didn't want to take on an armed rider with nothing more than a pocket knife and a bunch of crackers. All he had to do was make it to the slope he'd climbed up, which was going to be too steep for the motorcycle, and get into the cover of the trees at the bottom.

He relaxed his shoulders, lengthened his stride, let his breaths come deep and easy. He flew across the orange dirt and short sage. Then he risked a glance back.

The drone was moving, speeding toward him.

Frank turned back around and continued to hoof it. He was reaching out now, extending, landing on the balls of his feet, his pack with the binoculars, Leatherman, and crackers jostling on his back. He figured those crackers weren't going to be worth anything by the time he got back. So much for sunsets.

The slope at the back of Frank's turkey toe was just a hundred or so yards ahead. He ran like a linebacker who'd just intercepted a pass. And then he began to see the valley open up on the other side. A few more seconds, and he came to the dilapidated barbed-wire fence. Frank hurdled a strand of the old, rusty wire, then slowed as the tabletop began to fall away. He might have hoofed it up the hill, but it was too steep to run down. Given the proximity of the drone, he realized he wasn't going to make the trees, which meant the drone would just watch him all the way down and to the car with the operator calling in his position.

Frank didn't know how good the camera was on that thing. Maybe they didn't know who he was yet. Maybe they thought he might be a random tree-hugger out for a jog. He needed to keep it that way, and that wouldn't happen if he bee-lined for his car.

He looked back, scrambled down the slope a bit, until he couldn't see the drone, then worked his way across the incline to a little tower of rock he'd seen on the way up. There was a six foot slope between the tower of rock and a section of cliff that fell to the valley below. Frank carefully skirted around the base of the tower, the cliff yawning only a few feet away, and took position in a fold of the rock on the other side. The fold was only a few feet deep. A shallow cave. But better than running out in the open.

He waited. A few moments later he heard the drone approach. Heard it fly one way, then the other. But Frank's little fold in the rock was a good one. He heard the drone fly out to get a good look at the front of the slope. Then he heard the engine kick. A moment later the drone sped past his position on a direct line for the ranch.

Frank smiled and watched it go. It must have been running out of gas, which meant the way was clear. He waited a second more, then removed himself from the rock, and began to skirt back around the small tower, having time now to think about just how much fun it would be to slip off this narrow bit of slope, tumble over the edge of that cliff, and then fall to the big rocks at the bottom.

He focused on his footing instead of the fall, carefully finished skirting around, and began to work his way back toward a more friendly part of the slope. Then he heard another soft whine and froze.

A moment later one of the smaller electric drones came around the corner, flying no more than twelve feet away from the slope. It was white, in the shape of an X with four rotors, and about as big as a microwave. Underneath were four post legs and a camera.

It turned and pointed its camera right at him.

"Awesome," Frank said. "Just awesome."

Above, the sound of the motorcycle could be heard. It had surely reached the mesa tabletop by now.

He could run for the car. But the drone would simply follow him, and the operator would direct that group of men he'd seen in the canyon right to Frank.

Frank moved. The drone moved with him.

He flipped it off.

The drone just stayed there, watching him.

And then Frank got an idea.

10

Drone

FRANK HUSTLED a few yards back up the slope. The drone stayed with him, flying just off the slope at eye level, far enough away Frank couldn't reach it, close enough to weird him out, like some alien menace out of a science fiction movie.

It was unnerving. It would have been more unnerving if it had been mounted with a gun. Of course, in a way it was, because it was communicating with any number of men who did have guns.

Frank hurried back to the old barbed-wire fence. The drone followed, keeping about twelve feet in the air. In the distance to the north, Frank heard and saw the mystery man on the motorcycle. He was headed in Frank's direction, really giving his machine some gas. Frank didn't have much time.

He found a good length of wire that had come loose from the old fence, then pulled the Leatherman out of his pack, grabbed the one end of the wire and began bending it back and forth. The old wire snapped, and Frank now had a roughly four-foot length of barbed wire. He quickly began to work another two-foot section, which broke free even more quickly. It was show time.

He looked up at the drone in mock fear, ran back to the slope with more mock fear. The drone followed. Or maybe it was more accurate to say the operator of the drone followed, probably relishing the anticipation of what was going to happen when Mystery Man showed up.

Frank scanned the ground for three stones the size of apples. He found two that were rectangular, and another that was kind of long and flat. Not ideal, but they'd have to do. He connected the two-foot section of wire to the middle of the four-foot section, ending up with something like a peace sign, except Frank didn't have peace in mind. He took one of the stones and used his multi-tool to hastily wrench the wire at one of the three ends into a barrel hitch around the rock. Then he repeated the process at the other two ends with the other two rocks.

Frank looked back toward the mesa in the direction of the motorcycle. More mock fear. He acted like he was looking for a place to hide, then ran back down to where the slope started to get steep.

The drone raced after him and took its position twelve feet away, whining like a gigantic mosquito. Six feet away would have been better, but twelve wasn't bad. Not bad at all.

It was obvious that these people had been honing their drone operating skills in the canyons while looking after their goats. However, he didn't think they'd practiced for this.

He held one stone in his hand and swung the other two, up and around, a nice big circle to straighten the line and get things going. He swung a second time, faster, and, with a good flick, let his barbed-wire bola rip. This wasn't anything close to the quality of the smart, South American bolas used to capture running game, and wouldn't wrap as well, but it was a good strong cast, the three stones spinning end over end, the barbed-wire mostly good and straight between them.

The operator of the drone hesitated for just a moment. He obviously didn't know much about the old South American gauchos, but Frank had learned plenty on Uncle Sam's dime on a training gig in Paraguay. He'd taught a cadre of the government troops how to fire M-16s. In exchange, three of Paraguayans had taught him and the rest of the team how to wrap posts with bolas.

The operator should have tried to go left or right. He went up instead.

The barbed-wire and rock bola slammed into the little craft, carrying it backward. One of the lines swung around and conked the thing with a rock. All by itself, a conk wouldn't have been enough, but the bola tangled itself around two arms of the X, preventing the rotors from working properly, pulling the thing completely out of balance.

The bola carried the drone a bit farther out, and then gravity took over, and the bola dragged the drone toward the ground.

The operator probably couldn't see the drone was wrapped on the one arm because he was really pushing the accelerator on the other two rotors, making them whine in high gear. Or maybe the gyros were going wacky, and the thing's little computer brain was trying to level things out. Either way, the drone only succeeded in doing a little twist dance that flew it into the cliff on its way down. It bounced, tangled some more, then fell, buzzing, to the rocks below.

"Buenos días, Dronito," Frank said, then hurried down the slope as fast as the incline would allow.

When he got to the bottom, Frank found the drone upside down. He grabbed one of its legs and marveled at how light it was.

He removed his super-fine bola, and at that point, the little beast came to life again. It almost flew out of Frank's hand, but he tightened his grip and banged the thing a number of times against some rocks. Some bits of plastic came off, but it kept struggling. He slammed it upside down on the ground, choking out the rotors, then took one of his bola rocks and banged the camera. Two more smacks, and he heard a satisfying crunch and saw the camera's mounts loosen.

Up above, the sound of the motorcycle grew, and Frank knew he might have delayed just a little too long. Frank rose, drone in hand, and raced for the mouth of the little draw. As he ran, he ripped off the camera, then hucked the drone away.

He slid the camera into his pocket, then hauled butt out past the boulders the size of trucks, then to the left, so he was out of a direct line of sight from the top of the slope. From there he ran through the trees for the Nova.

Then Frank heard a whine. He glanced back and saw the drone rise shakily into the sky at a tilt, like some wounded bird, with only three of its rotors operable. It didn't come after him, but flew away, a weak and trembling version of its former self, in the direction of the ranch.

Frank was impressed with its cockroach-like survivability. Unfortunately, Frank himself didn't have any cockroach-like capabilities, so he ran into the trees.

The whine of the motorcycle grew even louder, and Frank doubted he was going to make it to his car. He ran over chunks of black igneous, past a pine, through cedars. He scared a bunch of magpies picking on some dead thing and, to his surprise, rounded the last bend to the Nova. He rushed up, unlocked the door, and slid in.

He glanced back and saw Mystery man pulling up to the top of the slope, his rifle still slung. It wasn't a long shot. Not for someone with a good scope and any amount of practice.

Alarm washed down Frank's back, pricking his hairs and skin. He started her up, threw the shifter in reverse, then looked back with his arm over the passenger's side of the car and floored it.

The car shot backward out of the trees and bumped onto the road. Frank hit the brakes and skidded to a halt.

Up on the slope, Mystery Man stopped his motorcycle, then unslung his rifle.

Hells bells, Frank thought, then threw it into first, and floored it again. The Nova's tires spun, kicking up dust, which really was no kind of smoke screen at all, and then he shot out along the road back the way he'd come.

He thought he heard a shot, but couldn't tell with the racing motor. And then he was racing behind a long stand of pines and cedars.

Mystery Man would have still been able to see him, flashing through the trees. If he was any good, he'd be able to lead him like a deer for when he reached the end of the cover.

Frank followed the road up, down into a little wash, up again. He fishtailed around one bend and almost had his meeting with Jesus, but he corrected and straightened out, and continued his escape down the road.

Luckily for Frank, the cover didn't really end until Frank was out of any line of fire the man would have had on the slope. But Frank kept up the pace, the dust rising behind him.

A mile or so later, he saw the Elkhorn turnoff ahead. He also saw a couple of vehicles making their way to the main road. He punched the gas, then saw the blue and red racks of lights on top of the vehicles and realized it wasn't Bill and a posse of shovel men coming out to get him. It was Sheriff Hood, moseying along.

Frank eased back off the gas.

The sheriff reached the turnoff well before he did, saw him, and stopped.

Frank slowed, the dust behind him giving away his previous hell-bent speed. He slowed some more. After all, there really was no sense in getting a ticket.

He motored past, the very model of an upstanding citizen out enjoying a drive in the wilderness.

Sheriff Hood gave him a you-idiot-what-do-you-think-you-are-doing stare.

Frank figured you caught more flies with honey than with vinegar, although he never saw flies mobbing honey. They seemed to go for poop, but he guessed that would ruin the expression. However, the idea was good, so he gave her a big smile and wave full of honey and moseyed on by.

Sheriff Hood narrowed her eyes.

Maybe she was regretting not having accepted his offer for lunch.

Maybe she was having a bad hair day.

Either way, stopping now and telling her a tale about drones and murderous goat graves and a mystery man on a motorcycle would sound exactly like one of those yarns spun by ex-cons who were too stupid to know when they weren't sounding very bright.

Frank did not stop. However, he did wonder what the odds were that she was working with Bill. He also wondered what the chances were of her turning and heading the other way.

He looked in his rearview mirror and saw the chances of that were exactly zero.

11
Bakery

THE SHERIFF PULLED out of Elkhorn lane and turned in right behind him as did the other two white SUVs driven by her deputies. But none of them flipped on their lights, yet, so maybe that was a good sign.

He decided to keep it just under forty, although he hadn't seen a sign posting a wilderness-approved speed limit, but he figured forty was a reasonable speed to avoid turtle and rabbit type pedestrians. Plus when was the last time forty ever bothered a cop on an open road?

Sheriff Hood fell back a little to avoid his dust, but not much. The two SUVs with her did just the opposite. They pulled out and accelerated. For a moment Frank wondered if this was some kind of maneuver, but they simply passed by in two clouds of dust, then pulled ahead and eventually disappeared over the next hill.

Sheriff Hood did not seem to want to do any NASCAR today, so she stuck a good three car lengths behind Frank, following him up and down the landscape.

Frank's mouth was dry. He popped open his cooler, pulled out a plastic water bottle, popped the lid, and noticed blood on his hand. He gave it a quick look and found a nice laceration right across the middle of his palm.

He realized it must have come from the barbed-wire, probably when he was breaking the camera free. He looked at the wound again. It was a good cut. And that had been old wire. He tried to remember when he'd had his last tetanus shot, and couldn't remember. Then he thought of all the manhandling he'd practiced on that drone, which had flown back to base with, he now knew, his blood on it.

And that was all kinds of dandy because not only was he now all set for a case of lockjaw, but they also had his DNA which would be a great help when corroborating whatever story they might concoct in any eventual court case.

He sighed and looked in the mirror.

Sheriff Hood was still there.

She was there when he bumped off the dirt road and back onto asphalt. She was there when he descended from the big wilderness stair step down into the great town of Glendale and drove past the car graveyard. She was there when he turned south, the direction of L.A.

Frank tried speeding up. Sheriff Hood sped up with him. He tried slowing down. But the good sheriff was obviously an expert with both her gas and brake pedals.

Frank drank his water and tried to enjoy the scenery as they exited Glendale and continued south. He tried to piece drones and goats and murder in the desert together.

He came up with blanks.

He fished the camera he'd ripped off the drone out of his cargo pocket and looked at it. If he had been Sherlock Holmes, he would have known the brand and model. He would have read the numbers on the side. And then he would have deduced that this was all connected to a racket run by three old knitting ladies who'd gone to the dark side.

Frank wasn't Sherlock Holmes, which meant Frank had squat. He looked at the camera one more time, then tossed it onto the passenger's seat.

Ahead, a sign announced he was approaching the town of Orderville. He also saw another sign advertising the artisan bakery the sheriff had told him about.

Had she not urged him to give it a try? Frank repented of his earlier disregard of following the sheriff's advice and decided it was now time to obey. He cruised around a few more bends, saw the bakery coming up on the left, then slowed and pulled into its parking lot.

The sheriff followed him and pulled into a stall two slots away.

Frank smiled. He told himself to assume she wanted lunch. He turned off the Nova and got out, ready to play it all friendly.

The sheriff called something in on her radio.

Frank turned up the watts on his smile and took a couple of steps closer to her vehicle to let her know he wanted to talk without getting in her space, then waited while she wrote something down.

She finished, looked up, and gave him that no-nonsense glance, then buzzed her window down part way.

She was a fine-looking woman. She seemed very capable. He said, "I suspected you'd change your mind. You coming in for that lunch?"

"Mr. Shaw," she said, "lunch was about seven hours ago."

He said, "I bet it's kind of close to lunch in Hawaii. Maybe this place has got pineapple. We could do a Hawaiian lunch."

She gave him a look that said she'd started the timer, and he'd just lost fifteen seconds. And she wasn't going to take any bull.

He gauged her. If she was working with Bill, maybe he could catch her in the lie. If not, she needed to know. But he knew he wasn't going to tell her the whole wild story. Not yet. So he said, "That wasn't the man in the tarp."

He watched her face for a tell.

But there wasn't one. She cocked her head instead and gave him one of those I'm not amused looks.

He gave her the "I'm serious" look back and waited.

When she saw he wasn't backing down from his position, she said, "Mr. Shaw, is this your idea of humor?"

He said, "They had a line on us from that upper window. They had another from Big Z and his rifle. Did you see his rifle?"

She said, "There was a cat in that upper window. And it's not against the law to own a rifle."

"A five-foot tall cat? Furthermore, there were more than seven of them there. I was not going to put us in danger."

"There's no us," Mr. Shaw.

"In their eyes, we were a team."

She just looked at him.

He said, "I'm telling you—the man they produced was not the man in the tarp. And that wasn't the truck. You saw the plates."

"We're a little low on evidence that there ever was a man in a tarp," she said. "But this is all beside the point. You were going to L.A."

"They're playing you," he said. "They have a police scanner. And they're using my ex-con status to muddy the waters. Tell me they're not."

A beat passed, which meant she was thinking, but it didn't budge her.

Frank had been watching her the whole time, but so far her body language and face hadn't betrayed anything.

She said, "We appreciate how helpful you've been. But we've got it now. And you have your family in L.A."

He was going to tell her they didn't have it, but something must have come over her ear piece because she held up her finger and started talking.

He waited for a bit, but when the time stretched long, he said, "I'll catch you next time." Then he turned and went inside the bakery because if she was going to bust him, she would have by this point. The key thing was letting her know their mystery had not been solved. Now that he'd done that, he figured she needed time for it to work on her. He hoped she'd sent someone out to the knoll, because she'd soon see he was telling the truth. But now was not the time to push it. Now was the time to wait for the evidence to arrive.

Inside the bakery, he found a glass counter with pastries. Behind it were shelves of dark European-looking breads. Some had nuts and seeds worked into them. One had sun-dried tomatoes. There were sandwich and soup items up on the menu.

Frank looked around at the half dozen groups in the dining area. Sitting at one table were three little old ladies. One of them was working a piece of cross stitch.

"Bingo," Frank said and grinned because cross stitch was definitely in the knitting family. What were the odds? Maybe he *was* Sherlock.

Then the old gal with the clearest view of the front door glanced up at him. She was wearing black sneakers, blue polyester pants, and a short red muumuu top with big flowers on it. She saw him and his tattoos, took his measure, but did not blanch and look away. Instead, she gave him a look, made eye contact, made sure he knew it, made sure he knew he didn't sweat her at all, then went back to her conversation.

Frank reconsidered his Knitters of Death theory. That look had taken him back to Coalinga. The groups of convicts radiating their territory with dead-eye, no sweat stares had nothing on that old gal in her muumuu. And it was a fact that some of those cons had been knitters too. If you looked at it that way, there was a whole underworld of knitters.

He glanced around to see if the Knitters of Death had any more members in the immediate area, but the rest of the folks were in sandals or biker shorts. Clearly visitors.

And those were clearly three old ladies who weren't scared of much. Frank decided he had nothing to gain by engaging in any male ape posturing with them. He was just one doughnut man, or ex-con, depending on where you decided to focus, and there were three of them. So he turned back to the menu.

He skipped over the chicken and arugula brioche, gave a big no to the fennel rubbed Italian roasted pork, then considered the Gobbler, which was wild turkey with alfalfa sprouts, avocado, and Swiss, all on a buttery croissant, and served with a side of cranberries.

The woman at the counter saw him looking and told him all the selections came with a giant pickle. She was in her mid-forties and had a heavy, rough voice, like maybe at one time she'd smoked like a chimney.

"A giant pickle is a plus," he said, but he wasn't thinking about food. He was thinking about the fact that she was a local and that the odds were good that she would know something. Everyone in a small community knew something. Or they knew someone who would. He continued to look over the selections and said, "You know the Elkhorn ranch?"

"Gorgeous place," she said.

"Indeed. How does one get there from here?"

She told him the route, which matched exactly the route Frank had taken.

He said, "You know how I might contact the owner?"

"It's owned by some foreigners," she said.

"Oh?" he asked.

"Germans," she said.

"You get a lot of Germans around here?"

"The parks bring in folks from all over. We had a bus full of Koreans just last week. They were doing a western circuit—Disneyland, Vegas, then here with Mother Nature."

"A triple threat," he said.

She nodded.

"Buses have got to be good for business," he said.

"They went for the soups," she said. "It appears Koreans are not big bread eaters."

"Rice is the staple in that part of the world," he agreed.

"And that stuff they bury in the ground. They all wanted kimchi."

Frank nodded. "I heard they rent the Elkhorn."

"The Koreans?"

"No, I mean I heard the owners rent it out."

"They used to, but they pulled it off the market about eighteen months ago. I have some friends who clean cabins and condos, and it used to be one of their accounts. But they don't send them up to Elkhorn anymore."

"Maybe the job went to someone else."

"No, it's pulled from the property management as well."

"That's disappointing," he said. "It looked like a real nice place."

"Gorgeous," she said again, then adjusted one of her heavy mascara eyelashes.

"They ever run any animals up there? Is it like a dude ranch?"

"The old owners used to ranch, but they died years ago. Some rich computer guy from California owned it for a few years. Then it went to rentals."

"With the Germans?"

"Foreigners are buying everything up," she said.

"Do the owners ever come around?"

She shrugged. "I don't know. It's not like the old days. Kind of sad in a way. But life moves on. You just hope the change is like a caterpillar in a chrysalis."

Frank thought about Coalinga. Maybe that had been his chrysalis. Maybe he'd emerged a new man. Maybe Frank was, at this very moment, a big butterfly.

Yeah, one that looked like Frankenstein. If he was anything, he was a moth, wasting his energy buzzing around some dumb light bulb instead of exploring the night and hooking up with a fine lady moth.

"You know who's up there now?"

"Nope," she shrugged.

Frank nodded, abandoned the sandwiches, and looked back down at the pastries and realized the lemon bars were calling out to him. He didn't want them to feel bad, and so he ordered one, paid her, and received his prize on a napkin. And then a new batch of customers walked in, and Frank stepped to the side.

The new folks began to pepper the gal at the counter with questions about the menu, and Frank looked out at the parking lot. The sheriff was gone, which was too bad. But then maybe she had actually taken his comment in the parking lot seriously. Maybe she'd called her posse and gone back to the ranch.

Frank should have told her about the draw farther up the canyon by the backhoe and all the drones buzzing around like wasps to keep an eye out. He should have told her Bill might be selling bad goat meat.

Frank got a water cup from the woman at the counter, then turned to get a seat. The only table available was by the three little old ladies, and so he made his way over and sat down next to them.

The one in the muumuu gave him a brief look. Her friends gave him a glance as well. One had short, elegant hair and was dressed in a sharp blouse and skirt. The other was a weathered gal who had her gray-streaked hair pulled back in a ponytail and was wearing a denim shirt with pearl buttons, jeans, and cowboy boots.

Frank waved hello. The sharp dresser gave him a polite wave, then the three of them turned back to their conversation.

Frank savored bites of the lemon bar and thought, but he was soon listening to the three women. The one in the muumuu had sheep. And either a pack of coyotes, or some dogs from an unnamed neighbor none of them liked, had been in her sheep, and she had been sitting up all night with her rifle and night vision scope trying to plug one of them. The sharp dresser said she'd come over with her own rifle tonight. The weathered cowgirl said they shouldn't mess with it and just set out traps.

Frank decided he liked the knitters of death. And then he wondered. He turned to them and said, “Excuse me.”

The three of them looked over at him.

He said, “I’m sorry, but I overheard you talking about coyotes.”

They waited.

He said, “Could a pack of coyotes kill a herd of goats? Just slaughter them. Dozens of them.”

The sharp dresser said, “They could, eventually.”

“But they’re not like wolves,” said the one in the muumuu. “Wolves just like to kill. They’ll chew on a dozen animals just for the fun of it and leave them to die.”

The sharp dresser said, “Coyotes will come in and kill a couple each night. If you’ve got kids, they can get a number of those.”

“Kids?”

“Goat kids.”

“Ah,” Frank said, realizing they were not talking about children.

The cowgirl spoke up, “They can get more if you don’t have dogs, but only a fool keeps a flock without dogs.”

“Or llamas,” said the sharp dresser.

“Overrated,” said the cowgirl. “But the best thing to do is get traps.”

“It’s legal to kill them.”

“You see a coyote, you run it over,” said the one in the muumuu.

Frank nodded. Clearly, there was no love-loss between these women and the desert canines. Frank thought about what he’d seen back at the ranch. There had been no sign of any dogs anywhere.

“Is there ever any reason why you’d want to keep goats without dogs to protect them?”

The one in the muumuu said, “You’re from the city, aren’t you? California?”

“No, I live in Wyoming.”

“In the city,” she said.

“In the city,” he granted.

“Well, out here Mother Nature is in control. And she can be one mean lady. She’s all about blood and guts and one thing eating another. So if you want your domesticated animals to stay alive, the ones we’ve bred the ability to run and flee out of, then you've got to have some protection."

"Right," Frank said.

The one in the muumuu pointed at the side of his face. "Where'd you get that tattoo?"

He could say prison, but he decided to be discrete. "California."

"Figures. It looks like hell," she said. "You should get it fixed. They can do that, you know."

He said, "I'll put it on my list of things to save up for. I'm sure the women will go wild."

She pursed her lips and assessed the idea of his face without it. "They just might," she agreed.

Frank stood. "Well, you three lovely ladies have been very helpful. Have a great day. I hope you fix your coyote problem."

The sharp dresser and cowgirl smiled discretely. The one in the muumuu gave him another appraising look and said to her friends, "Rock Hudson?"

The name tickled Frank's memory. It was some golden age movie star.

The sharp dresser considered, then said, "Not enough hair."

Frank smiled and left them to the assessment of his qualities and walked out, licking the last of the lemon bar off his fingers.

When he was outside, he looked north, towards Glendale and wondered if he should try to find the sheriff, but discarded that idea. Kanab was to the south. That's where the sheriff's office was, and that's where he'd leave his message about goats and the canyon. And then he'd be done with the matter. It wasn't his fight after all. The fine people of this area had their own dogs to protect them from Mother Nature and her blood and gore, and those sheepdogs were Sheriff Hood and her deputies. And if they'd gone to the coyote side, well, that wasn't his issue.

Just after he made his decision, he noticed a white Taurus with tinted windows down the road a bit. It was pulled off to the side by a field of alfalfa. A man sat behind the wheel. The Taurus hadn't been there when Frank pulled in. Furthermore, something about it was odd, and Frank immediately realized the shoulder there was super narrow. It was not a good place to stop, not with parking lots just ahead. However, it was a good spot from which to observe the front of the bakery at a distance that made it hard to see facial features.

Frank dusted the remaining powdered sugar off his hands, then got into the Nova and started her up. He made a three-point turn, drove to the sidewalk and looked both ways. He had a good break in the traffic, so he pulled out onto the road, heading south. He glanced in his rearview mirror, waited, glanced again and saw the white Taurus pull onto the road behind him.

12

Taurus

FRANK DROVE AWAY from the bakery and through the rest of the little town of Orderville with the white Taurus keeping its distance behind him. The houses petered out, and the fields began, as did a scenic view of a section of the White Cliffs. Frank looked at the cliffs, looked at the Taurus still in his rearview. One of the last places on the way out of town was a rock shop. Frank decided he'd just acquired a craving to go rock shopping and pulled into the parking lot out front.

The white Taurus pulled off a hundred yards back. The guy rolled down his window, held his phone out like he was taking pictures of the White Cliffs.

It could be a tourist, Frank thought. Time would tell.

There were tables of rocks set out front of the shop. Frank turned the Nova off, then got out and went to look at the rocks. He saw a collection of flat, polished rose-colored stones and figured someone could make a fancy rock family with such things.

The guy up the road stopped taking pictures and just sat there.

Frank browsed, found a box of dark ammonite, another of green malachite, and a third of honeycomb onyx that looked like butterscotch candies. Frank looked back up the road. Plenty of time had passed for someone to exhaust all the possible angles you might get by taking snaps from inside a car, but the Taurus was still there.

Frank fiddled around with a chunk of Utah zebra marble about half the size of his palm that had been carved into the shape of a buffalo, put it back, then walked to the Nova and gave the Taurus a stare.

Was that an unmarked vehicle? Sheriff Hood's replacement?

Frank got into the Nova, pulled out onto the road, but instead of heading south he decided he didn't need to stop at the sheriff's office in Kanab when Deputy Dan was right here with him. Frank turned his car around and headed for the Taurus.

But the Taurus suddenly pulled onto the road and accelerated.

As Frank approached, he looked at the plates, but they did not have the "EX" that signified it was a state-owned vehicle. So it wasn't a cop, unless the driver was an investigator or involved with some other special operation that required that he go undercover. Which could be a possibility. But why would Sheriff Hood put an unmarked car on him? Wouldn't your regular ne're-do-well be more motivated to leave the county if he knew a cop was riding his tail?

Frank and the Taurus approached each other. Frank slowed, but the guy in the Taurus was speeding up. He was also wearing a baseball cap and sunglasses and looking the other way so that all Frank got when they passed each other was a good view of his neck.

If the Taurus man had been a cop wanting to escort Frank, he would have flagged Frank down, given him a look, or turned to follow him—something. But this guy continued tooling down the road.

So maybe Mr. Taurus was just some tourist on his happy way south towards Arizona. Maybe he was a real estate agent, scoping out potential buys for a client.

Or maybe not. The Taurus had come from the north, from the direction of Glendale and the car graveyard. Make a turn there, and you could drive out and meet some fine folks who claimed to be renting a place that wasn't for rent. A place with drones and security cameras. And a backhoe and lots of dead goats. And a missing man who'd been walloped in the head with a shovel.

Frank slowed, cranked the wheel, and turned south again. He passed the rock shop, got the Taurus in his sights, but then had to ease off the gas because Mr. Taurus was going two miles an hour under the speed limit.

And Frank wondered again who it was. Who in their right mind went two under the speed limit?

Real estate agents scoping a place out might. And student drivers. And someone who wanted you to pass them might drive slowly as well.

Frank decided to hang back. Then he decided to pull over and search the sky for drones. He didn't see any. Not in the space up to the regulation 500 feet ceiling. But that didn't mean one wasn't up there at an illegal height, far too high for him to see easily.

Frank pulled back onto the road. A few miles later he cruised into Mt. Carmel Junction. He passed the RV park, the turnoff to Zion's National, the Thunderbird Cafe, the gas station. He looked for the Taurus, but it all looked exactly the same as it had when he'd come through the first time. The Taurus was nowhere to be seen.

He left Mt. Carmel Junction and entered the winding, hilly stretch where he'd caught up to the pickup earlier. Not too long after that, he cruised around a bend, and the area where he'd been earlier that day opened up before him. The sun was setting, lighting up the cliffs. They would soon be ablaze with light, then fade as the stars revealed themselves. In the distance stood the knoll where he'd found an excellent front row seat.

If Frank hurried, he might be able to make the last of the show. Except all that had been spoiled now. Even if his lizard companion returned, Frank wouldn't be watching the glory of nature. He'd be replaying the scene of the man being hit by the shovel. He'd be thinking of the canyon above the Elkhorn and the hasty grave that lay there. And the fact that his history had been dragged into this to let the perpetrators get away scot-free.

Frank drove along the stretch of highway. A few minutes later, he passed the dirt road turnoff where he'd parked the Nova. He continued along the highway, driving toward Kanab as the sun dipped toward the western mountains.

Frank drove into Kanab just after the sun had set. It was the time when there was still enough light to see by, but dark enough that all the neon signs for the restaurants and motels and gas stations shone in the twilight. The town wasn't big, just a few dozen crisscrossing streets nestled up against the foot of the Vermillion Cliffs. It was a main drag a mile or two long with a couple of turns in it. The town was mostly on this side of the river, but there were some homes on the other side in the cedars at the foot of a red rock mountain. North of Kanab was the wilderness. To the south were farms and ranches. For many it was a drive-through town as they made their way to the Grand Canyon or other parts of Arizona. But not always. A number of western movies had been shot in the area. For them, Kanab had been a destination.

Frank drove past a number of residences. Then saw some restaurants and inns up ahead. He found a place that looked cheap, went in and asked if they had any rooms. They did. He paid the woman and came back outside with the key and found the first stars had begun to appear in the sky.

He didn't go to his room. Instead, he followed the directions the desk clerk had given him and drove to the sheriff's office. The front door led to a small receiving room with a door and a service window. The locked door led to the rest of the office. The plexiglas service window gave view to a little office on the other side. In that office sat a woman. Frank figured that was Kathy, the dispatcher. He got her attention, then asked her if they had any Ford Taurus's in their fleet.

"No sir," she said.

"What about Highway Patrol?"

"You would have to talk to them," she said. "Is that what you came in for?"

"No," he said, "I came to talk to Sheriff Hood."

"She's not in. Do you want to leave a message?"

He had wanted to leave a message. But he didn't think the message would carry much weight if he left it on a piece of paper.

"When will she get back?"

"She's on call all night long."

"Tell her I've got something to say. She can call me on my cell number."

"Okay," the dispatcher said, and then she took his name and number and promised she'd get the message to Sheriff Hood.

Frank figured he had a ten percent chance she'd call him, ninety percent she'd listen to the message and tell Kathy to file it. Frank bid Kathy a good evening, then walked back outside into the twilight. The heat of the day had leached away. The air was soft and dry and cooler than during the day, but still warm. The crickets chirped. He heard the clopping of horse hooves on the asphalt and turned to see an old man wearing boots, jeans, a western-styled shirt, and a pale cowboy hat ride a horse with big white and brown patches, what horse people referred to as a paint, across an intersection a few houses down.

Frank watched him disappear behind a house, took in a big breath of clean desert air, then walked over to the Nova. As he was opening the door, he glanced down the road in the opposite direction and saw a white Taurus two blocks down at the curb on the main drag. It was in a spot that had been empty when he'd turned down this street.

Frank peered more closely. Shadows were falling, the first stars shining in the eastern sky, but it was not so dark that he couldn't see who was sitting behind the wheel. It was not just a Taurus. It was *the* Taurus. With the driver in the baseball cap.

Frank slid in behind his wheel, shut the door, and started her up. He backed out calmly. Pulled up to the sidewalk calmly. Then rolled out of the sheriff's little parking lot and onto the street.

Frank had seen what Bill's folks were capable of. He knew they were listening to their police scanner. He knew there was a good chance the sheriff had reported what he'd said in the parking lot of the bakery. On the other hand, that Taurus sitting there could all be coincidence.

But then the driver of the Taurus saw Frank approaching, cranked the wheel of his car, and shot out from the curb.

"I don't think so," Frank said. The Taurus was a decent car. But it didn't have near the horsepower the Nova did. "You and me are going to have ourselves a chat."

Then he punched it.

13

Edna's

THE MAN IN THE TAURUS accelerated down the main drag and out of view behind the buildings.

Frank turned on his headlights, roared toward the intersection, prepared to swing out after him, but saw an old couple in a huge motor coach lumbering right at him, the headlights big and blockish and halogen bright. He slammed on the brakes.

The front windshield of the coach was the size of a barn and gave Frank a clear view of the old guy at the wheel and the old gal in the passenger seat who glared and pointed at him, then brushed her finger at him in an old-fashioned scolding as they moseyed on by. The coach was as tall as a touring bus with a big full-color scene of Yosemite all down the side with a web address where fellow travelers could go to rent themselves such a fine vehicle and drive to such fine sights. And sleep in luxury with pop-out sides for extra living space. The back of the coach passed, and Frank saw they were towing a car behind them because a coach was no kind of thing to get around in once you reached your destination. For example, it would never fit in a McDonald's drive-through. If he recalled correctly, RV people called that car in the back a toad.

The toad passed by, but Frank still couldn't go because a blue Ford sedan was two car lengths behind the coach, and Frank wasn't too keen on being T-boned. The Ford was followed by a big yellow pickup.

A few streets ahead, the Taurus turned off onto a side street, down into the shadows of the fading twilight.

After the pickup, the road cleared, and Frank punched it out onto the main drag and floored it. One nice thing about all these small

Utah towns was that the old pioneer Mormons who laid them out had believed in order. So instead of building roads on top of cow trails, they'd laid out the town in a grid. If Frank was fast, he might be able to take a different route and cut the Taurus off. He turned down the next side street and accelerated hard.

When he came to the next intersection, he looked down the street and saw the Taurus, lights off, blowing through a quiet residential intersection three streets down. And that clinched it—Mr. Taurus was definitely not an undercover cop because a cop would have simply called in, saying his cover had been blown, and someone else would have been sent to take his place. Furthermore, a cop wouldn't run.

Frank turned into that part of the street grid, raced past the cross streets to that intersection and turned the direction the Taurus had gone, but the street was empty.

Frank raced down to the next intersection and looked both ways, but there was no Taurus. He sped to the next intersection and the next, but they were empty too.

He cursed, knowing he'd missed his opportunity, because while the grid had offered him one brief chance of catching up, it also gave the Taurus multiple chances of escape. Nevertheless, he spent twenty more minutes driving patterns through the grid as night fell. After his last turn, he thought he spotted the Taurus once more in the street lamps out on the main drag, but he was a number of intersections away, and when Frank finally got there, the car was gone.

His one consolation was that all this chasing around had confirmed his original assessment—Bill had sent someone after him, which in Frank's mind took this up a notch.

He turned onto Kanab's well-lit main street and drove back toward his hotel. He glanced at his phone. Sheriff Hood had not called. She had not texted.

He passed a couple of restaurants and another inn, and Frank decided he needed to have a think, so he slowed at the well-lit café ahead, and pulled into the parking it shared with a local pub and steak house. The lot was dark and there were a lot of cars, but Frank found a good spot in the shadows in the back, parked, and got out.

By this time, night had truly fallen. The stars were out in full force as were the neon signs of the various businesses. Loud music was coming out of the pub. Frank didn't think alcohol and lots of thumping bass would lend itself to thinking, so he chose the diner with the red neon sign that said Edna's.

When he opened the front door, he discovered most of the cars must have been there for the pub because the diner was a ghost town. But it smelled good, and the waitress gave him a warm smile as soon as he walked in, and so he stayed. She told him to find a spot, and he found one at the back and ordered a coffee. Then he pulled his phone out and began to examine the photos he'd taken, zooming in and searching around.

When he got to the ones he'd taken of the shed up the canyon by the goat graves, he noticed something at the peak of the eaves. He zoomed in and found more security cameras.

He looked at a few other photos with good angles and confirmed that's what they had to be. He thought of the three knitters of death and wondered what kind of rancher got security cameras for his goats instead of dogs or llamas.

No kind of farmer he knew. Besides, who would be close enough to respond to a predator if the cameras picked one up?

Maybe it wasn't predators they were worrying about. Maybe they were more concerned about something else. Frank thought about those drones zooming around that muckity-muck ranch. Drones were making new businesses possible. You could do search and rescue with a little squadron of networked drones. You could do crop dusting with far less pesticide. Naturalists could track animal populations better. You could deliver pizza. Drones were used for surveying and wedding photography. But Bill's drones hadn't been taking pictures of brides.

Maybe Bill had some new drone prototype. Maybe the man in the tarp was a competitor, or working for one, performing a little corporate espionage.

Frank thought about that. A 4,000 acre ranch in the middle of the wilderness was one heck of a place to keep something secret.

The waitress came by with his coffee and asked him if she could get him anything else. She was one of those friendly gals, treating him like they'd been neighbors for life.

He said, "I don't know. What have you got?"

She said, "We've got a cheeseburger that will knock your socks off."

"I didn't know burgers could do that," Frank said.

"You haven't had one of our burgers," she said.

What the heck, Frank thought. Somebody needed to support this diner, especially if everyone was going to the pub. And he was hungry. "It sounds like I'd better not miss it," he said.

"I'm going to have them put extra tomato on yours. A nice thick, perky slice. They're fresh from my garden."

"Maybe that's what's knocking the socks off."

"Oh, honey, we've got more than one trick up our sleeves," she said with a smile.

Frank decided he was looking forward to this cheeseburger.

About this time some cowboys walked in. From the dirt on their jeans and hats, these were the real deal. Their shirts were tucked in. Their hair was cut short, although one of them had a beard. They took a booth in the corner.

Not long after that an attractive woman in her twenties arrived. She had nice brown skin and dark hair parted into two braids that fell past her shoulders. She was wearing long pants with cargo pockets and boots. She too was told to find a spot and selected one equidistant from the cowboys and Frank. She had a ring on the index finger of her right hand, but none on her left.

She glanced over, and Frank smiled, but she looked away. Frank thought of the advice from the muumuued knitter, and figured she might be right: only a certain kind of woman went in for men with tattoos on the face.

Frank glanced over at the cowboys who had noticed the woman as well. They were polite boys. One gave him a little shrug of sympathy. Frank nodded, then made a small motion saying she was all theirs. But the cowboys either weren't interested or were still working their courage up because they just drank the waters the waitress brought and talked between themselves.

The woman sighed a few times heavily, then surprised him by getting up and walking over to his booth.

Frank looked up. She was pretty, and that was without wearing much makeup. Her teeth weren't movie star straight, but that only gave her a little extra charm.

She said, "I don't mean to bother you, but I'm wondering if you might help me."

She had an accent. Not Spanish.

"Where you from?" Frank asked.

She hesitated, clearly not comfortable giving a thug like him any personal details, then said, "I have cables. I just need a jump."

"You just sat down."

"I left my wallet back at the hotel."

Frank nodded and saw the cowboys watching them.

Then she must have reconsidered, now that she'd seen him up close. "It's okay; I can walk," she said and prepared to turn.

"No," he said and smiled big. "It will take ten seconds."

"I should have replaced the battery," she said.

Frank slid out of the booth and stood up. "You sure it's the battery and not the alternator?"

"I don't know," she said.

Frank nodded. "Well, lead the way. It's easy to figure out."

She turned and began to walk toward the front. One of the cowboys caught Frank's eye and gave him one of those I-thought-we-had-a-deal looks. Frank shrugged. You snooze, you lose. What could he say?

As they walked past the counter, Frank called to the waitress. "I'm coming right back for that cheeseburger," he said.

She nodded, then walked over to take the cowboys' order.

The woman pushed through the front door, and Frank followed her out. He said, "Denmark?"

"What?" she asked.

"Where you're from."

"Not quite."

"Your English is very good," he said.

"I've been studying at university," she said.

"Kanab has got a university?"

"I don't know," she said and turned the corner into the parking lot. "I'm not studying here." She unzipped her purse. "I probably will need a push out from the parking stall. That's why I asked you. You look very strong. You look like you know cars."

Ms. Mary, his doughnut shop boss, told him he looked like a serial killer the first time she saw him. This gal was obviously braver than Ms. Mary, and Ms. Mary was one tough nut.

"Which one is yours?" he asked.

"That one, sticking out," she said and pointed at a Cherokee toward the back.

Frank could have sworn he'd seen that Cherokee when he'd come in, so maybe she meant the Buick next to it. But that had been there too.

They walked past the Cherokee, past the Buick, almost to the end of the parking lot. Back into the shadows that were only illuminated by the neon strip along the side of the pub. Frank recognized all of the cars here. Then he saw the back end of a Lincoln parked in the alley behind the diner. He'd seen a Lincoln just like it a little earlier today. Exactly the same in every way, except this one had its big fat trunk standing open.

A faint and distant alarm sounded in his mind, and he slowed.

"I really appreciate this," she said and reached into her purse.

His alarms went on full.

"No problem," he said and decided to rush her, because he'd much rather be in close when the gun came out than backpedaling, but then a man wearing a balaclava stepped out from behind an SUV to join the woman. He was holding a club made from the long handle of an axe.

Frank stopped.

The woman whipped a little pink pepper spray pistol out of her purse and pointed its fat barrel at him. The LED light, designed to help the wielder aim the spray and momentarily distract the target, lit up.

Crap, he thought, then ducked. Pepper spray in the face took your vision away. Made it hard to breathe. He heard the spray eject and stream over his head. A number of drops hit his face and immediately began to burn.

Frank's adrenaline surged. He darted in between two cars, but the club man must have thought of that too when the woman had shot her spray and was already racing to stop Frank's progress.

There was another blast from the pink pistol which hit the side of the vehicle next to him and splashed down Frank's exposed arm and his ear and jaw.

The club man reached the end of the gap between the two cars. He held the club up in his left hand, which meant that was the side Frank would charge.

Then a shoe scraped on the asphalt close behind him. Before Frank could turn, a thin cord looped down over Frank's face, and his alarms went into full swing because back in the day, Frank had trained with garrotes, and once they were around your neck, you were pretty much done for.

14

Definitely Not Danish

FRANK IMMEDIATELY THREW his head back and his forearm up, knocking away the loop. The guy and Frank did a little roll, a twist like a dance move, and then Frank got his feet under him, growled in anger, and charged into the guy's middle, hitting him like a lineman hits the blocking sled.

The guy was big and strong, but he wasn't some monstrous Cornhusker, which meant he was far easier to move than a blocking sled, and Frank drove him back through the space between two cars at the club man.

The man grunted, tripped over the cement curb, and went down next to an arrangement of desert grass in the pub's gravel landscape.

Frank almost went down with him, but caught himself and stumbled over the guy in his balaclava.

Club man had stepped back. Now he waded in, stepping over the garrote guy, and swinging hard with his left at Frank's head, but Frank had been expecting it, and moved into it, catching the club about halfway down its shaft.

With his arm extended, the guy wasn't in the best position to fight much, so Frank stepped into him, slammed the palm of his hand into the guy's nose, and felt the septum collapse.

The guy's head flew back. Frank took the axe handle in a two-handed grip, wrenched it out of the guy's grip, then reversed and rammed the end at the guy's throat.

Except the adrenaline had really kicked in and wrecked Frank's aim, and he hit the guy high in the chest instead. But the blow was still strong, and it knocked the man back.

The big man with the garrote surged to his feet and reached behind his back, obviously for a gun.

Frank charged, swung for the man's head, but the guy ducked, and Frank's blow smashed into the back of a little SUV.

The garrotter spun, tried to raise his semiautomatic, but Frank swung again with the club, slashing down at an angle, and hit the guy in the forearm with a nice woody thunk.

The gun fell from his hand into the gravel.

A few feet away, the club man climbed to his feet.

Frank whirled, the club low, preparing to bring it up in a strong backhand into the guy's jaw, to jolt his brain, to shake it in its skull so severely the guy would pass out, and then a light flashed, like someone was taking his picture, but Frank knew the paparazzi hadn't taken over the parking lot.

The woman had come around the cars and onto the pub's pretty gravel. She was in a sturdy stance, her LED lit up, her pink pistol aimed right at him. She pulled the trigger.

Frank turned, and a stream of pepper spray shot out of the pistol and up his side, over his neck, jaw, and the side of his face. His one eye began to burn. There was mist in that stream, and he breathed it in, and the burning mist immediately started to choke him.

Frank swung at the club man, caught him with a glancing blow to the head, tried for another, but his one eye was streaming now, the other was stinging, and it felt like someone was closing his air passage.

The light flashed again.

Frank didn't have much time, and knew he couldn't take another dose of that pepper. He spun and dodged low, into the space between a pickup and a car.

The spray shot over his head and hit the truck.

One of the men shouted something, but it wasn't in English. The man who had tried to garrote him scrambled for his gun. The other one pulled a knife. They weren't as steady as they had been, but there was still enough juice left in them to do quite a bit of damage. The woman skirted across the gravel, trying to get an angle on Frank again. They were going to trap him.

Frank wheezed for breath. His eye was running like a river.

And then a group of people came out of the pub, talking loudly and laughing, and headed for the parking lot.

The three attackers turned to look at the group, just as he'd hoped they would, and Frank stepped back, then ducked behind the pickup—out of any kind of line of fire the garrote man might have.

Frank prepared himself with his club. He figured he'd have one chance, and it couldn't be a swing. It would have to be a two-handed shot with his two hundred and ten pounds coming at speed directly at the person, concentrated in the four square inches at the end of the axe handle. Enough force to do internal damage.

He wheezed and waited, his ear burning, then heard quick steps moving away on gravel, then across the asphalt. A moment later they shot out of the lanes between three cars and sprinted for the Lincoln.

Frank rose, took two steps, then hurled the axe handle at the garrote man. It flew end over end, missed the garrote man, but glanced off the woman's head.

She stumbled to the asphalt, the axe handled clattering beside her. The other two either didn't notice or didn't care and ran to the car, which was just fine by Frank because he was going to get some answers.

He lumbered toward her, but the hit must have been nothing more than a medium grade conking because the woman pushed herself to her feet. Then she saw the axe handle, lunged back for it, and ran with it toward the Lincoln. She reached the massive open trunk just as the car was pulling away, tossed the axe handle in, then jumped in with her purse. The car shot away. The lid slammed down over her. And then the Lincoln disappeared down the alley behind Edna's.

Frank stopped. His face felt like it was frying on a griddle. His one eye was watering like Niagara. He was wheezing, his throat threatening to close off any second now. He needed to take care of this spray, and what better place than the diner?

He turned and began to walk back toward the main entrance, breathing loudly.

The group from the pub was coming his way. One of them saw

him. Frank must have been a real sight, coming out of a dark lot with his running eye, wheezing, and tattoos.

"Whoa," one of the pub patrons said. The others stopped and sidled back. "Dude," the guy said.

Frank lumbered past, trying to keep himself going in the right direction, which was becoming increasingly difficult because the pain and watering of the one eye was making it hard to see with the other. He made it past the last of the cars and walked into the light of the sidewalk and to the front door of the diner.

He pulled it open and stumbled in.

"I need water and dish soap," he said loudly. "Where's the kitchen sink?"

The waitress was behind the counter. She looked up at him in alarm. "Oh my lord, did the battery explode?"

"Your sink," Frank said.

"Right," she said and hustled over to open the door that led to the kitchen. Frank followed her, knowing that if this was a hit, they just might circle round, see him standing in the well-lit windows, and send someone in who then might very easily exit out the back.

The door swung behind him, and Frank walked over to the sink which was deep with a high faucet. The liquid soap was standing in a bottle next to the side.

He needed to get as much of the pepper off him, and that started with his shirt, which was wet with it. He carefully pulled it over his head, keeping the sprayed side away from his face, and tossed the thing to the ground. The skin on his side where the pepper had soaked through felt like road rash.

He turned the water on semi-hot, grabbed a metal bowl with bits of flour and chicken still in it, then picked up the plastic bottle of liquid soap and squeezed it hard three times, squirting in at least a cup of the blue liquid. He put the bowl under the water and filled it up until it was a nice big frothy mess, and then he looked up at the ceiling and splashed the heavily soaped water onto the side of his face. He didn't rub. Rubbing at this stage would only spread the pepper oil, so he settled for saturating his head and skin with the soapy water over and over. When his bowl of chicken soap ran out, he made another and soap-rinsed again.

He soaped and rinsed half a dozen times. The waitress asked how she could help, and he told her she needed gloves. A few moments later she showed up with rubber gloves and took over rinsing. Then he turned to his neck and side and cleaned them the same way. By this time, the burn in his eye had reduced to a sting.

The floor around the sink was sopping wet. So were his pants and shoes. But the pepper burn had receded.

He turned off the faucet, and, thinking the waitress and cook were still there, said, "I'm sorry about the mess. Let me clean it up." But when he turned, he found Sheriff Hood instead, her arms folded, her eyes suggesting this town still hung drifters.

"Smells like pepper," she said and looked his bare chest and abs up and down.

A few paces behind the sheriff were two city cops. Farther back by the door stood the waitress, cook, and the three cowboys.

"According to everyone in the diner, Mr. Shaw, you escorted a woman out."

"Yes," Frank said.

"And then you came back in covered with pepper spray."

"I did," Frank said, and knew exactly what they were thinking.

"Mr. Shaw," she said, "are you messing with me?"

"No, ma'am," he said.

"Because you're causing a lot of problems. One of the people you passed who had just come from the pub had a concealed carry permit. You're lucky you weren't shot."

"I wasn't worried about the folks from the pub."

"Do you have a death wish, Mr. Shaw? That woman might have had a real gun."

"She didn't need one," Frank said. "Her buddy had that."

"Her buddy?"

"I told you it wasn't the man in the tarp."

"You told me you were going to L.A. But now I think you're going to come with me. And you're going to do it with cuffs on."

15

Questions

THEY PUT CUFFS on Frank, then took him on a nice three-minute ride down to the city police department instead of the sheriff's office, because the incident had happened in the city, not out in the unincorporated part of the county. They sat him on a chair in an air-conditioned interrogation room that was a bit cold for a man in damp pants and no top. The city cops obviously thought Sheriff Hood had the angle because it was she who came to visit with him and chat even though this was clearly out of her jurisdiction.

She brought a city officer with her, a big guy who looked like he knew how to handle himself. Mr. Don't-Mess removed Frank's cuffs, then stood by the door with a piece in his ear, which Frank figured allowed him to communicate with those watching. Sheriff Hood took a chair across from Frank.

She looked at the tattoo on his bare chest, then produced a plastic water bottle and said, "Water?"

He said, "Have you got milk?" He was thinking milk would help the residual burning in his throat.

"This isn't school lunch," she said.

Frank nodded and took the water, knowing it probably wasn't going to do anything.

She motioned at his naked chest and face and said, "Are you feeling better?"

The diner's sink had done wonders, but there was a spot on the side of his face just back from his eye that had somehow been missed, and that eye was still watering. Also there was some burning on the palm of his hand where the pepper had gotten into the cut from the barbed-wire, and there was another spot on his on his back. But these were small, so he said, "I feel capital."

She said matter-of-factly, "Mr. Shaw, I thought you and I had a deal."

He said, "Do you guys have a white Taurus in your fleet?"

"Mr. Shaw."

"Just humor me."

She smiled her pretty smile, gave him a look that said she knew all the games, all the cons that happened in these rooms. She said, "No, we don't."

"What about the city guys?"

"Not that I know of." She looked at the don't-mess city officer.

He shook his head.

She turned back to Frank and said, "You're trying my patience."

He said, "That's the last thing I would want to do."

She waited. He waited back. Finally she gave in and asked, "Does a white Taurus have anything to do with what happened in the parking lot?"

He said, "I'm thinking it does."

"So why don't you tell me what happened?"

Frank appreciated the police. They performed a valuable job. But he knew that job wasn't to protect his interests. It was their job to investigate and prosecute crimes. And if they thought they had enough to prosecute him, they'd send it on up to the DA, regardless of the actual facts. It didn't matter if their theory of what went down was true. It only mattered that it was possible. And right now they were working on a theory of attempted rape.

He said, "I went into the diner. I sat down. I ordered a knock-your-socks off cheeseburger. The waitress was going to put extra tomato from her garden on it. Some cowboys came in, then a woman. A few minutes later the woman came over and told me she'd left her wallet at the hotel, and she needed to jump her car to go get it. She asked if I would help her out. I said I'd be happy to. I followed her out. I asked her if she was from Denmark because she had a faint accent I couldn't place. She said Denmark wasn't quite it. She said she was going to college, but not around here." Frank paused because it was beyond this point, if he wasn't careful, he would hang himself.

"Okay," Sheriff Hood said. "Sounds innocent enough to me. Any guy would help her in your place."

Hood was polite. She'd put on her listening face. Her smile and eyes were all sympathy. Like maybe Frank was the victim here, which he was.

"So what happened then?" she asked.

Frank said, "Well that's the funny thing. See, after you left me at the bakery, a white Taurus started to tail me. Any ideas why someone would want to follow me?"

She said with more of that disarming sincerity, "You'll know better than I will. Why don't you tell me about that?"

Safety and kindness radiated from her, which was exactly what a good interrogator wanted to radiate. Most people, if they've done something wrong, want to confess. They want to share the burden of their guilt. They want to share their anger. All it takes is a little friendly sympathy, and they figure they're in a safe place and pour the story forth.

Frank had known a sincere, older cop who who'd regularly sympathized people into not only confessing their crimes, but also thanking him for listening when they finished. Frank figured Sheriff Hood's straight-forward feminine kindness probably broke plenty of the locals into spilling all sorts of beans. He said, "I know your Jedi mind tricks."

She smiled a very warm and disarming smile, and his lizard brain, the one in the back, totally fell for it. It started telling him that not only did she believe his innocence, but she was also interested in a date. It pointed out how fine she looked in the fluorescent, interrogation-room light. Luckily, Frank had a neo-cortex.

He said, "You've looked me up. You've run my information. I know what you're thinking, but if you're going to solve this, you're going to have to trust me."

She said, "I want to trust you, but trust is earned."

"I totally agree," he said.

She said, "I asked you to leave the county. You agreed. But when I drive out of the Elkhorn, I find you coming the other way. I then gave you the benefit of the doubt, but the next thing I know you're involved in an incident with a woman and pepper spray."

Frank nodded.

She said, "Somebody else might look at the situation and decide you pose a risk to the public safety."

He said, "You're reading this with the wrong lens. My crime is in the past. People change."

She said, "All crimes are in the past, but I think we've gotten a little off track. I'm not looking to probe your history. I'm just trying to find out what happened to the woman you walked out into the parking lot with."

Sheriff Hood might have a good heart. She might be straight up. But she didn't have all the facts, and that was usually dangerous.

She said, "The woman obviously had some type of pepper spray canister or gun. What would make her pull that on you? You said she was a foreigner. Did you say anything she might have misunderstood?"

Frank's lizard brain said she was truly trying to see it from his perspective. She just wanted to understand. This, of course, was more Jedi mind crap. The problem was that the woman and her two thugs needed to be sitting here, not Frank.

He said, "I know you don't have anything to hold me on. You don't even know if that woman I walked out with sprayed me. I might have accidentally discharged a canister myself."

"Many things are possible."

"You're making assumptions. You're letting irrelevancies color the facts. You've got a hypothesis about an ex-con convicted of a violent crime and a woman and pepper spray. You're trying to make it work. But you've started down the wrong path."

"I'm just collecting facts," she said. "And I let the facts determine what I do next."

"Let's go back over this then," he said. "I'm driving down to visit family in L.A., but the landscape is too gorgeous not to stop. So I stop. Late in the afternoon, I witness a man being knocked in the head with a shovel and put in the bed of a pickup truck. I call it in and follow the attackers to make sure you can find them. Did you send someone back out to the spot to confirm the tire tracks and the footprints down the slope?"

"We did."

Frank's hopes rose. "And?"

"And we saw exactly what you and the folks at the Elkhorn said we'd find."

"You found exactly what the Elkhorn folks heard discussed over their radio scanner and then spun into a lie," he said.

"That's one possibility," she said.

Frank blinked his stinging eye. "You and I talk to Bill. He did not produce the man in the tarp. Instead, he produced someone else dressed in his clothing. Then suddenly Bill's got a goat emergency, and a number of the renters, remember they said renters, rush up the canyon, following the pickup you and I both saw. The one with the shovel in the back. Have you checked to see if the folks there are actually renters? Because I was told the place had been taken off the market eighteen months ago."

"Who told you that?"

"The gal at the bakery where you missed a fine lemon bar with me and the knitting club. You can call her. She's the one with the heavy voice."

Sheriff Hood nodded, probably knew the gal by name. "We're still waiting to hear back from the property management company," she said.

So she hadn't just brushed him off. She was being thorough. That was evidence enough for Frank's lizard brain, and he found himself liking this woman despite the fact that she couldn't see past his ex-con status.

He said, "They don't have any goats. Not now."

"How do you know that?"

Did he tell her, or did he not? Trust had to be earned.

He said, "What's the biggest strike against me in your mind?"

She said, "There are no strikes. We're just trying to get to the bottom of this. We want to explain it, just like you, Frank."

When she said his name, his heart thunked a little bit, and Frank realized, right then, that his neo-cortex had been compromised. He'd been without the company of a woman too long. It had been years in prison, then all the time out. He was watching her fine eyes and lips and forgetting where he was, and his lizard brain was precariously close to running off with the show. Either that, or she really was a Jedi.

He punched his hulking lizard brain in the face and reasserted control. He said, "You don't have anything on me, and I'd like to get some rest."

She said, "Your recent entanglement in Colorado concerns me."

She was referring to the run-in he'd had with one of his old cellies. He said, "Did you call the DA of El Paso County? There's a reason he only brought one charge against me."

"Usually they don't charge unless they think they can win the case."

"Exactly, there was no case."

She nodded. "At the same time, it shows involvement with a criminal organization."

Frank sighed.

"I'm just being honest," she said. "And now I've got this. I've got a woman to locate. And I don't want anything else going on your record. But you need to help me. Tell me what was said in the parking lot."

How was he going to get her onto the right trail?

Frank considered the cards in his hand. He had his tale of his surveillance and trespassing. He had his phone pictures that didn't show anything except a trench with dead goats in it and a shed with security cameras. He had his account of the parking lot incident without any corroboration. And then there was his criminal past putting a nice big frame around the whole mess.

If he were in her shoes, he'd be pegging Frank for a scumbag himself.

He said, "Did you get any statements from the people who came out of the pub?"

"Yes," she said.

"What did they say?"

"I'm more interested in your version."

They had nothing on him. But they'd had nothing on him when

he'd called in the man on the tarp. And the outfit at the Elkhorn with their police radio scanners had been listening in and clever enough to get ahead of the story and turn it against him.

He wanted to trust Sheriff Hood, but he didn't trust this situation. And this wasn't her case anyway. It wasn't her jurisdiction, which meant he was dealing with Officer Don't Mess or whoever was behind the pretty one-way window, and who knew what they thought. Who knew what parts they might fail to include in their reports or miss because they already had their theory and were working on it.

He said, "I'm not going to file a complaint. And it doesn't sound like anyone else has filed a complaint, so there really isn't anything more for us to discuss."

If a complaint had been filed against him, she'd bring it up now, but she didn't. She just nodded her head, and Frank's hulking lizard brain said she definitely wanted a date. Frank sighed.

Sheriff Hood looked at Officer Don't Mess. He did a little shrug.

She said, "You know that refusing to talk makes you look suspicious."

Frank said, "According to you, I was suspicious from the get-go."

"What would make her want to spray you?"

"I never said anything about anyone spraying me," Frank said.

"We can help you, Mr. Shaw."

The lizard brain had no doubt she could. But Frank wasn't going to say anymore. If he talked about an axe-handle, and that was broadcast over the radio, then the Elkhorn bunch would find out, and they would say that Frank had gone to his car and pulled it out, and her friends has wrested it out of his grasp, then fled in fear. If he talked about the garrote, the cops would really think he was making it all up.

The only thing they'd listen to was hard evidence. And so that's what he'd need to bring.

He said, "You haven't told me I'm under arrest, so, I thank you for the water, but I think I'm going to go now."

She looked at Officer Don't Mess who cocked his head like he was listening. Whoever was on the other end must have had a discussion because he stood there for what must have been a minute, then finally turned to the sheriff and nodded.

Sheriff Hood pushed her chair back and stood. Frank stood as well.

She said, "Mr. Shaw, if you've gotten yourself entangled in something, the best thing to do is stop, and let us help you out of it."

"The only thing I was entangled with was a trip to L.A.," he said. "We were thinking about hitting Disneyland."

"Who does Disneyland in the heat of the summer?" she asked.

"Me and the Koreans," he said.

She gave him a quizzical look full of Jedi mind power, but at that moment Officer Don't Mess opened the door for him, and Frank just walked out, bare chest and all, into the hallway. He waved a friendly good-bye to the other folks in the office, then headed out into the night. His pants and shoes were still moist from his sink bath at Edna's, but the dry desert air would go to work on them as he walked the few blocks back to the diner to get to his car. Then he'd fetch a dark shirt out of his duffle and find out what was really going on.

16

Kit

HERE WERE THE FACTS. A group of killers had come at him with a garrote, and the choice of that uncommon weapon said a few things. Frank had done some training with a garrote in the Special Forces. The most common use was for quietly removing sentries. But it could remove more than sentries.

So the man wielding it was probably a professional, someone who was practiced at killing up close. He probably had a military or organized crime background.

Second, it said his attackers had wanted to keep the incident quiet because if they'd wanted to kill him, they could have started out with the gun.

Third, they actually could have started out with a gun. Could have used a silencer back there in the dark, and nobody would have been the wiser.

Which meant they probably hadn't wanted to kill him. Or at least not kill him there where they might leave blood behind.

A garrote was a nasty thing. Some, like those made of piano wire, were made to quickly crush the arteries and throat. Others, however, were used primarily to restrain a subject.

He thought about the attack. It had been dark, but when he'd brushed the garrote, it hadn't felt like wire. It had been a thicker cord. And then there had been that open trunk on the Lincoln. All of which confirmed the plan had been to spray him, take him around the neck, then drag him over to that trunk and evacuate him to some other place. To question him, then kill him. It was a neat little plan, cooked up by Bill and his happy bunch of scanner-listening renters.

Frank had to admit that Team Goat was winning the intelligence war. But that was soon going to change.

He turned into the town's grid and made his way through the dark residential streets, avoiding the bright areas under the street lamps as best he could, watching for any sign of a tail. His nose and lungs were still reacting to the pepper, as was that spot just back from his eye, but he'd have to deal with that later. He made a good circuit that led him to the shadows at the back of the diner's parking lot.

The pub still banged with music, and the lot was still mostly full of cars. However, it was not full of people. Whatever investigation the police had decided to conduct must have wrapped up, and all of the folks who had surely come out of the pub to gawk, had lost interest, including everyone in the diner because the diner's big sign out front had been turned off.

Frank watched the lot. If they were going to take him here, they'd have a lookout with a good view of the entrance to the lot. The team would be positioned in a van, or behind the building in some bushes, or maybe even across the street, waiting for the signal. Or they'd be back here.

But nothing was back here with Frank except the plants and a couple of crickets. So he waited in the deep shadows, watching and listening, and when he was satisfied it was safe, he slipped into the parking lot and over to the Nova.

Above, clouds scuttled across the moon, promising a desert rain, which wouldn't be bad for what he was about to do, although it would be cold. The highs here in June averaged just under ninety degrees, but the lows averaged just above fifty.

He unlocked the car and climbed in, then paused. These folks were part of an organization, comfortable not only with garrotes, but also with electronics, as witnessed by the drones. Which meant rigging a car wouldn't make them even break a sweat. He didn't think the probability was high, but better safe than sorry.

So instead of starting the Nova up, he took his flashlight out of his glove box and examined the ignition and steering column. Then he released the hood, got out, and checked the spark plug caps. In neither place did he find wires that shouldn't be there. He looked around the undercarriage to check for any signs of meddling or tracking devices, but she was clean. And he'd know because he knew every inch of her.

Having cleared the car, Frank got back in and started her up. The busted muffler roared to life, but there was nothing to do about that, so he pulled out of the parking space and onto the main street, and accelerated.

He checked his mirrors, then kept a good eye on them as he sped down the next few blocks, but nobody took the bait, which was just as well. The road bent, went a couple of blocks, then bent again, and then brought him to a stretch that included a nice establishment called Honey Bun's Marketplace that advertised its wares with a grocery cart out front that was big enough to have been used by Paul Bunyan.

He put on a dark tee-shirt from his duffle, then went in and walked the aisles and found they had enough to make do. He gathered the best items he could find and took them up to the cashier. He piled a dark wool blanket with an Indian-looking design onto the conveyor belt, then added a box of black plastic yard bags, a nice, long-sleeved dark blue shirt, a nice tan super absorbing micro-fiber towel, some Dawn dishwashing soap, a quart of milk, batteries, and a package of bobby pins that promised to hold back fly-aways and bangs and were great for securing up-dos. He spotted a sleeve of Blueberry Pop Tarts in the display at the checkout aisle and added those for good luck.

The mousy teen manning the cash register saw Frank's face and he grinned. "Whoa, dude, what did you do to get that burn? It's like a fall asleep at the pool scorcher."

"Battery acid," Frank said.

The grin was immediately replaced by shock and concern. "Whoa," he said. "You all right?"

"I've still got my face," Frank said.

"You should get some aloe."

"Actually, if you want to neutralize an acid, you need something on the other end of the ph scale, something like baking soda."

"Right," the guy said. "I learned about that."

He scanned the next item.

"Pop Tarts help too," Frank said deadpan.

The teen stopped the next scan and got a baffled look on his face. "What?"

"It's the fortified vitamins and minerals. B_{33} in particular. Helps all sorts of skin conditions. It's like a miracle drug."

"Whoa," the teen said thoughtfully, obviously wrestling with this stunning new information. "Pop Tarts?"

Frank nodded.

The guy shook his head and finished ringing Frank up. As Frank picked up his bags, the kid bid him good evening, then moved out from behind the cash register.

When Frank reached the front doors, he glanced back and saw the boy in front of the junk food display, studying the nutritional information on the back of a sleeve of Pop Tarts.

Frank smiled and walked out to his car. With these items added to his kit, he was now prepared to go back to the ranch and find out what was really going on.

He drove to a brightly-lit gas station and entered carrying two of his brand new black plastic bags, the blanket, the shirt, the tan microfiber towel, a pair of sweats he'd pulled from his luggage, and the Dawn soap to finish the spots he'd missed. He also had the bottle to his CamelBak back pack and his leather work gloves.

He said hello to the woman presiding over the aisles of candy bars and chips, then walked past the doughnuts and corn dogs to the little hallway next to the beer cooler and into the bathroom.

After taking care of business, he turned the water on at the sink and filled his bottle. Then he saturated, in turn, his sweats, the shirt, the gloves, and blanket and stuffed them into one of the bags. Then he stuffed that bag into the second to give it more support and walked back out past the shelves of chips to his car.

Before he slid back into the car, he looked up and down the street, but didn't see anyone. So he got in with his sack of wet clothes, and in the bright lights over the pumps, he removed two of the hairpins from their package, pulled off the plastic nubs on the ends, then used his multi-tool to bend them into the shapes necessary to be used as a lock pick.

With that completed, he started the Nova and pulled out, but instead of driving the main street, he turned into the residential grid. He drove through the grid with his lights off, using the light from the moon and street lamps. He made enough turns to satisfy himself that nobody was tailing him. Of course, with his blasted muffler, they could stay put and track him by sound, but he continued on, and soon came to the north end of town and stopped at the last intersection with Highway 89, the highway that ran back north.

He pulled out, his lights still off, and left Kanab behind. A mile down the road, he saw the headlights of a vehicle coming his way, so he turned on his own headlights.

He hoped it wasn't an officer. He was sure they would all know by now to look for his Nova. A minute or so later he passed the vehicle. It was a semi, which paid him no mind, leaving him to continue north, watching his mirrors, the dark desert slipping by on both sides. In the winding stretch just before Mt. Carmel Junction, he killed his lights and pulled down some private lane and waited a good ten minutes. Three late night cars passed by during that time, but he didn't recognize any of them. He gave it five more minutes before he pulled back onto the road and continued his journey.

He drove through Mt. Carmel Junction, past the dark farm fields on the other side, entered Orderville and saluted the bakery, den of the coyote-killing knitters, and then rumbled out of town and was soon rushing through the dark narrow fields in the canyon. When he got to Glendale, he turned at the car graveyard and climbed up out of the canyon onto the mesa, his muffler breaking the night silence and marking his progress up the slope.

About four miles away from the Elkhorn, as close as he dared go with his muffler, he pulled off the dirt road and bushwhacked it over a stretch of sparse, rocky grass and parked the Nova behind some cedars a couple dozen yards back.

Frank got out, changed from his cargo shorts to cargo pants and new long-sleeve shirt. Above him, the moon and stars shone in the night sky. To the north, clouds obscured great swaths of the sky, but the rain seemed reluctant to visit these parts. He opened his trunk.

He had an auto kit back here with jumper cables, flares, and snow chains for the fine Wyoming winters, which he'd forgotten to take out. He also had his bug-out kit because you never knew what might happen.

Mostly what happened was that Frank would see a place on a map or be driving along and get a hankering to leave all concrete and asphalt behind. There was clarity to be found in the solitudes that surrounded human habitation. There was something about living off the land that spoke to him deep in his bones. In the Special Forces, he'd loved the SE part of the SERE—survival, evasion, resistance, and escape. In prison, it had taken on a whole different meaning, and he'd longed for the day he'd get out of the box and could go back into the wild.

And now that Frank was out, he was determined not to miss another moment. His kit included survival items like a medical pouch, a compass, cordage, a foldable spade, poncho, Ibuprofen, fire steel, and fishing hooks and line.

It included a slim-jim, which was useful for helping pregnant women break into cars that they'd locked their keys, baby, and dog into. It was useful for the non-pregnant types as well, but it had been a pregnant woman the last time he'd used it. It had been dusk, and she'd been at the end of a mostly empty parking lot.

When he'd walked up and she'd seen his I'm-a-criminal tattoos, she hadn't gotten a look of fear or wariness in her eyes that many women would. Instead, she'd looked to heaven and said, "Thank you, Lord, for sending a professional," leaving Frank to wonder if she'd assumed the Lord had just sent her a criminal.

A higher tech item the road kit included was a used Gen-3 night vision monocular that he'd gotten off a hunter at a garage sale. Such monoculars had about a 10,000-hour life, give or take. Frank figured this one had no more than 600 hours left. It was on its last legs, and while it still worked, it produced an image that was a lot less bright than it would have been when it was new. It also had a significant scratch on the outside lens, but instead of the five thousand dollars it might have cost at full price, he'd talked the old boy down to a hundred.

Frank dreamed of having one of the latest FLIR imagers, but that, and many other things, were not to be had until he moved up from working two minimum wage jobs.

He removed the monocular from its case, opened his packet of AA batteries, inserted the four that were required, and set it aside. He opened his pocket 500 lumen tactical flashlight, inserted new batteries in it. Then he stashed the flashlight, hairpins, a little notebook, pen, and his cell phone into the copious pockets of his pants. He left the Pop Tarts in the car as a reward for when he got back.

His friendly neighborhood tree huggers had guns and garrotes. And shovels. As a felon, guns were out of the question for Frank. Some states specified other types of off-limits weapons like switch blades, monkey paws, or blackjacks. Other states just used the term "dangerous weapons," which covered a lot of ground.

Frank might be skating on the edge, but he had a slingshot in his survival kit. If you were going to be Mountain Man Joe, you needed a tool to acquire meat. Snares and fish hooks were good. But a modern slingshot with steel or lead ball bearings was murder on squirrels and rabbits.

There were some guys who could nail a cup at a hundred yards and shoot marbles out of the air. Frank had not yet reached ninja status, but he could hit a Coke can at fifty. And the bearings smoked along at surprising speeds. When they left the slingshot, depending on the bands you used, they might be traveling 140 to 200 miles per hour. Some folks got the speed up to 300 miles per hour, which was a little less than half the speed of sound. It was quite amazing, the power of these things. In fact, there were hunters who went deer hunting using arrows in their slingshots and liked them better than their bows.

But those speeds weren't anywhere near the muzzle velocity of a gun. The bullet from a thirty-eight pistol might go 650 miles per hour. Pellets from a twelve gauge flew 800 plus miles per hour. As effective as Frank's peashooter was at killing snakes and grasshoppers, getting nailed by one of his ball bearings was nothing like getting hit with a slug from a forty-four.

So the peashooter wasn't going to win any wars, but if Frank needed it to, it just might shoot out the lens of a security camera. He put his slingshot in a pocket with a tight leather bag of ball bearings and slipped his folding knife into its sheath on his belt.

He was loaded for bear, very small ones. But he figured this would be enough; the object of this mission was recon, not storming the castle.

He glugged a pint of water, then glugged some more. When he had drunk most of the bottle, he tossed it next to the jumper cables, and quietly snicked the trunk shut. He grabbed his plastic garbage bag with the saturated clothes out of the car and locked it. His pockets were already full, so he hid the keys in a jumble of lava rock a few yards away.

Around him, crickets chirped. Above him, the sky was black, the multitude of stars bright. More stars than you could imagine living in the city with its electric glow. Looking at the tiny lights that made up the ribbon of the Milky Way always made him wonder who else in the galactic neighborhood was up. He certainly hoped some of the desk jockeys in heaven were, wherever that was located on the map.

He took a breath of the desert air, then set out, carrying the plastic sack over his shoulder with one hand, holding the monocle to his eye with the other, and headed straight for the ranch.

17

Recon

FRANK CAREFULLY MADE his way through the desert cedars and pines, avoiding the open spaces as best he could. He traveled quietly, watching his step. Walking one-eyed in the green light of night vision was a skill that had taken him and most of the other Green Berets a little bit of time to get used to. But it was better this way than using goggles. A monocle not only allowed you to keep your night vision in one eye, it also allowed better peripheral vision too.

When he figured he was about a mile away from the Elkhorn, he moved up next to the base of the slope. He'd taken a good look at the cameras and fencing earlier when he'd been there with Sheriff Hood. The cameras had infrared illuminators. He was betting they were thermal detectors, not night vision cameras like his monocle that amplified ambient visible light from the stars and moon and shorter-wave infrared radiation. Instead of magnifying existing light, thermal cameras detected and displayed tiny differences in heat via mid- and long-wave infrared.

The surface of skin was above ninety degrees. The night air was in the low seventies and dropping. This meant a man walking around a landscape a number of degrees cooler shone like a beacon. Skin would be the brightest thing out here, so unless you could keep yourself behind something that covered your heat signature or reflected the infrared away from the camera, like glass did, you could not hide.

From what he'd seen, whoever had set this system had done a reasonable job. The ranch stood in an island of trees at the mouth of the canyon. They had cameras around the compound, but he'd also seen them at the edge of the island, watching the perimeter, creating something of a thermal fence.

Many of these systems had heat sensors to alert them when something crossed the thermal fence. A lot of critters would trip that, and if you didn't have a more advanced security system with logic to determine if the heat signature was a man, you grew tired of that feature and began to ignore it. Frank hoped this was a lower-end system, although he doubted it.

He kept to the thickest parts of the desert trees, which sometimes weren't very thick. When he was 1,000 yards out, he put on his saturated gloves and began to crawl across the sparse areas to keep his heat signature behind yards of sage and other scrub. Most thermal cameras had a range up to only 300 yards. But there were some that could detect a man 800 yards out, and Frank didn't want to take any chances.

His progress slowed. Every so often, he would stop, and scan the sky with his monocle, and then he'd close his eyes, and listen for the whine of a drone. But all he ever saw were the stars. All he ever heard were the crickets and the night breeze. If they had a big military- or police-grade drone, they could park the thing up there and let it watch for hours. But the drones he'd seen were all small, and he hoped that's all they had.

About forty-five minutes later, just before the trees petered out and broke onto the sage meadow around the ranch, he found a ravine that ran part way up the steep slope that led to the mesa above. The slope itself had only scattered vegetation, but the ravine would keep him hidden behind dirt and rock. At least from the eyes in the direction of the ranch. Someone patrolling the valley floor might see him, but they'd have to be close to do it.

He figured that was a risk he could take, so he crept up the shallow ravine, careful to not send any rocks tumbling down, until he was a few yards above the canopy of the short desert trees on the valley floor. He located a spot on the lip of the ravine with an outcropping of rock that would give him cover, and then he put on his wet baseball cap, tied the damp super-absorbing towel around his face like a highway robber, and peeked over the edge, exposing only enough of his head to see with the monocle.

He watched the ranch for three hours from that position, refreshing his hat, towel, and gloves with the water in the bag a number of times. In those three hours, he saw a little cabal of raccoons trundle up to the compound on their nightly rounds. He saw a great horned owl swoop over the trees, then take perch in the top of a tall cottonwood that overlooked the sage meadow in front of the ranch. He saw a small group of deer in the distance.

But around the ranch itself, things were more interesting. The grounds were fairly open with very little undergrowth. And while a number of trees shaded the place, there wasn't a forest of them. Instead, there were huge gaps in between the clumps and the solitary giants that didn't branch out until they were fifteen or twenty feet up. This left a lot of dirt, gravel, and some small shrubbery, which gave him a good view of the buildings.

What he observed were Bill's buddies going in and out of the barn like it was Grand Central. He counted two women and five men. One had gone in with food and come out with empty trays. Another had taken in a little stack of cardboard packing boxes. Each time the door opened, a blaze of light spilled into the night, as would the soft low sound of a radio. Sometimes it was music. Most of the time it was static and talk, but it was all too faint for him to make out what it was. Maybe they were listening to thrilling, wackadoo AM radio programming like Coast-to-Coast. Maybe they'd learned from tonight's special guest about the lizards of the hollow earth that were plotting to take over mankind.

He saw Bill, Big Zeke, and, his non-Danish student from the diner. Around two a.m., the woman he'd seen earlier today, the one that had run down the man in the tarp, turned off the light inside the barn, and locked the door. After some chat, they went inside. Lights in the ranch and bunk houses began to wink on.

Frank turned back to the barn. He was pretty sure there weren't any special needs cows in there. Or goats. They were working on something else. Something Frank figured would illuminate this whole situation, but it wasn't time to go down just yet because he was due for another visitor.

A quarter turn of the clock later, the guy on guard duty walked down past the big cottonwood to the edge of the ranch's tree island. This was his fourth time around. He carried a rifle over his shoulder and a radio on his hip. He sat down on the bench he'd used the previous two times and lit another cigarette. Then he proceeded to scan this side of the property with a monocle of his own. Frank had no idea what kind of night vision device that was, but he assumed the worst: a FLIR monocle with passive thermal detection.

The earliest night vision technology amplified existing light. Those early devices needed active infrared illumination to see much, but if the enemy had night vision, he'd see you when you turned on your infra-red flashlight. You could use such things around a building, but out in the field it was like turning on a spotlight to call attention to your location. Not a good thing. And so the military had created better amplifiers, passive ones like Frank's, that didn't need an infrared flashlight.

But these new FLIR thermal detection devices were a whole other ball of wax. They didn't amplify light—they detected variations in the heat objects radiated. They could detect a man hundreds of meters away. And they were almost impossible to fool.

Frank kept his head down as far as possible and watched the night patrol in the green light of his monocle.

The man yawned, put his monocle in his lap, pulled some kind of bar from his pocket, unwrapped it, and began to eat it. Then two coyotes yipped maybe a hundred yards away from Frank, out in front of the ranch.

The guy continued to eat, but brought up his monocle to scan for the coyotes.

An unwise and impatient intruder might try to go for it now, thinking the guy was preoccupied. But Frank was not impatient.

The man watched the coyotes for a while. He probably had good zoom. Probably had great optics.

Ten minutes later, the coyotes moved off, and the man, knowing patrolling included movement, got up from the bench and began to make his way to the next spot which was a little ways up the canyon.

Now was the time to go, Frank thought.

He carefully made his way back down to the bottom of the ravine, then untied the garbage bag and squeezed his sweats so they were damp, but not dripping, making sure the water went back into the bag. He did the same to the blanket and put it over his head. It draped over him, hiding his heat from the knees up, but it didn't make him invisible. Not by a long shot.

Tree trunks, foliage, grass, dirt, rocks—they all had different temperatures, which the thermal cameras could detect. The bag had been sitting on the ground for the last three hours, so the water was probably close to ground temperature, but it was still water, and he figured with the evaporation, it would make him a little cooler than his surroundings. And that difference would show up.

It was easiest to see a man when you set the camera to display the hotter objects with brighter colors. He figured that's what they'd have it set on, which meant he'd show up dark. Probably darker than the ground which would cool at a slower rate as the temperature fell. Darker than the foliage and trunks of the trees.

But Frank's Taliban cloaking device had a limited life because, every minute that passed, the desert air would be wicking away the moisture. Every minute, his 98-degree body furnace would be heating up the blanket and sweats from the inside. Within a very short time, he would go from being a dark object to being a mottled one with heat shadows for his eyes and skull, and he didn't think these guys would mistake such an object on their cameras for a ghost. Stay too long, and he'd show up like a kid coming for trick or treat.

Frank's sweats went right down to his ankles, but that left good portions of his boots exposed. It simply wouldn't do to present to the cameramen a pair bright feet stepping across the sparse desert ground. So he carefully cupped water from the garbage sack onto them until he felt the moisture seeping into his socks. He hoped it would be enough.

He put the monocle's lens through one of his eye slits and picked up the garbage bag, feeling the cold water seeping into his dry clothes. He would have to keep low, move slowly, but not at an inches per minute pace. He didn't have time for that because even if his cloak of darkness didn't evaporate, the night man would be back, and Frank had a strong suspicion the guard wouldn't be giving Frank a pass like he did the coyotes.

So he kicked it into turtle gear and slipped out of the ravine in a slow, low crouch.

18

Darth

THE CROUCHING TURTLE WALK was a real party. Ten minutes into this hall-of-fame heel-to-toe run, Frank's legs and back began protesting, so he did a slow-mo stretch of one leg. A slow-mo straightening of his lower back. And then he was crouch man again.

A quarter of the way across the seventy-five yards, he stopped and did a slow pan with his night vision. When he'd been up on the slope, he'd spotted two cameras on this stretch of the perimeter. The closer one had been affixed to the bare lower branch of a tree. The other, the one way down the perimeter, sat atop a pole. Frank had wanted to appear in as few views back at the command center as possible. He'd also wanted to avoid appearing in the foreground of any view. They probably had zoom, but it was one thing to catch a small object in the distance. It was quite another when Casper the friendly ghost walked in front of the camera. This meant that instead of splitting the distance between the two cameras, he'd selected a course with taller scrub as far away from the second camera as he could get.

But as he panned, he realized he'd made a mistake. He hadn't been able to see it from up on the slope, but it was clear as day from his current position. Under the eaves of the barn was a third camera, and he was picking his way across the open ground right in front of it.

He cursed under his breath, but there wasn't a better path, so he continued forward. Another minute and four steps later, one of Bill's buddies came out of the big house. The guy was wearing a baseball cap and carrying a rifle with a nice fat scope on top which surely had night vision.

Frank halted.

The guy came off the porch, but instead of turning to the bunk house, he began to walk in Frank's direction.

Frank silently cursed again. But just because the guy was coming this way didn't mean they'd seen him. The mind saw what it wanted to see, and he was hoping they were looking for bright thermal imaging.

The guy continued in Frank's direction.

Frank decided to take cover. So he began to sink, inch by painstaking inch, until he was squatting behind a scraggly salt brush. One that would have provided awesome cover for a squirrel.

The guy walked across the asphalt drive, then crunched onto some gravel and made his way between the barn of intrigue and some other shed. He continued all the way to the perimeter, then stopped on almost the exact spot where the first guard had stood. But instead of taking five on the bench, this guy brought his rifle up.

Frank's heart began to thump in his chest. Lord, he prayed silently, it would be a great favor to me if you struck him with blindness.

But the man did not cry out with a sudden lack of sight. Instead, he began to sweep the area with his scope.

Maybe Frank should have prayed for a diversion of bats. He'd seen enough of them flitting about the place earlier. But the bat brigade seemed to be occupied as well.

The guy continued to sweep the area with what looked like a nice AR-15.

It was one thing to observe the enemy up close while wearing a custom ghillie that blended in with the brush. It was quite another to be squatting with nothing but a little stick between you and your doom. Frank told himself he was a rock and held still.

The guy's sweep came closer and closer to Frank. He slowed when he passed Frank's position, came back.

Hell, Frank thought.

A beat passed.

Then the guy continued his sweep, and Frank almost fell over from the adrenaline. When his heart came back down into the normal human range, he focused his breathing and watched the guy finish.

Then the new guard turned and headed the direction the first had gone.

A huge relief washed over Frank, but he knew the cloak was evaporating, and he still had some distance to go. And the first guy might be back any time.

Frank gave the guard another minute, and then he slowly rose and began his heel-toe again, taking ten-counts for every move, making doubly sure not to crack twigs or knock rocks underfoot. He veered between cameras two and three.

Twenty minutes later, he was to the other side, sweating, his back, thighs, hamstrings, and shins, and the deltoid that had been helping keep the monocle up all burning.

He did not remove his disguise just yet. Instead, he swept the compound and saw only the cameras he'd seen earlier in the day, which meant he could cross behind the fence along the covered corral. Frank slowly picked his way along the fence which led him to a clump of quaking aspen, rustling in the night breeze, and then to the back of the shed next to the barn.

The sliver of moon shone above and illuminated a portion of this area, casting ghostly shadows from the trees. But at least this bit wasn't in view of any of the cameras. Frank held still and listened, but only heard the crickets and the quaking aspen.

He crept to the lane between the shed and the barn, out in open view of the camera on the house, and moved over close to the shed, thinking his heat signature would be less visible against it. He also moved to avoid the crunch of the gravel path. He crept down the wall, then crossed over to the steel-framed door all of these fine folks had been going in and out of.

Frank tried it and found both the deadbolt and the door itself locked. He took off one glove and felt around the door frame for keys, but found nothing. The good news was that the big strong door had regular locks. Obviously, these law-abiding renters had not thought they needed to replace the locks on all the doors. Not with night guards and night vision. Besides, they would hear anyone who tried to force it. Except Frank wasn't going to force it.

However, he needed an adjustment. He'd begun to notice that it was getting hot in the blanket. It was still damp, but he didn't know how much of his heat signature he'd passed through. It would not do to light up like a Christmas tree, so he lifted the side of the blanket away from the camera. The cooler night air rushed in, and the volume of the breeze in the trees increased. He slowly gathered that side of the blanket up on top of his head until the whole side away from the cameras was exposed.

Then he slid the monocle into one pocket and reached into another for the bobby pins. He would have brought his set of bump keys he kept in the road kit, but he'd loaned those to his happy Mormon neighbor Sam who said he'd needed to use them to help an old widow get into her house. The problem was that Sam seemed to have a lot of old widows to help, or he'd gone to the dark side and started pilfering his baking necessities from the neighborhood houses. Either way, they weren't here.

So Frank slipped into the keyhole the bobby pin he'd made into a tension wrench and turned it. Above his little wrench he inserted the other bobby pin he'd made into a pick and began to wiggle it back and forth, aligning the pins with a few audible clicks. A minute later, he felt the lock give, and he twisted the door knob. One down. He did the same on the deadbolt, and just as he turned it open, a man crunched onto the gravel at the back of the barn.

Frank froze.

It was the guard with the rifle and scope, and instead of walking past, he turned into the lane. He saw Frank and said something in German.

It sounded friendly. The guard finished with a rise in pitch like he'd just asked a question. Frank didn't know German. The guy asked his question again, and Frank swore he was talking about Darth Vader.

"Ja, ja, Darth Vader," Frank replied and reached into his pocket for his flash light.

The guy halted and said something else, which didn't sound like he was talking about Darth Vader at all.

Luckily, Frank didn't want to chat anyhow. He grabbed the

flashlight, brought it out, and shone the 500 lumen beam into the man's face. Then he charged.

The man shouted, blinded by the light, and tried to bring his rifle down.

But before he could get off a shot, Frank was on him. He shoved the barrel of the rifle up and away with his left hand, which left the guy's other side wide open.

The guy tried to wrestle his rifle free, which was the wrong move. A rifle was a long-range weapon, but Frank was in the guy's face. He should have let Frank push it up and reversed the weapon, striking Frank in the face with the stock.

But Frank wasn't about to let him work that out. He tightened his grip on the flashlight and slammed his fist into the bottom of the guard's rib cage.

The guard oofed and flinched, opening a target on his neck.

Frank jabbed him hard in the open spot, a sharp blow to the carotid artery.

The guard gasped, released his grip on the rifle.

Frank wrenched the rifle free, then struck the man in the jaw with the butt of the weapon.

The guard fell like a sack of potatoes, unconscious.

Frank was no longer wearing his Taliban cloak. Furthermore, the whole thing had gone down in high resolution in view of the camera on the house. But no alarms had sounded. He flicked off his flashlight.

He could run, or he could continue the mission and help this poor fellow. He decided on the latter and set the rifle against the barn. Then he crouched down, heaved the guy over his shoulders and stood. Next, he picked up the rifle and cloak and hustled into the barn, knocking the guard's head on the doorframe as he entered.

Once inside, Frank lay the man down on the cement floor, and then he carefully shut and locked the door and listened.

But there was no shouting or turning on of the yard lights.

He blew out a sigh in relief, then turned on the red LED light on his flashlight and looked around for something to tie the guard up with. There were racks of tools on the wall, a fridge, the radio he'd heard earlier. Then he spotted a roll of duct tape on a table against a wall, which he immediately appropriated.

A few minutes later, he finished hog-tying the still-unconscious, German-speaking guard. Frank stood, satisfied the man wouldn't be able to do more than open his eyes when he came to, and wondered what was in here because it didn't smell like a garage. It smelled like bleach.

He shone the dim red light about the place. There were three windows on the far side, two on this side with the door, but all of them had been boarded up. Around the walls were things you might expect—plywood shelves, saw horses, power tools, a desk, a big plastic trash can, stacks of cardboard moving boxes. At the back of the garage sat a huge drone with parts to one side like someone was working on it. It was as big as a man. Compared to the others he'd seen, this thing was King Kong. But it wasn't the drone that caught his attention. It was the other items in the middle of the floor.

There was a long plastic workbench with chairs around it. Rectangular cardboard moving boxes were stacked neatly at each end. Other boxes were stacked by the chairs. Frank walked over to the table. In the red light, he could see two electric heat knives attached to a socket that dangled from the ceiling. There were scissors. He looked in the boxes. One of the boxes had new cellophane wrappers. The other had big sheets of square thumbnail-sized stickers on it.

He used his shirt to pick one of the sheets up and corrected himself. These were not stickers, they were stamps. Tax stamps. And the sheet he was holding was for Arizona.

He stepped over and looked at the boxes at the end of the table. They were filled with cartons of Marlboros. Probably fifty cartons per box. And Frank was pretty sure Bill wasn't a licensed distributor.

He shined the dim red light at the boxes by the wall stacked at least eight feet high. He estimated there were at least thirty boxes here.

Thirty boxes times fifty cartons each, times ten packs per carton. That was around 15,000 packs of cigarettes.

He saw it now. The table in the middle of the floor was an assembly line. Actually two lines, one on either side. The first person put the pack in the cellophane. The second affixed the tax decal with a little bit of heat. He saw another box with thin rubber gloves, the kind a doctor might use. Good for keeping fingerprints off the packs.

A cigarette smuggling racket like this worked one of two ways. The first way exploited the different tax rates each state charged. Idaho and Wyoming only charged around sixty cents worth of tax per pack. But Arizona charged two whole dollars. So an enterprising soul might purchase a bunch of cigarettes in Idaho and then sell them in Arizona, pocketing the difference.

The only problem was that it was illegal to sell cigarettes in a state without that state's tax stamp. And the only way to get stamps was to buy the license for them from the state. So smugglers were forced to either sell them on the black market or replace the stamps.

Using his shirt, Frank flipped open a carton of cigarettes and examined a few of the packs. These had no cellophane wrapping and no stamp whatsoever. This meant they might have been stolen or skimmed from some warehouse. Or they might be knock-offs, not official Marlboros at all. Which led Frank to believe this was probably a smuggling operation of the second type. In these rackets, you smuggled in virgin cigarettes, ones for which you paid no tax at all. It was higher risk, but higher profits. Especially when the knock-offs were made on the cheap.

If Bill and his buddies were using the first method, and they'd just removed the cellophane with the other state's stamp on it, then these 15,000 packs might be worth 20,000 dollars. If they were using the second, they might be worth as much as 60,000 dollars.

A little group could meet and have a tax party once a month, and in five months they'd have themselves 300,000 dollars. Not bad for a few day's work.

And all that was hidden in moving boxes with "kitchen" and "bathroom" and "kid's closet" written on them. Some in black marker. Some in crayon.

Men had been killed over things as small as the price of a beer, and there was a lot more than a few beers in this barn. No wonder they'd taken out the man in the tarp.

Using his shirt, he collected a pack of the Marlboros, a cellophane wrapper, and folded up one of the sheets of stamps, careful to keep his prints off them. He figured this should point Sheriff Hood and her posse in the right direction.

Then he pulled out his cell phone, turned it on in mute mode, and snapped a number of shots—without the flash—of the table, the boxes, and the hot knives used to seal the tax stamps to the cellophane. The photos weren't the best in the red light, but they were clear enough. Frank also made sure none of them had Darth Vader in the background.

Frank stood, proud of himself, and then the radio on the guard's belt crackled, and someone said, "Hey, did you fall into the toilet?"

Darth Vader was awake, looking at Frank. He was also trying to get his hands around to depress a button on the radio. A few more inches, and he'd be calling in the cavalry.

19

Hunt

FRANK RAN ACROSS the garage, while Darth Vader yanked as hard as he could and reached the button. He depressed the button, moaned.

Then Frank was there and kicked his hand away.

The radio crackled. "What was that?"

But Frank snatched the radio up and turned it off.

The man began to buck like a fish out of water, trying to get out of his bonds.

"You should be careful in here," Frank said lowly. "You might knock something over. Might start a fire."

Feral anger burned in the German's eyes. If he wasn't all duct-taped up, Frank figured he'd be trying to bite Frank's throat out.

He couldn't leave the man on the ground because he'd just roll over to the garage door and start kicking it. But he didn't want to kill him. Frank looked around and spotted a spool of bailing twine and a rafter, and figured that would have to do.

He doubled a length of the twine four times. Three minutes later Darth Vader was hanging upside down about three feet off the ground. And then Frank realized he'd seen this guy before. He'd been the one to come at him with the axe handle in the diner's parking lot.

Frank struck him in the jaw with the butt of the rifle and knocked him out again. Then he went to dunk his blanket and sweats in the water remaining in the plastic garbage sack but found he didn't have as much water as he'd thought. He looked for a sink, but didn't see one. There was a door at the back with stairs up to another room and stairs going down to a basement. One could be a bathroom, but Frank was running out of time. He'd just have to hope he was damp enough to keep his clothing cool. He put his gear on, picked up the rifle, and went to the door.

He thought about just running for it, but knew patience was the best approach, so he slowly unlocked the door and opened it just a crack. He gave it another second, then opened it all the way and slowly stepped out, knowing he was in full view of the camera on the house, knowing whoever had been calling would be frustrated or alarmed at this point. They'd be scanning all the cameras to find the German. However, they'd be looking for a brightly lit object, which meant they might miss him.

Frank kept to the deep shadows along the wall of the barn and slow-walked back the way he'd come. He didn't hear any alarms or shouts when he reached the back of the barn. Didn't hear any when he crossed behind the corral. Didn't hear any when he walked out to where he'd entered the compound.

He did hear them as he was crossing the barbed-wire fence, but he didn't know if that meant they'd seen him or called out the troops to look for Darth Vader.

He did not panic, but slow-moed in a crouch out into the moonlit sage meadow.

Shouts rose behind him. Yard lights went on, casting shadows on some parts of the field, illuminating others.

He continued forward.

A deep-voiced man shouted for Marko. The others picked it up.

If Darth had come to again, he'd start moaning. If he wasn't, somebody still might check the barn.

Frank decided to pick up the pace just a little bit. He made twenty-five yards. He made fifty.

"I found him!" a woman yelled. "In the barn!"

Frank figured all eyes would now go there, so he picked up his pace again. He passed seventy-five yards and the stick he'd hid behind the first time. But just as he passed a solitary cedar, a man back at the compound said, "Hey, there! In the field!"

"Where?" another said.

They were both on this side of the compound.

"Out by that tree."

Frank slowed to a halt, then did the slow sink, hoping enough brush and grass was between him and the men to provide some cover.

"I don't see anything," the second man said.

The beam of a high-powered flashlight raked across the meadow.

Frank held perfectly still.

"Put that away," the first man said in accented English.

Frank turned slowly and looked out the slit of the blanket with his night vision. One of the men was the first guard with his nice monocle, panning the field and thin wood.

There were shouts by the barn, and then Frank heard Darth Vader shout in his German accent, "It's de ex-con! He vas here!"

Frank was only a few yards from the edge of a wash. He slow-crawled toward it, then eased himself in, and turned around to see what the men were doing. One was coming across the field with his rifle raised. The other, the guard with the good night vision, was hoofing it for the slope.

When he got up there, he'd be able to see a long ways and direct the others. Not good. Frank had to put some distance and a number of trees between him and the man immediately. He kept low and carefully followed the wash, knowing he could not afford to crack sticks or knock rocks. He traveled south, away from the slope and the man crossing the field, moving farther into the trees.

He figured he just needed a quarter of a mile, and that night vision wouldn't be worth squat.

And then he heard a high-pitched whine in the distance and realized they'd sent up one of their drones.

Splendid, Frank thought. Lord, he muttered under his breath, but knew pleas from a guy like him would mostly likely be routed to the desk jockeys.

On the bright side, at least the drone wasn't carrying a Hellfire missile.

He paused, trying to get its direction, then realized it was flying a slow pattern.

Another whine, and another drone lifted off from the compound and went searching, but this one went the other direction, which meant they didn't know for sure where he was.

Frank spotted the drone on this side by its small flying lights. It flew to the slope, then turned and headed back over the trees, right toward Frank.

He hunkered down under a pinyon, gathered himself under his blanket that had dried in a couple of spots, which was not good at all.

The drone approached with its annoying little whine.

The camera man was going to see brightness under the pine, he was going to fly past, then come back, investigate. And if the operator identified him, that would be it for Frank because that annoying little device would track him while all the others converged.

Frank listened and huddled in the close darkness of his blanket as the drone approached. He slipped the safety off the rifle and prepared to throw the blanket off.

It was dark, and the trees, though thin, would still present an obstacle, and the thing's flying lights were so small, they were hardly any target at all. He would only have a few seconds to get his shots off and down it. Kind of like pheasant shooting, except this prey had more brains behind it.

He waited. The volume of the drone's whine grew. And then it passed overhead.

And kept going.

He waited, but the drone continued its path. Clearly his drying blanket had still been able to disguise his signature enough to fool the operator.

Frank rose and made his way west, in the general direction of the Nova.

Back at the ranch, a truck started up, turned on its headlights, and drove out onto the road. There were more shouts as those at the ranch moved out, and then it became quiet, save for the breeze and the sound of the drone.

He continued now faster, knowing his cloak was running out of juice.

Over the next hour, Frank played a game of cat and mouse that included him evading the drone twice more as well as one of their searchers, but he eventually skirted around a hill and saw ahead the clump of trees where he'd parked the Nova.

It was a little past five a.m. There were still stars in the western sky, but the eastern horizon had begun to lighten, and the land was as bright in his monocle as day.

He put the device away and walked up a slope, carrying the rifle and garbage sack with the blanket and sweats.

There were still drones and men searching the woods. There were still headlights moving up and down the dirt roads. Soon enough, he figured they'd start to panic and decide it was time to bug out. Which meant he didn't have much time to call the sheriff.

He thought about keeping the rifle, but he could not afford to be caught with it. Not as an ex-con, and not with Sheriff Hood wanting any excuse to bring him in. So, using a gloved hand, he removed the chambered round and the magazine and tossed them. Then he disassembled the rifle, wiping down the magazine and barrel to remove any prints. He hid the barrel under some sage and tossed the receiver and stock the other direction.

He walked the final thirty or so yards to the car, fetched the keys from the lava rocks, and opened the driver's door, quickly shutting off the interior light. He threw his crap in, then pulled out the phone, saw he had one bar, and prepared to dial 911.

20

Bill

HE PUNCHED in the number nine.

"Mr. Shaw," the sheriff said, "what are you doing?"

Frank started with surprise, then spun around. He looked left and right, but nobody was there.

"Where are you?" he said.

"They're buzzing like wasps," she said.

The sound was coming from up in the tree. Frank stepped back and looked up, but couldn't see her. "What are you doing?"

"That's what I asked you," she said, then began to climb down with a bunch of pine branch rustling.

A moment later she came into view, backside first, which wasn't a bad view at all. She hopped from the last branch onto the ground.

"You're very nimble," he said.

"You should try it some time in a vest," she said. Then she squatted down to get some dirt to rub between her hands.

"Is that like an Indian thing?" he asked.

"It's the sap," she said. "I don't want it sticking to the cuffs I'm going to put on you."

"You don't want to put any cuffs on me."

She stood in the wan light. "Are you resisting arrest?"

"You're not arresting me."

"I'm not?"

"No, because if you had something, you would have said it right up front. And you would have brought backup because I'm betting it's standard procedure to never arrest a felon on your own unless you have to. But even if you did have something on me, which you don't, you wouldn't arrest me anyway. Not after hearing what I have to say."

"Remember when you talked about second chances and trying to fly straight?"

"Yeah."

"You're not doing so well with that, are you?"

"Just listen," he said.

"You've got ten seconds," she said.

He said, "Your opinion of me is going to change. And you're going to want to have that lunch."

"Highly unlikely," she said and put her hand on her taser. "I'm giving it less than a tenth of a percent."

"A free lunch with a guy who uses deodorant and wears manly shoes. And I guarantee you at least one laugh."

"You were in prison a little too long, weren't you?" she asked. "Was that the big thing that was going to change my mind?"

"No," Frank said. "That's just the promised reward. Now, I'm going to reach into my cargo pocket to pull out the answer to the man in the tarp. So don't zap me." Then he carefully used his shirt to grab the pack of contraband Marlboros. He pulled them out and tossed them to her.

She caught them with one hand, her other still on the taser.

"There you go."

She looked at it. "Cigarettes?" she asked. "The Mormons might not smoke them, but the last time I checked, they're not against the law in the state of Utah."

"Look at the tax stamp," Frank said.

"It's unwrapped," she said like she was pointing out the obvious.

"Exactly," he said. "So here's exhibit B." He extracted the cellophane from his pocket and held it out to her.

She took it.

"And exhibit C," he said and held out the sheet of stamps.

She took that as well and unfolded it. She held it up, then pulled out her flashlight to examine them.

He stepped back a pace to give her plenty of room and said, "Their barn is full of stamps and cigarettes and a nice little table for putting them all together. I took lots and lots of pictures. You should get yourself a quick e-warrant to search their place. But you'd better have your team together when you go in because we already know what these folks are capable of."

She finished examining the stamps and said, "You know it's a felony to possess these?"

"I was bringing them to you."

"I appreciate that," she said.

But Frank knew she wasn't accepting his story at face value because Frank was still an ex-con in her mind. For all she knew, they could have been his. Or he could have been trying to frame Bill and company. Or maybe the stamps had nothing to do with anything, and he was running some other con.

She said, "Let me have you sit down over there. I'm going to call this in, and we'll get it sorted out. This is really good evidence, Mr. Shaw."

Sheriff Hood was playing it all calm and cool, keeping her voice low and slow, keeping everything de-escalated, which meant she still didn't trust him. But at least she was calling it in. His estimation of her went up yet another notch.

And soon enough, she'd start reconsidering her profile of him. Frank sat down on the dirt. "Don't use your radio," he said. "Remember: they're listening to the police scanners."

And then he realized what he'd just said, and a little ping of alarm shot through him.

"How long have you been here?" he asked.

"About twenty minutes," she said.

"Did you call in when you found my car?"

"Yes," she said.

"On your normal radio?"

"What are you getting at?"

Frank's alarms went on full alert.

"We've got to get out of here," he said and stood.

"Mr. Shaw, I need you sit down."

"They know," he said.

They'd known his destination fifteen minutes ago when she had announced it over the radio and he was juking and hiding. If they were smart, they would have simply been heading straight here. No wonder the pursuit seemed to have let up. No wonder he'd been able to fool the drones.

"They have at least four guys on my tail with rifles, and they are going to be here any minute."

Sheriff Hood processed what he was saying, then glanced back toward the ranch.

Frank said, "I might be wrong, but I don't think someone running a cigarette smuggling organization is going to want to sit down with us for tea and crumpets."

She pulled out her cell phone to call it in, but before she could thumb a thing, a man said, "Drop the phone."

Frank turned. The first guard Frank had seen, the one who'd watched the coyotes with the FLIR monocle, was standing about twenty feet away, aiming a rifle right at the sheriff, and Frank wondered if he'd just arrived, or if he'd been hiding there all along.

"Drop the phone," he said again, "and put your hands in the air."

He too had an accent. A German one like his friend Darth.

And that was just odd. What were two Germans doing way out here?

"We can talk this out," the sheriff said calmly.

But that wasn't how this was going to go down. These guys were part of a cigarette smuggling operation, not some mom and pop thing. These were guys who used garrotes. These were guys who weren't going to leave any witnesses.

Frank trusted this sheriff knew her business, and when he distracted the gunman, she'd pull her piece and take care of the problem.

"How's your buddy doing?" Frank asked.

"He's doing fine," someone else said.

The new speaker had an accent, but it was not German.

Frank turned. Big Zeke was there with his rifle trained on Frank.

"You guys are multiplying like rabbits," Frank said.

"Get down on the ground," Zeke ordered.

Frank could try to run. If these guys were any good at all, he might have a twenty-five percent chance of getting out into the bush and not being shot. But then he saw a drone heading his way and knew that while he might evade the first shots, they had trucks and eyes in the sky and rifles, and he had nothing but his legs and a peashooter. The barrel and bullets to the AR-15 he'd taken from Darth weren't too far away, but there was no way he'd get them without being shot.

"Boys," Frank said. "You've made a huge mistake. The sheriff called this in. She disappears, and they'll come looking."

"Not for us," Zeke said. "For you. For the criminal."

Then Frank heard a car coming. A moment later, he saw headlights flickering in the early morning twilight through the trees. The car drove to where both the sheriff and Frank had pulled off the road and stopped, but the driver kept it running and the headlights shining down the road. The passenger doors opened. Two people got out and threaded their way between a couple of cedars and came into the clear.

It was Bill and the woman who'd attacked the man in the tarp.

Bill shook his head. "Well, shoot," he said. "I had hoped it wouldn't come to this."

"Tell your men to put their guns down," the sheriff said.

Bill said, "You're going to have to come with us. But maybe it isn't as bad as it seems. Maybe we can work a deal."

Yeah, a deal where they got to choose which desert plot they were buried in—the one with the goats or some other location.

Sheriff Hood said, "Whatever you're into, you don't want the trouble that taking a sheriff will bring down on you."

"Oh, you're just a little drop," Bill said. He motioned at the men and woman who closed in. "Now if you will kindly lie down, we can restrain you and be on our way so we can have our chat in a more private location."

The sheriff went for the distress button on her radio, but the German had expected that, and he slammed her in the back of the head with the butt of his rifle, and she went down.

Bill pulled a pistol and pointed it at Frank.

Frank should have run earlier. Both of them should have run the moment this started to go down. But that was then, and this was now, and Frank wasn't going to make the same mistake twice.

21

Ride

THERE WERE MAYBE twenty feet between Zeke and Bill. Frank immediately darted for that gap, hoping the angle led them to shoot each other or hesitate.

All he had to do was get ten or fifteen yards into the cedar and juniper, and his chances would start to climb. And then he could pour it on. Zeke was big, but he didn't look like he had the stamina to match Frank mile after mile. Bill looked like a noodle that had been sitting in a pot for three days. The German looked fit enough, and so did the woman, but Frank knew that if they were running to catch him, they wouldn't be shooting. They would be panting and sweating and their hearts would be pumping and making it mighty hard to get off a clean, well-aimed shot. And there would be trees and branches and rocks crowding the way.

Running didn't give him good odds, but it gave him and the sheriff much better odds than the sure death at the end of the line with Bill and his cigarette killers. All Frank had to do was hoof it a few miles to the next town or flag someone down on the road or find the truck or motorcycle some farmer had left at the side of a field. And then he could call in the Kanab cavalry.

He took five good strides, felt his luck rising, then heard a pop. A moment later two needles shot through his shirt into his back, and then the taser started clicking, sending 50,000 volts into him.

The muscles in his body reacted instantly, all of them contracting at the same time, turning him stiff as a board. Frank's forward momentum took him one more step, and then he crashed to the dirt, groaning with pain.

The electrical popping continued, burning as it went through his back, forcing his whole body to clench.

Someone called out for the sheriff's cuffs. They were tossed.

The popping continued, the pulsating electrical current overriding Frank's central nervous system, directly controlling all his muscles, telling them to fire, fire, fire.

Zeke approached, and then the popping stopped.

Immediately, all of Frank's muscles relaxed. He gulped a breath, tried to think.

The guy with the taser decided to give him another surge for good measure.

Frank stiffened again. And then the popping stopped, and Zeke was on him.

Frank tried to roll and get away, but Zeke was strong and had Frank's hands behind his back and in the cuffs before Frank could gather his wits or his limbs.

"On your feet," Zeke said and yanked on Frank's hands.

The torque on Frank's shoulders hurt, and he stood. When he did, he noticed a chunk of the prickly pear he'd smashed when he'd fallen was embedded in him just below his chest. It was a nasty little bugger, skewering him with half a dozen needles. Mother Nature's velcro.

Frank grimaced, still feeling dazed.

Bill shook his head, disappointed in Frank. "Get them in the car," he said. "Take them back to the barn."

Frank could see no way to get out of this, not with his hands cuffed behind his back. But he had to get out of this, because the trail back to the barn could lead to only one place. There would be no deal. There could be no deal. They'd crossed that threshold when the German had aimed his rifle at the sheriff.

Frank's only option was to play along for time and hope an opportunity presented itself. And pray.

Dear God, he prayed in his heart, give me the opportunity to wring their necks. Or save the sheriff, he amended. And he willed the desk jockeys to get the message upstairs.

Big Zeke walked him over to the Lincoln, but he didn't open the door. Instead, he popped the copious trunk.

"She called in my car," Frank said. "They're going to be wondering where she is. Your best bet is to leave us alive somewhere and scoot on out of town."

"Shut it," Zeke said with his accent and pushed Frank back to the trunk.

"I'll be happy to walk," Frank said.

"In," Zeke said.

"Really, I will. We can watch the sun rise together."

In response, Zeke slugged him in the gut.

His fist hit like the short end of a two-by-four, and Frank doubled over in pain.

Then Zeke shoved him in, knocking Frank's head painfully on the lip of the trunk on the way down.

Frank groaned. "The manhunt they're going to raise isn't worth a few cigarettes," he said. "Zeke, don't listen to the others. You need to get out. Now."

Zeke answered with a back-fisted pop at Frank's eye.

Frank saw it coming and turned his head, but he couldn't avoid it altogether, and the blow walloped him on his cheek bone and bounced his head off the steel bottom of the trunk.

Frank now definitely had a headache. He groaned again and decided that maybe Zeke wasn't the right one to talk to.

A few moments later, the still-limp sheriff was thrown on top of him. They moved her around a bit to make her fit, then forced the trunk shut, pressing her down into Frank. It was close and dark, and the uneven ridges in the trunk pressed into his back.

"Sheriff," he said. But the sheriff didn't respond.

Had they broken her neck? Killed her?

Frank focused, but couldn't feel her breathing and certainly couldn't feel her heartbeat through her ballistic vest. He wished she still had her duty belt, but they'd already taken that.

He heard Bill tell the woman to take the sheriff's vehicle. Then Zeke, the German, and Bill got in the Lincoln. Frank felt the car bounce as each sat down. The doors shut. The engine started. Bill made a nice three-point turn, and then they were rolling across the dirt. The suspension on the old Lincoln was nice and soft, which meant Frank and the sheriff got a slow beating by the bumps in the road instead of a fast one.

There was a turn, and another turn, and Frank figured they were now on the little lane that ran to the ranch, the place where he'd first met the sheriff and then Bill. He heard the thrump of them crossing the cattle guard under the tall pine gate mounted with elk horns, and then they were heading up hill. Moments later the crunch of the gravel ended, and they rolled onto the asphalt.

Time is what he needed. And his wits, which he was happy to report were coming back to him. The electric daze had faded. He was a little sore, but that was to be expected when you did the full-body clench.

The Lincoln stopped. The doors opened, and the men got out. A few moments later the trunk popped open, revealing the faces of Zeke and Bill backed by the tops of the trees and the pre-dawn sky.

Zeke pulled the sheriff out, who they'd handcuffed, slung her over his shoulder, and carried her away.

Bill took a step back, pulled out his pistol, and motioned for Frank to get out. "I'd give you a hand," Bill said, "but somehow I don't think that's a good idea."

"I think I can manage it," Frank said and threw his legs over the lip. He executed a little snaky roll and stood, cuffed hands behind his back.

"Impressive," Bill said.

"You should see my limbo," Frank replied.

"We're really not the dancing types."

"And all this time I thought you guys were out here getting ready for the big square dancing competition down in St. George."

"I don't think you properly appreciate your situation," Bill said, smiling with his big bleached, corn teeth.

"Leave us tied, pack up your goods, and go," Frank said. "You can be two states away before anyone's the wiser."

"That's definitely an option," Bill said. "Let's go over to the barn and talk about it."

Frank didn't want to go to the barn, but Bill had his pistol out. So Frank skirted around the car and headed for the barn.

One of the pickups was out front. A twin mattress leaned up against the bed. In the bed of the truck itself were a couple of moving boxes. Ones Frank suspected had been in the barn.

Behind him, the woman from the diner came out of the house with a vacuum, an extension cord, and a stiff brush. Frank continued toward the barn. A few moments later, she turned on the vacuum and started going to town on the trunk.

"Can't be too clean," Frank said.

"Cleanliness is next to godliness," Bill replied.

"So that's how you get into heaven," Frank said. "And all this time I thought it was about faith, hope, and charity. I guess I've got to start taking me some more showers."

Up ahead, Darth Vader held the barn door open for them. The bruise on his face looked great in the morning light. Big, mottled, purple.

"Darth," Frank said. "Long time, no see."

Darth smiled, and when Frank got within range, Darth wound up and let go with a big haymaker. Frank tried to duck it, but there wasn't much space to move, and the tight fist of bone and sinew smashed into the side of Frank's face.

Frank's head whipped to the side and down.

Darth pulled back and slugged him hard in the ribs, sending pain flashing along Frank's side.

Frank winced. Darth was definitely not a noodle.

Darth pulled back for another blow, but Bill waved him off. "Not now," he said. "Just wait."

Frank took a breath. Yes, just wait, he thought.

Then Darth shoved him toward the doorway, and Frank stumbled inside.

22

Offers

FRANK FOUND THE SHERIFF lying on the floor in the middle where the little assembly line had been. Zeke was kneeling over her, removing the sheriff's shirt and revealing a black ballistic vest worn over a white sleeveless undershirt.

Zeke finished removing the shirt, then cuffed her again.

"Sit down next to her," Bill said.

Frank walked over, arms behind his back, his jaw still throbbing in pain from Darth Vader's blow, and sat on the gritty concrete next to the sheriff. He was definitely going to need an Ibuprofen.

"Hey," he said and nudged her with his foot. "No sleeping on the job."

Surprisingly, she groaned.

Groaning was good, much better than the silence of a coma.

"Can you sit?" he asked.

"Oh," she said in some pain. "Ow."

"That's it," he said.

The sheriff worked her eyes open, looked around in a squint. She tried to get up, found she was cuffed, then struggled up and finally got herself sitting Indian style.

Sitting was good. It meant her neck wasn't broken.

"Look at me," he said to her.

She looked over.

He said, "How many eyes do you see in my head?"

"Two and a half," she replied.

"How do you feel?"

"A bit out of body."

"You've had your bell rung," Frank said. "A rifle butt will do that to you. But it will pass." He just hoped it passed quickly.

He looked around the barn. The assembly line table was folded up and stowed neatly against one wall. However, most of the moving boxes hiding the cigarettes were still stacked in the corner.

That was not good. It meant they weren't interested in playing innocent.

He motioned at the boxes with his chin. "Shouldn't you be loading those up?"

Bill said, "Put your ankles together. We're going to tape them."

Frank did as he was told, and then Zeke came to bind their ankles with silver duct tape. Zeke did a good tight job of it. Then he searched Frank and removed the tactical flashlight, the knife, the ball bearings in their leather pouch, the cell phone, and the notepad and pen. Last of all, he pulled out the slingshot.

Bill saw it and said, "What is that?"

Zeke held it up, flapped the bands about with a grin on his face like the slingshot was just too rich.

He said, "We've got some big fire power here, boss."

Bill said in mock worry, "I don't know what we've gotten ourselves into, Zeke. I think we might be in over our heads."

"Give it to me," Frank said. "I'll show you how it works." He'd show them what 200 miles per hour of ball bearing could do to Bill's head at close range. Show him what it could do to an eye.

Bill said, "Maybe some other time when I get bored and feel like knocking off some bugs." Then he directed Zeke to put Frank's items on the work table up against one wall. Zeke did, then came back and searched the cargo pockets on the sheriff's pants. He came up with some keys, a stick of gum, and some latex gloves, and then pulled out a rock figure no bigger than a man's thumb and held it up.

It was made of three little stones glued together. A small one for the head, another for the body, and another for the legs and feet. It had been painted with dark boots, brown cargo pants, a duty belt, a brown shirt with name tag, auburn hair, and a cap that said "Sheriff." Big googly eyes had been glued to the face.

Her daughter Lily must have made that. A little girl all proud of her mama.

Zeke looked at the little rock sheriff, then at Sheriff Hood. "This you?"

"What does the name tag say?"

He held it so he could read it. "Hood," he read.

"Well, look at you. I bet you got a lot of advanced reading points in school."

He narrowed his eyes. "Sass killed the cat."

"No, I think that was curiosity," Frank said.

"Either way, the cat was dead," Zeke said all self-satisfied.

"Zeke, don't provoke them," Bill said.

"Whatever," Zeke said, then picked up the rest of the items and dumped them with Frank's on the workbench.

He came back and removed their boots and made sure nothing was in them. When he finished, he stood back and said, "They're clean."

Frank motioned at the cactus stuck to his chest and said, "How about you remove this? Someone resourceful might use it as a weapon."

Zeke looked at Bill.

Bill said, "Thanks for pointing that out. We'll get right on it. But first I've got to make sure the sheriff's okay." He brought over a chair, set it down, then sat, holding his cell phone upright on his thigh. He said, "Sheriff, can you count to twenty for me?"

She said, "Can you say a lot of years in prison?"

He said, "I'm very sorry about what happened, and I want to make sure everything's all right."

She said, "Take the cuffs off, and things will get a lot better."

"I need to know you're in your right mind before we talk. Please count to twenty. Go slowly."

The sheriff growled a bit in anger.

Bill waited.

Then she gave in with a sigh of irritation and counted to twenty.

Bill nodded. "I'm so happy to hear that. Now, let's check your memory. Just humor me. You were called out a few days ago on a drunken disturbance. Some guy off his meds threatening some campers. Where was that?"

The sheriff narrowed her eyes.

"Do you not remember?"

"Oh, I remember."

"Before we discuss anything, I need to know I'm talking to someone who is all there. Please name the place."

"It was out by Clear Creek."

"Very good. One more," Bill said. "Count down from one hundred."

"You need to undo these cuffs right now," Sheriff Hood said.

"Just count," Bill said.

The sheriff gritted her teeth, then counted all the way down to fifteen before Bill stopped her.

"Very good," he said.

"Hey," Frank said. "I can sing a hundred bottles of beer on the wall. You want me to do that?"

"If you start singing," Bill said, "I think Zeke will indeed have to shoot you."

"I can do it in Spanish," Frank offered.

Bill said, "I've got a better idea. Zeke, hand me Mr. Shaw's phone."

Zeke fetched it for him. Bill took it, tapped the screen, and said, "What's the pass code?"

"There's no service out here," Frank said.

Bill said, "Do you have any connection to a man who calls himself Emilio Cruz?"

Frank shook his head. "Never heard of him."

"The man who had the unfortunate accident yesterday. The one you just happened to be waiting for out in the desert."

"I wasn't waiting for anyone in the desert," Frank said. "I was waiting to see the sunset and commune with my maker with some crackers and a little lizard buddy, and then you guys screwed it all up."

Bill smiled with his big white corn teeth. "So give me your pass code and let me see who you talked to yesterday."

Frank didn't want these men rifling through his contacts. He certainly didn't want them finding the contact information for Tony, his nephew, or Kim, his sister, but he needed time. He shrugged. "Double zero ninety-nine."

Bill tapped it in, brought up the call log, and began thumbing through. "What's this 4378 number?"

"It's the sheriff's office," he said.

"Oh, really?" Bill asked.

"Ask the sheriff."

Bill asked the sheriff to recite the office number. She rattled it off. Bill nodded and continued scrolling and scrolling.

"Are you looking back five years?" Frank asked.

"Who's Kim?" Bill asked.

"An old military buddy," Frank lied.

Bill opened up Frank's messaging and thumbed through. He opened a thread, then read aloud, "Disneyland will be fun. Love ya, bro."

"I was supposed to call him today," Frank said. "You want to get him on the line for me? I think he'd be really interested in meeting you."

"You and your military pals go to Disneyland for kicks, eh?"

"Sure," Frank said. "Bear Country is an awesome place to pick up women."

Bill was not impressed.

"Really, you'd be surprised," Frank said. "Of course, the best hang-out is by the Jungle Book ride." He said it as matter-of-factly as he could.

"Huh," Bill said, like he might be storing that bit of data for future use, and then he shrugged and continued thumbing through the log. He closed messaging and said, "I see you've got email." He opened it. "Oh, yes, here we go. More from Kim. I'm beginning to think you and Kim have a special relationship."

"Sure," Frank said. "When you hide out in spider holes for a few days at a time together and poop in plastic sacks, it forms a special bond."

"Was Cruz part of that?" Bill asked.

"I don't know any Cruz."

"Did you meet him in Special Forces?"

"You've got my phone. Do you see a Cruz in it?"

"Maybe you use Snapchat. Maybe you've got some Google account and you post messages in the drafts folder."

"Yeah, me and the generals and their mistresses. We're all in the drafts folder, hiding out from the NSA."

Bill finished with the phone and looked up. "Why did you come back?"

"To prove to her I wasn't the criminal. And because I wanted to thank your yahoos for kindly spraying me with pepper and trying to garrote me."

Bill turned to the sheriff. "He's working for you then? Is that why you were waiting for him?"

"Mr. Shaw has no relationship with us."

"But the man who called himself Emilio Cruz did?"

"Yesterday you said there was no man," the sheriff said.

"Answer my question."

"You have a police scanner. You know exactly what's going on. Nobody in my department, or any department I know of, knew Mr. Shaw before he showed up yesterday."

Bill looked at them.

He wasn't a very good interrogator, and that was bad because that meant sooner or later he was going to resort to pain.

Frank said, "Bill, all the deputies in the county, plus the city police, plus the game wardens, plus the dog catcher are going to be wondering where their sheriff is. Do you really think it's wise to hang around here trying to figure out who this Cruz guy is? Your cigarette operation is busted. Save yourself from having to wear an orange jumpsuit. Put the boxes in the trucks and get out."

Bill sat back and looked at the two of them. "You're both being real clever, but it isn't going to get you where you want to go. Let me show you something." He reached into his pants pocket and pulled out some paper which he unfolded to regular size. He thumbed out most of the creases, then turned it around so they could see the head-and-shoulders picture of a girl maybe eight or nine years old. She was standing in front of a building, maybe a school. She was blowing a bubble with some pink bubble gum.

Sheriff Hood took in a breath and tensed.

"This here girl's name is Lilly. She has swimming practice today at nine a.m., just a few hours away. She's an independent girl and likes to ride her bike to the pool. Likes to get there early."

Bill paused and looked at the sheriff. "Are you ready to talk? Or do we need to go get some leverage?"

The sheriff's eyes sparked with anger hot enough to arc weld.

Bill said, "Is Cruz ATF?"

She replied through gritted teeth, "If he is, we don't know about it."

"Is he associated with any law enforcement?"

She said, "If he were, then this place would be swarming with officers and agents."

"Only if he'd made contact."

"I'm telling you everything I know," the sheriff said.

She sounded like she was about to fry eggs with the heat of her anger, but Frank knew that deep down there was a little black hole of fear waiting to suck her in. It was clear she loved her daughter; that had been clear in the first few seconds of hearing her talk about her and her pet rocks. And Bill's threat against her was probably this cop's worst nightmare.

Bill looked at Frank.

Frank said, "I'm a felon, which means I can't work in law enforcement. So there's no government plot here. You guys can get away clean. Just leave us tied up. Someone will come along eventually. Or they won't. Either way, you're free and clear."

Except for some odd reason they didn't seem to want to go. If Frank had been in their shoes, he would have been out last night. So what was keeping them here?

Zeke picked the sheriff's shirt up off the cement. He said, "You want me to take this?"

Bill nodded.

Frank said, "What are you going to do with her shirt?"

"Give the hounds something to follow," Bill said. Then he smiled and stood.

Which was definitely not good.

23

Baling Twine

FRANK FIGURED they'd put one of the women behind the wheel of the sheriff's SUV. Too many people would recognize the sheriff's vehicle around here, and seeing a man behind the wheel would draw attention. But a woman wearing the sheriff's shirt and wearing the sheriff's cap down low so you couldn't really see her face, that wouldn't attract much attention at all.

And she'd be carrying the sheriff's voice in her hand. In fact, Frank was sure someone back at the house was editing all sorts of ten-code from the numbers the sheriff had recited for Bill.

Bill ordered Darth in, then left him and Zeke to finish securing the two of them. And Frank knew in his gut that Bill wasn't giving them time to think about the errors of their ways. He wasn't going to give the threat to little Lilly time to grow in their minds. He didn't have the time.

So when Bill came back, there wouldn't be any more talk. There would only be shovels, or baseball bats, or guns, or garrotes, and then a nice trip with Frank and the sheriff wrapped in his and her tarps.

Zeke said, "Where are we going to put them?"

Darth smiled, half his face a bruise, and pointed up at the uncovered roof beams above. He motioned at Frank. "He goes feet first."

"That's so last night," Frank said.

"Payback is the daughter of a pig," Darth said, "isn't it?"

Frank looked at him. Darth was either trying to be very creative and failing because very few in English-speaking lands thought the daughters of pigs were anything but good sources of bacon, or he was speaking from a very specific ethnic background, one that Frank had encountered before, but not in Germany.

"The daughter of a whoring pig," Frank agreed.

"Sit down and put your feet in the air," Zeke said.

There was no sense in fighting. What was he going to do—inch worm them to death? He rolled onto his back and put his feet into the air.

It didn't take them long to double a long length of twine, then double that three more times to end up with a nice eight-strand rope. They lashed Frank's taped ankles with it, then hauled him up until he was hanging two feet off the floor, his hands cuffed behind his back, the blood rushing to his head, which was a fine position for bats, but humans had evolved to work the other way.

For instance, humans actually had three hearts, three pumps. There was the big one in your chest, but each calf muscle also acted as a pump when you were moving, squeezing the popliteal and tibial veins, forcing the blood back up to the heart. Frank had learned about that when the medical sergeant on his team in Afghanistan had treated a local who was trying to deal with swelling feet.

The problem was there were no calf muscles in your head. Or your lungs. And so gravity caused the blood to pool. Pool long enough, and all the added pressure caused fluid to leak out of the blood vessels in the lungs, making it hard to breathe, which was bad, but pooling in the head was worse. In the head, the pooling eventually led the blood to clot, which starved the brain of oxygen, which caused strokes, which turned off parts of the body. Create enough clots, and one of them would eventually flip the switch to the heart, and then it was sayonara.

Zeke and Darth stood back and admired their handiwork.

Frank twisted a little at the end of his rope. The twine constricted and cut into his ankles. He said, "Does this spa do cucumber and avocado treatments as well?"

In answer, Darth stepped over to Frank and hammer punched him in the crotch, a nice solid blow that sent an asphalt roller of pain through Frank's nether regions.

Frank groaned, writhed like a big, slow caterpillar.

Darth hammer punched him again, but thankfully was off by an inch, and Frank's inner thigh took most of the blow.

Darth said something in German, and then he and Zeke moved over to the sheriff, leaving Frank to slowly spin with his pain.

They didn't lash the sheriff's ankles and string her up like a hog. Instead they wound the twine around her neck a number of times and tied that line to a beam above.

They smirked, then Zeke canted his head at a lecturing angle and said to the sheriff, "America is weak because America is run by women."

The sheriff didn't respond.

Frank wanted to say he was willing to bet money the sheriff could break Zeke's leg and stomp him into a mud hole, but he kept his mouth shut.

Darth glanced at the padlocked door at the back of the garage, then at Zeke, and the two of them shared a smug, knowing look. Then they exited the garage and shut the door behind them, their feet crunching on the gravel as they walked away.

Frank immediately looked around for an escape. He was too far away from the walls to swing to the workbench or shelves. He was too far away from Sheriff Hood to swing over to her. He looked up at the rafters. There were some old boards and lengths of PVC stored up there. There were a couple of bits of wire tied around some of the rafters like maybe the previous owners had once strung up a banner or something in here. Down at the back, to let people know when they'd driven their vehicles far enough in, a tennis ball hung from a string, much like Frank was hanging from this rafter.

He said, "I don't think your boys are going to come looking for us."

She said, "They'll come."

He said, "I think I know why Bill was recording you."

She looked at him.

"He now has the name of the destination where they're going to leave your SUV stated in your voice as well as all the numbers to relay that destination over the radio in ten-code."

She cursed. "And they have my shirt."

"Just about as bad as losing your duty weapon," he said.

"In this situation, it just might be worse."

Frank was feeling the twine cut into his ankles. He was feeling the pin pricks of his feet falling asleep. He was also feeling the corresponding flush of blood into his neck and face, although brain death by hanging would probably take a number of hours. He said, "I'm betting they put the shirt on the one who chases men down in the desert, the wildcat. She's taller than the one who isn't Danish. More your height and build. She's just missing your fabulous auburn hair."

The sheriff blew out a breath. "It will be hours before anyone thinks to come looking here."

"If they think to come looking at all."

She glanced over at him. "We've got to get out." Then she bent down, trying to see if the twine was loose enough to allow her to pull her cuffs around her feet and bring her hands up in front of her. But the give in the twine wasn't even close.

Frank said, "It's going to tighten around your neck, and you'll either pass out or choke."

"I'm not going to just stand here."

"Think about it. You'll have one shot. Maybe two. Because you're going to have to hop, and then you're going to have to hope you're quick enough to loop those cuffs around to the front. Otherwise, you'll be supporting your whole body weight with your neck. And while you're fit, I don't think you've been working that neck out to support a twine hanging."

"You've got a better plan, Bat Boy?" she asked.

"Indeed I do," he said. "Just give me a minute."

She said, "You're wrapped up like a fly, waiting for a spider."

"One that shouldn't have walked away," he said, and then he folded himself up with a nice vertical sit-up, despite the ball-smasher he'd just received, bringing his cuffed hands up behind his legs, and grabbed his pants at the back of his thighs. He curled up farther and grabbed his pants higher, at the back of his calves, but the pants pulled down, and he had to try again, this time grabbing onto his legs just above his ankles.

"You're not going to be able to untie it."

"Oh ye of little faith," Frank said, and then he reached farther and grabbed the taut strands of twine leading from his ankles to the rafters above. Together, the strands didn't come anywhere near to being as big as a fat climbing rope, but they would do. They would have to. He reached up again, and then he bent his knees and began to pull himself up.

Below, the sheriff watched him, feet tied, hands behind her back, the orange twine noose around her neck.

The cuffs didn't allow him much room, so there was no ascending hand over hand like a monkey. Instead, he had to hold on, one hand under the other, and slide his way up two inches at a time. After a couple of feet of that, he switched lead hands and continued, but his biceps and shoulders were burning. Frank ignored them, just as he was trying to ignore the twine tourniquet around his ankles and his oxygen-starved feet, and continued inching up until he reached the turning point and was suddenly kneeling upright in midair. He stopped to take a breather and let the muscles in his arms calm down, hoping the twine held because dropping eight feet to the concrete would not be anything any respectable doctor would recommend for the knees. He also stopped to remove the cactus from his chest.

"Impressive," she said and looked at the door. "Now what?"

Frank held himself steady with one cuffed hand and with the other plucked a chunk of the cactus from his chest, the little barbs ripping away pricks of skin. "If I get out of this, you buy me lunch. Deal?"

She said, "My previous assessment still stands."

He flicked the cactus chunk away. "Come on," he said and pulled out another chunk with its accompanying barbed needles.

"You get out, and then we'll talk."

"I'm thinking I want that burger from Edna's I missed out on. The one with the zesty garden tomato."

She said, "There won't be any burgers, with or without tomatoes, if you're still hanging there when they come back."

He began picking the remaining needles out and cast them aside, his chest stinging. It was like ripping hairs off with tape, except he wasn't ripping hair—he was ripping skin.

He motioned with an elbow at the moving boxes stacked in the corner. "You see the boxes?"

"I see them."

"Don't you think it's all a little odd?"

"This whole situation is a little odd, including you."

"Think about our friends," he said and stuck his finger with a needle that he then had to pluck out. "We've got a bunch of Germans coming half way around the world to smuggle cigarettes in, of all places, Utah."

"They're smuggling them to Arizona."

"I know, but why come all this way? There are hundreds of smuggling opportunities in their back yard. Europe is a smuggler's heaven." He felt around for any remaining needles.

"Maybe it's a German mafia thing."

"You ever heard of a German mafia over here?"

"No," she admitted.

"Right," Frank said and found the last big one and tugged. It was deep and bit on the way out.

He held the needle up and said, "You think Bill will let me stick this in his eye?"

"We'll make the offer when he comes back," she said.

With the cactus out, he felt much better about climbing, reached up, then stood, wondering when foot death by twine tourniquets was going to set in.

She said, "So if it's not the German mafia, what is it?"

"I have no idea," he said, reached as high as he could, and pulled.

"You're climbing up to the rafter?" she asked.

"Like a really big inchworm," he said and began to pull himself up, little bit by cuffed little bit.

She said, "It looks like something CrossFit crazies would put into their routines."

He said, "When we get out, we'll post it on the internet. Maybe it will go viral." He pulled himself up another couple of inches. "We can make a DVD. Call it the mafia workout."

She said, "More speed, less chatter."

"You're kind of demanding," he said. "Maybe lunch isn't such a good idea."

"Maybe not," she agreed.

He pulled himself up another hand span, straining. "Cancel that. You're not wiggling out of it that easy," he said.

But she was right. He was feeling his alarms, suspecting Bill would crunch his way over the gravel to the door any second now, and so redoubled his efforts. He continued, another ten, then twelve pulls, until he was six inches or so under the rafter and paused.

His biceps and shoulders burned like little camp fires, and he knew that sooner or later the lactic acid would build to the point where the shoulders and arms wouldn't work. But Frank wasn't close to that point with those muscles. It was his hands, gripping this thin twine rope. He hung by one hand and flexed the other to work the burn out of it. Then switched and figured now was as good as it was going to get. So he took the twine rope in both hands and swung himself forward, back, forward, back, putting his body into it and getting some good arc. With the third swing forward he tensed, mustered his strength, and waited until he was at the apex of his arc.

The moment came, and Frank bucked like a big fish, pulled with all his might, then released the twine rope to make a twisting, cuffed leap to the rafter like some ungainly gymnast in a high bar routine.

If he missed the rafter, he would fall, and when he reached the end of his rope, the twine would yank his feet up, stretch, possibly break, and send him head first into the cement.

He flew up, his cuffed hands brushed the wood, and he caught the rafter with the tips of his fingers, one hand a little more securely than the other. But it was enough, and he swung back, gripping the rafter. Relief surged through him, and he extended his arms for a second to let some of the burn drain out. Then he swung his lashed and pin-pricking feet up, hooked the backs of his ankles over the beam, then pulled and twisted himself up until he was sitting on the rafter, his legs dangling, his cuffed hands now in front of him, the twine hanging down in a big loop.

"Ha," he said.

Outside, the gravel crunched as someone approached.

The sheriff groaned. "God, please."

The footsteps drew nearer, and Frank knew he was had. They'd open the door and see him perched up here like some idiot chicken.

The sheriff looked over at him. "Why did I listen to you?"

The crunching footsteps came to the door, then continued on.

Frank held his breath. But the crunching continued down the side of the barn, and then whoever it was must have left the gravel trail because the crunching turned to normal footsteps. Frank blew out a sigh of relief and looked down at her.

He said, "You listened to me because if you hadn't, you'd be swinging by your twine rope right now."

"How are you going to undo those knots?" she hissed. "Your weight has probably pulled them so tight they might as well be glued together."

"We'll figure out the knots in a second," Frank said. "First we do the cuffs."

She looked at him like he'd just started to talk about vegetables. "With what?"

"With higher technology," he said, then scooted over as far as he could, looping his legs around the rafter for balance, and leaned out at a precarious angle to the one piece of wire he was able to reach.

24
Barn

IT WAS A decent gauge wire, and Frank grabbed it with both hands and began to bend one spot back and forth. The wire soon broke, and Frank pulled himself back to sitting upright, wire in hand, then lost his balance and immediately had to do a weird fanny-sag off one side and brace himself with his foot on the other to keep from falling. It was not comfortable. Sitting on the narrow end of a two-by-four was a literal pain in the butt.

"Daughter of a stinking pig," he said.

"What?" the sheriff asked.

"When in Rome, speak as the Romans," he said and put the wire in his teeth. He repositioned himself until he felt secure, then took the wire again. He curled one end down into the key slot, and bent it. Then he repositioned the wire and bent it again so that it had a spoon-like shape at the end.

"You learn that in felon school?" she asked.

"Kind of," he said. "I learned it in Special Forces, which some in the Army might classify as a federally funded school for non-conformists." Then he repositioned the wire in the cuff slot to release the teeth and twisted.

The wire bowed with the pressure. He twisted a bit more, and with the torsion and odd angle of his hand, the wire suddenly sprang free. It flitted up, out, and then down.

Frank's heart did a triple beat and gave up the ghost.

Then the wire landed on the top and side of his thigh, almost at the point where it was going to fall off, and lay there.

Frank froze. "Lord," he murmured, "please assign me a different desk jockey." Then he unthawed his arms, and slowly reached out to grab the wire, balancing with every muscle known to man, keeping his legs perfectly still.

The wire did not spring to the ground, but allowed Frank to approach and pick it up with two fingers.

He blew out a sigh. Blew out another. "It's like playing freaking Operation."

"You're killing me," she said.

"Tell me about it," he said, then curled the unruly cuff pick down into the key slot on one of the cuffs for a second try. These cuffs were double-lock Smith and Wesson's, but Zeke hadn't engaged the second lock. It wouldn't have mattered if he had. Frank took a solid grip, then moved the wire around, felt the sweet spot, and twisted, lifting the locking mechanism away from the teeth.

He pulled his hand free, felt a surge of triumph, then went for the other cuff. That one came off even faster.

A little wave of relief washed over him, and then he glanced up at the door, knowing he was still a sitting chicken. But a chicken with a tool.

He stowed the wire in his pants pocket, then with one hand, he grabbed a rafter crossbeam. With the other, he took the pointed ratchet end of one cuff and worked it into the twine knot at his ankles and tried to loosen it up.

It was tight, almost as tight as Sheriff Hood had feared it would be, but he finally worked the point of the cuff in. He moved it back and forth. Tried a different spot. Tried a third, struck pay dirt, and the knot loosened. He continued to work it until it was loose, and then he stowed the cuffs in his pants with the wire and went at the knot with his fingers. Soon enough, he unraveled the knot and began unlooping the lashes from around his rejoicing ankles.

"Okay," she said. "Now I'm impressed."

"How did you find my car?" he asked, continuing to unloop the orange twine.

She said, "We got some footage from a security camera across from the diner. It seemed to corroborate your story. I came by your motel to talk to you, but you weren't there."

Frank finished with the last few loops and let the twine fall to the floor. Like flowing needles, the blood began to pump back into his feet again. He rubbed his ankles to speed it along. "What time did you come by?"

"A little after four a.m."

He picked the end of the duct tape under the twine free, then began to unwind it, going slow to keep the ripping sound down. "That's late. How did you know I hadn't gone south?"

"Night Owl Ned."

"Night Owl Ned?"

"He lives in the little white bungalow on the north end of town. Right on the main road. He's lived there for almost sixty years. Ned doesn't sleep much. I found him in his front yard fertilizing his flowers."

"In the dark?" Frank asked, hurrying with the duct tape.

"In the dark."

"What is he, a vampire?"

"Vampires bite people and suck their blood. Ned just putters about. He's an owl, not a blood sucker. So I asked him how long he'd been up. He said he'd taken a nap around two. I described your car. He asked me if it was the one with a muffler problem. I said yes. He told me you'd driven by sometime around eleven, heading north, with your lights off."

Frank shook his head. "That blasted muffler," he said and pulled away another loop of tape.

"It didn't take a genius to know where you were going. On my way into the ranch, the SUV's brights glinted off something in the bush. I backed up and found your car."

"Lucky you've got yourself a little spy network," he said.

"You think that's luck?"

Probably not, Frank thought. She probably knew almost everyone in her little town. "You know you gave away my position," he said and kicked free of the last bit of tape.

"Hide your car better next time. Now get down here and get me out of this."

Frank grabbed the rafter with both hands, then swung down like Tarzan and landed right in front of her on his still-recovering feet. He said, "I can taste that Edna burger right now."

"Just get me out."

He unpicked her cuffs and removed them first.

She sighed and rubbed her wrists, and he walked over to the work table.

"Where you going?"

He retrieved his gear and came back, finding her trying to pick the knot of twine and not making much headway. He said, "Here, let me get that for you," and cut her free of the twine and the duct tape.

She rubbed her throat, then scrambled for the boots. Frank followed her lead. They pulled their boots on and hastily laced them up. Next, the sheriff went over to the table, grabbed the little rock sheriff, and put her back into her cargo pocket. Then the sheriff took her keys, gum, and box of latex gloves and stowed them as well. Too bad they hadn't left her duty belt, but this was a barn with tools, and she walked over to a shelf and grabbed a ball peen hammer.

Frank looked around the garage. He said, "This can't be just about cigarettes. They could have easily blown out of here if this was about a bunch of boxes, but they didn't because there was something else they couldn't move that quickly."

She said, "I don't want to be here when they come back."

He said, "Did you notice that bleach smell when we came in?"

"Maybe they're tidy."

He motioned at the stairway and doors at the back of the barn and said, "It will only take a second."

"I'll give you seven," she said.

Not a lot of time. He hoped she added a lot between each count.

Frank headed for the back of the big garage-barn. The sheriff went to the side door, quietly wedged the ball of her foot up against the bottom, and slowly turned the deadbolt home.

Frank passed the big drone he'd seen earlier. It looked a lot like a mini stealth bomber with three propellers for vertical power and one in the back for speed.

That was another question—what were cigarette smugglers doing with drones? Maybe they smuggled goods across the border with them.

He paused for a second to make a choice. He had a mystery door at the bottom of the stairwell in front of him, another off to the side with a padlock that looked like it hadn't been opened in some time, and another mystery door at the top of the stairs on the second level. He was sure the answer to his questions was behind one of them.

He saw dust prints and some packing tape on the stairs going up and decided to take the road more traveled. He ascended the stairs softly, taking them three at a time.

Frank tried the door and found it unlocked, so he opened it and stepped into the room. It was dark. He found the light switch on the wall and flipped it. The lights went on, revealing a room that ran the length of the back of the garage. Like below, the windows had been covered over with sheets of plywood. Under the windows were two long tables with a couple of padded and wheeled office chairs. On one table stood a dozen or so round canisters the size of plastic protein powder jars on top of sheets of newspaper.

The canisters had been painted red, white, and blue, and from the drips and overspray on the newsprint, it looked like that had happened recently. Frank looked closer and discovered they were made of stainless steel. Each canister had a steel top on it with a round hole in the middle big enough to insert a thin straw. Next to the canisters were tubes and other mechanical parts. Some looked like parts to the drones.

Across from the table, a brand new map of the United States hung on one wall. He knew it was new because not only were the creases still sharp, it had this year's date printed on it. Frank walked over to look at it. He did it quietly because the last thing he wanted was for someone outside to hear him clomping about.

On the map, someone had used pink highlighter to circle the cities of San Diego and Huntington Beach. Huntington Beach was one of the stops on Frank's L.A. vacation plan. Kim said they had a huge Fourth of July parade there with hundreds of thousands of spectators. Farther up by San Francisco, Alameda was circled. North from there was another circle around Seattle. Moving east, there were circles around Provo, Utah, Houston, St. Louis, Oklahoma City, Chicago, Nashville, Philadelphia, Boston.

Frank tried to see a pattern, but couldn't. They weren't big-ticket cigarette smuggling destinations. San Francisco and Oakland were port towns and close to Alameda, but that wasn't the profile of Provo, Mormon central and home of BYU. And what did any of these have to do with the singing culture in Nashville?

Frank turned and looked at the tables. He found some tourist printouts for San Diego. He found a box of tools for use with small screws. He found some more white cardboard boxes. One contained a manual remote control for a hobby airplane. One held little brass nozzles like you'd find on an insect sprayer or mister.

He turned and looked around, waiting for something to pop out at him, but nothing did, and so he exited the room, turned out the light, and shut the door behind him.

The sheriff held up seven fingers, whispered, "Seven," and gave him a look that meant business.

Frank quietly took the stairs three at a time back down. When he got to the bottom, he pitched his voice low and said, "It's got to be in the basement."

"No," she whispered and shook her head. "We're going now."

He wanted to try that mystery door, but she was right. They couldn't afford to be caught in here. The sheriff might lock the door, but Zeke or one of the others would shoot out the locks, then come and shoot them. Or shoot him, then have a rape party with her.

Frank glanced at the stairway to the basement, then hurried over to join the sheriff at the door. On the way, he saw a tire iron leaning up against some shelves and picked it up.

She said in a low voice, "Were there any cars parked out front when they brought us in?"

He said, "There was the Lincoln, but I'm pretty sure Bill pocketed the keys."

"You know how to hot-wire?"

"No self-respecting mechanic doesn't. But we've got to get across the asphalt, get into the car, then I've got to get the wires. The problem is I'm not practiced, and I don't know the Lincoln. We'll be sitting ducks in full view while I figure it out."

"So we make a run for the cedars. Should we split up?"

It was hard to fight a mob on your own, but if you had a second body, you suddenly cut your risk in half. "I'm thinking our odds are better together."

She nodded and quietly turned the deadbolt.

Outside the barn, someone whistled to get someone else's attention.

She froze.

Frank whispered, "We go down to the end of the barn. You'll see a clump of quaking aspen. Go around them to the north, jump the barbed-wire fence, and haul across that field. When you get out in the field, don't run a straight line all the way across. Pick three points, equally spaced, and alter your direction slightly at each. You don't want to make it easy for them to get a bead on you and lead you like some dumb deer."

"I'm not worried," she said. "They're going to shoot you first. You're the bigger target. And I'm betting I'm faster."

"The things some women will do to get out of a date."

"Lunch isn't a date."

"It could be a date."

"Maybe I'll hit you with the ball peen hammer now. Take my chances."

"Then you'd be the only target."

"Dang," she said. "It was such a good plan."

"We're going to make it," he said.

"You just keep up," she replied and put her hand on the doorknob.

"You open. I'll look to see if it's clear. Then we go."

She nodded.

"Ready?" he said.

"Oh, I'm ready," she said and tightened her grip on the hammer.

25

Plan B

SHERIFF HOOD TURNED the knob, then stepped back, and slowly opened the door.

Frank did not peek out, but moved in an arc to see the lane between the barn and the building next door. The lane was clear. He moved in an arc the other way, like walking the rim of a circle, and looked down the lane toward the cedars and freedom.

Darth and Zeke stood down at that end of the barn, Darth's bruise looking outstanding. Darth sucked in on his cigarette, then blew out a trail of smoke and glanced in Frank's and the sheriff's direction.

"Hey!" He shouted.

"We've just been made," Frank said. "Plan B." And he stepped out and cocked the tire iron.

Zeke turned. Darth's expression slid from surprise to anger.

"Run toward the house," Frank said, then hurled the tire iron at Zeke and Darth.

Darth and Zeke lunged out of the path of the flying hunk of metal.

The sheriff shot out of the garage toward the asphalt and the big house. Frank spun and took off after her, the gravel crunching under his feet.

Up ahead, the sheriff shouted, "Lincoln's no good!" Then she turned and disappeared around the corner of the big shed.

And, indeed, the woman who was not Danish was coming out of the house and down the porch steps. She saw Sheriff Hood, shouted, and went for a gun behind her back.

Down at the other end of the barn, a pistol cracked, and the bullet whistled past, inches from Frank's head. The hair on the back of his neck stood on end.

"Hell a-mighty," he said and raced around the corner, a few paces behind the sheriff.

Ahead, there was a long chicken coop, followed by an animal pen, followed by trees and the dirt road cutting up the canyon.

Another shot rang out, this time from Ms. Pink Pepper Pistol, and slammed into the shed above Frank, cracking the wood.

The sheriff turned the corner of the coop. Frank turned the corner of the coop two strides after her. He looked at the meadow that led to the cedars and freedom and saw one of Bill's men moving across the meadow toward them.

The sheriff slowed, then stopped. Frank just about ran into her.

"Where now?" she asked.

Behind them, Darth and Zeke shouted, raising the alarm. In less than a minute, Frank figured, he and the sheriff were going to be surrounded.

Frank looked beyond her and saw an ATV parked behind the animal pen. It had a trailer attached. On the trailer sat a bale of hay speared with a pitchfork. He thought he saw the key still in the ignition.

"There," he said. "We head up the canyon."

"Count of three," she said.

Back by the asphalt Ms. Pink Pistol was yelling, telling the men to circle round. Then Frank heard a light crunch of gravel along the side of the coop they'd just ran down. Frank turned and saw the top of a man's shadow, advancing across the ground all slow like he was sneaking up. It was a good move. If the man turned the corner, he'd have Frank and the sheriff dead in his sights. But it was the wrong time of day to approach from that direction.

Frank turned to the sheriff and motioned her to continue on. "Go," he whispered. "I'll catch up."

The sheriff nodded, then crouched low and ran for the ATV.

Frank looked around for a board or pipe to hit the guy with. There was no board or pipe. There were only two faded, pink, plastic, garden flamingos standing in an attractive arrangement of landscape rock and wild flowers. One of the flamingos had a little sign hanging from its beak that said, "Bloom Where You're Planted."

Frank plucked the aphoristic bird out of the ground and cocked it back, watching the shadow progress closer, then hesitate at the corner.

Ms. Pink Pistol yelled that the sheriff was running behind the animal pen. Shots were fired from the direction of the front of the ranch house, but Frank didn't know if it was Pink Pistol or someone else.

The man obviously thought this was his chance, and quickly advanced, gun drawn.

The gun, a nine millimeter Beretta, appeared first, held in a two-handed grip. Then came the arms. And that's when Frank swung his flamingo by the metal posts and nailed Darth in the face.

The flamingo cracked. Darth stumbled back, raised his arms to protect himself, and shot three rounds into the sky.

Frank tossed the flamingo, strode forward, saw Darth's ankle present itself, then took another step and smashed down with his boot heel just above the joint. He felt the ankle give way and knew he'd at least partially broken it.

Darth fell back, arms flying wide, and lost control of his pistol, which flew a couple of yards and landed in the gravel.

Frank dove for the weapon and rolled up into one-knee stance with the gun in his hands. He saw something out of the corner of his eye and turned.

Back by the asphalt, a new guy rounded the corner with a rifle.

Frank swung the pistol around.

The guy went wide-eyed, stopped, and wheeled back.

Frank aimed and squeezed off a round, slow and smooth, but the guy ran behind the corner of the shed, and the bullet shot past.

Frank heard the ATV starting up. Then he heard a number of shots coming from the back of the barn toward the sheriff.

In front of Frank, Darth rolled over and pushed himself to his knees.

Frank shot him in the torso, and then he gave the corner of the shed a wide berth, gun up, and moved around in a semi-circle to see what was down by the barn. He saw Zeke with his pistol raised, shooting past Frank's position at the sheriff.

Frank shot. Missed. Cursed his eroding skills. Cursed the Beretta, then adjusted and shot again. This time he hit Zeke's arm.

Zeke cried out, flinched, and staggered back.

The guy out in the meadow raised his semiautomatic and began firing at the sheriff as well, although he was too far out.

"Shaw!" the sheriff yelled.

Frank watched for shooters and began to back up toward the ATV.

The sheriff pushed the ATV's throttle lever and lurched forward with the trailer and hay.

"Shaw!" she yelled.

Frank turned and ran to catch her.

Behind him Zeke opened up again, the bullets sounding like the crack of a whip as they sped past.

The sheriff was now taking fire from three sides, and she gunned it.

Frank dashed past the chicken coop and animal pen, chased her for a few paces, and caught up just as she was approaching the dirt road that ran up the canyon. He dove onto the two-wheeled, flatbed trailer just as she was pulling onto the dirt road. Frank moved to join her up on the ATV, but she turned, knocking him off balance and sending him flying. He landed on his back, his shoulders and head off the side of the trailer about an inch from the ground.

He abandoned the idea of joining the sheriff up front and pulled himself back onto the trailer.

The sheriff gave the thing all the gas it had. The motor whined. The knobby wheels kicked up dust, and the ATV sped up the trail, the tiny hay wagon bouncing and jostling over the bumps.

The canyon was narrower here, the slopes steep and topped with cliffs. The dry streambed ran a dozen or so yards to the side of the road. Stretches of willow ran in thick patches there. But the rest of the ground was mostly open with a variety of trees here and there. Not a lot of cover to find a good spot to return fire. And an arsenal consisting of one semiautomatic and a pea shooter wasn't going to do the job anyway.

Back down by the bunk house across from the animal pen, yet another man Frank had not seen got on a newer, shinier ATV, put it in gear, and came after them, a rifle slung across his shoulder. That made person number ten.

Bill was such the liar. Frank wondered how many more of them there were. He wondered if some of them were up this canyon. Getting sandwiched between a group in front and one behind would not be good.

Frank knew this magazine for the Beretta would have carried fifteen rounds when full, but he didn't have a full magazine. He'd used four rounds back at the ranch, which meant he had eleven at the most, but the weight didn't feel right for even that.

The sheriff rounded a bend, then hit a bit of rock. The trailer bounced, the back end kicking up like a mule, and Frank and the bale of hay next to him were suddenly airborne. A moment later, both landed back on the bed with a good thump.

The sheriff continued on at full throttle. Dust from the knobby ATV and trailer tires billowed up around Frank, coating his teeth and making him squint. Behind him, the guy on the shiny new ATV began to draw closer, his machine roaring with a nice high, clean whine.

"Faster!" Frank yelled.

"I'm going as fast as I can," the sheriff yelled back.

Then she went around a sharp bend, and, as if to prove her point, two wheels of the ATV lifted up a bit. The sheriff stood and leaned out as far as she could to counteract it. A moment later, the ATV's two wheels slammed back down, and Frank didn't know if Bill's guys or the sheriff were going to kill him first.

She slowed and went around another bend, and the guy behind them narrowed their lead another ten yards.

Frank cursed and pushed himself up to his knees. There was no way he would get any kind of good shot bouncing along on his belly.

The sheriff turned out into an open stretch, and Frank figured this would be his chance.

He let her put some distance between them and the last bend, the dust billowing up along the trail, then yelled, "Stop!"

"What?"

"Stop. So I can get a shot."

The sheriff let off the throttle. The ATV chugged and geared down. Dust filled the air around them.

A few moments later, the man on the new ATV rounded the corner through the dust. He was about fifty yards back, leaning way out to keep his vehicle from rolling. But the dust was so thick, he probably didn't realize Frank and the sheriff had stopped.

Frank took aim, waited for the guy to straighten out, and squeezed off a round. The muzzle flashed. The gun kicked. And the bullet sailed who knew where, certainly not where Frank had been aiming, the freaking crap gun. Frank adjusted his aim and fired again and this time hit the fender.

If their pursuer hadn't understood what was going on with the first shot, he certainly did now. He slammed on his brakes, skidded to a halt, and reached for his rifle.

A rifle was not fair, Frank thought. Not at all. If the man got that rifle and was any kind of shot, this game would be over.

Frank adjusted again and fired. The Beretta banged and kicked. A moment later the man jerked and dropped his weapon into the dry grass, then grabbed his lower torso.

Frank adjusted his aim ever so slightly and squeezed the trigger again.

The Beretta clicked.

He squeezed again.

Another click.

Awesome, he thought. They had a horde of killers on their tails and no weapon. He needed the ATV guy's rifle, but just as he moved to run back, a helmetless rider on a motorcycle roared up from the ranch, flashing through the dust and trees, and Frank knew there was no way he'd make it in time.

"Go!" he yelled and waved at the sheriff. "Go!"

The sheriff punched it. The ATV and trailer lurched forward, and Frank almost fell off a third time.

Behind them, the man on the ATV slumped over, and then the motorcyclist approached the corner, took it at speed, the guy laying into it, looking all cool and smooth in his sunglasses, and Frank knew there was no way they were going to outrun that.

The motorcyclist finished his turn, straightened back up and gunned it, blowing past his ailing tobacco-smuggling buddy without giving him a second glance.

The sheriff and her little hay wagon and passenger zoomed along, but the motorcyclist screamed across the distance between them, nothing but sunglasses and business.

Frank needed a weapon. A rock. Something.

The breeze was blowing the dust Frank and the sheriff made to one side of the road, so the motorcyclist moved to the other side, out of the dust, shifted, and twisted the throttle all the way. He sped forward. Forty, then thirty, then twenty yards behind, which is when he pulled his own semiautomatic and pointed it one-handed at Frank.

Frank took a solid stance, cocked his arm back, and hucked the Beretta at him. The gun spun end over end, and looked like it might hit the motorcyclist. But the guy leaned, and the gun flew past.

The motorcyclist brought his semiautomatic back up and fired twice. The bullets cracked past Frank on his right.

Frank grabbed the pitch fork and hurled it at the man.

This time the motorcyclist had to grab both handle bars and swerve. The pitchfork flew harmlessly by, and the man swerved back onto the road.

Frank ripped one of the loops of twine off the bale of hay, grabbed a thick flake, and tossed it in the air, trying to spread it. He grabbed another, tossed it.

The motorcyclist ducked his head and blew through the first toss. He blew through the second. But part of the third flake hit him in the face, and flecks of hay must have gotten past his sunglasses and into his eyes because he suddenly braked to a stop and put a leg down to steady himself. He ripped off his sunglasses and began to wipe at his eyes.

Hail, the power of hay.

The sheriff hit a little rise, Frank almost caught air, and he realized standing on this trailer was a little less than secure. He sank to his knees, and then he and the sheriff raced to the end of the straight-away, her bending low over the handlebars, him kneeling on the trailer, squinting to keep the dust and hay from blinding him like the motorcyclist.

The straight-away ended. The trail bent. The sheriff took it at speed, and Frank had to brace himself with his knees to keep from falling off. They climbed a little hill and flew over the top. Frank, the hay, and the trailer again caught air.

The trailer slammed down. Frank landed with it. However, the remaining half bale of hay did not have his catlike reflexes and did a half bounce, half roll, then lost its shape. One end tumbled off the trailer, dragging the rest with it.

They hit another bump, and Frank flattened himself on the trailer. They raced like that down this side of the hill and across a dry streambed, over some flat ground, then up another longer hill. The steep slope of the canyon wall rose to their right. To their left, the hill they were on fell away to a steep ravine with the streambed at the bottom.

As they neared the top of the hill, the motorcyclist came flying over the first hill that lead down to the streambed behind them. He caught good air, then landed solidly on the other side.

Frank and the sheriff crested the top of their hill and started heading down the far side. And that's when Frank got an idea. He turned and yelled for the sheriff to stop. Yelled again.

She brought them to a skidding halt.

Behind them, on the other side of the hill, the motorcyclist approached, his machine whining in high gear.

"What are we doing?" she asked.

"We're dumping the trailer," he said and jumped off.

And they were going to place it for maximum crash effect so that when the motorcyclist came roaring over this hill, he'd hit it.

A triangle of metal posts extended from the front of the trailer forming a neck. At the end of the neck was a coupler, an upside-down cup, that fitted over a ball hitch on the ATV. There were two safety chains as well running from the ATV's hitch to the trailer. Frank went to the coupler first, removed the pin, then lifted the lever releasing the coupler from the ball. The sheriff jumped off the ATV and began to remove one chain. Frank began to remove the other, but the whine of the motorcycle had been growing. It was loud, just over the hill, and he knew they'd been too slow. There was no time to remove the chains and move the trailer into place.

He looked around, saw a stone lying off the side of the trail away from the ravine, and went for it.

Frank figured the motorcyclist would see the trailer and slow. At that point, Frank would nail him with the rock and charge.

Frank grabbed the stone and positioned himself just when the motorcyclist flew over the crest of the hill. He landed a number of yards up from the trailer, skid-braked to avoid the obstacle, then gunned it to blow past them.

Frank hurled his stone and watched it fly wide.

The sheriff had her ball peen hammer cocked back. She lunged forward with one leg, wheeled her arm around like a pitcher throwing a fast ball. The hammer spun twice, the metal winking in the sunlight, then nailed the guy in the side of the face.

The rider yanked his handle bars to the left, his sunglasses askew, and shot away from the road toward the ravine. He hit a bump, continued forward, the throttle on full. And then the ground dropped out from underneath him, and the rider and motorcycle flew out over the ravine in a smooth arc. And then gravity took hold, and the flying rider and motorcycle dropped out of sight behind the curve of the hill.

A moment later, there was a loud crunch, followed by another. Frank ran over to the side of the slope and peered down.

Fifty or so feet below, the man lay sprawled at a bad angle. The motorcycle lay on its side with bent forks, but still running.

Two points for team sheriff, he thought.

Then he heard the sound of a different motor and looked down the dry streambed in the direction of the ranch and saw a white pickup crest the first hill.

He hustled back and found the sheriff had removed the safety chains. Frank pulled out his tactical knife and punctured both tires, then left the back end of the trailer sticking up, the whole thing blocking the road. It wouldn't save him and the sheriff, but it just might give them a little more time.

The sheriff climbed back up on the ATV. "Come on!" she yelled and motioned at him.

Frank folded his knife, stuffed it in his pocket, and ran to the ATV. He jumped on behind her, and she gunned it before he'd fully sat down. He almost flipped over the back, but grabbed one of the cargo bars and held on.

They sped down the hill through the sparse trees, wound around some snaky bends, crossed the canyon's streambed again, then followed the trail up onto the side of the slope and back down. Frank figured they had another half a mile before this canyon would start to open up.

But then the ATV chugged. It ran a little farther, chugged again, then cut out entirely and rolled to a squeaky, fat-tired stop.

The sheriff unscrewed the gas cap. "Empty," she said.

They heard some shouts echo up the canyon and a pickup engine roar. Frank figured their pursuers had just cleared the trailer out of the way.

He looked to his right. The slope there was a couple hundred feet high and steep. And provided almost no cover. Up there, they'd be easy shots for someone with a rifle. Running straight along the dirt road wasn't an option either. Joggers simply never fared well against pickup trucks.

He looked over to the left. There was a narrow canyon feeding into this one. The orange rock slopes around it were steep and topped with cliffs. But there wasn't any road to it or through it that a pickup might travel, just a little trail wide enough for a person or a horse.

"The canyon," the sheriff said. "And we'd better hustle."

26

Bighorn

FRANK STEPPED OFF the ATV. "We can't just run to the canyon. We've got to lose them now."

The sheriff got off as well. "I don't think we have the time. I say we get ahead. We outrun them. And then we scuttle our tracks."

"Except you're forgetting that these guys use drones. If they don't know where we went, they'll have to split up to search. If we leave clear tracks, they'll know exactly where we went. And then all they'll need to do is send a drone to keep an eye on us, send a few guns to come behind, and a few others to circle around and ahead. That's what happened to the man in the tarp."

She sighed.

"You know I'm right," he said.

"You're killing me."

Frank pointed ahead. "We can use that patch of rock up there running across the road. We stomp on past it for a few yards and turn off the road like we're heading up into the fold of the slope and those trees. We'll go just a bit, then stop, back track, and use the rocky patch across the road to hide our true direction."

She sighed. "Okay, let's get moving."

"Follow my lead," Franks said and sprinted up the road, making sure to set his footprints nice and hard.

She snatched the key from the ATV and hucked it into the weeds, then followed.

They passed the rock that spanned the road, and Frank said, "Now slow. Like we just realized we need to get off the road. Stride over here with me."

He could hear the truck coming up the canyon and knew this was going to be close.

They walked off the road. Frank stomped a few good ones so they'd see, and when they got to another rocky stretch a few yards later, she said, "It's time to back track. Walk backwards in your footprints. Lead with your toes."

"You've done this before," Frank said.

"Honey," she said. "The Kane County sheriff's department puts on a man tracking class every year."

He couldn't help himself and said, "And how do the ladies like it?"

She grunted and rolled her eyes. "It's for law enforcement. They come from all over the nation." And then she began to backtrack in expert fashion.

Frank followed her to the swath of red rock that crossed the road, and then they both turned toward the dry creek bed and the canyon beyond. A finger of the red rock extended maybe fifteen feet off the road in the direction they were heading. They followed it right to the edge, where the sheriff said, "Take off your boots. They're going to be looking for the tread they saw before. You and I are going to walk in socks. Keep off the dirt as best you can. Use the little clumps of weeds. They're dry and won't show any bruising or breaking."

She really did know what she was talking about.

They both shucked their boots and stood. Between them and the creek bed was sage and salt brush and lots and lots of dry, dull-orange dirt that would capture their footprints marvelously if they weren't careful.

They began to half-jog half-pick their way through the brush. Such a pace was not ideal for camouflaging tracks, but all of their counter-tracking wasn't going to help a bit if they were still out here when the pickup topped the rise. Their pursuers had rifles, and if they were any kinds of shots at all, they'd stop and bag Frank and the sheriff like two rabbits too dumb to go to ground.

The noise of the truck increased.

They came to the creek bed, which stretched thirty feet across. Farther upstream, there were stretches of willow along the banks.

Downstream, there was a clump of cottonwoods. But here the bank just cut away and dropped a sheer six feet down. That was good because the drop would give them cover. It was also bad because he could tell the bed was softer here. Great for making footprints, but they didn't have time to be choosey.

They jumped down and made two sets of awesome, deep footprints in the moist, sandy soil. They scuffed them over, but anyone with any tracking sense would see it for what it was. Even when the heat dried the dirt, it still wouldn't look right. But it was better than nothing.

"How about another fake?" he asked and pointed at a good swath of river stone. "Right there. It goes a long ways. They'll think we tried to circle down."

"You *are* going to get us killed."

"Look on the bright side. If we get caught, you won't have to take me to lunch."

She shook her head, but quickly led him the ten yards downstream to the river stone, got to a dry, hard part, and turned upstream again. The creek bed was rocky and mostly dry, but there were a handful of stagnant, little puddles with water skeeters flitting over the surface, which the sheriff was careful to avoid.

The sound of the truck's motor was getting closer. They were on the other side of the hill behind the sheriff and Frank.

"I think we need to run," she said.

"Patience," he said. Their pursuers were going to come to the creek to look for them, and he and the sheriff needed to leave as few prints as possible; they simply didn't want to ruin all their counter-tracking now.

But the truck was coming up the rise, its motor revving, and unless they hid right up against the sheer drop of the bank, they would still be visible to someone up on the hill.

Moving around when the enemy was active was not a good way to stay hidden. But hiding this close to the road wouldn't do much because someone was going to get the idea to search the creek bed, and then it would only be a matter of time. They needed to get to the narrow canyon upstream.

It was fifty yards of river stone to the mouth of the narrow canyon.

Stones were buggers to run across in bare feet. Not much better in socks.

But the truck was almost to the top of the hill.

She said, "It's time to make haste."

"You're right," he said, and they set off running across the stone, which wasn't bad for the first few strides, but then he got a nice point on the sole of one foot and a few strides later jammed a toe. The sheriff grunted in pain ahead of him, her bare arms shining in the hot morning sun.

Up ahead, there was a little dry streambed running out of the narrow canyon into this bigger one. It was the logical place to enter the canyon, which is why they weren't going to take it.

"Not the streambed," he hissed. "Let's go up here, by the log. I'll give you a leg up."

She ran to a section of the bank that was five feet tall and as sheer as the rest of the creek had been. He came up behind her and took another point of river stone in the ball of his foot and winced. He threw his boots up, then made a stirrup with his hands. She stepped into his stirrup, and when she went to step up to the bank, he gave her a big heave.

She let out a little exclamation of surprise as she flew way up and over the bank. When she moved off, he took two steps back, then made a run at the bank. He planted his hands up on the edge, then vaulted onto the bank in his socks and rolled away from the drop.

The narrow canyon's slopes rose a few hundred feet to either side. Above them, the sky was bright and blue. Down in the canyon, there were shadows. They were on the south side of this little canyon, the part that didn't get as much sun, which meant the ground didn't parch as quickly, which meant the brush here could grow higher, except nobody had told the brush because this bit of ground was barren.

"Find cover," she said and ran for the bushes a number of yards ahead.

Frank grabbed his boots and followed her.

A few strides later they passed into the canyon shadow.

Behind them, the pickup topped the rise.

"Down!" he hissed, and they both dropped behind some shin-high weeds and a little bit of rock.

The pickup stopped.

"Stay perfectly still," he said. "Don't move your feet, your arms, don't turn your head faster than thirty-seconds per quarter turn."

"Did you think I was going to pole dance for them?" she asked.

She didn't need to pole dance. Her pants were a good brown color, but her light skin didn't really blend in with the rock. Nor did her white tube socks. And while the black of her vest wasn't shocking orange, it would stand out to a careful eye. Worst still was her all-too-human form. Humans were made to spot other humans.

Which meant his outfit and form wasn't any better. But color and even pattern were both secondary. Movement was the biggest thing that drew the eye. And so they stayed there frozen.

There were five of them up on the hill—three in the cab, two in the bed of the pickup. Caterpillar Brow was driving. His skinny sidekick was in the cab with him, along with the wildcat woman who chased down the man in the tarp. In the bed, sitting down, was the German as well as the guy who'd said he was the man in the tarp. Both held rifles.

Lord, he prayed, let them look the other way, but the crew didn't seemed to be tuned into the right channel.

Instead, each of them surveyed the scene around them. Then the German said something, and the driver gave it some gas, and the pickup moved forward and began to make its way down the hill.

When the truck passed behind a stretch of cedars, she said, "We go now. Hands and knees, up into the brush up ahead."

"Keep it slow," he said.

And they crawled forward. A dozen or so yards later, they made it to some sagebrush that could actually hide them.

Back out in the main canyon, the pickup stopped, which meant they'd come to the abandoned ATV. So now they knew Frank and the sheriff were on foot. He heard doors open. Moments later he heard them push the ATV off to the side. Frank couldn't see them, but he knew they'd be looking around.

Frank wasn't going to be happy until he and the sheriff were completely out of the direct line of sight of the road.

Back at the main road, someone shouted, "Here!"

Frank said, "Keep going." And he and the sheriff kept crawling, threading their way through the rather large gaps between the bushes until they came to the trail leading up the canyon.

The sheriff halted, examined the trail, then pointed at footprints with the light tread of a boot.

Frank changed his angle and saw that the edges had weakened a bit.

He said, "Somebody's been here. Probably yesterday. This is still Elkhorn land, right?"

"We've got a long way to go before we're off this ranch," she said.

The prints went up the trail, but there was another set of prints coming back down.

She said, "We can use this. Let's not disturb the trail. I'm betting there will be strands of spider web across it. If anyone comes after us, I want them getting the strands and seeing this set of prints going in and coming out and thinking nobody has been here since."

"Good call," he said. "Let's cross over then. There's more cover on the other side."

"Keep your eyes peeled for some place to hide," she said, and then they stepped over the trail, making the barest of sock prints on the other side, and continued in a crouch into the taller brush and deadfall, carrying their boots in their hands.

The canyon here was probably a hundred feet wide. Frank looked up to the first bend. The slopes on the right side there were still topped with cliffs. On the left, however, it looked like the cliffs began to break up. There were chutes between some of the steep parts, but he couldn't see if any actually went to the top.

Back out on the main road one of the men shouted, "No," like he was reporting something. Probably that he hadn't found any additional tracks in the direction they'd sent him. Frank figured it would be at this point that his tobacco friends would be looking around, trying to decide where he and the sheriff had gone. Had they continued up the main canyon, or jumped into the creek bed and tried to loop back down? Were they hiding behind some brush, or had they gone into the side canyon?

Frank and the sheriff continued to carefully move forward.

He figured two of their pursuers would stay with the truck and race ahead of the farthest point they thought Frank and the sheriff might have been able to run, then work their way back down. The other three would start searching where they were. The wildcat woman with her braids would be one of those.

If it were him, the creek bed and narrow canyon were no-brainers. They would be the first spots he'd check. He'd also send someone back up the rise to get some elevation and direct the others. And to make sure Frank and the sheriff didn't circle around them and head back down the canyon. Or maybe not. Maybe they had called in the drones and were waiting for the little eyes in the sky to find them.

And if the drones did come, this canyon would be one of the first places they'd look. Right now, he and the sheriff needed to be finding a hiding spot. But the bottom of this canyon presented no such place. It consisted of the streambed, dirt, boulders that had tumbled down from above, and precious little cover. If he had a shovel and a net, he could make a spider hole nobody would see. Too bad he wasn't back in the Special Forces days with exactly such items packed on the Bat Belt.

He turned to the steep slope on his left again and scanned it. It was mostly barren, nothing more than little dots of scrub here and there and an animal trail with a mountain sheep on it. The sheep was a ewe, looking back at him. No, it was two ewes, and beyond them was a bend above which poked the tops of some pines. The animal trail led up and across the face of the slope toward those pines and the broken chutes above.

Frank said, "Option A is to go down to the little streambed and try to bury ourselves. It's close. On the other hand, that's the first place they'll look. And the dirt down there is full of rocks, so we're going to have to dig with rock spades, and even if we could cover all signs of our digging, we might not finish in time."

"What's option B?" she asked.

Frank looked at the animal trail and the mountain sheep. He said, "Animals don't walk a route over and over just for the heck of it. That trail leads to some destination. I'm willing to bet they use it to come down from the top for water and feed. We need to go up," he said.

"Onto the bare slopes where it will be easy to spot us?"

"That path has got to lead to those trees. I say we follow those two honeys out of here."

The sheriff looked at the thin animal trail and the two brown sheep still looking back at them. "Crap," she said.

"We're not going to outrun the drones," he said. "Besides, do we even know if there's a way out at the end of this thing. Is this a blind canyon?"

She sighed. "I don't know."

"There you go," he said.

"You know this is not what I had on the agenda for today."

"No, but if we're quick, we can still do lunch."

"That was not on the agenda either."

He shrugged and motioned at the trail. "How about escape? We could do it on the double."

She sighed in frustration, obviously not liking the situation he'd dragged her into, but turned and faced the slope. "Sometimes goat trails don't really go anywhere," she said, then took off at a good lope for the trail anyway.

Frank followed. She was full of spring and had a fine-looking stride which would have been awesome to contemplate in another situation. She was also surprisingly fast and started to pull away from him, and Frank lengthened his own stride to keep up.

On the slope, the two ewes saw them and began to trot away.

Frank and the sheriff crossed back over the trail heading up the canyon and quickly came to the foot of the slope. The sheriff began the climb to the animal trail in her now very dirty socks, but she was smart and slowed down, making sure to keep her footprints light, to step on stones and weeds, because it would not do to sneak all the way here and then leave two clear sets of prints in the dirt up the side of the steep slope. Frank followed, watching his step. Maybe thirty feet up, they came to the animal trail that, at its best, was no more than six inches wide, and they began to traverse along it.

Frank pitched his voice low. "We've got to get around that bend before someone gets to the mouth of this canyon."

"You know you're a pain in the neck," she whispered.

"I'm going to save our buckets," he whispered back.

The sheriff grunted, but she put on the speed and began to run. She didn't clomp along like some tired jogger. She was landing on the balls of her feet, reaching out with long strides, placing her steps smartly, softly. Voices would echo off these rocky canyon walls as would the thudding of running feet, but she was keeping it quiet. Her arms moved with power and grace. Her single braid jounced back and forth.

Frank tried to keep up. They rose along the slope, two ghosts in socks. The canyon floor receded below, and he realized this slope was very steep indeed. From this perspective, it looked like it ran almost straight down.

Frank didn't dare look back. He couldn't. If he glanced while running, he would miss the path and either take a flight to the bottom, which was now some distance below or send rocks and dirt to tumble noisily down the steep incline.

They ran another dozen yards, and then he heard two people talking to each other as they approached the mouth of the narrow canyon, their voices carrying up the steep slopes.

The sheriff lengthened her stride, running as gracefully as a deer. He lumbered behind. Not a moose or cow, maybe a mule. They leapt a fallen branch, then passed behind a large stone, and then they were rounding the bend, and Frank saw his guess had been right. The cliffs at the top of the slope broke up a bit here with some chutes and hoodoos. And trees. The trail led up to a break maybe fifty yards away.

The two ewes were on the trail up there, as were a couple of juveniles. They were all watching as Frank and the sheriff rounded the bend. Upon seeing the two humans coming full steam in their direction, the mountain sheep turned and ran in single file for the break.

Frank's breath was coming hard, making it difficult to hear if any drone was approaching. He wished there were some cover closer, but he was happy they'd taken this trail because he could see now that there really was nothing below along this stretch of the canyon that would have hidden them.

The sheriff was striding out, gaining speed. She *was* a deer. Frank tried to keep pace, brushing past a little pine tree that barely came up to his waist, but she pulled farther ahead.

Above, the trail ran toward a narrow break in a line of jagged bluffs maybe twenty feet high. There were trees above the gap, a couple below, and Frank figured the gap was the way out.

The sheriff reached the gap between the cliffs and shot into it. Frank was a number of strides behind her. He poured on as much speed as he dared on this narrow trail and entered the mouth of the gap, which was maybe six or seven feet wide. He was hoping to see a trail up through the cliffs. What he found was a little refuge with tall rock walls around three sides. And no way out.

It was a dead end.

Furthermore, it was occupied. The sheriff had her back to the wall, alarm on her face. Opposite her a few yards up the slope was a mature bighorn ram, the whites of its eyes showing all crazy. Behind it was a small herd of sheep, all bunched up. Maybe a dozen ewes and their young'uns in the back, milling in fear.

The ram was a big boy. Five feet long. Probably three hundred pounds and full of muscle. Its rack of thick curving horns flowed back and around to point forward again. They looked almost a yard across. They probably weighed thirty pounds all by themselves. With its position up the slope and its height, it was tall enough to look the sheriff in the eye. And it was all tensed up like it was going to charge.

Frank halted. "Good Lord," he said.

The ram turned to face the new and bigger threat.

"Whoa," Frank said and held out his hands.

But the ram didn't speak that language. All it knew was that Frank probably wanted to eat him or one of his women for lunch. It bristled, arched.

Frank's alarms went on full because these things could hit with bone-breaking force.

"Hey," Frank said and took a step back, waving the ram off.

But the ram didn't speak that language either. It was fight, flight, or freeze, and these two humans had him and his family cornered.

Its nostrils flared, and then it rose up a bit on its hind legs and lowered its head.

"No," Frank said, and backed away another step, but the ram charged, its heavy horns propelled by hundreds of pounds of wild muscle that had to contend with bear and cougar and other well-equipped rams wanting to push in on his game.

Frank tried to juke left, but the ram nailed him right at the waist. It was like being hit by a truck. The blow sent Frank reeling backwards, arms flailing.

He tried to slow down, but the slope was too steep, and he continued in his wild backpedal, unable to get his feet underneath him. He stumbled back out of the alcove, took a step, completely unable to regain his balance, and then he stepped backwards off the little animal trail entirely. The slope dropped out from underneath him, and suddenly all Frank saw were the pines at the top of the bluff and the blue sky receding from him.

And all he could think was that it was a hundred feet down, with a lot of big rocks along the way, and a lot more waiting at the bottom. He would land on his head and crack his skull. Or crack his spine across a fat stone. Or snap his neck. Or break his face. There really wasn't an option that was going to be good.

He thought he shouted, but wasn't sure. Then he struck the slope with his hip, then shoulder, head pointing down. His legs flew pell-mell over him. The world spun. He tumbled, lost his boots, flew again, hit a little pine, and figured he would now drop the yawning distance to the bottom, but instead of flying to a hard landing, he slammed into the trunk of a much bigger pine that stopped him dead.

He oofed, then began to roll, and realized this pine was the end of the line, and he flailed out and caught the trunk and held on while his senses came back to him.

Up on the trail, the ram came over and peered down at him like maybe he ought to knock Frank about a bit more while he was down. That's what the street fighter would have done, but the ram apparently wasn't interested in stomping. Instead, he chuffed, then turned and trotted down the trail, head held high. His honeys and young'uns exited the alcove right behind him in an orderly manner, a nice big family procession in single file.

If Frank hadn't been backing away, that polygamist probably would have dislocated his hip. As it was, Frank was going to have a massive bruise.

Frank looked down and realized one more bounce would have taken him on a very short and nasty flight.

A moment later, the sheriff peered over the edge of the trail above. "Holy cow," she said.

"Holy goat," Frank groaned.

"Technically sheep," she said.

"Whatever."

"Are you okay?"

Frank did a limb check. "I think so."

Just then voices rose at the mouth of the canyon. Frank turned and saw the bighorns had stopped their parade and were watching something in that direction.

"Get on up here," she hissed and held out a hand.

The slope was steep, but it wasn't a cliff. And Frank's legs worked just fine. He dug in with his stocking feet and hands and scrambled up on all fours.

The sheep were now filing down another trail that hooked up with this one, clearly wanting to steer clear of the second set of humans moving up the canyon.

Frank reached the top of the slope and crawled onto the narrow animal trail. The sheriff helped steady him as he stood.

"You first," she said and held her arm out at the chute. "Quickly."

"Are there any more sheep up there?"

"Nope, you pretty much cleared them out."

Frank took the lead, and they both hurried back up between the gap into the now empty alcove.

The alcove was shaped like a stretched out and ragged tear drop, big enough to accommodate two large SUVs side by side. The seamed and fracturing orange rock walls rose up around them fifteen or twenty feet to the sky. In the back at one spot, the rock curved inward to a smaller alcove. Running down the face of the rock into that smaller space was a big black smear flecked with green. And in that smear was a trickle of water that seeped more than ran over the face of the rock. It followed the curve, creeping down to a small rocky puddle in the back. One that didn't have enough volume to do more than run another two yards before seeping back into the ground.

Frank surveyed the rock walls around them. They were too high with way too few hand and toe holds. He saw the root of a tree way up, but it was too far away to reach. Maybe if he had gear, they could make it out. But he and the sheriff were going nowhere.

Frank kept his voice low. "A tight little spot for that bighorn clan. At least we won't die of thirst."

"Dying is not on the agenda."

In addition to his hip, Frank felt a twinge in his side, and winced. It appeared his polygamous friend had caused more damage than he thought. He gingerly probed his ribs.

"Broken?" she asked.

"Bruised."

"I've never seen that before. That ram cleaned your clock."

"I'm sure the Mountain Goat Gazette will have a big write up on the front page. Hero Knocks Human On His Can. He's going to be very popular. Might even get a couple more wives out of it."

The sheriff looked him over. "Where are your boots?"

"I'm thinking they're at the bottom of the little fork. Most likely lying in plain sight."

Then a man called out. "Frank! Sheriff Hood!"

Frank and the sheriff froze. The man sounded all friendly, concerned, like someone in a rescue party, but a rescue party would be calling with Southern Utah accents, not one tinged with German.

"Sheriff," another man called. "We've taken care of Bill. We're here to help."

They were there, hoping Frank and the sheriff were idiots and would pop out to check to see if they really were friendlies.

Frank looked around, wondering how best to make a defense in this little mountain castle with its open front door.

He had his rabbit-killing slingshot. The sheriff had her hammer-throwing arm. It would be a battle of sticks and stones until the bullets started flying, and then he didn't think it would be much of a battle after that.

The sheriff blew out a long breath of stress and looked at Frank.

He whispered, "Dying is not on the agenda."

"Not today," she agreed, then looked about her and selected a few stones appropriate for caveman tactics.

The first man called again. "Frank, Sheriff Hood, come on out. You're safe."

With the way the sound carried up the slopes and rock, Frank couldn't tell if they were on the animal trail or down at the bottom. He pulled out his slingshot and thought about using one of his ball bearings, but there were some smooth almond-shaped stones on the ground about him. They would provide greater mass, and while a rock going a hundred or a hundred and fifty miles per hour wasn't a bullet, it was still traveling mighty fast.

He was thinking their best bet would be to step back into the alcove, inviting the men to enter the front door of their open-air fortress, then nail them in that narrow space.

"Frank," the first guy called, his voice echoing in the canyon. "Come on."

"Sheriff Hood," his companion called.

But the direction of their voice was off. Like they'd walked passed Frank's and the sheriff's position.

"Bill is in custody," one of the men said.

They were definitely past Frank's and the sheriff's position. They were still heading up the main canyon, which meant they weren't on the animal trail, and they hadn't seen his boots. They were just fishing for some response.

Frank smiled. So far, the little trip up the hill had worked.

Then the second man spoke to the first. It was in a normal tone, but the rock and slope carried the sound. And what he said wasn't in English. And it wasn't in German, Danish, or Spanish. Frank actually didn't believe his ears.

The sheriff cocked her head and mouthed, "What is that?"

He held his hand up for silence and turned his head to hear better.

The two exchanged a couple more comments, the rock walls carrying the sound up to them, and he clearly heard the one man say, "Lays ladayna waqt. Ayn Marko?" Which Frank thought meant, "We haven't got time. Where's Marko?"

And while he wasn't sure just how good his translation was, he was positive which language had been spoken. "That's Arabic," he whispered.

"Arabic?" she said, trying to process the new info. "Are you sure?"

Frank had heard it back in his Special Forces glory days on the other side of the world in a mountainous desert with steep slopes, sheep, and lots of goats. Most of the folks there spoke Pashto or Dari. But there were enough who spoke this as well. And everyone he'd met in Iraq had spoken it.

One of the men spoke again and said, "Aetani nurana." And Frank knew that one. He'd heard it a hundred times when training the locals. Give me a light, as in lighting a cigarette.

There was no doubt what it was they were speaking, and suddenly all the facts of this situation began reshuffling in his mind.

This cigarette thing wasn't German mafia. And it wasn't some racket run by regular criminals looking for an easy buck.

No, the most likely scenario was that this was a financing operation. And what brought together Bill, an American, the Germans, who were probably Arab-Germans, and these two was a deep-seated belief they all shared about the path of righteousness.

"We need to get out," she said. "And then bring some big guns back with us."

He nodded, but Frank wasn't thinking about big FBI or Homeland guns. He was thinking of that map on the wall of the room at the back of the garage.

27
Mud

FRANK DESPERATELY WANTED to get eyes on the two men. He started to step forward, then heard the whine of a very large mosquito. It appeared that Marko's drones had arrived.

There was only one place here to hide. Frank and the sheriff moved to the smaller alcove at the back. Frank backed up into the deepest part and flattened himself against the wall. She followed, squatted to see if the sky was visible because if it was visible from her knees, then their knees and feet would be visible to something up there.

"Scoot back," she said.

"I'm against the wall," he said. "This is all we're going to get."

She made a sigh of resignation and pressed back into him, trying to get as far away from the edge as possible. The back of her ballistic vest was hard against Frank's lower chest. But the warm skin of her arm was smooth where it touched his. He got a whiff of something fruity. He sniffed. It was her hair. It smelled like peaches. It smelled fabulous.

And that could be a problem. The last thing they needed was for someone following them to get a whiff of that. Peach shampoo was pretty much a dead giveaway. He supposed he hadn't smelled it before because he'd been recovering from his electrical Frankenstein treatment, or maybe he'd been too focused on not dying.

He said, "Where's the closest phone?"

She said, "If we get on the road to Glendale, before too long we'll run into someone. That's the closest."

The road to Glendale was the one that ran in front of the ranch. "They'll be watching the road. I would be."

"Then we go overland to Alton. It's six or eight miles. With this mountain and maybe two more in between us, maybe it's ten."

"Once we put some distance between us and them, we can jog."

"Can you keep up?" she asked.

"I can run between five to six miles per hour for as long as it takes. If we're lucky, we'll be there in time for a late lunch."

"Alton it is then."

He got another whiff of the peaches, looked down and noticed a small curl of hair sticking to the moisture on her neck. He hadn't noticed it before, but she had a fine neck, and he decided her lovely scent was problematic for more than one reason.

He said, "Have they got any burger joints there?"

"Nope. But you can get chicken strips and deep fried potato logs at the gas station."

"Well, that isn't going to work," Frank said. "I'm not going to waste your treat on potato logs."

She shook her head. "A terrorist money cell. It's unbelievable."

Clearly she wasn't thinking about lunch or being distracted by the manly smell of the big, strong guy at her back. He said, "Do you think it's just financing? They could have easily bugged out last night. And what does a money cell want with drones?"

"Security," she said.

"Yeah, but these aren't the types of drones you send up for five or eight hours at a time. These are little microwave and lawn-mower-sized units. If they wanted security, wouldn't they want it round the clock?"

"Maybe," she said.

"Maybe," he agreed, but it just didn't fit.

The sound of the drone grew.

He said, "Our eye in the sky might have a microphone in addition to a camera."

She nodded, and they both fell silent.

The whine of the drone continued to increase in volume. Then the sound grew loud. Really loud. A moment later, a small shadow flitted over the ground inside the alcove, then was gone. Then the whine began to recede.

The sheriff blew out a little sigh of relief. But they waited to speak until it sounded like the thing had flown around a bend.

Frank said, "I saw a map in that back room. Twelve cities were circled—San Diego, Huntington Beach, Alameda, Seattle, Provo, Oklahoma City, Houston, St. Louis, Chicago, Nashville, Philly, Boston. What do they have in common?"

She thought for a moment. "Nothing."

"So why circle them?"

"Maybe the map was from before. Maybe renters were circling where they came from."

"It was a new map. This year's date was printed on it. And there haven't been renters in there for eighteen months. You confirmed that."

"I did."

"So did these guys put it up there, or someone else?"

She said, "You know what those cities have in common?"

"What?"

"They're not what you think of when you think of terrorist targets. Maybe Chicago is. But they're not New York. They're not D.C."

"No, but San Diego has military bases. The SEALs train there. Seattle and Chicago have big naval bases close by too. Nashville's got Fort Campbell with the 101st Airborne in the area. Philly's got Fort Dix."

She said, "What's in Alameda, California?"

Frank thought. "Lawrence Livermore Labs is just down the road. Lots of classified military research is done there." He began to think they were seeing a pattern.

"What about Huntington Beach?"

He thought, racked his brain. "Disneyland," he finally said. "That's what's close. And what's in Provo, Utah except a bunch of happy Mormons? Nothing really by Houston either." And what was in Boston? "Maybe they aren't targets," he said.

She said, "Homeland can figure that out. Our goal is to get out to a phone. Maybe now's the time to go. Get behind them and run like hell the other way."

"Alton's in the direction the drone and our two friends headed, right?"

"Yeah."

Frank thought about it. They could make a run back down to the mouth of this narrow canyon, hope nobody was there, and then what? He was not going to go back down to the ranch. That was too risky. They could hike up the streambed, but that's exactly where he suspected other groups were looking because the vegetation along its banks provided the most cover.

"I don't know," he said, "When the wasps are buzzing, it's best to simply lie low."

"They're terrorists," she said.

"Which only means they'll shoot us faster. Better for us to take three days to get out of here than rush it and get shot. Because if we get shot, there won't be any phone call at all."

"We can't just sit here."

They could. Unless the wild polygamist returned and went all sheep crazy, but Frank didn't think that was going to happen.

He said, "Let's give it a couple of hours. Give them some time to start thinking they lost us."

She said, "And in the meantime a bunch of terrorists fade into the population."

"Maybe it isn't terrorists. Maybe it's a politically correct crime gang of diverse nationalities from New York City. Maybe they were sick of the big urban life. Maybe they're out West trying to recruit more diversity into their ranks."

"Mormons and cowboys?"

"You've got to admit that's pretty diverse."

She rolled her eyes.

"Look," he said, "I don't know what to believe just yet. But I do know we're missing something."

She said, "I'm going to go nuts sitting up here all day."

He said, "The good news is we've got some water. I say we fill up while we can."

She nodded. "That's actually a good idea."

So they cupped handfuls from the little pool. It was cold, pure, and delicious with just a hint of mineral. Water was a scarce resource in these parts, and when they started to move, they might not find another source until they got to Alton, and it wouldn't do to be fainting along the way from heat exhaustion. They drank until neither could drink anymore.

She said, "We ought to camo up."

"You got paint in those pockets?" he asked.

She pointed at the pool. "We've got Mother Nature's makeup right there."

"Mud," Frank said and nodded. "Great for toning down skin shine and contrasting colors." And the truth was her vest was just a little too black, her socks and arms a little too white. But they needed to disguise more than color because it wasn't like his head blended in.

In good camo fashion, she removed her simple ring and two stud earrings and put them in her pocket to prevent any shine.

Meanwhile, Frank took off his dark button up shirt he'd gotten at the store with the acne kid, then his white undershirt.

She looked at his bare chest and abs and said, "For some reason I don't think that's going to blend in."

"The idea is to stun them with my manliness."

"That work for you in the Army?" she asked. Then she pointed at a scar on one side of his ribs. "That one looks fairly new. Looks like the pucker from a bullet."

He nodded. "The witch of Lullaby Lane gave me that one. A spiteful shot from a twenty-two revolver from about three yards away. Broke a rib."

"What happened?"

"It's a long story," he said and handed her his tactical knife. Then he grabbed the undershirt and pulled the bottom of one side tight. "I want you to cut it up to the armpit," he said.

"What are we doing?"

"Trust me."

"Trusting you got me tied up in a barn."

"Trusting me got you untied."

She shrugged, then opened the knife.

"Just slice it right up to the arm pit."

She did. Then they did the other side, then across the shoulders.

They ended up with two rather large, squarish pieces of fabric, with little flaps of half sleeves.

He said, "Do you know where the word khaki comes from?"

"Men's casual pants?"

"Hindi. The root of the word means something like dust or earth. Some British Lieutenant was over in Pakistan with his troops in the mid-1800s and realized his soldiers would do better blending with the local color than standing out in bright uniform. So he got some white cloth and took it down to the river to be soaked and rubbed with mud. Mud dye is basically what it was. Turned them the color of dust. Dust-colored uniforms for a land of dust."

She looked over at the little slick of water and mud and back at the pieces of cloth. "That's a good story; however, I don't think you've got enough fabric to make uniforms for anyone but Hobbits."

He said, "I'm going to make us some masks. Break up the patterns of our heads."

"Oh," she said and nodded appreciatively.

Frank had learned early on in his military career that one of the strongest patterns used to identify humans was the face and head. Humans were keyed to subconsciously scan for them all the time. Making theirs look like something else would help them blend in.

"Let's make some khaki," he said and walked over to the little puddle, knelt down, and pushed the tannish orangish mud back to make a reservoir almost a yard across. He waited for the water to pool a bit, then plunged the pieces of his undershirt in to let them soak. When they were good and saturated, he began to knead them with the tan-orange mud, working it in.

She took one from him and began to work it separately. They quickly plunged and scrubbed in the loose mud until the large blocks of cloth were nothing at all anyone would want to put in their mama's wash.

He said, "Your white undershirt and black vest make a very distinct contrast. We need to change that."

She said, "Turn around."

He turned and observed one of the craggy rock walls and the blue sky beyond.

Her vest was secured with velcro straps. He heard the ripping of one strap. Then another. And then the sound of her removing the vest. And then the sound of her removing her undershirt.

His lizard brain kicked in and began to imagine a whole set of sleek, strong, and fabulous curves with nothing but a bra to cover them.

He sighed, half because they really didn't have time for his man brain to get all excited and half because, holy cow, all that sleekness, which surely was glorious, was right there behind him.

"Chop chop," he said, aware of her every movement.

The tee-shirt suddenly flew onto his shoulder, and she said, "Plunge and scrub, camo master."

He sighed again, then realized he couldn't fully turn back to their little mud reservoir without ruining her privacy, so he started plunging one-handed.

"Wickaway fabric," he said. "You like it?"

"It's the best I've found so far."

"What I wouldn't have given for a bit of this back in Afghanistan carrying around seventy pounds of gear in the heat of summer."

Behind him, he heard her slip into her vest, then secure one strap, and finally the other.

She said, "Okay."

He said, "You sure? I don't want to get a ticket or anything."

"I think I can write you up for five things already. I'm giving you a break on this one."

He turned and glanced over at her. The smooth curves at the base of her throat and the strong curves of her naked arms and shoulders were stunning in her blocky vest. His blood thumped, a surge of attraction washed over him, but he told himself there were men trying to kill him, and he ought to pay attention to that.

Frank turned to the task of transforming her undershirt into khaki and said, "That's not your everyday armor. You've got rifle plate in there."

She said, "In the city it's mostly handguns, and level two armor covers that. But in the country, very often it's not *if* there are going to be rifles, it's how many. And given what I saw the first time we visited Bill, I thought rifle armor was prudent."

"Are those trauma pads behind the plate?"

She took his long-sleeve shirt and plunged it in the mud soup. "Yes. But nothing like the titanium I heard Special Forces used as a backstop in Afghanistan. Is that true?"

"Sometimes you need to take more than one hit. And the titanium backstops did the job."

He pressed more mud into her undershirt, then glanced over at her again, working next to him, and noticed an old scar high up on one of her arms. It was long and slashed almost halfway around.

He said, "Where did you get that?"

She glanced down at the scar. "That one? Barbed wire. I was a teen, riding an ATV at dusk, and didn't see the barbed-wire fence."

"Ouch."

"It could have been my neck. I thank God regularly for my little arm scar."

He said, "You sound like you've got others."

"Wouldn't you like to know," she said and rubbed more mud into his button-up shirt. "This is fairly dark fabric. You think this is going to blend?"

"It will dry and be lighter than it would have been. And I'll get you to smear the back. It will do better in shady spots." Then he held his hand out for the shirt.

She gave it to him and said, "I assume the masks are for when we're stationary or moving slow."

"When we're trying to observe without being seen, we'll wear our muddy head coverings. The rest of the time they will be down as neck gaiters."

"Then I'm going to do my face and hair."

"Make it a complete mud mask facial."

She scooped up some tan-orange mud on her fingers and said, "Is that what you guys do in the Army, give each other facials?"

"Oh, it's a complete beauty salon."

She smeared the mud over her cheek and across her brow and went for more.

She said, "The dirt in those shirts is going to chafe like sandpaper."

"Like a loofah. Like artesian spring exfoliation," he said.

She said, "You're starting to worry me."

He grinned and said, "Your braid is too regular a pattern. You probably want to undo it."

"Right," she said, then undid it and used her elastics to bind her hair toward the bottom. Then she scooped up another large glop of tan-orange mud and smeared it over her hair. She looked over at him, her fingers working the glop in like it was shampoo.

Frank got his own glop of mud and spread it over his face, head, and neck, making sure to get behind his ears so those spots didn't shine like two bright eyes. Then he put on his shirt. It was cold and heavy with mud and water and sagged with the weight.

He handed her the transformed tee shirt she'd taken off earlier. It was not the latest high-tech camo pattern, but it was a heck of a lot better than bleach white.

She took the filthy tan-orange wad of shirt from him. "There goes thirty bucks," she said and pulled the shirt over her head and ballistic vest. It was tight, but it covered the vest and the rest of her torso just fine.

"That's going to dry up nicely," he said and buttoned up his shirt. Their camo wasn't going to make them invisible, but it would help some. And that little bit just might be the thing that saved their lives.

She scooped up more mud and began to smear it over her arms. Frank also scooped up handfuls and began to smear it in thick slashes across the front of his shirt.

She said, keeping her voice low, "What is it with Islam?"

He asked, "You religious?"

"Yeah, I grew up Lutheran," she said and began to work the mud across her pants.

Frank took a clump of mud and smeared it into a sleeve. "Okay. Let me ask you: do you think if you submit to the Lord's will, you'll be blessed?"

"I guess that's the basic premise."

"It's the same with Muslims. In fact, the name Muslim means submission. Sincere submission. Their whole religion is about submitting to God. Doing what he wants. Doing the right thing."

She picked up more mud. "God could be a she, you know."

"Some people think God's an it, that god isn't involved with gender or breeding at all."

"A eunuch? I thought we were made in his image, male and female, which makes you wonder."

"I'm not even going to touch that," he said and moved down the sleeve of his shirt with more mud. "The point is that Muslims have the same basic premise we all do. So they try to find God's will by looking at the revelations they believe were given to Muhammad, which is the Koran, plus the collections of ancient reports claiming to quote what Muhammad said and did in various situations."

"I don't think Muhammad said to kill Americans."

"But did he say to kill folks that are like Americans? It's up for interpretation. Islam isn't like the Catholic Church with a pope who can make declarations for everyone. Muslims believe Muhammad was the last prophet, and so there's nobody to make the final decision. They're more like the Protestants with every believer interpreting the scriptures a bit differently, but often leaning heavily on the opinions of those who have degrees in religion. Muslim theologians from the various schools of thought research and write theo-legal opinions, which are called fatwas, about God's will on everything from underwear to car insurance."

"No, they don't."

"They do."

"Underwear?"

"Hey, the Bible proscribes certain hairdos."

"Does God really care about underwear?"

"Look, nobody has to follow any of these fatwas. They're just opinions from people in various schools of thought, but if you're going to claim to be doing God's will, it's nice to have a good fatwa with a lot of consensus among the authorities supporting it. Still, most Muslim authorities aren't writing American-killing opinions."

Frank had worked with one of those in Afghanistan, helping in his pear orchard when his team wasn't on patrol. He'd been a smart man with kids and a wife who loved him.

He said, "But some of them do. This well-regarded, piece of work named Abdullah Azzam issued one of the most famous fatwas. He was buddies with Osama Bin Laden and officially opined that it was the individual duty of every Muslim to kill Americans whenever and wherever possible. Another Bin Laden buddy ruled that it was legally okay to kill up to ten million Americans. Women, children, men—it didn't matter. Beyond that number, however, there was only iffy legal support."

"That was his legal opinion?"

"In their eyes, the church is the state and the state is the church. Sharia is the law for everything. End of story."

"So it's the law of the land to kill ten million Americans?"

"According to those legal opinions."

"What did any little kids or civilians ever do to them?"

Frank took one of the mudded squares of cloth that used to be his tee-shirt and began to cut a line down at the bottom. Keeping his voice low, he said, "You have to identify who the them is. The core of Islam stretches from Indonesia, up through Burma and India, across the Stans to the Middle East, then west to Egypt, North Africa, and Morocco. There are somewhere around 1.5 billion Muslims in the fifty or so Muslim-majority countries that make up that huge swath of the earth.

"But where are most of the terrorists coming from? It's not Indonesia. That country has the fourth largest population in the world and is ninety percent Muslim. Almost a quarter billion Muslims, but you don't see them pulling ISIS and al-Qaeda crap. It's not the Muslims in Malaysia, Bangladesh, or India, which hold almost another quarter billion of the faith. It's not Morocco on the other end with its thirty million Muslims, or even Turkey with its seventy-five, although Turkey is changing."

"It's the Middle East."

"The main seedbed for the extremism is in Egypt and Saudi Arabia because they are the main sources of Islamism."

"That's not the same thing as Islam?"

"There are many different kinds of Islam. Islamists are those who believe democracy is sinful and want to set up an Islamic theocracy that uses their theo-legal opinions as the law of the land. For everything."

"Including underwear."

"They want to get back to the pure religion of the salafs, the first Muslims. Egypt's contribution is the Muslim Brotherhood, a huge international organization hell-bent on setting up a theocracy, and not just in Muslim lands. Saudi Arabia's contribution, along with its neighbors Kuwait and Qatar, is big money and Wahabbism, their version of Islamism."

She said, "The 9/11 attackers were overwhelmingly Egyptian and Saudi."

"That wasn't on accident. The Muslim Brotherhood and Saudi Wahabbists have been spreading their version of Islam for years. Saudi Arabia has promoted its ultra conservative version of Islam with hundreds of millions of dollars. Some peg it close to ninety percent of the expenses of the Muslim faith in the world for schools, scholarships, textbooks, mosques, teachers—you name it. Heck, they've set up Wahabbist schools and mosques in California."

"I'm betting it's not pray and surf," she said.

"Alas," he said and cut another line in his head wrap next to the first, making a flapping strip. He began to cut another strip on the opposite side. "Instead of sponsoring up-and-coming surfers, they keep sponsoring up-and-coming monsters. Saudi Arabia sponsored the Taliban, which is based on another strain of Islamism. They sponsored Al Qaeda, more Islamists. They sponsored ISIS. Sometimes it's official government aid. But there are plenty of individuals with lots of money over there who are quite happy to make private donations."

"But I thought Saudi Arabia was fighting against ISIS," she said and began to smudge up the whites of her socks. "I don't get it."

"Sunni Islamists aren't just against the West. They also want to get rid of what they see as corruptions to the true Islam that Muhammad lived. And to the radical Sunni, one of the biggest corruptions in all of Islam is the Shia Muslim."

"Iran?"

"And its satellites. They're heretic central. But it's not just that they're apostates, which their theocratic law says you can kill. The problem is that the Iranian Ayatollahs are Islamists too and want to establish a Shia caliphate to rule the Islamic world. If you're a hard core Sunni Islamist, you've got to stop that. So they supported ISIS to fight the Shia government in Syria, which has close ties to Shia Iran. They supported Saddam Hussein to keep the Shias in his country and in Shia Iran at bay. They supported the Taliban to keep Shia Iran out of Afghanistan. It's Saudi Arabia versus Iran. Like the United States versus the old Soviet Union."

"And then all of their monsters turned."

"Exactly," he said and began to cut more strips in his hood mask.

She finished her socks. "But that's all Muslim stuff."

"We're corrupting them from the outside. We're the secular Satan, the tempters. Not only tempting them into sins like booze and porn, but tempting them to set up democracies, where you submit to men and the laws of men, instead of the caliphate, where you submit to God and his laws."

"Because that always works so well."

Frank finished cutting the strips on the first cloth, and began cutting more on the second. "Back in the days of the pure religion, Islam spread from a little persecuted group in an Arabian town to controlling an empire that stretched from the western part of India all the way to Spain. In those days, the Roman Empire and Persian Empire were the big powers in the area. And this band of Arabs totally defeated the Persian Empire, something Rome had been unable to do for centuries, and then they took out most of the Roman Empire. A bunch of nobodies from the desert. And they did it in seventy or so years. The blink of an eye. It worked back in the glory days. You can see their logic."

"It's bad logic. 700 AD was a long time ago. And they're now all struggling. If everyone else is prospering, you'd think they'd look around and figure out that maybe the rest of the world was onto something."

He said, "Some did. By the early 1900s, Europe was controlling most of the Islamic states as parts of their empires. The fact that they had fallen behind the West was staring Muslims in the face, and many of them concluded they'd lost their supremacy because they'd been too bound in a tradition that prevented them from better industry and technology. Others thought it was the political setup that needed to change. Others thought it was that they'd strayed from the original religion. But the modernizing reformers had the momentum and the volume."

The sheriff grabbed one of her boots and began to mud it.

Frank finished cutting the last strip on the second head covering and said, "They tried to change things, but most of them failed and ended up with tyrants, a series of folks like Saddam Hussein. Then in the 1950s and 1960s, the voices of those who thought the issue was the fact that they'd strayed from the pure, original religion, grew in volume. Israel had humiliated the armies of all the Muslim nations around it, which the various strains of Islamism saw as one more clear sign that Allah had withdrawn his help because the nations of Islam were trying to ape the great Satan in the West. And guess where those voices were the loudest?"

"Saudi Arabia and Egypt."

"And they cross-pollinated. Saudi Arabia was growing as a kingdom. They needed teachers. So they brought thousands of the Muslim Brotherhood in to fill the gap. That was also the time when Saudi Arabia's oil money started to pour in. Right on schedule to funnel those hundreds of millions of oil dollars into spreading the message of the pure religion far and wide."

"The pure religion that says we're their problem."

Frank stood and began to mud up the back of his legs. "It's not very different from what some preachers say in America when a crisis hits. Ebola, Hurricane Katrina in New Orleans, AIDS—each time one of those things raises its head, we've got American preachers standing up and claiming the calamity was sent because we've strayed from the pure religion."

"You think the problem is religion?"

"I love religion. It's what saved me in prison. But I had to fight these folks in Afghanistan. And one of the first things you want to do when trying to defeat an enemy is figure out what makes them tick. What I found is that it wasn't too far off from what makes some of us tick."

"Maybe, but we aren't breeding terrorists like they are."

"I think the only reason we don't is because of our political and religious freedom. Take that away, and you start to prepare the ground for groups like ISIS to grow. You get a religious police that gets rather zealous in commanding what is good and forbidding what is wrong. We all have this tendency. This temptation. There's something in us. We get so righteous for our own causes. It's so easy to start to feel justified in stamping out other beliefs by force."

"That's the heart of this thing," she said. "That's what the founders of this nation saw. We've never been perfect, but, praise the Lord, at least they got that right."

Frank nodded. "Islamism is as anti-American as it gets. To them, democracy is anti-God. I've heard a number refer to democracy as a train that you ride to a destination and then get off. You ride it to get into power. And once you have that power, you get off and set up a theocracy. Can you imagine what would not have been possible if we'd been set up as a government that enforced one set of beliefs—socialism, communism, atheism, the wearing of kilts."

She said, "Or what foods you eat or don't. Or who you subsidize and who you don't. Or what you can teach in schools and can't."

He stopped spreading mud. "Am I hanging out with a Libertarian?"

"I'm not anti-government. I'm anti-governmentism. I'm a cop. I believe we need a government for many things. But I don't think it's just the religious and political freedoms we were set up with that help keep the terrorist weeds down."

Frank looked at her.

She said, "It's the fact that in dozens of ways we were set up to keep power from accumulating into one spot. When we let it accumulate, those political and religious and civil freedoms start to suddenly disappear. The founders saw firsthand the fruits of monolithic governments. We've seen them as well. Look at North Korea. Communist Russia. Communist China. We saw it with the Taliban. And yet we don't see. It's like we're blind. We've always got someone wanting the federal government to take more power. We're imbeciles, always forgetting what the whole revolution was all about."

"Give me liberty, or give me processed meats," Frank said.

She looked at him, obviously assessing the intelligence of that comment on the low end of the scale. "And that's why we are very happy women got the vote."

"Hey," he said.

"Which, by the way, was another separation of powers."

"A good one," he said.

"An overdue one," she said.

"You know what this conversation proves?" he asked.

"What?"

"You and I have lots of common ground. Who knows what may develop?"

"What we have in common is mud. And I believe I need someone to help me finish. You want to do my back?"

"Ooh," he said. "Just like at the beach, except I think you're wearing too many clothes."

She rolled her eyes and groaned, then turned around.

He slathered the orangish mud in slashes over her wet and muddy undershirt.

While he was working, she reached into one of the cargo pockets of her pants and pulled out the little rock sheriff that Lily had made and looked at it in her open hand.

Frank said, "And how much do those sell for?"

"The sheriff is not for sale. It's a one of a kind."

Frank looked at the figure's big googly eyes and slightly crooked smiling mouth. He thought of the time her little girl must have spent on it. "I bet she's proud of her mama."

"She's something," the sheriff said. Then she tightened her fist around the little rock.

Frank said, "You're going to be eating dinner with her tonight."

"That's the plan."

That was indeed the plan. And Frank realized that if nothing else happened, he was going to make sure this woman was going to get back to her girl.

He finished painting up her back and asked her to return the favor.

She worked from top to bottom. She had strong hands and took a matter of fact approach, but they were still a woman's hands, and by the time she finished, he was wishing he had a longer back.

He blew out a breath. It had been a long time since Blanca had left him. A very long time. He'd loved his time in Special Forces, but the time away from home took its toll on the team members. Many groups had ninety percent divorce rates. He'd thought his and Blanca's relationship had some kind of special protection from that, but he'd realized his mistake too late.

She said, "What are the strips you cut in those cloths for?"

He put the cloth over his head, a big fold with open sides, and grabbed two of the strips that were opposite each other. "You're going to use them to tie the sides closed."

"Smart," she said.

Frank positioned his cloth, marked where his eyes were, then took it off and cut horizontal slits in the cloth there. He put it back on.

"Can you see?"

"Good enough for government work," he said and handed her the knife to cut her own slits. While she was cutting, he went to the back of the area, to a small sagebrush growing there, and broke off a branch. He unlaced one of her boots and used the lace to tie the branch to one arm.

She handed him the knife back. "Fancy," she said and motioned at his vegetation.

"A little goes a long way," he said. "And now that I'm all dressed up, I think I'd like to get some eyes on the situation." Because it was entirely possible that their two pursuers had devised a ploy to make Frank and the sheriff think they'd gone farther up the canyon. It was possible they'd taken up excellent positions with their weapons and were simply waiting for their prey to show themselves.

28

Slot

FRANK SHOWED HER the hand and finger signals he'd use for "coast is clear," "hostiles," the number and direction of hostiles, "drone," and "hide." Then he turned and began to carefully and quietly make his way down to the mouth of the chute.

He crept until he was about five feet from the opening, then dropped to his hands and knees and pulled up his hood and secured it. Then he lay on his belly, and from there he used a slow mini push-up to advance: barely rising up on his hands and toes, then moving forward a few inches and lowering himself again. He crossed the five feet a few slow inches at a time until he saw a section of the canyon floor, then more, and then was able to see up and down the length of this part of the canyon with just the smallest movement of his head.

There was nobody there.

He looked again, more closely, more slowly. But it was clear, so he reached back with one hand and gave her the thumbs up. He decided that the pattern of a human lying prone would be too easy to spot from above. The sheriff would have to cover him with rocks or dirt, or he could use a little outcropping at the mouth of the chute. He could sit behind it and still see the canyon. The bottoms of his legs and feet would be in shadow. His head would look nothing like a head. And the sage on his outside arm would break the pattern there.

Frank decided on the outcropping of rock. He positioned himself, then quietly called back to the sheriff and said, "There's a spot up a little higher. I think you'll fit right into it."

"One odd pattern is enough," she said. "Let's not give them two opportunities to see us. I think it's best I stay hidden back here."

He nodded. She retreated to the back of the alcove, and Frank waited and watched, slightly shifting his position now and again because it was, after all, jagged rock he was sitting on.

Thirty minutes passed that way, the sun rising higher, the shadows in the canyon changing. Squirrels came out to gambol in the pines farther along the slope. Chipmunks ventured out from places on the ground, one just below his position. A buzzard flew overhead, its shadow streaking across the canyon floor and then up the other side. A few minutes after that, a pair of pale yellow butterflies flittered out toward the center of the canyon, circling round each other.

The pressure from the rock point in his butt started to hurt, so he moved again, then saw a flash of white, two bends up the canyon. The drone cruised across the open sky, then behind the curve of the mountain slope.

He gave the sheriff the hand signal, the slightest of movements, and she retreated into the smaller alcove.

A squirrel chittered up in the pines, its voice echoing in the canyon. A moment later, Frank heard the whine of the drone. And then it appeared around the bend. It was flying maybe fifty or sixty feet up, slowly following the dry little creek bed, scanning.

The part of the canyon where Frank and the sheriff were was a little offshoot, a little tributary to the main canyon. The drone came over to sniff, flying right above the dancing yellow butterflies, and began to scan the pines. Then it moved in Frank's direction.

He made sure his hands were hidden and froze.

The drone dropped in elevation, rotated, then flew what sounded like only a few yards above the chute. Frank wanted to see how far above him it was, but any movement would give him away, so he remained still.

The drone slowly moved across the chute, then continued on back to the main part of the canyon and picked up where it left off, examining the streambed.

A minute later, he heard a voice echo off the canyon's rock walls. He waited for what seemed a very long time, then the two who had gone up before came striding around the corner in a half jog. They were not scanning the trail or the slopes. They were simply covering ground, the one's rifle slung across his shoulder. They tramped past, trying to catch up to the drone, obviously having concluded that he and the sheriff had not come this way.

Frank signaled their number and direction and waited, watching them until they disappeared around the bend farther down.

The canyon fell quiet. The chipmunks began to move on the slope again. The butterflies landed on some brush clinging to a cleft in the rock.

Frank waited a few minutes, then stood up and stepped out of his crevice, the rocks pressing through his socks.

"We're clear," he whispered.

The sheriff stepped out, her face a vision of mud, and said, "Let's get to Alton. We have some scumbags to take down."

"Yes, ma'am," Frank said.

Of course those scumbags might always send a drone back up the canyon. But for the next little while that wouldn't make any sense. This was his and the sheriff's chance.

They exited the mountain sheep watering hole, then descended the narrow animal trail back down toward the canyon floor. When they got to the bottom, the sheriff sat down and began to put on her boots. He removed his vegetation and gave her the lace back, and then he ran up the little offshoot, found his boots lying hidden between some large rocks, and put them on. When he came back, she was ready to go.

He reminded her that they still needed to practice noise control because they didn't want the stone walls carrying their noise back to the mouth of the canyon or up to someone on top. That meant they wouldn't talk; they would snap if they needed to get each other's attention, then communicate using the signals they'd agreed on back up at the watering hole.

Frank set off at a brisk walk. The sheriff followed behind. The prints of the terrorists were easy to follow along the path. They led around the bend, across the creek bed, around another bend, over a straight stretch with wild flowers, then past a couple of tall cottonwoods, their green leaves fabulous against a sunlit backdrop of orange stone.

He stopped a few times at irregular intervals to step into the shadows to look, listen, and smell and thought he caught a whiff of cigarette smoke, but neither he nor the sheriff could catch it again. It was probably from the two who had come looking for them.

After crossing the dry creek bed once again, she snapped. He turned and looked at her.

"Should we start to jog?" she whispered.

"The minute we start," he whispered, "it will cut down on our ability to hear someone coming. Or notice someone or something up high. And our movement will draw the eye."

"At some point we've got to take the risk," she said.

"Another mile," he said, resisting the urge to start hoofing it as fast as they could.

She nodded, and they started up again, keeping the noise down and watching the slopes.

The canyon itself was lovely with rock and more rock—orange, pale, and gray—as well as sparse brush, trees, and wildflowers. The dry creek and dirt on the valley floor made it feel like some kind of Zen garden. It would be an awesome spot to commune with the power upstairs and eat some crackers. Too bad Frank couldn't enjoy it.

They continued on under the shade of a thin tree, passed by a squadron of large, dark blue dragonflies that were feasting on winged ants as they took flight. Frank had thought prison was bad, but he supposed it could be worse. He could be a male ant whose whole purpose in life was to mate once in one flight and die. He watched another ant launch only to be eaten by a dragonfly two seconds later.

Frank silently thanked the Lord he wasn't an ant and stepped over a fallen, whitened tree trunk. The trail led forward, then rounded a bend of rock. Frank followed the trail, keeping quiet. He caught a whiff of cigarette smoke again. It was stronger, and Frank slowed, wondering. Just before he rounded the bend, the rock gave way, giving a view up the trail.

Thirty yards farther on stood a man, one of the men who had gone to help Zeke with his goat problem the day before. He was reading a small book with one hand, smoking a cigarette with the other. His rifle was leaning against a boulder.

Frank froze, then flicked his hand for the sheriff to halt. He signaled one hostile. Then he slowly began to inch back. He took a step, toe to heel. Took another painstaking step, then began to slowly squat, sinking below the jut of rock between him and the man. Just before he disappeared completely, the man cocked his head like he'd heard something, and began to turn.

Frank sank below the lip of the rock and froze, listening.

He heard the guy take a step.

Frank waited, straining to hear him take the next one, but it never came. Instead, he heard the clacking of some grasshoppers farther up the canyon. The lack of noise could mean the man had seen them and knew how to practice noise control himself and had picked up his rifle. It could be he was making his way toward them in a slow heel-to-toe. Or getting in a better position.

What was this guy doing here? Frank thought back. Had three of them come up the canyon?

No, there had only been two men.

So had this guy circled around and come down?

Frank didn't think so. Why would he be just standing there? If he were on the hunt, he'd be patrolling, looking, not standing out in plain sight, taking a smoke break with a book.

The sheriff motioned at Frank, her hands out asking what he wanted to do.

He drew a quick aerial picture in the dust of the trail with a line for the trail and dots for each human.

He pointed back down the trail, motioned for her to go slow.

She shook her head and wrote "Go" in the dirt with an arrow pointing toward the guy.

Frank mimed a rifle.

The sheriff pointed at the cargo pocket in his pants. The one with the sling shot. She mimed shooting it.

Frank looked at her. He was not going to go up against a rifle with ball bearings and elastics.

She motioned at herself, drew a line indicating she'd rush the guy. She pointed at Frank and mimed him using his slingshot. She pointed at herself and made a motion like tackling, then slowly hit her palm with her fist.

She was proposing that Frank distract the guy with his mighty rabbit murdering weapon while she rushed him and took him out.

Frank shook his head and pointed back down the trail.

She shook her head, pulled her tee-shirt down a bit at the neck to reveal her ballistic vest.

A ballistic vest was not magical armor. They both knew that. Furthermore, it did not cover her head or her legs or arms. And it didn't stop all bullets.

She put a finger to the back of her wrist and mouthed, "No time."

The guy was roughly eighty or ninety feet away. This was not the average twenty-one feet at which someone could charge another and get to them before they could fully draw their weapon.

But his rifle, when Frank saw him last, was a few feet away, leaning against a rock.

So Frank would hit the guy with a bearing. It would take the guy a second to react. Maybe two seconds to grab his rifle and swing it around. Another second to raise it and take aim. Four seconds. Olympic sprinters ran forty yards in 4.5 seconds, so an Olympic sprinter just might make it. But how fast could the sheriff run?

She would be running in a straight line at him, so all the guy had to do was turn and raise his weapon. An easy shot. Point blank.

She gave him a look and pointed. It was an order to turn around and get ready. She reminded Frank of a woman he'd met in Afghanistan, a villager who had an AK from when the Soviets had been there. She hated the Taliban and had a little squad of boys she directed who also carried guns. She'd been one hard lady, but she learned well and had those boys practicing good squad fire. All with the point of her finger.

Frank thought about this plan. It was going to be close. And if she was hit, if she was only wounded, it would still make Alton very difficult because he wasn't going to leave her behind.

She pointed to her wrist, indicating they were losing time.

If the guy already had his rifle, then they were going to lose more than time. They needed to know where he was.

Frank nodded an okay, then held his hand up for her to wait, and listened.

A moment later, the guy farted, which could be a ploy, but probably meant the guy didn't know they were there.

Frank motioned the sheriff to wait, and then he prostrated himself, and crept forward in his half-pushup crawl, until he slowly moved one eye around the base of the bend in the rock.

The guy was now leaning against the boulder next to his rifle. He was facing Frank's direction but still had his nose in his book.

Frank did a slow three-inch push up backwards a yard or so, then sat up and nodded at the sheriff. He motioned her forward.

When she came close, he bent over close to her ear, smelling dirt where once had been the lovely peach scent. "When I shoot," he barely whispered. "Not a second before."

She nodded, then shook her wrists to loosen them up.

Frank slowly pulled his sling shot out of his pocket. He used double flat bands made of Theraband black, which had a definite kick. He could send his ten millimeter steel bearings close to 150 to 200 miles per hour. Ten millimeters was about the size of Franklin's head on a dime. About the diameter of a forty caliber bullet. If he hit the guy in any exposed place, it would penetrate the skin. Not super deep, but deep enough. If he hit the guy's clothing, he doubted it would break the skin. But it would hurt like a mother. A heavier rock might hurt more.

He looked about, found a squarish looking gray rock a little smaller than a golf ball with rounded edges. It had been tumbled by the water, but not enough to make it completely river-stone smooth.

Frank needed to make a shot that would distract the guy. He could aim for the head and use his steel bearing. If it hit, he could crack a tooth, ruin an eye, ding the skull. Definitely distract him. But if he missed, the guy would only hear a whistle, turn, and immediately pick up his rifle. And he'd find the sheriff charging him.

Better to go for a bigger projectile, something that would make the guy pause. Better to aim at a bigger target, to nail him in the chest with solid rock traveling maybe 120 miles per hour. Then Frank could follow up with his ten millimeter shot, which would travel faster and straighter.

Frank loaded the rock into the pouch of the slingshot, put a bearing in his mouth, then nodded at the sheriff. It was go time. He scooted over to the edge of the jut of rock and slowly peeked up. The man was still reading. Frank hoped the guy was really enjoying it and began to slowly stand.

The guy looked up.

Frank stood, pulled the rock back to full extension, and released. The bands thwapped. The little gray rock shot forth.

The sheriff raced out from behind Frank like a sprinter coming out of the blocks.

The guy saw the rock, flung himself away, and the rock flew past.

Frank strode out into the open, away from the sheriff, to force the guy to choose one target over the other, to make him hesitate, and spit the bearing out into his hand.

The guy scrambled back for his rifle.

Frank loaded the bearing into the pouch.

The sheriff sprinted for the man, another mad woman hell-bent on revenge in the desert, which seem to be par for the course in these parts.

The guy grabbed his rifle.

Frank brought the slingshot up, pulled the ball bearing back.

The man swung his weapon around, raised it.

Frank released the doubled-up black bands. The steel ball flashed in the sun. It had to be streaking close to 200 miles per hour.

The guy made the smart choice and aimed at the sheriff, the closer threat. But the bearing nailed him in the chest first.

He flinched.

And the sheriff barreled into him. She wasn't kidding when she'd told Frank baseball wasn't her sport. This was football, a full-on body hit, and the two of them slammed to the ground.

The rifle fired. The bullet cracked somewhere over to Frank's right.

Frank charged to help her.

The sheriff and the man scrambled, but she scrambled faster and stuck her fingers in his eye.

The guy cried out, flinched, raising his arms to protect his face. But he'd left the rest of himself open. The crotch in particular.

The sheriff raised her arm, then dropped her full weight, swinging down with her ulna, the nasty hard part of the forearm opposite of the thumb, and struck his terror-loving manlies.

The guy jolted, groaned, let go of the rifle.

The sheriff lunged for it.

But the guy wasn't out. He yelled in rage and struck at her, a wild, back-handed hammer that connected with her face, knocking her to the side, and scrambled on his hands and knees for his weapon.

And then Frank arrived and kicked the man in the side of the head like he was punting a football in boots.

The man's head whiplashed to the side. His body twisted, and he sprawled to the ground, groaning. And then he went for something in his pocket.

Was it a pistol? A knife? A radio?

They couldn't have any more noise. It had to be over now. Frank stepped close to the guy and stomped down with all his force onto the back of the guy's neck.

The cervical vertebrae fractured or gave way, and the guy jerked, then collapsed, his eyes large, pain and dismay written all over his face.

Frank was pretty sure this guy wasn't going anywhere anytime soon, not unless someone dragged him there.

The sheriff stood, her one arm bleeding from the fall, and looked down at the man. "They teach you that in facial school?"

"Some of us," he said. "Where did you learn to tackle like that?"

"Rugby," she said, then put a finger in her mouth to feel a tooth.

"Loose?" Frank asked.

"Yeah."

"It will tighten back up, probably."

"It had better," she said and retrieved the rifle.

"Rugby?" he asked. "Really?"

"Ruck and roll," she said.

Frank looked at her. No doubt about it—she was one tough cookie. But her rugby moves wouldn't help at long range. He scanned the hill-sides, then the canyon in both directions. Nobody seemed to have heard their scuffle, but there was no doubt someone had heard that rifle shot.

She said, "What was he doing out here?"

Frank looked around. There were many cigarette butts lying on the ground. There was also a fire pit with lots of ash. He spied the remains of some half-burned food wrappers among the ash of the fire pit. On the ground by where the rifle had been was a pack.

Frank scanned the wider area, saw lots of footprints. He walked a few paces up the trail leading farther up the canyon and saw the end of the canyon in the distance, which was nothing more than the steep slopes narrowing to a steep dead end. He doubted there was a road up there. He doubted there was even an outlet. Frank came back.

He said, "There are no fresh prints on the trail. So he didn't come from that direction. Not today. And either he's been here a long time, or a number of people have been here in turns. Those other two must have walked to this point, asked him if he'd seen anyone. And when he said no, they assumed their job was done."

"But what was he doing here in the first place?" she asked.

"No idea," Frank said, "but maybe the pack has some answers."

The guy was still alive, but not looking so well. He clearly wasn't focused on them anymore, and so didn't protest their search of him and the pack.

They found more cigarettes, a lighter, a wallet with a Texas driver's license for one Ralf Kunz with this guy's picture on it, and seventy-eight dollars in cash. The book he'd been reading was a paperback about grow box gardening. The thing he'd been going for in his pocket was indeed a knife. Over by his pack was a two-way radio, which was dead, and a milk jug a quarter of the way full with a blue sports drink. Inside the pack was a thermal poncho, a box of ammo for the rifle, and three tins of Vienna sausages.

Frank held up the baby sausages and said, "He's got seventy-eight dollars in his pocket, and he goes and buys these? Not a protein bar, not a bag of jerky or trail mix, but a bunch of baby hotdogs in gelatin?"

"I used to love those when I was a kid," she said.

"Dogs in mucus," Frank said.

"We'd eat them with Cheese Whiz."

Frank groaned, then looked around for any other clues. "All this tells us is that he has bad taste in snack foods."

The sheriff looked around, then stopped. "I think I've found something," she said. It hadn't been in view before, but now Frank saw a small dry streambed that led to a narrow little ravine that quickly turned into a slot maybe eight feet wide.

Frank and the sheriff walked over to get a better look. There were dozens of footprints heading in and out of the slot.

"A lot of traffic," she said.

"Maybe they're keeping something in there."

She shrugged. "A slot's not a good place for keeping things. You get a big rainstorm, and the water's going to blast right through there. Fill it right up."

Frank looked at all the prints leading in and out. "It's a lot of traffic."

She said, "Well, there's only one way to find out what they've got in there. Lend me your flashlight. I'll take point."

"I can do it."

"Just give me the flashlight," she said.

"You want to go first because you have the vest."

"I want to go first because who can see around your bulk?"

He sighed, fetched the flashlight out of his pocket and held it out to her.

She took it. There were all sorts of ways to attach small flash lights to barrel hand guards and rails, but this rifle didn't have one. So she simply held the light and the barrel guard in her left hand and brought the barrel up.

"You think this guy's buddy's in there?"

"Who knows?" she asked. "Better safe than sorry." And she walked up the little dry streambed toward the narrow ravine. Frank gave her a few strides, then followed.

They entered the ravine, which narrowed. Then narrowed some more. Ahead was the slot, a shadow cut in the rock. The sheriff turned on the 500 lumens and shone them into the slot, then proceeded forward and entered the narrow path. Forty feet above was a thin ribbon of blue sky. Down in the slot, it was like twilight. The slot quickly narrowed until it was just over two feet wide in some places, which forced Frank to turn sideways. They traveled a few dozen yards in, following a bend one way, then the other. The shadows grew deeper. It was cool in the slot and smelled of water, so maybe the sheriff was right, and weren't storing anything in here.

He looked at the walls for signs of scuffing and said, "Maybe there's some ledge up there. Do you think they went up?"

"It's narrow enough. Maybe too narrow. But look at all the footprints," she said and pointed the flashlight down, shining it on the ground, which looked like a marathon had come through. "If they went up, they did it farther in."

"Maybe this is a tourist destination," he said.

"On Elkhorn land? Probably more their own little Robber's Roost," she said and brought the flashlight back up and moved forward again.

They followed the slot for another minute or so. It grew narrower, darker. Frank found himself having to turn sideways more often.

She shined the light at the ground and said, "I still see footprints."

Frank said, "How far do you think this goes?"

"If it's a full blown tributary, it could go a long way."

He said, "I say we come back later with some skinny teenager. I say we prioritize and get to Alton."

She looked down the rocky passageway. "I think you're right," she said.

But then something moved in the shadows a number of yards ahead. It wasn't clear what it was because the bright light on the rocks was casting deep, odd shadows. Frank looked at the object and thought it was a rock.

The sheriff swung the barrel of the rifle and flashlight at it.

And then someone's shoulder and arm moved in and out of the light. The skin shine and crook of the elbow were unmistakable.

"You see that?" he said.

She raised her voice a bit. "This is the sheriff. Come out with your hands on your head."

The person did not respond.

She said, "We've already dealt with your friend Kunz."

They waited.

And then the man spoke. He said something in Arabic.

The sheriff said, "Show yourself and put your hands on your head."

He said something in a weak voice.

The sheriff moved forward a step, the rifle ready.

"We've already captured your entire cell," Frank said. "The game's up."

"Help me," the man said weakly.

A classic ploy, Frank thought. In a tactically bad spot. If that guy had a gun, he had a straight shot at both of them. If he hit the sheriff's vest, it would most likely stop the bullet. But if it went through some other part, the bullet would hit Frank as well. And if the guy missed, the bullets could still ricochet off the walls. Bullets liked to hug walls. But maybe this guy had more firepower. If he had a grenade, Frank and the sheriff were mangled toast.

Frank tapped the sheriff on the shoulder and said, "I don't know if we want to get too close."

"The goats," the man slurred.

"Come out so we can see you," the sheriff said.

There was movement, then the man slowly stepped out into view. He was hunched, unsteady. He was holding a semiautomatic pistol in one hand down at his side.

Alarm raced up Frank's back.

"Drop your weapon!" the sheriff ordered, the rifle stock up against her cheek, the man in the weapon's sights.

The man dropped his gun, then raised his face so they could see it in the bright beam of the flashlight.

Frank stared, not processing what he saw.

"What the . . ." he trailed off.

"What? Who is it?"

There was no mistaking him. Frank said, "That right there is the man in the tarp."

29

Intel

"WALK THIS WAY," the sheriff ordered.

The man took a halting step forward.

"Back up," the sheriff said to Frank.

Frank moved back.

"Keep walking," she called to him. "Keep your hands up."

The man shambled forward, his arms dangling.

"He looks like some kind of zombie," Frank said.

"I'm clean," the man moaned. "I'm clean."

"He sounds like a zombie."

The sheriff took another step backward, her rifle still trained on the man in the tarp, and said, "Keep coming. Keep coming."

But the man didn't have it in him. He fell to his knees in the narrow space, banging his shoulder on the rock wall as he collapsed.

He muttered something in Arabic.

"Get up," she ordered.

He pushed up onto one elbow, but couldn't do more.

"Let me get past you," Frank said. "I'll help him out."

"It could be a ruse."

"I don't think so," Frank said.

But there wasn't enough room for Frank to press past her, so they backed out to a spot where the slot widened, then came back in with Frank in the lead.

The man hadn't moved.

Frank went to him, the sheriff staying back with the rifle, although to hit the man, the sheriff would have to shoot through Frank.

The man had a goatee, wore a tee-shirt, pants, and boots.

The tee-shirt was bloody on one side.

Frank said, “Let me help you.”

The man said, “Abdul?”

Frank crouched down. “Abdul is not here. I’m Frank.”

“Na’am,” the man said weakly. Yes.

The guy was definitely not faking. He was banged up and bloody and looked like he was well past his expiration date.

The gun lay a few paces behind the man on the sandy soil. Frank quickly stepped over him and picked it up. It was another Beretta nine millimeter. He stuffed it into his pants behind his back and said, “I’m going to pick you up under your arms. Can you turn a bit?”

The man said, “There is no time.”

Frank knelt next to him and slipped his arms like the two tines of a forklift under the guy’s armpits. “We’re going up,” he said. Then he gathered himself and lifted the guy up.

The man moaned in pain, but he didn’t fight. And he wasn’t too heavy either.

“Got him,” Frank called to the sheriff. “Coming your way.” Then he turned to the man. “We’ll just walk out together. I’ll call the steps.”

Frank called the steps, but the man was too weak to even manage that, and Frank ended up dragging him out of the slot and into the sun.

The guy looked like he’d been worked over. He had bruises all over his face. And where he wasn’t bruised, his skin had a gray cast to it. His eyes were glassy. His lips dry. And then there was the blood. He had a number of cuts and scrapes over his face and arms, but the real source was a stab wound high on his right pectoral.

Frank pulled the collar of his shirt aside to examine the wound, which was scabbed and angry. It looked like the blade had gone in at an angle and been turned by the ribs; however, there were lines of infection radiating outward from the cut.

Frank said, “I think it’s gone septic.”

The sheriff grabbed a roll of skin on the back of the man’s hand. She pulled it and let it go. It stayed where she pulled it for a moment, then slowly returned. “He’s also dehydrated,” she said.

Dehydrated and definitely in the first stages of shock. Frank walked back to the pile of stuff they'd recovered from the guard, who was lying in the exact same position they'd left him. Definitely a broken neck. Frank retrieved the jug of sports drink and brought it back to the man.

Frank knelt down next to him and put the jug to his lips. "Here," he said. "Drink this."

The guy pushed his dry lips out, and Frank tipped the jug, just a little at a time so the man could keep up.

When he'd had a number of swallows, Frank pulled the jug away.

"What's your name?" The sheriff said.

The man took a weak breath, looked at the sheriff, then at Frank, and got a confused and wary look in his eyes. Then he saw the guard lying on the ground.

"What happened to Ralf?"

He had to be talking about Ralf Kunz, the guard, because how many Ralfs would be running around this place? Frank said, "Ralf tried to shoot the sheriff. Then he tried to stab her."

"Sheriff?" he said and looked around.

"She's the sheriff," Frank said and pointed.

The man looked at her and her lack of uniform, and couldn't make it compute.

"Your people are in a lot of trouble," the sheriff said.

"You can tell Bill"—he paused to take a breath—"I don't know anything."

The dehydration and blood loss had made him stupid.

"We're not with Bill," Frank said.

"What is your name?" the sheriff asked.

"You know," the man said and looked over at Ralf again, still not computing how he could be lying there.

She said, "We received a report that you were hit on the head with a shovel. Is that true?"

He just looked at her.

"Were you hit in the head with a shovel?"

He looked over at Ralf again. "Did you kill Ralf?"

"We broke his neck," Frank said.

The guy closed his eyes and started to fall over.

Frank caught him and straightened him back up again.

"Were you hit in the head with a shovel?" the sheriff asked.

The guy looked the sheriff in the eyes, and then something must have finally turned over in his brain.

"Hakim hit me," he said.

"With a shovel?"

"Yes."

She looked down at Frank. "Your story seems to be checking out."

"You still don't trust me?"

"I'm gathering evidence," she said. "They're going to want evidence. Now you have someone trustworthy who has verified it firsthand. That's called corroboration."

Sheriff Hood wasn't thinking two steps ahead. She was thinking five. A very smart cookie. And he decided once again that he liked her.

She pointed at Frank and said, "Do you recognize this man?"

"I don't know him."

"Is he part of the cell?"

"No."

"Why did Hakim hit you?"

He looked at her.

"How big is the cell?"

He hesitated. "Why did you kill Ralf?"

"We didn't kill Ralf. I'm the sheriff, and he and your other buddies wanted to kill me so they could cover up their smuggling. So Mr. Shaw here broke his neck."

"You're the sheriff?"

Frank said, "I don't think we're going to get anywhere with this guy. I say we tie him up, stuff him and Ralf back in the slot, and let the FBI talk to them when they get here."

She nodded and turned back to the man. "You came into the wrong country. You and your cockroach friends. The FBI is going to have a heyday with you. Maybe CIA. And you're going to spill all your secrets."

The guy said, "You killed Ralf." He said it definitively. Like it had just sunk in. Like it was an important discovery.

"Tie him up," said the sheriff.

Frank looked around and decided he'd use the laces from their shoes.

"You don't have any time," the man said. He closed his eyes.

Frank knelt down and began to untie the man's shoes.

"You must stop them."

Frank pulled one shoe off.

"Muk," the man said and mumbled something in Arabic.

Frank pulled off the other shoe and began to loosen the laces. "I say we pour as much of the sports drink into him as we can and hope he makes it. He might have a good motive to rat the others out." Although the question about what he'd done to deserve their ire loomed large.

The sheriff nodded and picked up the jug. She lifted it to the man's mouth. "Drink," she said.

He refused it. "No. The goats." He took a breath. "They killed the goats."

"Yeah," she said.

He closed his eyes again, opened them. "No. I am Mukhabarat."

"I'll make sure we note your name," she said and lifted the jug again.

"Mukhabarat," he said more forcefully.

Frank stopped pulling the shoe laces. He knew that name. Where did he know that name?

"I am Mukhabarat."

"Yes," she said and held the jug to his lips. "Now drink."

"Listen," he said, frustrated, exhausted.

She pulled the jug away.

"I am . . ."

"I know," she said. "We got your name."

And then it came to Frank. "You're Mukhabarat?" he asked.

"Na'am," the man said.

"You're undercover?"

The man nodded.

"Undercover?" the sheriff asked.

Frank said, "Mukhabarat is Saudi Arabia's intelligence agency. It's their CIA."

The sheriff looked at the man. "Well, that's a first," she said. "I guess if you're going to lie, you ought to go big."

"He could be telling the truth," Frank said. "It would explain why they decided he needed a whack on the head with a shovel and an armed guard. It would explain his hiding."

"I don't know what I believe," she said.

"What's your name?" Frank asked.

"Sayyid."

"I don't buy it," the sheriff said.

"They are going to kill," Sayyid said. "There will be more graves."

"What graves?" she asked.

"The goats."

"They're going to kill more goats?" she asked.

"They killed the goats," he said exhausted and exasperated.

"There you go," she said. "It's a cell of goat terrorists."

But Frank was thinking of the animal pens and the mass goat grave in the canyon. He said, "How are they going to kill?"

"The drones," Sayyid said. Then he mumbled something in Arabic that Frank didn't understand.

You could attach explosives to a drone. You could attach automatic weapons. A drone would be much easier to use than a suicide bomber. "How are they going to use the drones?"

"They put them in the graves."

The sheriff looked at Frank, as confused as he was.

"Sayyid," Frank said slowly. "What is the target?"

"Big."

"What is it?"

"Big."

"And they're going to use drones?"

"There is no time," he said. "They're going to send it all out. San Diego. Huntington Beach. Nashville."

The cities on the map.

"What are they going to send?" Frank asked.

Sayyid slumped again, grabbed his shoulder in pain.

"Sayyid, what are they going to send?"

“Aljumrat alkhabitha.”

“In English,” Frank said and thought about weapons you could attach to drones. Small weapons that could pack a lot of punch.

Sayyid thought, squinted his eyes in concentration, then opened them. “Onthraks,” he said. “Aljumrat alkhabitha.”

“Good lord,” Frank said, knowing now what the brass pesticide nozzles back at the ranch were for.

“What?” she asked.

“Anthrax?” Frank asked Sayyid. “Is it anthrax?”

“Na’am,” Sayyid said. “Anthrax.”

30

Rifle and Gun

"AND THAT EXPLAINS the smell of bleach," Frank said. Bill's gang wasn't a bunch of neat freaks. They were using the bleach to sterilize. They must have their lab down in the basement. Then he thought about the mass goat grave up the canyon. He said, "Sayyid, were they testing the delivery on the goats?"

Sayyid grimaced. "Water."

Frank asked again, "Were they testing the anthrax on the goats?"

"They killed them all," he said. "Highly effective."

Frank thought of all those dead goats. A mass grave of them. The tests had apparently been very successful. He thought again of what he'd seen back in the garage with the brass insect sprayer nozzles. He thought of the stainless steel canisters that had been painted red, white, and blue.

The sheriff tipped the jug. Sayyid took a long drink.

Frank said, "They're going to use the drones to spray the anthrax. That's the delivery mechanism."

Sayyid nodded.

After 9/11, Homeland had been worried about airplane crop dusters, but drones were beginning to be used to spray crops. These were simply smaller versions of the industrial crop models. They were things you could build with a kit. Parts anyone could purchase online. Harmless little drones, spraying weaponized anthrax.

"When?" the sheriff asked.

"They are sending it out," said Sayyid.

"What?"

Sayyid's head lolled to the side.

"When are they going to send it out?" Frank asked. "Sayyid?"

"Wednesday morning."

Today was Wednesday, and the morning was almost gone.

Each of the cities on the map was a big place. Frank had been trained on bio-warfare, and he knew that anthrax that was the right size carried on the wind like pollen. A little over two hundred pounds of it, a quantity roughly equivalent to four bags of fertilizer, if released in the air, upwind of the target, could theoretically cover 180 square miles with deadly effect.

But that was theory. Even if you had a lethal strain of anthrax, winds didn't flow uniformly. Some areas would have more of it, some would have less, some none at all. But none of the drones would be able to carry 200 pounds. Not even the big King Kong drone they had on the floor of the barn. Furthermore, the canisters he'd seen had been the size of big plastic protein powder jars. They could carry maybe two to four pounds each. Not enough for a city. Maybe enough, in optimal conditions, for one and a half to three miles. But they wouldn't be looking to blanket some general area. He wouldn't be. If it were him, he'd be looking for something smaller.

"What's the target?" Frank asked.

Sayyid fell forward.

Frank helped him up. "Sayyid," he said.

But Sayyid was blinking, trying to gather his rapidly deteriorating wits.

The sheriff said, "You could fly those little drones anywhere."

He thought about the map. There were all those military installations, but they'd already discarded that idea.

She said, "They could fly them over schools; some kids go year round. They could fly them over parks, beaches. They could try to get it into the food supply. Spray crops with it. Spray cattle in a feed lot maybe."

"Beach," Frank said, and suddenly the image of thousands of people lined up shot like a bolt of electricity right through him. But he wasn't thinking about the sea.

Huntington Beach, the city, not the physical beach itself, had a huge Fourth of July parade. He and his sister Kim and nephew Tony were planning on attending it along with hundreds of thousands of others. Drones would just be part of the show.

He said, "Does Provo, Utah have a big Fourth of July celebration?"

She said, "Huge. It's called Stadium of Fire. I would assume forty or fifty thousand people attend."

"Alameda has a huge parade," he said. He'd seen it on the list of major Fourth of July celebrations in California when he'd been planning the trip. San Diego had fireworks. Seattle. Boston had a large one. St. Louis. They all did. What big city didn't? There could easily be a million, maybe two, at the celebrations at all of those places circled on the map.

The hair on the back of Frank's neck stood up.

He said, "They're going for the Fourth of July crowds." He imagined the thousands of people lined up along the parade routes, the little children with popsicles, the babies in strollers or slung in front of their mothers. The fathers wearing sunglasses and patriotic shirts. And the drones would fly maybe only a foot above their heads, all red, white, and blue, part of the festivities, releasing death that none of them could see, taste, or smell.

Why spray some big general area when the people would line up for you? Why do some big fly over when you could release just a few feet over their heads?

And the mothers, fathers, and children would inhale the bacterial spores. And if they had been milled to the right size, they would go deep, and when the people exhaled, the anthrax spores would stay, clinging to the sides of the lungs. Other particles would stick to ice cream cones or hot dogs or get caught in cotton candy, and the parade-goers would ingest them. And then in the evening the drones would do it all over again, flying the stadiums, flying over face after face after face, the freedom-lovers pointing at the little Fourth of July drone making its rounds just a few feet above the crowds.

"Dear God," he said. "How many hours to Alton?"

"You figured it," she said. "Four to six."

"Where can you drive to in six hours from here?"

"Phoenix, San Bernardino, Provo, most of the way to Denver."

"That's almost the whole western part of the United States. Close to a million square miles. We'd never catch them. They'd change vehicles. And then they would just change targets. Maybe the delivery mechanism."

"Don't we have vaccines for this?" she asked.

He said, "The anthrax vaccine the government has been stockpiling is old. It's never been approved for use in children. Most importantly, they don't have doses for everyone in the United States. They don't have doses for even a fraction of us. They do some inoculation in the Army. I received one of those shots, but it's one thing to inoculate 15,000 Special Forces troops. It's something else to take care of a major metropolitan area. The CDC might be able to treat an attack on two major metropolitan areas, but not the dozen on the map."

"There will be panic," she said. "Even if they only killed a few thousand."

"Or even a few hundred because millions of moms and dads would be wanting their kids to be safe, not knowing if or when the next strike might occur. It only takes a few thousand going Rambo to get their kids vaccinated to turn it all into a nightmare. There would be attacks on hospitals, people taking hostages. And the black marketeers would come in with fakes. The state National Guards would be called out to provide security. Biological weapons are the poor man's nuclear bomb. And they're about to release one."

"Not one," she said. "How many canisters did you see?"

"We can't let them get six hours on us."

"No, we can't," she said.

"We have a rifle," he said, thinking.

"A box of ammo," she added. "You've got a semiautomatic. It's two of us against, what, six or seven of them?"

"Seven that we know of," Frank said. "Although I don't think they'd have more because they usually like to keep their cells small."

"And their drones," she added.

"If we're lucky, they won't be looking close to the ranch. They'll be looking past our current position. If we're not lucky, then they will see us coming. And they'll set up an ambush."

"How do you defeat an ambush?"

"Avoid it," he said. "Or call in air support."

"Or outflank them," she said.

"Yeah," he said, knowing that was going to be mighty hard with just the two of them.

"It's time we got moving," she said.

"Right."

Then she hesitated. "Do you think our friend Sayyid is making it up? Have we been played?"

Frank looked at Sayyid, struggling to drink out of the jug. "There's a chance," he said, "but he'd have to be the best actor I've ever seen."

"What about the women? I thought these hard core Islamic terrorist cells were all male."

"Sometimes. Sometimes they use women."

"As suicide bombers. Did those women look or act like women brought in because they were willing to wear explosives?"

He had to admit they had not. They were trained. In fact, the one had taken a lead role in hunting Sayyid down. "I don't know," Frank said. "Women fought with Muhammad. Maybe some theologian has written a fatwa sanctioning it."

"Well, acting or not, I don't think he's in any condition to work his way out of knots. Let's tie them both up for safe keeping and go."

Frank nodded. They helped Sayyid to the shade and tied him up with shoelaces to keep him from wandering off. They left the guard where he was but splayed his book over his face to keep the sun off him. Then they took his pack with the box of ammo in it and began to speed walk back down the path, Frank with the semiautomatic, the sheriff with the rifle.

They could have run, but Frank didn't want the noise it would make. It would do them no good to hurry back to a number of men who had been able to set up a good killing field because they'd heard Frank and the sheriff coming. However, with the urgency of the situation, it was hard to walk, and Frank found himself doing a half-jog before they'd gone a hundred yards.

They hurried down the bends in this canyon, Frank trying to keep the pace quiet, stopping them at irregular intervals to listen, look, and smell. They passed the alcove they'd hidden in high up on the slope and slowed to a walk, then quietly made their way down into the dry streambed and carefully crawled forward until they could see the other valley.

They waited and listened and watched for two or three minutes and saw nothing but a solitary red-tailed hawk riding the air currents above.

The mouth of this side canyon was maybe only fifty or seventy-five yards away. They slowly crawled forward over the rocks, sand, drift wood, and other detritus, happy that this part of the streambed was in shadow, which would make them harder to see. They stopped again and scanned the slopes of the main canyon as well as the road and sage and cedar on the valley floor.

Nobody was there. No pickup. No ATVs. No drones. There was, however, the sound of rushing water. They crept the last distance and soon saw the source of the sound. The dry creek bed that they had crossed before was now running with muddy water. Judging by the height of the water on the banks, it was probably only a foot deep.

"What's this?" he asked.

"Rain storms north of us. I suggest we get across before it gets any deeper."

"Roger that," Frank said, but he paused again to scan the canyon. They were about to step out of the shadow and into the sun with no cover whatsoever. He scanned the ridgelines. If it were him, he would place someone up there. He shaded his eyes and scanned for drones. But he didn't see anything.

He said, "I'm going to cross. Do not come out until I've safely made it to the other side." He supposed if there was someone out there, he'd be too big a bait not to bite.

She nodded.

Then Frank slipped out of the shadow and stepped down into the muddy water. It was cold and came to his shin. He waited for a rifle to crack, but none did. Nevertheless, he wasn't about to announce his presence, so he picked his way across with as little splashing as possible, then climbed up into some willows on the far side. He looked for danger, found none, and motioned the sheriff to cross.

She came out of the shadow and stepped into the water and began to cross the muddy flow. While she was moving, Frank scanned the slopes. If a shot was going to come, he wanted to see the muzzle flash and the location. But no shot came, and the sheriff was soon below him, asking him to take the rifle so she could use both hands to climb up the sheer bank.

He took the rifle, helped her up.

He said, "They're either farther north, trying to find us up there, or they gave it up and all headed back to the ranch."

"If it were me," she said, "I'd start to worry that our prisoners had escaped for good. I'd send some eyes into the sky and get everyone else packing up."

"I think you're right," he said. He hoped they had a lot of packing, but he was guessing they didn't. He was guessing they'd already started that process when Frank had broken in last night, which meant he and the sheriff did not have a lot of time.

Frank said, "Let's keep a few yards apart so if someone is watching, it's not an easy shot to get both of us."

She nodded, and they headed south in their wet boots, toward the ranch, keeping well away from the road. They'd only gone a short distance through the sage when a deep rumbling sounded farther up the canyon.

Frank turned, saw dark storm clouds miles to the north, and thought it might be distant thunder, but the rumbling continued. The sheriff was standing still, listening, her head cocked.

The sound was growing, coming right down the canyon.

The sheriff finally recognized it, and her eyes went wide in alarm.

"What is it?"

"Run!" she said. "We've got to beat it to the crossing." And she took off and sprinted past him.

Frank turned and ran after her. "What is it?"

"Flood," she said.

How were they going to outrun a flood?

But the sheriff wasn't letting up. If anything, she put on more speed.

The grinding, low rumble grew louder. Frank glanced back and saw a darkness come around the creek bend farther up. Saw a thick tree limb stand up on end and crash over. Knew that what was coming down the creek bed was chaos.

"Good night," he said and turned and booked it through the sage after her.

They ran a hundred yards across the sandy flat and into the junipers, Frank knowing that running like this would only make them stand out. The ground turned rocky, then sandy, then rocky again. The fingers of the bushes scraped against his legs and exposed arms.

Up the creek in the approaching wave, large stones tumbled and knocked.

Frank and the sheriff made it to the base of the hill, and then the sheriff, who was still in the lead, decided that the road was worth the risk and broke out from the junipers and sage and lengthened her stride.

They sprint-jogged up the slope. Frank's lungs began to work like bellows. His legs began to burn. But he pushed himself, his boots kicking up the dust and sand.

They ran another fifty yards and approached the trailer that they'd left as an obstacle, which had been pushed off to the side of the road.

Ahead of him, the sheriff slowed, then stopped. She took two big breaths, then took off again. Frank continued to run after her, his lungs burning.

They pushed themselves up the last few dozen yards to the top. The sheriff stopped again to get her breath. Frank stopped with her, both of them blowing hard, and they glanced back at the creek.

The flood looked nothing like he expected. The front edge for maybe twenty or thirty yards was not a wall of frothing, rushing water. Instead, it was thick—a dark, wild ogre jumble of black dirt, mud, and branches crushing everything in its path. It looked like some monster moving down the creek bed, rumbling with stone.

"Crap," she said in alarm and took off down the road.

Crap didn't begin to describe it.

Frank took off after her, not knowing if he was more worried about having just presented their silhouettes at the top of a ridge for all to see, or that they were trying to beat this thing like some idiot teenager beating a rushing train.

They ran down the road, their feet thudding on the dirt, making sure they avoided ruts and stones that might cause them to twist an ankle. They had maybe 200 yards to go to reach the crossing. Frank glanced upstream to the bend around the hill. The crushing ogre edge of the flood hadn't made it that far yet, but the knocking and cracking of stone and wood was growing louder.

They ran down into a dip, passed a number of cedars. The sheriff switched the rifle to her other hand, her boots kicking up little puffs of dust and sand with every long stride.

This side of the hill had a longer slope that grew more gentle as it approached the bottom. They finished the steep part and began to hoof it across the flatter ground.

The view to the bend opened up again. Frank glanced that way. It was still clear, and his hopes soared. They were going to make it. And then the black edge of the flood came gnashing around the corner, and Frank realized it was moving faster than he had first estimated.

Both of them picked up their pace, dried mud shaking off their filthy clothes as they ran.

The waist-high wall of branches and mud and stone rumbled down the creek bed toward them.

Frank gritted his teeth and put on a surge of speed, just like he would the last fifty yards at the end of a race. The sheriff heard him coming and did the same. His body was protesting, but they had to make it across. If they didn't, they wouldn't make it back to the ranch. And while they might hike their way out of the canyon, the creek would still be between them and Glendale, and it would probably take hours for the flow of muddy water behind the dark front to diminish enough for them to cross it. Which meant Bill and Company would be long gone.

The creek bed came into view ahead of them. It was maybe seventy feet across with a sand bar off center.

The front wall of the flood pushed down the bed, seething, tumbling the branches in it.

Holy hell, this was going to be close.

The sheriff sprinted across the last bit of ground, the oncoming wreck just yards upstream. She ran out into the creek bed, splashing into the shallow water.

Frank followed.

The thick dark wall of sticks and earth and stone cracked and rumbled so loudly the hairs on the back of Frank's neck stood on end. This wasn't happy bunny nature. This was stark nature that tore rock and earth to make canyons. This was the nature that didn't care what was in its way. It was going to grind, wrench, and break whatever was in its path.

To be caught in that grind of branches and stones would be death. It would be too thick to fight. Too thick to get out of.

The sheriff angled slightly away from the leading edge of the flood, but she couldn't simply race to a point downstream because the far side of the creek bed quickly turned sheer. They had to make it across here where the road on the far side would let them easily escape the creek bed.

The sheriff sprinted across, ten or twelve paces, splashing through the shallow water. Frank followed. She reached the exposed sand and rock bar. The far side of the creek was only maybe twenty feet away. Just another five or six good running strides.

The sheriff ran across the bar, but before she could cross the last bit of the creek, the leading edge of the flood split in two around the bar of rock and sand, and the dark flow ground past, closing the way before her.

She turned downstream and began to run, trying to get far enough ahead of the flow to skirt around the front of it. Frank followed. The front edge of the gnashing flow was only moving maybe ten miles per hour. An Olympic sprinter might run twenty-three miles per hour. Frank and the sheriff were not Olympic sprinters, but they were moving fast enough that it looked like they might make it. But then the sand bar ran out.

The sheriff splashed into the water. Frank followed. But there were too many stones in this stretch. The sheriff slipped. Frank stumbled and barely kept himself from going down. The sheriff tried to run a few more paces, but the flood pulled ahead.

"Sheriff!" he yelled.

Behind them the other part of the mad black flow cut off their escape to the side they'd come from. It was like a pincer, closing in on them.

"Sheriff!" he yelled.

She stopped. The slopes farther down the creek were sheer for as far as he could see—they'd lost their chance to outrun this.

He dashed forward, grabbed her hand, then dragged her back to the rock and sand bar. Together, they scrambled to the highest point.

The thick debris flowed past them, inches away, like some weird stick and dirt lava. The ground shook with the tumbling stones. For some reason he thought the flood might stink, but it didn't. It smelled like loam, like vegetation, like wet earth and wood, except far more intense.

A muddy twenty-foot trunk of tree flowed past amidst a clog of smaller sticks. Then a sagebrush. Large stones banged under the water.

A small wave of sticks and dirt washed up over the sandbar and their boots. The flow was heavy, full of mud.

Frank and the sheriff began lifting their feet to get out of it.

The thick plug of debris looked like it continued for another ten or fifteen yards upstream before it began to thin.

Lord, Frank prayed.

And then Frank felt the sand bar start to give way underneath him. He suddenly sank down to his knee, and the flow grabbed him. It was as if some primordial hand had his leg and was pulling it downstream.

He spun, cried out. Slipped. But the sheriff grabbed his arm and pulled.

"Here!" she said and dragged him up to a more solid part of the sand bar.

Frank yanked his leg free. As he did, some force shoved a muddy branch as thick as his wrist up out of the water right at them.

Frank tried to move, but the branch took their legs out from underneath them.

They fell into the muddy flow at their feet, splashing into the shallow muck. The black mud washed over them, but the sand and rock bar was still holding, and they climbed back to their feet.

"Good Lord," he said. It was trying to kill them.

There was mud on half his face, and he wiped it away.

And then the debris flow began to thin. The water following the plug was chocolate brown and heavy with mud. There were still large stones rumbling past and debris being carried along. But the massive grinding wall was beyond them, moving downstream.

He said, "Thank you, God."

She said, "The water's going to rise."

"That wasn't the worst?"

"A flood comes like a long wave."

He looked at her.

"It will probably rise to double the height of that front edge."

That would be to his chest. Maybe his neck.

"It might only do that for a hundred yards or so, unless this is from a longer rain event or multiple events upstream. But we won't make it to the back end of the wave."

He sighed in dismay. They did not want to get caught in this. He'd seen how powerful water became in narrow channels. He knew the stories of Western desert flood victims, their broken bodies with clothes torn from them, their eye sockets packed with clay and sand. Or bodies that simply disappeared.

"We've got to get out," she said. "Now."

31

Water

THE WATER RUSHED around them, then, just as the sheriff predicted, began to rise. It was the color of dark cocoa, turgid, full of sediment and silt and still carrying branches and logs, still rumbling with stones.

They were only five or six good strides from freedom. Five or six strides through a rush that was thick with sediment. A rush more powerful than mere water. A rush strong enough to tumble large stones.

The muddy water rose to their ankles, then began to lap at their shins.

"If you go under, screw your eyes shut," she said.

"Because something will poke them out?" he asked.

"Because of the clay," she said and stepped down off the sand bar into the flow to her mid-thigh and almost lost her balance. She turned herself sideways, so the force of the stream pushed only against her side instead of the full width of her torso. She braced herself, took a sideways step.

Frank didn't know what the problem was with the clay, but he figured she knew what she was talking about.

The water rose another few inches.

Frank stepped into the flow up to his thigh. It was cold and massively strong, as if it were trying to rip him off his feet. A branch followed by a train of sticks flowed between him and the sheriff.

He braced himself, shuffled a small step forward. The water was heavy, so very heavy.

She lost her footing, cried out, then stopped herself.

The water rose to her waist.

She shuffled a step forward.

A large, deep knocking approached from upstream, some large stone or boulder thundering down at them under the waves.

"It's getting too high!" she said.

"You can do it!" he said.

She pushed forward.

The dirty, chocolate water rose to her belly.

The bank was so close!

Frank took another short step, braced himself, the sound of the massive boulder growing in volume.

They were going to make it—all he needed to do was get past her to the bank, grab the willows with one hand and her with the other. He stepped forward and, to his shock, sank into a deep hole, the water almost to his ribs.

The power of the flow knocked him back. He cried out. Flailed. Was forced back a step, then another.

The sheriff saw him, reached out her hand, but that exposed more of her trunk to the river. The water slammed into her, and she reeled back.

She tried to catch herself, but the swell rose to her chest, and then she cried out and was swept off her feet and went under.

A part of her side and back surfaced, then disappeared again in the muddy water. He fought for another step to grab her as she slipped past, but the chest-high swell of water surged against him and carried him off his feet.

And then he was under the water, the rumbling of stones knocking in his ears. He screwed his eyes shut. Briefly felt the bottom. Kicked and shot up.

He broke the surface, sputtering, just another bit of detritus being carried along in the raging flow. He tread the thick water with his arms, but everything was gauzy. He wiped his eyes, but could still barely see, and then he realized why she'd said to screw his eyes shut—the super fine clay had formed a film over his eyes.

He blinked, wiped his eyes, blinked again, tread water with his arms and tried to keep his feet up.

"Sheriff!" he called.

The only reply was the sound of the seething water.

He blinked furiously to get the filmy clay out of his eyes and turned in the water, looking upstream, downstream, trying to find her.

There was nothing but the muddy water and the willows speeding by.

Fear began to fill him. There was that old ceramic plate in her vest that would be dragging her down. Or maybe she'd snagged on something deeper along the bottom, gotten a foot or leg stuck between two boulders. It was almost impossible to survive something like that because as the snag held you, the current pressed you down and drowned you.

He kicked and pushed hard, propelling himself partially up out of the water, trying to get a higher view, but there was nothing, and he sank back, the current carrying him along like a cork.

Lord, he prayed.

And then he saw something out of the corner of his eye just a few yards downstream. He turned just as the top of her head broke the chocolate surface. She pawed at the water, then went under again.

There was no splashing. No waving. No theatrics. Contrary to what's portrayed sometimes on film, a person who is drowning does not call out. They very often don't look like they're struggling at all, which is why so many kids drown within ten feet of their parents.

Frank kicked hard and swam toward her, his hands striking twigs and sticks.

She surfaced again, her filthy hair masking her face. Rolled. Then she must have struck something underneath because she suddenly jerked back under.

Frank stroked for all he was worth. He hadn't done a lot of swimming since he went into prison. But the years of practice while in the Special Forces had burned the form into him. It was like riding a bicycle, and he cut through the water.

She surfaced again just a little upstream from his position, and he stroked the last distance to her and grabbed her arm.

She flailed, tried to turn and grab onto him.

He knew in her panic that she'd try to climb him and shove him under. On the teams, they'd been taught to grab the man's collar from behind and stroke away to get him horizontal. He went to grab the back collar of her vest, but it was gone. Her tee-shirt was bunched up around her neck.

He wasn't going to choke her with her shirt, so he turned her so she was facing downstream, cupped her chin, and stroked against the cold, thick current.

Her hair-strewn face rose out of the water. Her body rose to the horizontal with it.

She gasped, choked.

Frank continued to hold her chin, but with the other arm reached across her front and held her by her bare armpit. Then he let go of her chin and continued to stroke into the current.

She gasped again. Coughed. He felt her convulse, and she turned her head and vomited muddy water.

Frank scissor-kicked and stroked, the cold, dirty current carrying them along with stones knocking below.

"You're going to be all right," he said, still not able to see clearly.

She blew out. Heaved in another breath.

"Just relax and breathe," he said. "We're going to be fine." Which was a laugh.

She continued to breathe, holding onto his arm with one hand, stroking with the other. She pulled her hair out of her eyes and blinked.

"I can't see," she said.

"Try using some spit," he said.

She brought the fingers of one hand to her mouth, spit, and tried to wipe her eyes.

Frank's own vision was still a bit gauzy, but he could see well enough to make out the banks of the creek and the dry slopes rushing past, and the two big waves just ahead, which could only be caused by the water rushing over something big below.

"Get your legs up!" Frank said, and lay back.

She lay back with him and kicked her feet up. A moment later they bobbed over the two waves, which might have been fun if they'd been in a raft.

He continued to blink and got one eye mostly clear. Ahead, the water surged around a wide bend.

Frank stroked them closer to the inside of the turn to keep them from being mixed in with the detritus that the fast water was carrying and smashing into the bank.

She was breathing normal now. She said, "Something caught the bottom of the vest. It went straight up my back."

He said, "Are you okay?"

"I'm good," she said but didn't let him go.

She had her sports bra on, which would provide a little insulation. But the skin of her belly and arms was exposed to the full impact of the cold water.

"Where does this creek lead?"

She said, "Past the ranch, out onto the mesa. A little after that, it shoots down into some rough spots. Into a narrow. There are some falls. Lots of big hard boulders and rocks below."

The fall and rocks would certainly be scary, but he and the sheriff would be dead before they ever made it that far. When a river was forced into a narrow channel, the flow's speed and pressure increased violently. It would thrash and bang them around like a giant would a doll. A narrow was a coffin in a flash flood.

"I don't think I want to take that rubber boat adventure," he said.

"No," she said.

"Good thing we're getting out before then," he said.

She said, "I lost the rifle and pack."

"A rifle and pack can be replaced."

"I'd kind of like body armor in a situation like this."

"The one with me holding you in a river?"

She groaned. "The one with the terrorists."

"By the time we get out, we just might have enough dirt and mud in our clothes it will be like armor," he said.

She said, "Hang on." And she let him go. Then she pulled her tee-shirt down from her neck and slipped one arm into it, then the other.

They rounded another bend, and Frank looked again for an exit, but the banks were sheer without anything to hold onto. They needed an eddy, but the dirty water was flowing too high for the normal bends and eddies. And it was flowing fast.

"The smell reminds me of Walmart," he said. "When a semi comes in with pallets of bark that have gotten wet. And potting soil. Wet potting soil and sage."

"I'm freezing," she said.

They both were. And in this cold, hypothermia wasn't far away.

He looked to the other side for a way out, but there was none. He turned and saw a big branch upstream a bit, speeding along in the fast water.

They needed that tree. The water was cold, and he knew his muscles would eventually stiffen and slow. And if they didn't slow, they would tire.

He said, "I believe I see a flotation device. You any kind of swimmer?"

"I'm awesome in backyard kiddie pools," she said.

"Well, we need that tree. Scissor-kick and stroke. I'll keep a hold of you."

"I'm doing fine," she said.

"I know," he said, but he also knew that he didn't want to lose her to the current again. However, she showed a good stroke. So he didn't grab her, but stayed close until the two of them reached the weathered branch, which was as big around as a man's thigh.

As they grabbed onto it, he realized just how cold and stiff he was becoming, and the branch brought a welcome break from having to keep him and her afloat. They both took a breather, the water rushing with the sound of stones and the crash of the flow against the banks.

She said, "Keep your feet up."

"Roger," he said and kicked them up.

"I still can't see well," she said.

His own eyes were stinging, but he looked up at the slopes of the canyon. "One of mine is fairly clear. I'm thinking we're not too far away from the ranch."

"You still have that Beretta?"

He could feel its weight in his pocket. "Yes, ma'am."

"And your slingshot?"

He patted a pocket on the other side, but the pocket was flat and empty. The slingshot was made out of materials that floated, and it appeared they'd decided now was a good time to make an escape. He said brightly, "I still have the ball bearings."

"Great."

"The good news is that we're approaching the enemy via a route they will not expect."

"So we're down to rocks."

"And the Beretta with its three rounds."

"Which probably won't fire because it's been filled with creek grit and silt."

"Probably," he said.

"How many of them are there?"

"I'm thinking six or eight."

"Are we still sure this is a good idea?"

He thought of the children looking up as the drones flew feet from their faces, breathing in the almost invisible spray of death.

He said, "All we need to do is take one of them. Get his weapon. Two of us. One of them. That's pretty good odds."

"And the other seven?"

"One at a time," he said.

"Yeah," she said.

But Frank knew there was no way that's how it was going to go down.

She pointed at his neck and said, "You've still got your mask."

"A mask and ball bearings and the Beretta, which is going to fire."

"Right," she said, and then something caught her eye. She looked over her shoulder, made a small sound of disgust, and moved down the log.

"What?" Frank asked. Then he saw them—a family of eight or nine drowned ground squirrels floating along with him and the sheriff.

The sheriff began to scissor kick, trying to push herself and the log away from them, but the current just brought the dead family along, and she finally gave up.

Frank, the sheriff, and the dead ground squirrels rushed around another bend with their log, then along a straight section with large boulders for banks and nothing but rock to grab onto. Ahead was a drop.

Frank said, "Let's move to the back of the branch. Loop your feet over it."

They did, and went over the three-foot drop, their weight keeping the front of the log in the air. The log lagged a bit. But the squirrels continued on, separating from Frank and the sheriff.

"At least it wasn't a family of snakes," he said.

"Ug," she said. "Don't even start."

And then Frank saw they were coming to the mouth of the canyon. "I think we're close to the ranch," he said. "I think I see the tops of the trees around the compound."

"We need to get out of this water," she said, "because that rubber boat ride starts just below the ranch."

Up ahead, the creek bed widened and swung toward the ranch. Wide was good. Wide meant slower. Probably shallower. Farther down, the river swung away again.

"We need to get to the inside curve, or we'll miss it," he said, and the two of them began to kick and stroke to get to that side of the creek.

They rounded the bend with their log, still kicking and stroking to keep themselves on the inside part of the turn. The flood made an oxbow that bent toward the ranch, then away. Ahead on their side of the surge was a small stretch where the bank sloped gently up out of the water. After that stretch, the banks turned to solid rock that rose eight feet straight up.

"There," he said and began to scissor-kick to get the log as close as they could to the sage-dotted shore. They made another yard, and Frank realized the branch was making it hard to move.

He pushed away. The sheriff did as well, and they began to swim for all they were worth for the little stretch, but Frank's muscles were cold and stiff and didn't move as quickly as he needed. The water was moving too fast, and carried them right past the first part. It was going to carry them right past the last. Fear ran through him.

The sheriff reached the bank and started grabbing at the sage, but she was getting just the ends of the branches, which slipped through her fingers, and Frank realized they were going to miss it.

Like hell, he thought. They were *not* going to miss it. All she needed was some height. And she needed it now before the slope turned into a sheer wall again.

She grabbed for another bush. At the same time, he moved behind her, grabbed her just under her rear with both hands, then heaved up with all his might.

She sailed up and forward onto the bank.

He shot down under the surface, touched bottom, and pushed off hard, launching himself up and toward the shore. He broke the surface just past the tail end of the flat stretch, saw something through the clay film over his eyes and grabbed at it.

They were the stems of river willows. He latched on with all his strength.

The water dragged his body, turning him sideways. The willows bent.

But Frank didn't let go. Instead, he scrabbled with his feet and knees, pulled with his stiff arms, and hauled himself higher, the muddy flow sucking and splashing.

He grabbed a clutch of trunks farther in, pulled, scrabbled with stiff legs, but the willow branches were almost like a wall. He reached farther in and pulled, trying to part the branches with his arm.

The loud water dragged at his legs, but Frank wasn't letting go of the willows. He scrabbled with his knees, pulled himself farther in, and was suddenly out of the water.

He took a breath. Some bug fell down the back of his shirt and began to scrabble around. Frank ignored it and thrashed his way forward. Another bug landed on his face.

Frank brushed it away and pulled the first out of his shirt. Then he remembered what the sheriff had said about the flood being like a long wave and realized it might be rising right now to the willows.

He wriggled the rest of the way through the thin trunks, got a spiderweb in his face for his effort, and pulled himself out on the other side.

His eyes stung. He was freezing, shivering, and stiff as wood. His hands were banged from the willows. And he was grateful for all of it because it meant he was still alive.

He blinked, climbed to his knees, and gave his eyes a spit and finger bath. He blinked again, spit and bathed again, blinked. The clay film was still there, but he could make out much of what was around him.

He looked up the bank and saw the sheriff kneeling in shallow water, looking at him, shivering, the noisy flood surging a few yards behind her.

He gave her an exhausted thumbs up.

She shook her head in shock and relief. And Frank knew that with their limbs growing cold and stiff, they probably would not have made the next landing, if there had even been a next one.

He pulled his arms around his trunk to warm himself, happy the sun was blazing down on his cold wet back, and crouch-walked his way over to her. "Let's get a little higher," he said.

She nodded, and they climbed completely out of the water.

"Are you okay?" he asked.

Her eyes were rimmed in red. "I'm freezing," she said, holding her arms close. "But I'm out of that water. Holy cow."

He nodded. What else was there to say?

She said, "I got a sudden boost from behind. It was like some circus trick. They teach you that in the Army?"

"The bum lift," he said. "It's a classic immediate action drill." He said it like he had everything in control, but the fact of the matter was that the bottom could very well have been deeper, or he could have hit something down there and tumbled, or he might have miscalculated his jump and speared the side of the bank with his head and fallen back in. And it would have been him following their squirrel friends on the rubber boat ride.

"I still can't see well," she said.

"We'll probably be crying clay for a few days," he said and looked around to verify their position. They were still down in the creek basin. And from the tops of the trees, he figured the ranch was just on the other side of the short hill.

He studied the slope to identify the best route to the crest. "We're going to be approaching in broad daylight. I sure hope there's cover on the other side."

Next to him, the sheriff crawled back down to the mud, then

dropped and began some weird roll and squirm thing, jerking this way and that.

He stared at her, wondering if she was having some kind of seizure.

Then she rolled up on her knees, took a big handful of mud, and slathered it over the front of her now muddy-brown tee-shirt. She smeared another glob over her chest and caught him staring. "What are you looking at?"

And he realized she was camoing up.

He grinned, relieved, and said, "I guess it's not every day I get to see a law enforcement, wet tee-shirt, mud wrestling event. Please continue."

She gave him a look and said, "You remember that I'm the only one that can vouch you're not part of the terrorist cell, right?"

"Yes, ma'am," he said. "Do you want me to do your back?"

"How about you be useful and do the gun."

He grinned again, then moved up stream to a spot where the muddy water was eddying instead of raging. He pulled the Beretta out of his cargo pocket and examined it. Mud dripped out of the barrel.

He looked at the water which didn't look much cleaner. What he needed was an AK-47, built for mud, but you worked with what you had. He removed the magazine, his hands still cold, removed the rounds, tried to clean them as best he could. He opened the chamber and rinsed it out, then worked the action a couple of times. He rinsed some more, blew out a piece of wet grass, and figured this thing was as clean as it was going to get.

He fed the rounds back into the magazine, slid that back into the grip, then walked back to her and held the weapon out to her handle first.

"Is it going to fire?"

"Only one way to find out," he said.

She took it. "Splendid."

He pulled off his head mask and held it out to her as well. She'd lost hers in the flood, and she was now the shooter. If Frank was spotted, he could run off and create a diversion, but she needed to be as hard to spot as possible.

He said, "I think I'll do my own mud thing. You want to show me that squirm technique again, just so I get it right?"

She rolled her eyes.

Frank dropped to his knees. They didn't have time for Hollywood, and the water had been so full of mud they already looked like earth people. So he drew some slashes of mud across his head and face to match hers and called it good.

When he finished, he wiped his filthy hands on his filthy shirt.

She said, "What's the plan?"

"It depends on what we see when we get to the top of the hill."

She nodded, gun pointing up. "Then let's get to the top. I've got a date with some international terrorists."

32

Bullets and Beans

FRANK IDENTIFIED a good point on the crest of the bank of the creek with some sage to hide behind, and they crept up until they were maybe a dozen feet from the top, then got on their bellies. As they did, Frank heard the sound of voices, car doors slamming shut, and at least two vehicles start up and drive away.

Not good, he thought.

She pulled up her head mask, and they slowly bellied their way up to their lookout. They found themselves just north of the back of the big ranch house, south of the bunk house. They had a wide view across the asphalt in front of the ranch house to the barn. Frank looked for the vehicles and thought he saw dust rising up from the dirt lane leading to the main road, but he was low and his view was obscured by bushes.

They needed to hurry, but it was always best to do a little recon, so they lay there, peeking through the gaps in the sage for a good five minutes.

North of the ranch compound, there was a drone hovering three hundred feet up, watching the canyon. There was another hovering even higher south of the ranch, watching the dirt road that ran to Glendale in one direction and deeper into the miles and miles of desert wilderness in the other.

At the ranch itself, the main activity was out in front of the barn. The barn's doors were open, and three men, including Zeke with his arm bandaged, were loading boxes. The boxes weren't the cigarette boxes. Those were all gone. These were different, metal or plastic. The men were bringing them out from the back of the barn. Then Frank saw one guy exit the basement wearing a yellow hazmat suit and bio mask and carrying a long-handled brush. The kind of brush you used to wipe things down with bleach or some other agent meant to kill bacteria.

In the barn, just about where the King Kong drone had been, the man removed the mask, suit, and booties, and deposited them into a plastic garbage can which looked like it had other material in it.

Frank glanced over at the sheriff. She looked at him. He couldn't see her eyes because of her muddy, slit-eye mask, but he knew she was thinking exactly what he was—that hazmat suit confirmed Sayyid's claims and put to rest the last doubts they might have had about them.

A man came out of the back of the house with a rifle and black garbage sack. He was wearing rubber surgeon's gloves. He leaned his rifle up against the patio table, then began to walk along the back of the house. He picked up a cigarette butt and put it in his sack. Picked up a scrap of paper. A plastic cup. While he continued his yard patrol, a woman came out with a bottle of spray cleaner. She too wore rubber surgeon's gloves. She sprayed and wiped down the door and door handle and glass, the patio table, the chairs, then went back in.

These were not super conscientious renters cleaning up after themselves. They were wiping away evidence of their stay. They would probably order in a full cleaning of the house, top to bottom, including shampooing the carpets, from one of their own teams, if their organization was big enough, or some group outside the area, maybe from St. George or Cedar City. Maybe even Las Vegas. Frank suspected the heavy duty cleaners would arrive later today.

Frank looked back out to the barn. The pickup had a camper shell over the bed. He figured it was just the right size to carry a dozen small drones and their happy red, white, and blue steel canisters of death.

Frank counted six people: Zeke and his two crew, Mr. Bio Suit, the garbage man, and the woman cleaning the house. He wondered if Bill and the others were somewhere in the house where he couldn't see, or maybe out front on the porch.

The guy in the back yard bent over and picked up another piece of trash.

Frank slowly leaned over to the sheriff's ear, partially covered by the slit-eye mask, and said in a voice below a whisper, "He's our man. When he gets close, I charge him. You go for the rifle."

She gave him the thumbs up.

They waited. Mr. Clean made a pass across the yard, like someone mowing a lawn might, except there was no lawn, just cobblestone, gravel, and displays of large stones and ornamental desert grass framed with a couple of Ponderosa pines. The man turned and made another pass, scanning maybe a yard of ground. Frank figured two more passes would put him in range, but the guy finished his pass, looked out at the edges of the xeriscape, looked right at Frank's position, then turned and walked straight back to the patio table.

A huge urge to sprint for the guy shot through Frank, but he knew the play was broken, the man was too far away. Too close to his weapon.

Mr. Clean picked up his rifle, walked over to the door, grabbed the handle with his gloved hand, and went inside.

The sheriff turned her bagged head and looked at Frank with the little slits they'd cut in the material.

"Plan D," Frank whispered. "We get him in the house. No knock, no announce. We slip in like ghosts."

"You breach; I go in with the gun."

Frank gave her the thumbs up.

The mud from the creek was drying on them, lightening, making them more part of the desert. They would need to be apart for just a little longer as they crept forward because the windows at the back of the house were big, and if they weren't careful, anyone walking past would spot them.

They moved turtle-slow, watching the house and yard, both taking a slightly different route through the sagebrush. Twice, someone inside walked past the big windows causing Frank and the sheriff to freeze, but they weren't looking for muddy intruders from the river and therefore didn't see them.

Not long after they began, the sheriff ended up at the edge of the cobblestone in the shade behind a thin-leafed shrub with small, pale yellow flowers. Frank ended up a number of yards away next to a good patch of tall ornamental grass. They were directly behind the house with nothing but cobblestone between them and the back door.

Frank rose to a crouch. She followed his lead and pulled down her hood-mask. He could hear the voices of men around front, but he hadn't heard the front door open and close, so he figured their target was still inside.

He signaled to her, asking if everything was clear from her perspective. She signaled back the all clear. Frank scanned the area one more time, heard the men still out front, heard the breeze through one of the big pines at the border of the yard, heard a cupboard bang shut inside the kitchen.

He nodded, counted to three with his fingers, then slowly rose and moved forward, walking a slow heel to toe, watching the windows. The sheriff rose from her hiding spot and did the same, except she had the Beretta up in a two-handed grip in front of her.

They converged on the back door, their feet making only the slightest of sounds. Frank grabbed the handle.

Another cupboard banged shut. Someone called from out front, asking for tape.

The sheriff nodded, and Frank slowly turned the handle, and pulled the screen door open. The weather stripping on the bottom of the door made a scraping sound. The hinges creaked.

Frank winced.

Both of them froze, listened.

A man from inside shouted the tape was on the porch.

The sheriff looked at Frank, her gun ready, and gave him a nod to open the door.

He nodded back. He doubted she'd done any entries with nothing but a muddy tee-shirt and pants for protection. Today was her lucky day.

Frank held the screen door open with his back, grabbed the knob of the house door with one hand. He turned the knob, thrust the door open, and stepped back. The sheriff moved into the house, gun in a two-handed grip. Frank waited one second and followed.

There was a big kitchen to the right, a nice granite counter and bar separating it from the fine dining area to the left. Beyond the dining table the floor wrapped around to the front room. Directly ahead, a hallway ran past a stairway to the front room and led directly to the front door.

Mr. Clean was standing just past the stairs, looking their way. He was peeling an orange, still wearing his surgical gloves. His rifle was leaned up against the wall.

The sheriff swung the gun to shoot.

Mr. Clean's eyes went wide, and he lunged for the front room.

The sheriff fired, a nice big loud bang that set Frank's ears ringing. But the bullet missed, shattered the glass of the front door, and sped out somewhere in the direction of the barn.

The man darted out at knee level, grabbed the butt of his rifle, and darted back.

The sheriff hurried forward, gun up, to take him.

Frank turned left into the dining room, thinking he could distract the man into thinking they were coming round the end that way and give the sheriff a good opportunity to shoot the guy in the back. As he hustled forward, he tossed a chair, which clattered to the tile floor, then shoved the heavy table still loaded with an electric pancake griddle and breakfast dishes, which made a fine groan. He knocked another chair, heard someone running toward him from the front room.

He expected to see Mr. Clean pop out with his rifle at any second. But it wasn't Mr. Clean. It was Mrs. Clean, murder on her face. She was holding a big Bowie knife, probably bought at one of the local shops. It was at least a foot long, an excellent size for cutting people's heads off. She saw Frank, saw he had no weapon, and charged.

He took a step back, reached for a plate to huck at her, grabbed a spoon instead. He hurled the spoon. She batted it away, a snarl on her face, and kept coming. He took another step back, grabbed the griddle.

She lunged at him.

He swung the electric pancake griddle round and knocked her knife hand away.

She slashed back at him.

He moved the griddle, parrying the blow.

She moved to stab him, but he grabbed the griddle with both

hands, took a step forward, and jabbed the griddle hard into her face. All of Frank's weight was concentrated in that metal edge, and she reeled back, then fell to the tile floor. Her knife went flying.

Frank stepped forward again, stomped her ribs with all his weight and felt them crack. She moved her arms to protect her torso, leaving her head and neck undefended. Frank prepared to stomp her neck, but from the front room the sheriff yelled, "Watch out!"

A bang rang out from the front room, but it was not the sound of a Beretta. Mr. Clean shouted something, and another shot rang out from the front room. A moment later, the sheriff raced back out of the hallway and darted into the kitchen, Beretta still in hand.

And then Mr. Clean opened up with his rifle from the front room. He had it on semi-auto, firing a rapid series of shots through the walls and stairway between him and them. The first bullet blasted a chunk of drywall out of the wall next to Frank. The next blew another hole in this side of the drywall and shattered the big window looking out on the back yard.

Frank tossed the griddle and hit the deck. The bullets marched down the wall, shooting over Frank into the table, the door, the cupboards.

The sheriff was on one knee in the kitchen, trying to get the action of the Beretta to go back, but it had jammed. A nice present from their muddy creek ride.

Frank knew the combat was going to get even closer and looked around for a weapon. He spotted the electric griddle a few feet away, rose up on his hands and knees to get it, and reached through the legs of a chair, but it was too far away.

Then Mr. Clean came out of the hallway, rifle at the ready. He spotted Frank. Swung the rifle around and aimed. And Frank knew this was this was the end of the line.

But the sheriff must not have gotten that message because she yelled and hurled the Beretta.

Mr. Clean stepped back to dodge, then swung the rifle toward her.

And that's when she followed her first throw with a fifteen ounce can of garbanzo beans. It was a tremendous throw. The can flew the five feet between Mr. Clean and the sheriff and nailed him in the face. Point blank.

He fell back, raised his arms to protect himself, and shot a round into the ceiling.

Frank and the sheriff both charged to get the rifle, but then someone from outside opened up. More than one someone. Glass shattered, drywall exploded, bullets cracked through the house.

Frank dropped and knew it was just a matter of time before someone came around the side of the house to the big window at the end of the dining room and started shooting at them from that position.

The sheriff retreated back to the kitchen, then motioned for him to join her.

There was no other cover, so Frank scrambled that way.

More shots rang out. Above him, a clock exploded. The plastic picture of water on the table was hit and flew out the window and into the back yard. Frank scrambled to the hallway, saw Mr. Clean lying in his own blood past the stairs, shot by one of his own. He saw the rifle lying on the floor just beyond Mr. Clean, but also saw Zeke out the front door with a rifle, looking right at him.

Zeke swung his weapon.

Frank lunged past the hallway and dove the rest of the way into the kitchen, then rolled and joined the sheriff behind the dishwasher.

A few more shots were fired, then those outside stopped.

"Coward dogs!" Zeke called in. "And you'll die like dogs, huddled in some corner."

Frank turned to the sheriff. "That was a classic fast ball pitch. Although I don't think the league would approve of beans. Are you sure you don't like baseball?"

She said, "I hate baseball."

He said, "Well, I'm sure if someone had clocked it with your radar, that strike you just threw must have been going at least sixty miles per hour. Not bad for the bean league."

She said, "Unfortunately, I don't think a sturdy defense of beans and diced tomatoes is going to get us out of here."

Frank said, "The rifle is right there in the hallway."

“They’ll shoot us before we take two steps down that hallway.”

He said, “Maybe, but what if I don’t go for the rifle? What if I run down and leap out the window at the far end of the dining room, which they have shot out. They’ll be worried about me. They won’t be thinking of She Who Kills With Beans.”

“That isn’t a very good plan,” she said.

“It’s the best I’ve got,” he said.

“You’re going to play the target, and I’m going for the gun?”

“I’m thinking we’d better do it before someone comes around to look in the window over the sink.”

She sighed. “Okay. Here goes nothing.”

“Count of three?” he asked.

“Count of three.”

He got up into a crouch, told himself it was just a sprint, told himself that action was always faster than reaction.

“One,” she said. “Two. Three.”

Frank rose and sprinted for the far window. He passed the hallway, crushed over glass. Someone outside shouted. He ran past the wall between the front room and kitchen that now looked like it belonged in the gulag. He took another stride, leapt over Mrs. Clean, who was either out or dead.

And then one of Zeke’s men finished running down the side of the house with his rifle and stopped just outside the big empty window pane. He saw Frank and raised his weapon.

There was no turning back. And there was now no jumping out the window and into the yard. But there was the front room. Frank planted his next stride and changed direction.

The guy at the window opened up.

Frank ran into the front room, the bullets cracking around him, ran across the nice cedar floor, past the custom cedar coffee table and leather couches with southwestern throw pillows, and found Zeke and two others standing out front crouching low, probably because the man on the side had gotten a little too loose with his aim. But when they saw Frank, they raised their weapons.

There was no way out the front, so Frank headed in the only

direction there weren't any bad guys, and that was for the hallway back to the kitchen. He hoped the sheriff had gotten the rifle because he didn't think he could do another lap around this tiny track.

He reached the end of the front room, turned to go down the hallway, and saw the sheriff running with the rifle back into the kitchen. And then Zeke and his buddies opened up.

The bullets cracked. Drywall exploded. But Zeke and his friends weren't going all insurgent and wasting their ammo. They had slowed down and were trying to take better shots.

A bullet sang by his ear, and Frank knew the corridor was too long for him to make it back to the kitchen without taking some lead in the back. However, the stairs leading to the second floor were right in front of him.

He pivoted, launched up the stair well, banged into the wall. He grabbed the railing to steady himself and shot up—two steps, then two more, then something burst through the wall and nailed him in the thigh. He faltered to his hands and knees and scrambled up the stairs on all four to the top, monkey style.

Ahead of him was a bedroom on his left, a bathroom, then another bedroom on his right. Frank looked down at his leg, fearing the worst. But there wasn't a bullet hole. Instead he saw a gash with a big chip of two-by-four embedded in it.

"Situation?" the sheriff yelled from below.

He raised his voice. "One at the south window. Three out front."

"Roger," she said.

But he knew if she stood up, the guy at the south window would have the first-mover advantage. All he'd have to do is adjust his aim to nail her.

Then Frank saw the solution in the bathroom in front of him.

"Wait for my signal," he shouted.

Someone fired another round that came up through the floor a few feet away. Then another. They were taking guess shots now, but they'd soon come in. He needed to get moving, now.

He tested his leg and found the gash was just a gash, so he hustled into the bathroom and retrieved the heavy ceramic toilet lid. There was a nice-sized window on the shower. Frank peeked out of it and saw the man covering the kitchen from the south window. He had his rifle snugged into his shoulder, waiting for the sheriff to pop up.

Frank hobbled out of the bathroom, back into the hallway, and then into the bedroom next door with his lid. The room had a window on the south side, directly above the man's position. It was a good-sized window with a great view of the mesa. Someone had dressed it up with fat wooden blinds that were half drawn. Frank hobbled past the bed and carefully pulled the blind cord, quietly lifting the blinds the rest of the way.

"Shaw?" the sheriff shouted.

Frank figured there was no reason to wait. He slammed the double-paned glass with the toilet lid. The glass shattered, falling outward.

"Now!" he yelled, and peered out the broken window to find his target.

The man was looking up, rifle partially raised.

Frank hurled the toilet lid down at him.

Before it hit, a shot rang out from the kitchen, and the man below the window stuttered a step back. Another shot cracked, and Frank saw a spray exit the man's upper back, which was usually not very good for a person's circulation.

The guy fell—sheriff one, bad guys nothing. Then another man came scurrying around from the front.

"You've got another on the south wall!" Frank yelled, then ducked back and hurried toward the door.

Outside, the man's rifle cracked, and bullets slammed into and through the wall behind him. But they were all at the wrong angle and did nothing more than careen into the ceiling.

Another shot from the kitchen rang out. Outside, the ceiling shooter cried out, and the sheriff yelled up, "That's two."

Which meant that there were only two left. At least that he knew about. But they could still pin her. Easy. And he was plum out of toilet lids.

He needed to get a weapon from one of the men the sheriff had hit. Or at least a can of the sheriff's wicked beans.

He headed for the stairs and saw something small and dark fly through the hallway at the bottom. A moment later there was a terrific blast and flash of light.

A flashbang. They'd just thrown a flashbang.

Frank couldn't hear. He could barely see anything other than the afterimage of the light. But he knew that a flashbang meant they were coming in. And the sheriff had been closer to the explosion. She would probably be totally blind, maybe on the floor. She would certainly be disoriented.

He started to make his way down the stairs, blinking madly, feeling a bit off balance, knowing he had to get down. His leg throbbed, and anger welled up in him against Zeke and his scum.

He could just make out the general shape of the stairway around the white afterimage, but it was enough. He took another step, three more, keeping to the side that would be closest to the front of the house. He was halfway down when he saw the barrel of the first man's rifle appear. Or, at least, that's what he thought he saw.

He blinked, figured that had to be what it was, and launched himself.

The guy came around the corner, swung his rifle to clear the stairway, but before he could get the rifle all the way around, 220 pounds of flying Frank slammed into him.

Frank had greater mass. He had greater velocity. And the physics of the situation really wouldn't allow for the two of them to do anything but crash into the far wall. Most homes spaced the two-by-four studs inside the walls eighteen inches apart. Nailed vertically between the studs, about four feet above the ground, are eighteen inch long sections of two-by-four that act as fire blocks.

The guy's ribs slammed into the wall roughly where the fire block should be and cracked. His head knocked a nice little hole in the drywall above it. The rest of his body cushioned Frank's fall and kept him mostly upright, which was a swell favor.

The guy groaned. And Frank figured he was out for a moment, which was good because Zeke had been behind the guy and was bringing up his rifle to aim and shoot.

Frank pivoted off the guy, swept Zeke's rifle barrel to the side with one hand, and stepped into him, trying to slam his ulna through Zeke's throat.

Zeke brought his bandaged arm up in reflex and deflected the blow, but Frank still hit Zeke with his body, knocking him back a step.

Frank took another step, went for Zeke's throat, but Zeke rocked forward with the butt of his rifle and struck Frank in the chest like a sledgehammer.

Frank winced.

Zeke pulled back to strike again.

But Frank stepped forward and slammed his palm into Zeke's face.

Zeke's head snapped back, and Frank grabbed the back of Zeke's hair with one hand, held him like a lover. With his other hand, he grabbed Zeke's brow, then shoved his thumb hard into Zeke's eye.

Zeke cried out, dropped his rifle, and pulled back to protect his ruined eye with his hands. The reaction was an automatic reflex. There was nothing Zeke could have done to prevent it. More importantly, it opened up other targets for attack.

Frank saw the next two moves. A kick to the groin, then a blow to the back of the neck, and Zeke would be down. He took a step and prepared to punt Zeke's gonads, and was struck from behind, a blow to the back of his head that send Frank reeling. He crashed to the floor.

Behind him, the man he'd slammed into the wall pulled back the butt of the rifle he'd struck Frank with and reversed the weapon so he could shoot Frank with the other end.

Frank tried to move, but the hallway was spinning and his body wasn't responding.

The guy brought the rifle up to his shoulder, pointed it at Frank.

There was a bang and a flash, and then the man fell to the ground, revealing the sheriff standing behind him down the hallway with her own rifle, her face a grimace of pain.

Relief and admiration flooded through Frank—how many times was that woman going to save his bacon?

Behind Frank, Zeke cried out in pain, then bent to snatch up his rifle from the floor.

Frank grabbed the rifle first, then kicked Zeke in the knee, knocking him down.

The sheriff strode over, her face full of fury, and aimed down at Zeke to blow a hole in his head.

"Don't kill him!" Frank yelled. "We want to question him!" He could barely hear himself. "Don't kill him!"

33

Zeke

THE SHERIFF'S FINGER was on the trigger, her eyes sparking with fury. She was clenching the rifle, baring her teeth. A wave of murderous intent washed over her face. But she did not pull the trigger. She snarled instead and said, "Find something to tie him up with. And wrap the wound."

At first Frank didn't know what she was talking about, and then he saw that Zeke was indeed bleeding from his side and realized the bullet that had hit the guy who had been prepared to kill Frank must have exited that guy and struck Zeke as well. A twofer.

Frank started to get up to look for some cord to tie Zeke up with, but before he could get to his feet, Mrs. Clean rounded the corner with surgical gloves and Bowie knife in hand. She didn't come yelling like a banshee. She came quiet, ready to kill. She cocked her arm to throw the monster.

"Look out!" Frank cried.

The sheriff turned.

Mrs. Clean hurled the knife.

It missed the sheriff by inches and sank into the wall.

Mrs. Clean charged, but the sheriff reversed her rifle and rammed the butt of it into Mrs. Clean's bloody face.

She went down, Frank was sure, with some kind of skull fracture.

Out front, the door to a vehicle opened and then slammed shut.

Frank and the sheriff turned.

Over by the barn, the guy who'd been in the hazmat suit started the pickup they'd been loading boxes into.

"I don't think so," the sheriff said and took two steps forward into the front room and raised her rifle.

The hazmat guy put it into gear and punched it.

The sheriff pulled the trigger a number of times. The rifle banged and kicked.

The bangs sounded distant, which meant Frank was pretty sure he'd lost another tone in his audio range today.

Outside, the pickup sped forward down the road, and it looked like maybe the sheriff had missed, but when the road bent, the pickup did not follow. It bounced off the shoulder, the engine roaring like the guy was preparing to jump the Grand Canyon, and slammed into a massive cottonwood.

The thick tree shuddered. The guy inside flew forward, breaking the windshield with his head. Then he bounced back. The engine continued to roar, and Frank figured the hazmat man had cleaned up his last bacterial spill.

Frank said, "I've got Zeke. You'd better clear the yard."

The sheriff nodded, then went to the big front window, stepped one way, her rifle up, and scanned one half of the yard, then turned and did the other.

"Clear," she said.

There had been a white van when they'd made their prison break this morning. And the Lincoln. "You see any other vehicles?"

"Nothing," she said, then stepped over the broken glass and through the window frame, rifle up. She cleared the sides of the house, then moved out toward the pickup, its engine still racing, howling like it was going to explode.

Frank picked up the rifle the first guy had been carrying, removed the magazine from it and pocketed it, cycled the action and removed the shell in the chamber, then saw a box on the floor in the front room. It contained a smaller box of surgical gloves, a bottle of Dawn, and some cleaning cloths. It also had some electrical tape.

Zeke moaned. "Inshallah," he said. God willing.

Frank walked over to the box. He set the rifles down, took the tape, and walked back.

Zeke was bleeding on the floor. It wasn't a fast wound, but if he lost enough blood, the pressure in the old pulmonary system would drop, which would stop or slow the delivery of oxygen to the organs. And when that happened, Zeke's systems would shut down. It would be lights out.

The first guy had already reached that point, leaving a pool of blood on the floor. But Frank was not going to let Zeke go to his black-eyed virgin paradise.

Frank grabbed Zeke's arm.

Zeke tried to resist, but Frank wrenched the arm back, shoved Zeke over onto his face, and grabbed the other arm. He wound the black tape around his wrists a number of times, good and tight. Then did the same to his ankles. Then he rolled him back over, sat him up, and wrapped his chest, a couple of big black bands around the man to apply direct pressure to the entry and exit wounds. Of course there would be all sorts of internal bleeding, but the tape might keep him alive until the cavalry could arrive and fix it properly.

Zeke spit at Frank.

Frank said, "I think a spit jihad is about all you're going to be able to wage from here on out. Because from here on out I think your struggle for righteousness will be conducted in a concrete cell with a couple of folks from the CIA."

Zeke glared at him, and Frank knew that if they left Zeke here as he was, he'd just scoot over to the glass, get a shard and probably cut through the tape. If his wound didn't kill him, he'd be long gone when the Feds arrived.

So Frank dragged Zeke by the legs over to the stairs and hog-tied him to the bottom baluster with a copious amount of tape. It wasn't Fort Knox, but it was a lot of tape, and it would have to do.

Outside, the roaring pickup engine cut out. Frank looked up and saw the sheriff had opened the door to it and reached inside to turn it off. She then moved around to the pickup bed, removed one of the ties holding the boxes down, then jumped up into the bed to inspect the contents.

Frank turned to his leg, pulled out the wood, and knew that if he just wrapped the tape around his pant leg, it would move up and down as he tried to walk. So he brushed some glass off the corner of the fat-legged, cedar coffee table, dropped his pants, and sat on the glass. He wrapped the bleeding leg a number of times.

The sheriff came back up to the porch. She had a Glock nine millimeter she must have taken from the truck driver in one hand, her rifle in the other. She was filthy and glorious and loaded for bear.

She looked at him and said, "What are you doing with your pants?"

"When I was a kid, I wanted to be Tarzan. I don't think I ever got over it."

"What?"

"You don't think the Hanes make me look like Tarzan?"

"Did that guy hit you in the head?"

Frank grinned and pointed out his field-wrapped knee.

She said, "Get your pants on."

"Yes, ma'am," he said.

She said, "There were no drones or anthrax in the bed of the truck. Just some equipment."

Zeke coughed wetly and said, "They've got miles on you. Hours on you. Allah's sword is gone, and you will not find it."

Frank thought about the two vehicles they'd heard when moving up from the creek. He said, "Nice try, Zeke. But they just barely left. Furthermore, we know about San Diego, Huntington Beach, Alameda, Boston, Provo—we know them all."

Zeke said, "You know nothing. The United States is, how do you say it? A target-rich environment."

"You're fools," Frank said. "You think you have seen the full response of the United States? You think that's what you saw in Afghanistan and Iraq? You think that's what the on-going drone strikes on your buddies are? That's nothing. Unleash biological weapons, and you will arouse Nagasaki and Hiroshima. The United States will consume your people."

"The United States," Zeke said in disgust. "Did the United States consume the Soviet Union? Did it consume China? Why will the United States invade Afghanistan, but forbear invading Pakistan, which is full of Taliban? Why will you never strike North Korea?"

Frank knew the answer.

"Mutually assured destruction," Zeke continued. "That is the only thing that the United States listens to. How do you stop a bully? You demonstrate there will be more pain in it for him, more than he thinks it's worth."

"By killing children," the sheriff said.

"Like the children and mothers you've killed," Zeke said. "Like the families you have destroyed in your obsession for cheap oil. And what of the souls of the children and mothers and sons and daughters the Great Satan has led into torment? You kill both body and soul. That is what you do. You glory in destruction so you can sit at ease in your wealth. You started with a dream of freedom, but that dream was built on sand, on humans. Instead of submitting to the creator of the universe, you submit yourselves to man. And so you give power to your politicians who submit to no god but the vote. You give power to companies who submit to no god but capital. And you give power to your media which does nothing but corrupt. You have become sepulchers."

Zeke coughed and winced at the pain.

"Mutually assured destruction does not require you to use any weapons," Frank said. "That's how it worked with the Soviets. So tell us where they went, Zeke. America will see you have weapons. They will have the intended effect. And America will forbear."

"Some must die. Otherwise there will be no mutual assurance."

"You don't need to kill to assure."

"The United States had to drop the bomb on Hiroshima, didn't it, before Japan would listen. But we won't kill like you. We are not heartless. We will let you know who we've sprayed. In time, but not before some die."

Even if they warned them the day the attack occurred, there were not enough vaccinations. "We cannot inoculate them all," Frank said. "Tens of thousands will die. Your war is not with them."

"If you were a dictatorship, we would decapitate you. But every citizen in this country votes. They are as responsible as your president and legislature. They authorize the killing of our people and the war against our religion. You cannot push the blame to your president. And so you must learn there are consequences to interfering in our efforts to simply do God's will."

"Are you Al-Qaeda or ISIS?" Frank asked.

"We are the Lions of God," Zeke said. "We fight for Allah. We help those who seek Allah's will."

The sheriff said, "He's trying to keep us here. Keep us talking. Buy his people some time."

Frank looked at Zeke and knew it was true.

Zeke said, "You cannot stop God's will."

She said, "There are a lot of roads out here. A lot of ways to slip through the nets."

Frank said, "Then we find them. They don't have hours on us. They couldn't leave early this morning because they were too busy tying us up. And then they were giving chase. I think we heard them leave when we first climbed out of the river."

She said, "We've got nothing but Bill's bicycle."

"The pickup?" he asked.

"The radiator is totally smashed."

If one of them got on the bicycle, they might be able to ride out to Glendale. Maybe they'd come across someone driving the road, but maybe they wouldn't, in which case it would be an hour or two. And then Bill's guys really would have miles on them.

Frank looked across the asphalt into the empty barn. There had to be something. And then he heard the distant whine of a motor.

"I think we need to get outside," he said. "I think we might be able to upgrade Bill's bike for something better."

34
Pirate

THEY LEFT ZEKE tied to the baluster and hurried to the front door. The sheriff went out first, her rifle ready, turning to verify nobody had popped up in her absence. Frank followed, doing the same in the other direction, and found the area clear.

The sound was coming from the south of the ranch. Frank thought it might be a motorcycle or maybe someone on an ATV. Best case was someone they could stop who had a phone. He scanned the mesa for the tell-tale dust plume that would give him the position of the mystery vehicle, but saw none.

"There," the sheriff said and pointed high.

Frank followed her finger and saw, up in the sky, flying west to east, a motorized paraglider. Some motorized paragliders attached a framed motorized propeller to their backs with a harness. In principle, they were nothing more than a man with a big fan on his back. Others attached the motor to a trike. This particular paraglider was one of the trike versions, a little frame with three wheels and a way to attach both the parachute glider and the motor. The circular motor frame at the back was five or six feet wide in diameter. The parachute glider was long and rectangular and black with a white pirate's skull and cross-bones on it.

The guy was just tooling along in the distance, kind of swinging from side to side.

Frank said, "That's our ticket."

"He's more than a mile away. He'll never see us."

"Higher technology," he said, then hustled back into the house because he'd seen some higher technology on the floor. There'd been a big full-length mirror up by the doorway. It, of course, had been shot. But it hadn't shattered into a million pieces. A huge section of it remained.

Frank bent down and picked up a section of the mirror that was as big as a platter.

Zeke curled his lip and said, "Pig."

"Daughter of a pig," Frank corrected. "But you keep up that jihad. We're going to need you later." And then he ran outside, down the porch steps, and out to the front of the ranch so he wouldn't be obstructed by trees.

The sheriff said, "You'd better hurry."

Frank pointed the mirror slightly down and angled it until it reflected a good-sized square of sun on the ground. Then he angled the mirror up, leading the reflection toward the paraglider. When he figured he was on target, he began to flash it, three quick flashes, followed by three long ones, then by three more quick ones, which was the classic code for SOS.

The guy just kept swinging.

Frank adjusted his position slightly. "Come on," he said and repeated his Morse code.

But the guy just kept on flying.

"He's oblivious," the sheriff said.

But Frank kept flashing. The guy passed their position, and Frank figured their chance was gone, then suddenly the guy stopped swinging. He flew straight for a few seconds, then began to bank toward them.

"Hallelujah," said the sheriff.

Frank kept flashing the code, until he knew the guy was coming. And then they stood there and waited. It took the pirate on a trike almost two minutes to get to the ranch.

He came in low.

Frank and the sheriff waved the distress signal with their arms.

The guy circled around the ranch, buzzing just above the treetops, the big silk skull and crossbones shining in the sun. He was wearing sunglasses and an open-face helmet which allowed his long salt and pepper moustache and beard to flow freely. The guy waved, then pointed out front of the ranch to the meadow.

The sheriff started to jog down the path, but Frank's leg was twinging with pain. He saw Bill's bike right there in the garage, so he picked up his rifle, then hustled over and grabbed the Almira Gulch mobile. He wheeled it out of the barn, put a foot on one pedal, then gave it a scooter-like start, and swung his other leg up and over. It only took a few pedals to get out of the yard to the sloped road in front of the house, and gravity took over.

He slung his rifle over his shoulder and caught up to the sheriff who was running along.

She heard him and looked over.

"Hey, baby. Wanna ride?"

"Not my type of vehicle."

He shrugged and bounced past. A few yards later, he turned off the dirt road and onto the dry grass and headed for the spot where he figured the guy would land. He didn't go very far before he hit a rock. With his one hand holding the rifle and the other the handlebar, the bike almost bounced out of control, so he figured right here was a grand place to stop, and he braked and got off.

The sheriff caught up and said, "That was real sexy, Mr. Shaw."

"And you missed it," he said.

"How will I ever recover?" she asked.

Above them, the trike pirate circled the small meadow, then found his approach, one without any sage. He came in low, cut the motor, and a few seconds later touched down, bouncing along on his small pneumatic tires. He used the glider to brake to a stop, then let it fall behind.

The trike was a two-seater. There were some two-seater trikes that had a tall frame that the riders sat inside. On others, the frame was only shoulder-high, and their heads popped up above it. This wasn't either of those. There were no upper frame posts at all. This was simply a Y-frame made of aluminum tubes, with two fat little pneumatic wheels in back and one in front. It looked barely bigger than the trike Frank had ridden as a kid.

The driver sat at the back, in front of the motor, and the passenger sat in front of the driver on a flat seat with little handles at the sides. Whoever sat there was basically going up on a seat cushion with a little rod and cross post sticking out front for a foot rest. But the old bearded sky pirate didn't have a passenger with him today. Instead, he had a blue cooler strapped in.

The sheriff and Frank began to walk toward him.

The guy looked at their rifles, looked at Frank, and then he grabbed the engine starter.

"He's going to bug out," Frank said.

The sheriff called out. "It's okay. I'm the Kane County sheriff. We need your help."

The guy hesitated, and then it was too late for him to take off because they were now too close. He'd have to take off right into them.

The sheriff said, "Have you got a phone?"

The guy looked like a cornered cat.

"We need a phone," the sheriff said.

"There ain't no bars out here," he said.

"It depends on where you are," she said.

He looked the sheriff and Frank up and down. Frank knew they didn't look very good in their mud and blood.

Frank walked up to the trike. "We've got a situation. The sheriff here needs your phone."

"She's the sheriff?"

"She's the sheriff."

"You don't look much like the law."

She said, "We've got a bad situation. Do you have a phone?"

The guy was wearing a leather vest. He reached in and pulled out a phone and handed it to the sheriff.

She took it. "Thank you, mister . . ."

"I'm Gary."

She looked at the phone.

"It's on the blink," he said.

"Has it got an access code?" she asked.

"No, ma'am."

Frank said, "Did you see a white cargo van or white pickup on the road running from Glendale up onto the mesa?"

"No," he said. "I came up from Orderville."

"Nothing on the road?"

"No."

"How about an old brown Lincoln?"

"Nothing."

Frank couldn't see the guy's eyes behind his sunglasses, so he couldn't read the man as easily, but he wasn't getting a bad vibe. Frank said, "I saw a few paramotors yesterday down by Kanab. You up here in a group?"

"Yeah, some of us." He hesitated, then said, "What happened over at that house?"

The sheriff held the phone up, then shaded it from the sun. "I think your battery's out."

"Probably."

"Great," she said.

"Will any others in your group be coming this way?" Frank asked.

"Naw, they all left yesterday. I was just heading out for one more flight and a lunch at this spot we found."

"It's a big park," the sheriff said. "No service. What if you had troubles?"

The guy shrugged. "One of the gals rented a satellite phone from a shop in Kanab, but she left."

"Do you have a satellite phone?"

"Nope."

Frank said, "How high can you go in this thing?"

"How high do you want to go? I think the highest anyone has gone is way up where the airlines cruise at around 37,000 feet, seven miles above sea level. Lots of folks go to 18,000 when they're making a cross-country trip. You get up that high and you can glide a long ways. But you need oxygen if you want to fly above 12,500 feet for any length of time."

Frank had learned all about oxygen and altitude when jumping for the Army. Part of the Special Forces skill set was inserting into an area with high-altitude, low-opening jumps from 15,000 feet or higher.

Frank said, "I don't see an oxygen tank."

"Nope. Today is cliff-gazing day."

Frank figured the area here was around 5,000 feet in elevation, which meant Gary had another 7,500 feet to play with. Almost a mile and a half. You could see quite some distance from that far up. And that gave him an idea.

Frank turned to the sheriff, "They can't be that far ahead. We get some height, we can find them."

Gary said, "You want me to look for somebody?"

Frank noticed he didn't offer to take one of them up, but even if he had, looking wasn't enough. If they had a satellite phone, which various places rented to the folks going into this area, it would be different because they could call in Bill's position. But they didn't have a phone, which meant they couldn't just look because even if they did find Zeke's friends, Frank and the sheriff would eventually have to turn around or run out of gas. And the hour or two it might take to get back to some place with a phone would give Bill and the others time to slip away again.

Frank turned to the sheriff. "We're going to have to both go."

She nodded, obviously having had the same thoughts.

Gary said, "I can only take one."

She said, "Gary, I have an important mission for you."

"I can take you up," he said.

"I appreciate that," she said. "But that isn't what I need you to do. I need you to take the bicycle and start pedaling to Glendale. I need you to make a phone call. Flag down anyone you see on the road. This is a national security situation."

"Why don't I just fly?"

"Because I'm going to need the trike. Mr. Shaw and I are going to go after some folks who need to be caught. I'm going to have to commandeer it."

"My trike?"

"Gary," she said.

"Do either of you even know how to fly one of these?"

"Me and the glider are old friends," the sheriff said.

Gary just sat there, then got a wary look on his face. "Can I see your badge?"

"I don't have my identification with me."

"How do I know this is legit?"

"Gary, you'll know it's legit when you call the sheriff's office."

"I don't know," he said doubtfully.

"Gary," Frank said with a bit of iron in his voice. "Those dead guys you saw on the south side are terrorists. And we're going after the rest of them."

Gary looked up at Frank looming over him, paused a second, then relented.

"Man," he said, "this is just my luck." Then he undid his buckle and stepped out of the trike.

"Thank you," the sheriff said.

"Terrorists?" he asked.

She said, "You're going to get a message to the Kane County sheriff's office. Lives depend on you, Gary."

"Okay," he said, then realized the import what she'd just said. "Okay. I'll do it."

"You tell them you talked to Sheriff Hood. You tell them we had a terrorist cell at the Elkhorn ranch and that the subjects are on the move."

She looked at Frank. "East or west?"

He said, "I think the road will tell us the way to go."

35

Desert Sky

GARY REMOVED HIS helmet, revealing a bald head. "You'll need this," he said and put it down on the driver's seat. He took off his sunglasses and held them out to the sheriff. "And these."

She took them and slid them on top of her head, then looked the trike and motor over. "Emergency chute?" she asked.

"Right there," Gary said and pointed at a pouch at the back.

"How many gallons are in the tank?"

"Three gallons or so. You've got about two hour's worth of flying."

The sheriff nodded. "Let's go see where they went."

The three of them fetched the bicycle, then walked it with haste up the road out of the meadow, Frank knowing that every minute let Bill get farther away.

On his way up, he spotted the tire tracks from the ranch. It was clear there were three sets. One had big wide tires with an aggressive pattern. Too wide for a car. It had to be for the pickup. Another one had a wide tire, but with a much less aggressive pattern. He assumed that was for the utility van that had been parked out front. The third was clearly for the Lincoln. They reached the intersection of the drive to the ranch and the main road.

And it appeared all three had turned west, toward Glendale. In a short time they could be traveling the highway into Arizona, or out to I-15 which ran all the way from Canada to San Diego. Or up to I-70 which ran east all the way to Maryland.

It seemed like an open and shut case, but just for kicks Frank ran up the road a few dozen yards to a place where the road widened and saw a little scrunch where the pickup had swung wide then turned.

He found another scrunch for the Lincoln. The van had continued forward, but the pickup and Lincoln seemed to have turned.

He followed their treads off the shoulder on the far side and back to Gary and the sheriff. He waved them over, and the sheriff and Gary looked with him.

"Sneaking back," Gary said.

"Looks like it," said Frank. Then they all walked about a dozen yards farther and saw the tracks ride back up onto the road.

"They went west and east," Gary said.

"Crap," the sheriff said.

Frank said, "So which way do you send the material? If you go west, you get out onto the roads quickly. You can be in California before dark. If you go east, you head into some iffy backcountry."

"Where nobody would look," Gary said. "I would go east."

The sheriff said, "The back roads aren't regularly maintained, but they're passable, sometimes even for a Lincoln. You can easily get up to Cannonville. From there, you're on nice paved roads, off the main highways."

Frank said, "I'm with Gary."

The sheriff turned to Gary and said, "You tell them you talked to Sheriff Hood. You tell them we had a terrorist cell at the Elkhorn ranch. You tell them there are three vehicles. A white utility van—"

"A Dodge," Frank said.

"A white Dodge utility van heading west. A brown Lincoln—"

"A '90s brown Lincoln," he said. "And a white 2000 to 2005 Ford F150 with a shell over the bed. They're heading east."

The sheriff said, "You got all that?"

Gary blinked. "Sheriff Hood. Elkheart ranch—"

"No," the sheriff said. "Elkhorn." She motioned with her hands.

"Elkhorn," he said. "Dodge utility, white. Brown Lincoln, '90s. Ford F150 with a shell."

"A *white* F150," Frank said.

"I got this," Gary said. He pointed at the sheriff. "Sheriff in the hood." He motioned with his hand like he had antlers. "Elkhorn ranch." He mimicked a big guy driving. "White Dodge utility." He acted like a grandpa. "Brown '90s Lincoln." Then he gave a thumbs up. "White Ford F150 with a shell, 2003'ish."

"Thumb's up?" asked Frank.

"That's me going camping with my honey," he said all happy-like.

"Right," Frank said, not wanting to think about Gary and his honey. "As long as it works. Now I think we've gotta move."

Frank did some rough calculations. The trucks had driven off maybe fifteen minutes before the fighting. There was another fifteen minutes fighting with beans and toilet lids. Another fifteen with Gary. He was thinking it had been forty-five minutes since they'd come up from the creek. If the vehicles had headed east, it was going to be slower going, but they would still have a good head start.

Gary repeated his set of actions with full concentration.

"Gary," the sheriff said, "you've got to get moving, my friend. We don't have a second to waste."

"Right," he said, then hurried over to where he'd laid the bicycle. He picked it up and said, "It's only a three-speeder."

"Go," said the sheriff.

"Right," he said, then awkwardly mounted the bike and started pedaling.

"There goes the hope of the nation," she said.

"It's men like Gary that win wars," Frank said, which was actually true.

The sheriff looked over at him, then looked at his leg. "You good?"

"I'm good," he said. "It's time for us to fly the friendly skies."

They hurried back to the meadow and the trike which looked even smaller than it had before. Frank unloaded the cooler and put it in the grass while the sheriff moved Gary's sunglasses down to her face and pulled on his black pirate helmet.

Frank said, "I don't suppose he has an extra pair of sunglasses anywhere?"

"Cooler?" she suggested, fastening the buckle on the helmet.

He expected to find pot in the cooler, but there was only water, chips, and three tins of Vienna sausages.

"What is it with people and the booger dogs?" he asked.

"No sunglasses?" she asked.

"No," he said. It appeared he would just have to take the wind in the face, although watery eyes were going to mess with his aim.

They settled on one rifle, which Frank would use. He would also carry the extra magazine of ammo he'd taken from the rifle at the house as well as the one from the sheriff's weapon. She would use the nine millimeter Glock she pilfered from the unfortunate driver of the crashed pickup.

Frank examined the rifle. It was a standard AR-15. Frank figured these guys for AK-47s. That's what most of the world used, especially in the Middle East. And you could get them cheap enough in the states. But maybe the Middle East part of this cell hadn't purchased them. Maybe it was Bill, their American buddy.

The rifle looked well-cared for; however, it didn't have a fancy scope, just the standard iron sights. But back in the day Frank had shot plenty without the fancy stuff. This would have to do. He looked around, spotted a section of the log fence fronting the property that was close to them and began walking toward it.

"Hey," she called, "where you going?"

"No sense taking me up if I'm shooting blind."

He walked to a point about twenty-five yards away from the post, then sat cross-legged, brought the rifle up, and stabilized his elbows on his thighs.

If it came to it, he figured it would go down inside 300 meters. If he sighted in at the Army's standard twenty-five meters, which, because of the bullet's arc with this rifle, would also sight him in at 300 meters, he'd have to do more compensation for all the distances in between. However, if he sighted in at 100 meters, what they'd sometimes done on the teams, that would keep him fairly close to what he aimed at out to 200 meters. At 300, he'd probably drop a little over a foot. Beyond that things dropped rapidly, but he just didn't think he'd be out that far.

He snugged the butt into his shoulder, flipped off the safety, calmed himself, and lollipopped the knot in the fence on the tip of the iron post of his sight. He fired. The rifle banged, a few shards of wood flew from the post, and he had a bit of déjà vu with an assignment in Peru.

He sent two more rounds into the post, then quickly walked over to examine his cluster.

It was low and to the left, so he went back, took a round out of one of the spare magazines and adjusted the front sight with it to drop his aim another two inches. If he was going to zero in at 100, he needed to be low at twenty-five. He adjusted the rear sight to bring everything to the right. Then he sat down and put two more rounds into the post right where he wanted them.

It wasn't going to be exact. Every rifle and round were a bit different. He was assuming the shots fired from this rifle would follow the average rise and drop, but he couldn't be sure how closely this one would adhere to that average. He could have dialed things in much better at a firing range with a chair for himself and a nice support for the rifle and time to test shots at various distances. But this would have to do.

Frank rose and quick-limped back to the trike.

The sheriff was already in her seat and motioned for Frank to take his in front of her.

He straddled the trike, sat down on his flying seat cushion, and buckled the seatbelt.

The sheriff started the motor which roared to life. "You ready?" she shouted.

He felt like he was sitting on a little pie plate with handles. He used the last of the electrical tape and made a quick safety cord with one end wrapped around his wrist and the other around the ring the rifle strap attached to.

"Ready," he shouted back and put his feet up on the little aluminum foot rest sticking out beyond the front wheel of this contraption.

The sheriff squeezed the hand throttle. The motor whined, the trike began to roll forward over the grass. She squeezed the throttle more. Behind them, the glider filled and began to rise.

Frank called back over the sound of the motor, "Do you really know how to fly one of these things?"

"How hard can it be?" she yelled back and squeezed the throttle more. The motor whine jumped in volume and pitch. The little three-wheeled,

Y-frame, go-kart trike bounced along over the grass like some fly-by-night amusement park ride.

"You're joking, right?" he shouted back.

"Desperate times, desperate measures," she said and squeezed the throttle more.

They took another little bounce and then were airborne, a whopping three feet off the ground. Frank figured if he was going to bail out, now was the moment. But then the sheriff pulled on the glider, and they quickly swung up, and Frank was looking at a much higher drop.

The little Y-frame trike slewed forward and to the side, then rose again, and suddenly they were twenty feet up, and Frank realized he'd missed his opportunity.

The sheriff banked the little trike, and Frank found himself heading straight for the tall cottonwoods around the ranch.

"There are trees," he said.

"Is that what those are?"

She was giving the motor full throttle, and they were rising, but it didn't look like they were rising fast enough. He braced himself as they rushed toward the trees. And Frank knew they weren't going to make it. They were going to crash right into the top of a grand old tree.

But the sheriff pulled, and they suddenly cleared the trees, the leaves close enough for Frank to reach his boot down and touch. He heaved out a sigh, looked back, and saw Gary straddling his bike on the road watching them. He gave Frank and the sheriff a big thumbs up.

Frank gave him one back, and Gary seemed satisfied enough to get back on the bike and start pedaling again.

They picked up speed, zooming to a whopping twenty or thirty miles per hour and flew past the ranch, over the swollen, rushing creek, and continued to climb. Frank looked back at the bend where he and the sheriff had exited the water and saw the willows were gone.

He turned back around. The juniper and pinyon mesa stretched out before them. The cliffs rose on their left. The sheriff took them over by the cliffs and caught a thermal and rose higher, climbing into the late morning sky. Below him, Frank saw the spot where he had taken the drone out with his barbed-wire bolo. They continued to climb, the country spreading out before them. A minute or so later, they were probably half a mile up with a great view.

To the north the sky was dark with rain clouds. Here and to the south it was blue and sunny. The brooding sky in the distance, the mesa, and cliffs—it was all quite spectacular. It would have been a joy to view if he had ear plugs and wasn't perched on a seat the size of a laptop.

The sheriff leaned forward and shouted, "Having fun yet?"

"A blast," he shouted back. "Let's find these morons. I'll look north. You look south."

"Roger," she said.

Frank began to scan in a pattern, but before he'd gotten far, she said, "What's that? Two o'clock."

Frank looked and saw a plume of dust six or so miles away. "Let's check it out," he shouted.

"Roger," she said and banked them and their little black pirate go-kart in the sky. Below, the dirt road itself wound over and down and around, but Frank and the sheriff had the luxury of flying straight. Ten precious minutes later they had cut the distance to a little over a mile, and Frank could finally make out the vehicle—a nice Jeep Wrangler with no top. It looked like it was transporting four women in shorts. It was definitely not a pickup or Lincoln with drones and anthrax.

Frank shook his head, and the sheriff turned and climbed higher. There were more dust plumes in the distance. More roads leading south. Too many for them to check out at thirty miles per hour. Too many even if they had the wind at their backs. It would take an hour at the least to search them.

He shouted back, "All those go to Highway 89?"

"Most of them," she shouted. "The others are dead ends."

"If you're trying to hide, are you going to go south on the main road into Arizona?"

The sheriff thought a moment.

"No," she said.

"Where?"

"Cannonville," she said.

"How far?"

"Thirty or so miles as the crow flies."

"How long does it take to get from the ranch to Cannonville?"

"An hour and a half if they don't run into trouble. Two or more if they do."

They couldn't search all the area they needed to. They could go north or south, but not both. "What do you think?" he asked.

"I think we're wasting our time down here," she said and banked the trike north.

They traveled that way for another fifteen minutes, flying over a number of wilderness roads, pale lines of dirt winding through desert canyons. They flew over and past ravines and washes and narrow slot canyons. The rock was orange and white and gray and brown. He saw some deer, cattle, a line of hikers with walking sticks. And during all of this he decided to consolidate the ammo. Each magazine could hold thirty rounds, but there weren't thirty rounds between them. He ended up with twenty-three rounds total all loaded in the first magazine. Twenty-three wasn't ninety, but it was a heck of a lot better than rocks and ball bearings, although it would be awesome to drop a can of beans or a toilet lid onto Bill from this height. He snicked the loaded magazine into his rifle and slipped the empty two in the little fly bag under the sheriff's seat

They continued to fly toward the big clouds still miles away, white on top, and dark blue and purple below. He pointed and shouted, "Our flash flood."

"Probably," she said.

The sheriff tapped him on the shoulder. "Ten o'clock."

Frank looked in that direction and saw a road running in a northerly direction. "That's the main route," she shouted.

"To Cannonville?" Frank asked.

"Roger," she said.

Beyond it in one direction were spectacular pink and orange cliffs. In the other were the massive storm clouds.

They flew a little farther, and then the sheriff turned and began to track the main route, which was really nothing more than a dirt road winding through the desert wilderness. Frank spotted vultures circling below him and off to the right and wondered what they had noticed on the ground. After the vultures, he spotted an Isuzu parked off to the side of the road, the car as small as an ant. Its occupants had found a nice spot under a pine not far from the road to lay out a cloth and stop for a snack.

He continued to scan for dust plumes. He saw a trio of ATVs with older, heavyset folks on them on some narrow trail. He saw more canyons. More juniper. More sage. More bare rock. More washes. And he began to worry they'd made the wrong decision to go north. Or they'd just been too slow.

They continued on, the big fan at their backs whining like the big brother to a weed eater. Frank watched the snaking road, the feeling that they'd gone the wrong way knotting in his gut.

Suddenly, a blast of cooler air hit the trike. It caught the glider and pulled them up and off course. And then a crosswind blasted past them, turning the trike and making them sway.

The motor whined higher, then lower. The sheriff tried to bring them round again, but the wind was fighting her, dragging them off course. And Frank realized the closer they got to that big dark storm system, the more unpredictable the winds would be.

Another cold gust blasted into them, dragging them out into the wilderness.

The sheriff shouted, "These aren't the best winds."

"You think?"

"We'll go lower," she said, then spiraled the trike down a few hundred feet. The air was cold, then suddenly warm. The wind wasn't as strong, but they were still fighting partway against it, which meant they weren't going to be able to go as fast.

He said, "Are you sure about Cannonville?"

"I'm sure about nothing," she said.

They flew over a hill. The road below them wound up, then down the other side. At the bottom of the hill the road led to a creek, flowing with muddy rushing water. Just up from the water's edge on the side of the road was parked a large brown sedan. A '90s brown Lincoln to be exact.

Frank's hopes rose.

The sheriff said, "Looks like that storm hit more than one drainage basin."

And Frank's hopes rose even more because that probably meant they had been forced to stop here and wait until the flow had dropped.

Frank scanned the area. There was no sign of the pickup. No sign of anyone around, but he'd learned it was better to be safe than sorry.

He brought his rifle up

The interior of the Lincoln was dark. There were dark shadows under cedars. Shadows in the folds of the ravines. Plenty of places for people to hide. Except they wouldn't be hiding. He wouldn't. They were either sitting in the Lincoln, hoping the river dropped enough for them to drive over. Or they'd abandoned it.

He said, "Go lower. I want to see inside."

The sheriff spiraled them down a few hundred feet, and Frank got a good look inside. It was empty.

"The creek must have been too full for the car to cross," he shouted. Which meant whoever and whatever they'd been transporting in the Lincoln had probably been transferred to the pickup.

And indeed, at this height, he could see wet truck tracks coming up out of the far side of the creek. Water dried up pretty quickly in these parts, which meant they couldn't be too far ahead.

"We're close," he shouted.

"Roger," she said.

They continued north, tracking the road. There were more hills, more cedars, more stretches of dirt, more wind. And then a white pickup, climbing the dirt road up a hill and out of the juniper. It had a shell and three people up front in the cab.

"One o'clock!" Frank shouted.

"Thank you, Lord," she said. "Are you ready?"

"I want to come at them head on," he said. A straight shot right into the cab. "Can you get in front of them?"

"I'll put you right on their hood," she said, then angled them down and gave the little trike full throttle. They yawed and pitched in the wind and dropped at an angle toward the pickup.

Bill was driving. The wild woman was in the cab with him along with a man Frank hadn't seen. They were all looking up, watching the trike pass by. The road wound down the other side of the hill, crossed over another creek, then ran straight for a bit along a section with lots of rock and a few junipers.

Frank pointed at the straight section. "That's the stretch," he shouted. "Get to the end of that. When they enter, you drop down, and fly right at them."

"Roger," she said and flew over the creek.

Behind them the pickup crested the hill. Then it stopped. The doors flew open, and Bill and the new man from the cab hopped out and ran to the back. They lifted the back window of the camper shell and lowered the gate on the pickup. Then they reached in and hauled out the massive five-foot drone Frank had seen in the garage and set it on the ground.

They were going to send it up to attack, and Frank wanted no part of that. Frank wanted to take that threat out before it got airborne.

"Turn around!" he shouted.

"Now?"

"Turn now!" he said and pointed. "They're taking out King Kong!"

The sheriff banked, fighting and sliding against the wind.

On the ground, the man fiddled with something on the big drone, then its motor started and blasted a circle of dust off the dirt road. The man reached into the bed of the pickup, grabbed his controls, and stepped away.

The trike turned. Frank prepared to shoot.

Then the drone's engine revved. Another larger puff of road dust flew up, and the drone shot into the sky.

"No!" Frank shouted.

The droned climbed to fifty feet, then seventy-five. High enough for Frank to see something long and black underneath it.

He squinted against the wind, then swore.

"What?"

"It's got weaponry," he said.

She looked over. "What is that?"

"I'm thinking an AR-15. And that's a high-capacity magazine. Probably a hundred rounds." The rifle and loaded magazine probably added another eleven or twelve pounds, but that was nothing for a drone the size of King Kong.

"God help us."

"God's going to have to do some fancy shooting," said Frank. "Because I think that other black thing on top is a camera, which probably means object tracking."

"Of course it is," she said. "Moron Germans!" And turned the trike.

36

King Kong

FRANK HAD TWO TARGETS—the drone and the operator. The drone was shooting up to their altitude. But the operator with his moron German killer drone gear was just standing there. The choice between the two was a no-brainer.

Frank wanted as stable a platform as possible, so he pressed both feet solidly against the footrest bar sticking out in front of the trike and wedged his rear into the seat. Then he spread his knees, rested his elbows on the soft part on the inside, and snugged the butt of the rifle into his shoulder. He looked down the sights and moved the barrel until he found the operator. Or tried. The trike was still moving from the turn, still slewing from the wind. And the guy was a hundred yards off. This was not what you would call a steady platform.

"Can you hold it straight?" Frank asked.

"Trying," the sheriff said, evening the trike out. The drone rose toward them. Frank ignored it, calmed himself, slowed his breath, relaxed.

The sights moved on and off the operator. Back on, back off. Frank adjusted, got them back on. Kept them. Wished he was lying prone on a rock somewhere high.

He squeezed the trigger. The rifle banged and bucked.

A moment later, a puff of dust kicked up just past the operator. He flinched, then dodged to the side and ran like a weenie to get behind the pickup, but he would have had to almost go under the pickup for Frank not to see him.

Frank got him in the sight again. Squeezed the trigger. The rifle banged and kicked just as they caught another bit of the wind.

A moment later, the dirt puffed up about six yards to the left of the guy. Another miss. And Frank now had twenty-one rounds.

The drone operator realized his mistake and ran with his tablet and game controller to take cover under a dense cluster of cedar.

"Take us forty yards, five o'clock," Frank said. That ought to give him a good view of the guy's position.

The sheriff gave the paramotor gas, and the little trike battled against the wind.

Then Bill and the Wild Woman got out of the truck with weapons of their own.

"Almost there," Frank said.

The operator's shoe came into view, sticking out from under the cedar. But Frank wasn't going to take pot shots at a foot. He wanted a big target. He wanted center mass.

"Lower," Frank said.

"You're kind of demanding," she said, and let off the throttle.

The drone was almost to their height, but it wasn't the drone that fired. It was Bill and the Wild Woman. The whisper of the bullets came first, and then the bangs from below. And Frank knew he could no longer wait.

The operator's knees came into view, and Frank took the shot, crappy as it was.

The ground puffed up behind the operator. Frank had missed by less than a foot. He adjusted his aim, but the operator moved back out of sight.

More shots cracked up from the truck. A bullet ripped a hole through the glider.

Frank swung his rifle over, aimed down at Bill, who was standing behind the open door, and fired.

The bullet struck the door in front of Bill with a nice clang, and Bill ducked down.

Frank swung the rifle and shot at the Wild Woman. He hit the glass in the window of the door she was hiding behind. The window burst, and she ducked into the cab.

"The drone!" the sheriff shouted.

Frank looked up. It had risen level with them, about a hundred yards away.

Frank swung his rifle back to the clump of cedar where the operator was hiding. He had nineteen rounds left. Plenty to take out the geek on the ground. He just needed a target.

Then he saw an elbow.

Frank guessed where the center mass of the operator was. It was a long shot with the bushy part of a cedar in the way, but he was out of options. He fired.

Fired again, and was down to seventeen rounds.

And then the drone rotated, pointing its rifle at them.

"Crap!" the sheriff said and gave the motor full throttle. The engine whined, the trike banked.

And the muzzle of the drone's rifle flashed and banged, a quick bap-bap-bap. They had obviously figured a way to convert it to full auto.

The rounds cracked around them. One sped past. Another hit a cord attaching the glider to the trike. It broke with a loud ping. The third slug clanked somewhere on the paramotor itself.

"Hells bells," Frank muttered, wanting to shoot, but they were banking, and he had no kind of platform to do anything but waste ammo.

The sheriff yanked one side of the glider, and the trike whipped around in the sky like a weight at the end of a string.

The drone had some spring mechanism to dampen the rifle's recoil, but each shot still caused the drone's front to rise just a little. The drone adjusted back down, then let out another burst of bap-bap-bap.

The bullets approached like angry insects. One pinged off the frame of the trike, another took out the wheel just under Frank's legs. Another flew right in front of Frank's face, so close to his nose that he felt the concussion of air like someone had slapped him, so close that every follicle on his head and down his back stood on end.

"He's dialing it in," Frank said and knew there was no way they were going to be able to compete with that thing in their Y-frame go-kart.

Another burst exploded from the drone's muzzle. Followed by a second.

"Hold on!" the sheriff said and slewed them left, then right, then right again.

Two bullets cracked past. Another hit the trike frame. Another nailed Frank in the foot, delivering a white hot burst of pain. Behind him, the sheriff cried out.

The trike swung left, high on its side.

Another burst flashed from the drone.

The trike continued to swing higher, as if the sheriff were doing some kind of barrel roll.

Bullets tore through the skull and crossbones fabric of the glider.

And then they were no longer gliding. They were upside down, and then they were spiraling, the paramotor still running full out, glider and trike spinning round each other, corkscrewing like mad toward the ground.

Frank lost his footing. His legs flew wide, and he grabbed onto the handles of his flying seat cushion. The rifle spun out of his hands, and he couldn't tell if it had broken his electrical tape safety cord or not.

They dropped like a spinning propeller, the ground rushing up at them. The fly-by-night amusement park ride had just become a horror. And Frank saw his spinning doom at the bottom of a jagged rocky canyon which he figured they'd smash into at more than a hundred miles per hour, which was a swell speed for cracking spines, breaking skulls, and jarring organs to literal death.

He shouted, tried to look back, thinking if he could get the controls from the sheriff, who surely was dying as they fell, he might be able to even the trike out. But looking back only put him off balance. He lost his grip on one of the sides of his seat, spun sideways, and flailed with his arm and legs like some bull rider about to meet his death at the rodeo.

They dropped down below a rocky ridge, death rushing up at them. He thought of Kim and Tony waiting in Los Angeles. He thought of all his plans. His new future. His life outside of the cement box. He thought about the faces of the innocent moms and dads and children this Fourth of July.

Dammit! He thought.

And then the glider caught air. The spin slowed. The trike swung out in a wide circle, almost clanging against a rock face. It rocked the other way, then back again, and then they were flying straight, threading between the slopes, the paramotor pushing them along.

Relief rushed through him.

"Get on your seat!" the sheriff shouted.

"You're not dead?"

"You're throwing off the balance. Get on your seat!"

Frank looked back.

"Your seat!" she commanded.

She was most definitely not dead.

Frank was sideways, just about to fall out of his seat belt, his legs hanging off one side, his chest and head the other. He grabbed both seat handles, righted himself, and found his rifle was still dangling at the end of his electrical tape safety cord. He got his feet back on the lousy foot rest, realizing that his injured foot was burning like a red hot poker, and hauled his weapon back up.

"What happened?" he asked.

"Controlled descent," she said. "There was no way we were going to out-fly that gun."

"You didn't faint?"

"Fainting is not on the plan," she said. "We were sitting ducks up there."

"I've done controlled descent before," he said. "That was not controlled descent."

"Did we descend? Did I have it in control?"

"You could have said something," he said.

"I'll buy you a new pair of shorts when we get out of here."

"My shorts are just fine," he said.

"You sure?"

"Where did you learn how to do that?"

"We can do the life history later," she said, "because I don't think that drone is going to stay put."

They were down below a ridge now, out of sight. But the operator would soon fly the drone over, and that would be the end of it. And they couldn't out-race the drone. They were much too slow; it was much too fast. If they were a few miles away from the operator, maybe they might have a chance of flying out of his range. But range wasn't a problem here.

The sheriff groaned. "You got any more tape?"

Frank turned and saw her leg. She'd been shot on the inside. The blood was soaking through. He suspected it was a good hit, which meant she could go into shock or faint at any moment, regardless of whether it was on the plan or not.

He said, "I don't have any more tape. But you've got my nasty do-rag. Hand it to me."

She realized he was talking about his head mask and pulled it off and held it out to him.

He took it, yanked it out to one piece of cloth again, then folded it length-wise and wrapped it around her wounded leg and tied it tight. Nothing sanitary about it, but it did provide direct pressure.

She said, "What are we going to do?"

"Two against one. That is what we're going to do. We've got an outstanding record at two against one."

"How are we going to do that?"

He looked around at the slopes. They were steep. Some parts sheer. But he knew that he and the sheriff had to separate.

He said, "You see that bit of slope up there with that lone bent pine? You're going to swing over and let me jump off."

"Then what?"

He thought about this canyon, thought about the position of the drone and operator. He did not want the drone flying over and getting above her.

He said, "You're going to flip up and turn around. Expose yourself. Let the operator know you're coming back the same way. Make him think you're trying to be sneaky. He'll expect you to appear where the ridge falls away."

"And?" she said over the motor.

"And while the drone is watching you, I shoot it out of the sky."

And if he didn't, the drone would shoot her to pieces. Then come looking for him.

"That's the plan?"

"You got anything better?"

"I think I liked the toilet lid plan better."

"Me too." Frank knew it wasn't much of a plan, but was else was there? If they landed and tried to run, the drone would see them. The operator would select them with his visual object tracking, and that would be that. They could turn around and try to shoot it out, but the drone would be a moving object at 900 feet or higher. An impossible shot with bullets raining down on them.

"Get me close," he said.

"You'd better pick up your aim," she said.

"Just don't get shot before I get into position."

"I'll be sure to pass that up the chain of command," she said, then let off the throttle and moved them over close to the slope. They glided, the motor idling.

Frank undid his seat belt.

They approached the slope with the small lone pine.

Frank tried to stand, but the blasted trike was too wiggly, and his foot was still on fire, and he quickly sat back down before he fell off.

They passed the pine.

"We're running out of slope," she said.

How the heck was he going to get off this thing? He couldn't leap. He couldn't roll.

He rose up part of the way, holding onto the handle next to the seat, and braced himself with his good foot on the crap foot rest. Then he slung his arm through the rifle strap and pulled it up on his back.

"We haven't got any more time, Romeo," she said. "I'm going to give you a swing, and you're going to have to make it work."

Frank imagined leaping out of a swing as a kid at school. "I think that will work nicely," he said.

She slowed even further, swung the trike away from the slope, then swung back toward it.

At the apex of the swing, Frank launched himself from his cockeyed sideways crouch. He flew from the trike, a nice little arc with a ten mile per hour forward momentum, then crashed into the hill. He bounced and rolled across the steep face, and then a tough sagebrush caught him, and he latched onto it. He gave her the thumbs up.

She gave him one back, turned and faced forward in her seat, and gave the motor full throttle. The motor whined. The trike picked up speed, and she climbed, and when she was a little from the top, she executed a turn that swung the trike up high and back down again. A little hide and peek. A little pirate bait.

Frank began to scramble up the slope, his injured foot yelling the whole way.

The sheriff buzzed by behind him, and he told himself to ignore his freaking foot because that woman was going home to her kid tonight. And Bill's gang of morons were either going into the ground or to the CIA.

He grabbed a rock, a cluster of green rabbit brush, another rock. The slope grew steeper, and he just scrabbled and clawed harder. He had to be in position before she exposed herself. Or, if the drone operator had decided not to wait, before King Kong reached an angle where the operator could see the pirate glider working its way back along the canyon.

He passed a little bunch of prickly pear, continued to climb, rocks and dirt sliding down behind him.

The whine of the trike moved down the canyon.

Frank paused next to an outcropping of rock and scanned the sky for King Kong. He didn't see anything, so he continued to climb. When he reached a spot a dozen feet below the crest of the ridge, he finally spotted the thing, a dark rectangle against the big sky.

King Kong was moving, not staying stationary, as he'd hoped. It was maybe 1,200 feet up, which was 400 yards, which was four football fields, which wasn't a super long shot when you were lying down, but shooting up was another matter.

The drone was sliding across the sky to let the operator see down this side of the ridge. And it was going to see the sheriff before she got to her gap.

Frank looked around. He needed something to brace the barrel of the rifle on. He spotted a jut of rock almost at the top, up where he would be exposed, but there was no way he was going to make the shot down here, holding the rifle up and breathing hard.

He scrambled up to the rock. The little valley on the other side came into view along with the road and the pickup and Bill and the Wild Woman, who were watching the drone. Farther back was the clump of cedars where the weenie operator had taken cover.

There was no cover on this ridge, and the human silhouette was one of the strongest patterns that drew the human eye, which meant that if any of them looked this way, they'd probably see him straight out.

He braced his rifle on the rock, found the drone, then got it in his sights. It was hovering now, sounding like a weed whacker.

Farther along the canyon, heading towards trouble, was the sheriff and the paramotor's throatier whine.

The drone suddenly rotated, dipped its front end. And Frank figured the operator must have just spotted the sheriff, which meant he was right now clicking, locking in the visual object tracking, preparing to let loose with what was essentially a machine gun.

Frank relaxed, blew out, made an adjustment for the distance, aiming to the right of the drone to compensate for the windage.

And then Frank squeezed the trigger.

37

Flier

THE RIFLE in Frank's hands kicked and banged.

Up in the sky, nothing happened. The drone moved not an inch.

He'd missed, and was now down to sixteen rounds.

He made another adjustment farther right. Squeezed. Another kick and bang.

Nothing. Sixteen rounds.

And then the drone opened up, its muzzle flashing.

The sheriff suddenly swung up out of the canyon, her motor rising in pitch. She banked wildly in one direction, then the other, but she was too slow, even without Frank's weight.

The drone tracked her with fire, bullets ripping into the fabric of the trike and sending sparks flying from the cage surrounding the paramotor and puffs of dust and rock from the slope behind. The shots moved higher, slicing a few more strings and then tore through the black glider above.

King Kong's nose was now pointing too high. The firing stopped. The drone angled back down.

Smoke began to pour out of the motor.

Frank breathed out. Adjusted left this time.

The drone locked onto the sheriff again.

Frank squeezed. The rifle banged and flashed. A moment later, two chunks of plastic on the left end of the drone blew away. Definitely part of the housing, maybe part of one of the rotors.

The drone dipped. Lost altitude. Its three remaining motors whined erratically, trying to balance it back out and maintain the tracking.

Frank took another breath, tried to get the drone in his sights again, but it was moving in unpredictable directions.

"Hold still," he said.

Bill and the Wild Woman began shouting over by the pickup.

A moment later a bullet cracked past over Frank's head, followed by the report of a rifle.

Frank ignored it, thought he saw a pattern in King Kong's movements.

Then another shot rang out, followed by a burst. Bullets zinged past, struck the dirt on the hill in front of him.

Up in the sky, the drone's motors and computer brain finally figured it out, and the craft stabilized with a little tilt.

"Thank you," Frank said and adjusted his aim.

Another burst of shots rang out from the direction of Bill and the woman. The bullets were closer this time. One slammed into the rock in front of Frank with a loud smack. A shard of rock struck Frank violently in the cheek, slicing open the skin.

He flinched, lost the drone in the sight.

The drone opened up again on the sheriff, the muzzle flashing, the report a terrible tat-tat-tat.

She swung the craft wildly to the left.

Bullets pinged off the little Y-frame and sent puffs of dirt and rock up from the slope below her.

The paramotor shuddered, poured out a larger plume of black smoke, then cut out.

She swung back again, the drone tracking her, the muzzle flashing, the bullets cutting into the fabric of the trike. And then the trike itself broke mostly away from the sheriff and glider to hang down, all shot to pieces. It snagged on an outcropping of rock, violently jerking the glider around.

The sheriff was limp, one arm hanging down, the glider essentially pilotless. Then the ragged trike broke free of the rock, but the sheriff didn't correct, and she and the glider dropped behind the ridge in a flutter of black silk.

Frank's heart stopped.

No.

No, no, no!

He listened for the motor to start back up, but it was silent. In his mind's eye, he saw her crash on the bottom of the canyon, the glider shot to pieces, the motor leaking gasoline from a number of holes, and her bleeding out in a dozen places. Grief and anger welled up in him.

He'd sent her right into the mouth of danger. And he'd failed her. Failed her kid.

"Damn them!" he thought. "Damn them to hell!"

The drone rotated, pointing its rifle at Frank.

Frank yelled in rage and opened up on it. Seven pulls, seven bangs, seven misses.

And then it was the drone's turn. The muzzle flashed. The bullets cracked. And Frank ducked down behind his rock.

All around him the bullets pinged and smacked, sending up puffs of dust, throwing up shards of rock and grit.

He'd just wasted seven rounds. He needed to get himself together.

The drone stopped, probably to right itself after all those shots, but Bill and the Wild Woman started up, their rifles cracking by the road.

A bullet struck the dirt a few feet away and whinged past. Another missed him by inches.

Frank realized he was presenting a great target and scooted down and behind the rock, but he couldn't completely hide from Bill and the woman because it would expose him to the drone.

He thought about the sheriff again and felt a new wave of grief and rage course through him. And then the drone started firing again. The bullets slammed into the dirt and rock all around him. More shards flew. They were joined by the shards and grit from the lead Bill and the Wild Woman were sending his way.

He looked around, desperate for something else to hide him. But there wasn't any other cover close enough for him to run to, not with his injured foot. He could try to run back down the slope, taking him out of view from Bill and the woman, but the slope was so steep he'd have to try sliding down it, except he'd probably lose control and start rolling. And even if he made it to the bottom, there was hardly any cover down there, which meant the drone would just pin him after his tumble.

A bullet cracked into the dirt close to him, sending some piece of grit straight into his eye. He flinched, bringing his arm up, and was rewarded with some piece of flying lead or rock grazing his arm.

He blinked, blinked again, trying to clear his eye. An excellent scope was required to zero in on a target from a long distance. The drone would need that and high-quality software, and maybe it didn't have quite the quality it needed for its current distance to hit the small target he presented. But the drone was now approaching, and Frank suspected the drone's software was going to do just fine when it got within seventy-five yards, especially when it got the angle and had his whole body in its camera. He could wait until it ran out of ammo, but he didn't think it had expended even fifty rounds yet.

He knew Bill and the woman were probably also each moving to get a better angle. All of which meant he had only seconds before his cover was gone, and he'd be hanged if he was going to go out of this life quailing behind some rock.

He steeled himself. Prepared to stand, take aim, and start firing.

And then he heard the sound of a lawn mower, except it wasn't a mower. Was it another drone?

No, it sounded like—but there was no way. He'd seen her fall. Seen her and the trike shot to ribbons.

But there was no mistaking the sound. He peeked around the rock. A moment later, the pirate glider suddenly rose up from behind the ridge, well beyond the drone, closer to the other end of the little valley where the road ran down from the hill.

The glider's fabric had holes and tears in it, ragged bits of fabric hanging down. A number of the cords were cut and flapped like broken kite strings. The Y-frame trike was gone. It was just the sheriff in her harness with the smoking paramotor roaring on her back with a slight whistle, which probably meant a bullet had punched a hole through one of the propellers. But despite all the damage, there was enough glider to fly, and enough power to propel her into the sky.

Frank's heart soared.

That woman was iron! Freaking iron. She must have cut the motor on purpose, must have faked the fall.

She whipped up over the top of the ridge, clearing it by only a few feet, banked sharply, then zoomed, full throttle, for the road. Zoomed for the operator, the dark smoke pouring out behind her.

Two against one.

The drone hesitated, then rotated to target the threat, and Frank saw his chance.

He rose up and laid the barrel of the rifle on the rock in front of him.

Shots cracked from Bill and the Wild Woman. A bullet smacked into the dirt beside him. Grit struck him in the hand.

Frank blew out, breathed in, got the drone in his sights. Dropped his aim to adjust for the high angle.

Another shot rang out from the road and slammed into the dirt inches away.

He breathed out slowly, held his aim, felt the small surge flow up his back, along his arm, and into his finger. He squeezed.

The rifle kicked.

He brought the rifle back on target. Squeezed again.

The first shot missed. The second nailed the drone, flipping it on end, which presented a nice fat picture. Frank had the drone in his sights. He squeezed a third time. A moment later the third bullet blew away a large, ragged chunk close to King Kong's middle.

The drone shuddered. The gas-powered motors whined, flipping and rotating the vehicle, and then the motor chugged once, twice, and then cut out altogether.

King Kong hung for a moment in the air, and then one side dipped, and the drone began to fall, sliding out of the sky, the weight of its motor and rifle and remaining ammo pulling it down.

Frank watched it fall, then crash onto some rocks toward the bottom of the ridge. It bounced and flipped, gasoline flying in a little arc, and landed on its back, rifle up. A second later, the gas caught fire.

Across the valley, the sheriff came to the road on the hill, banked and sped down it, flying no more than three feet off the ground.

The operator moved out of his trees, gun in hand.

Frank swung his rifle that way. He was down to five rounds and knew he needed to make them count.

The operator stopped in front of the trees and raised his weapon.

Frank didn't know what the sheriff was thinking. Maybe she still had her semiautomatic. Maybe she was simply planning on landing and shooting, but she'd have to land first, and that would give the operator plenty of time to take aim.

What Frank did know was that he had a clear line of sight on the man who was probably around 350 yards away. Frank got the operator in his sights, made his adjustment, fired.

He saw the puff of the first bullet as it slammed into the dirt to the side of the man.

Frank adjusted and fired again.

The man turned, and the second bullet hit him in the torso, and he arched his back and twisted in pain.

Frank was going to fire again, but the sheriff was closing in on the operator.

The man hunched, holding his wound, then looked up at her. He began to raise his weapon, but he was too late. The sheriff bore down on him at full throttle, and as he tried to straighten to shoot her, she kicked him in the face with her boot.

The man flew back, his arms wheeling, and slammed into the ground. The sheriff blew past, pulling up to avoid the cedar trees.

Frank took aim, but the operator wasn't moving, and Frank figured the kick had probably broken the guy's neck.

By the pickup, a rifle cracked. The shot zinged past Frank. Then Frank heard the pickup start.

He turned and saw Bill already behind the wheel. The Wild Woman jumped into the passenger's side and slammed her door shut. Bill put it in gear and floored it. The truck's engine roared, and the pickup peeled out on the dirt road.

Frank got the front windshield in his sights, led it. Fired.

He heard the pop as the bullet hit the metal.

He led it a bit more. Fired.

Missed.

Adjusted. Fired the third time.

The headlamp blew out with a crunch, doing nothing to stop the pickup.

Frank squeezed the trigger again, but the weapon clicked. He was out of ammo, and Bill was getting away. But maybe the shot to the headlamp had hit something. Maybe a belt would suddenly give way. And Frank wanted to be there if it did.

The road ran in the shape of a horseshoe through the valley. Maybe he could get them on this end. He rose and began to run down the slope, his foot burning with every step. But it didn't take a rocket scientist to know he and the sheriff had lost. The pickup was moving along just fine. And at his lame speed there was no way he was going to be able to get close enough to the road to even huck a rock at them as they sped past.

But he continued down the slope anyway, cursing, knowing it was fruitless.

And then the sheriff flew across the tops of the ponderosas and sage, her paramotor smoking, taking a straight route across the valley while the pickup had to follow the horseshoe. She executed a banking turn that brought her down and around to the end of this part of the shoe.

At the other end, the pickup came around the bend and straightened out.

She'd been flying with the wind, now it was blowing across her, and she had to turn the glider partially into it to move down the road, but move down the road she did, heading right for the truck, and Frank realized she was going to kamikaze herself into it.

Her 140 pounds plus the sixty pounds of the paramotor, all going forty miles per hour and striking Bill and the pickup going sixty the other way. 200 pounds versus 5,000 at a hundred miles per hour. Not really a contest. Not one that any flier was going to walk away from. Not even Sheriff Hood.

Frank doubled his limping speed.

38

Bird of Prey

THE TRUCK AND THE SHERIFF flew at each other.

And then the sheriff took both of the glider controls in one hand. With the other she pulled out the Glock and pointed it at the truck.

She fired as she flew. Five loud cracks, the gun jerking in her hand.

Chrome exploded. The hood pinged. And then the windshield shattered.

Bill swerved.

The sheriff pulled the trigger again, but she was out of bullets, and she tossed the gun and took the controls in two hands.

Bill careened back the other way, right into her path. He was going to hit her.

She put on the throttle, pulled the sides of the glider in, and swung up.

Bill and the Wild Woman barreled at sixty miles per hour just underneath her feet, dust billowing up behind them. Then the pickup drifted the other way, to the right side of the road, to the part that sloped steeply down into the sage meadow. And then the passenger's front tire went off the shoulder.

Bill tried to correct. He was good. He was doing it slowly, keeping it in control. No over-reacting. The truck slewed only a bit, and Frank figured he would make it back up onto the road.

But a big, half-buried rock had different ideas. The passenger's side tire hit it at speed, and it launched the front of the truck up, almost vertical, high enough to see the pipes and undercarriage. And then the pickup turned, like it was doing a slow pirouette, except it didn't make the full 360 degrees. It made maybe ninety-five, then tumbled onto its back on the slope.

The camper shell on the back cracked with a large crash. The top of the cab crunched. And then the pickup flipped, plastic and glass flying, and its back end came up and over, like a domino tumbling lengthwise. It landed, bounced again, and this time it hit the side. Air bags deployed. It rolled, rolled again. The camper shell flew off. The contents went flying. And, in a cloud of dust, the truck slammed down on all four tires in the desert brush of the meadow, wobbled, and stood still.

The cab was smashed. Two tires were flat. One was buckled underneath the truck. The shell was lying on its back a number of yards away. Drones, and canisters, and boxes littered the field.

Lady Al Qaeda, the Wild Woman, was somewhere below the dashboard and her deflating airbag. Bill was sitting upright in his seat belt and was apparently only a bit dazed because he moved his mushy airbag aside, then reached down to his side and undid his belt buckle. He tried the side door, but it was smashed and would need some heavy bending to open it. So he climbed out the front of the cab where the windshield used to be with a rifle, slid across the dented hood, and fell to the ground. He rose a moment later, a bit unsteady and surveyed the scene. Then he turned and began to lumber away.

Frank continued to hustle down the slope, his foot jolting in pain with each step. Bill was looking around, acting a bit disoriented. And then he saw Frank.

Frank limp-ran to the bottom of the slope, hoping Bill was still too shaken to take a good aim.

Bill raised his rifle.

Frank continued his gimpy charge, using his rifle like a cane, and then a large shadow moved across the meadow toward Bill.

Frank looked up. The sheriff was maybe fifty feet up, gliding without the aid of the paramotor which must have finally cut out. The wind was against her, and she soared like a bird of prey.

The shadow passed over Bill. He looked up, saw her.

And then the sheriff pulled in her wings and dove at him.

Bill raised his rifle, but the sheriff had had the sense to come at him with the sun at her back. He aimed, but even Frank could see that Bill's aim was off. He fired. The rifle boomed and kicked. He fired again.

But the sheriff was moving too fast. She spread her black pirate wings at the last moment, swung around at speed, and kicked Bill in the chest with both feet.

The blow knocked Bill backward, slamming him onto the hard desert meadow of rock and grass and sending his rifle flying.

The sheriff landed in a hop shuffle on one leg, favoring the one that had been shot. Frank thought he saw other wounds as well, dark spots of blood. He thought she would stumble, but she stayed upright as the black glider fell behind her. She shucked her harness, then limped forward toward Bill who was trying to pick himself up.

Frank started into the rock and sage meadow, then caught movement out of the corner of his eye back by the pickup. Lady Al Qaeda was extracting herself from the cab, and Frank cursed the freaking air bags.

She crawled over the smashed hood and slid down to the ground. Her hair was askew. There was blood on her face. She saw the sheriff and drew a knife, a big one like the one Mrs. Clean used back at the house.

What was it with these jihadists and knives? Was it part of the training to always be prepared to saw someone's head off?

Lady Al Qaeda stumbled, then began to run toward the sheriff, her one big braid down her back swinging to and fro. She was fast, as fast as she'd been the first day he'd seen her, running the man in the tarp down.

"Behind you!" Frank called. Frank was now well into the sage and rock meadow doing his awkward heel run, using his rifle as a support, his foot protesting every moment. "Behind you!"

But the sheriff didn't hear him.

Instead, she picked up a stick, limped over to Bill who was still struggling up, raised it high, and then swung with all her might, hitting him in the head.

Bill fell to one side. The stick, which wasn't big to begin with, broke, leaving her just a stump.

Frank sprint-limped toward them, closing the distance, but he knew he couldn't reach her in time. "Behind you!" he yelled, then tossed his rifle to run faster.

The sheriff finally heard and looked over at him.

"Behind you!" he shouted again and pointed.

The sheriff turned, all gimpy and unstable on her one leg and saw the woman charging, full of wrath.

There was no time for the sheriff to run. She wouldn't have been able to anyway. She threw the stump of her stick at the woman, bared her own teeth in anger, and took a step forward.

The woman raised her arm and deflected the stick, then threw herself at the sheriff.

The sheriff tried to side-step her, but she wasn't quick or stable enough to execute the maneuver, and the woman plowed into her, slamming her to the ground.

They tussled. The sheriff tried to scramble away, but the woman grabbed the sheriff's mud-dried hair and yanked her head back, forcing her to expose her neck.

Frank was maybe ten yards away.

The woman raised her knife high.

Frank roared. A primal war cry.

The woman looked up and saw him, hate written across her face. Then she turned back to the sheriff and stabbed down.

Frank launched himself at the woman, hitting her solidly. If she'd been standing, he would have pancaked her into oblivion. As it was, he ripped her off the sheriff and bore her to the ground with all of his weight.

She growled, tried to scramble free.

Frank grabbed her knife hand, wrenched it up, then slammed it on a rock. He slammed it again, and again, and again, breaking bone. The knife flew free.

The woman tried to stab him in the eyes with her free fingers, but Frank knocked the arm away, then uppercut her chin with his elbow.

Her head flew back, and she went limp.

Frank struck her again, then realized she was unconscious.

"Frank!" the sheriff shouted.

He turned back to the sheriff and saw that her neck was dirty, beautiful, and whole. Relief rushed through him.

"Bill!" she said.

Frank looked beyond her and saw Bill crawling for his rifle. Frank scrambled to his feet and did his funky limp run, racing Bill to the weapon.

Bill reached out for it, but Frank was faster. He kicked the weapon away from Bill, then snatched it up.

Bill yelled in anger and frustration. "May God slay you, ant kalab, ant khanzeer" You dog, you pig. Then he rose and surged at Frank.

Frank grabbed the rifle two-handed and lunged, striking Bill in the gut with the butt of the weapon.

Bill doubled over and cried out in pain.

Frank hit him again in the back, knocking him to the ground.

Bill looked up at him, anger and pain on his face, and let loose with a string of Arabic Frank could not understand but knew was directed at him.

"Bill," Frank said. "You might as well call me an avocado. If you want to insult me, do it in English, you son of a shoe."

Bill snarled.

Frank said, "We've got Zeke. And now we have you and Lady Al Qaeda. And you're all going to sing."

"You have won nothing," Bill spat.

"We've won enough to stop you," Frank said.

"You'll never stop us because we love death more than you love life."

"What is that—Muslim Brotherhood crap? Do you know how stupid that sounds, Bill? I mean, really. Think about it."

The sheriff groaned.

Frank said, "How you doing?"

She said, "Tie them up."

And Frank saw she wasn't doing well at all. There was blood on her shirt. Blood on her arm. Blood on her face. But he needed to secure the area before he tended to her, so he appropriated Lady Al Qaeda's knife, which was actually a decent piece of equipment, cut cords from the glider, then lashed Bill's wrists behind his back. He went over to the woman and did the same. She came to while he was tying her up and tried to struggle free, but parachute cord is tough stuff.

He turned to the sheriff. "Maybe we can patch up that gas tank, and you can fly out of here."

"I don't know," she said.

He walked over to her and assessed her wounds. She was shot in the leg from before. Shot in the side. She was bleeding, scraped, and dinged. He cut off one of the pieces of the glider that was hanging loose and tied it around her like a sash over the new bullet wound.

He said, "You're going to be fine. If you can't fly out, I'll do it."

Bill got to his knees and moaned and sucked in his breath.

"I think you broke his ribs," Frank said.

"I sure hope so," she replied.

Frank handed her the rifle. "Watch them."

"They love death," she warned, meaning they'd probably welcome a bullet.

"Right," Frank said, which meant he needed something else. So he cut off another length of cord, walked over to the woman, and lashed her ankles. And knowing she could just fold her legs behind her and reach the knots with her hands, he dislocated each of her thumbs. She yelled and cursed him, and then he went over and did the same to Bill. When he finished, he went to look at the paramotor which had been shot in multiple places.

"It's out of gas," she said.

"Maybe we can patch it," he said, looking at the hole in the tank. He'd have to mend the gas line as well, which had been cut.

"What are you going to use as a siphon for the truck?" she asked.

"Don't need one. We've got a knife. I can poke a hole in the tank. We can catch it in our hands if we have to." Then he looked at the truck and sighed heavily. "That is we could have, but the truck is a diesel. And this runs on gasoline."

It looked like the sky pirate was out of business for today, which meant one of them was going to have to get back up on the road and hike for who knew how many miles, hoping someone was coming this way. She was in no shape to hike, and so it was going to be up to Frank.

He said, "I'll wrap my foot. Make a crutch."

She said, "You could light one of those ponderosas on fire. Someone will see the smoke."

"We can do both."

And then he noticed four or five spots around the pickup where thin trails of smoke were rising a number of feet from the meadow, then disappearing. The thin trails of disappearing smoke were blowing in Frank's and the sheriff's direction. Except they weren't smoke because nothing was on fire. And smoke didn't dissipate that way.

He sniffed. And there was no smell of any kind of smoke on the air.

Frank walked a few paces closer to investigate and saw the source of one of the disappearing wisps. Then he saw another, and another. Littering the ground were fat, stainless steel canisters painted red, white, and blue. Canisters with their lids off, and the white powder contents spilled onto the ground. White powder as light as air. Light enough for the breeze to pick it up like pollen. And he and the sheriff were right in the path.

Frank looked at the sheriff.

The most common way to weaponize anthrax was to turn it into an aerosol, something that would float in the air. Something you could dust a whole lot of people with. It started with a soup of spores that you fed and grew. When you had enough, you dried it. Then you milled the material that was left into small particles that would float in the air. Such particles were just a few micrometers across, so small they might contain a cluster of only three to five spores. Any smaller than that, and the particles would be exhaled out of the lungs. Any larger, and they might not reach the lower parts of the lungs, which was where you wanted them to lodge for maximum lethality.

There were a million micrometers in a meter. Frank couldn't tell how dense the air was with the particles. But even if it was just a fraction, he guessed that with each breath they'd been inhaling thousands of spores. Fifteen breaths per minute at rest. Forty in heavy activity like fighting terrorists and beating them with sticks.

Anthrax started killing in doses of 8,000 inhaled spores.

When had he hit that number? Ten breaths ago? Twenty? A hundred?

The spores activated in the presence of liquid. Incubation took one to seven days, but it wasn't the anthrax bacteria itself that killed, it was the toxins the bacteria produced. It was like having thousands of little poison factories inside your body, factories that multiplied. It started with a mild fever and a vague weakness and discomfort. That was followed by severe respiratory distress—labored breathing, wheezing, a bluish discoloration of the skin from the lack of oxygen. If you weren't treated, death followed twenty-four to thirty-six hours later in seventy-five to ninety percent of the cases. With aggressive, early treatment, the death rate fell to forty-five percent. About the odds of a flip of a coin.

Frank said, "We need to get up and out of this sage meadow. We need to get out of the dust."

39

Lycra

FRANK SAID, “Can you stand at all?”

She said, “I’m starting to get a little dizzy.”

He nodded, that would be from the blood loss. He said, “Raise one of your arms. I’m going to help you up.”

She raised an arm and cradled the rifle to her chest with the other. Frank squatted beside her, slipped an arm behind her back and the other under her legs, then rose.

With his limp, he carried her through the scrub, across the rock and dirt, up the short slope to the dirt road, and made sure she was upwind of the anthrax and set her down in front of a large, fine orange-red rock with a smooth flat side that she could use as a back brace. Then he went back down into the field because there was no way he wanted Bill or Lady Al Qaeda dying and taking their secrets to the grave.

He carried Lady Al Qaeda out next, his injured foot less happy about that load. Then hauled Bill.

The sheriff sat in front of the rock holding the rifle.

He said, “You going to be able to cover these two?”

“I want to say yes,” she said, grimacing from her pain. “But I’m pretty dizzy.”

Frank looked at their captives. “The cord will hold ‘em. Either way, somebody has got to get some help.”

“Isn’t your foot killing you?”

“It’s nothing,” he lied. The whole thing still burned like a red hot poker, one squishy with blood, and he knew if he stopped, he just might not get up again.

She said, "Maybe we should pray."

He said, "You're the praying type?"

She said, "Why not?"

"Indeed," he agreed.

Then Frank looked up. He did not see God or angels. What he did see were five people standing in a row on the top of the little hill next to the road. It was like in some of the old Western movies where the Indians show up on a ridge all spooky-like, except these were no kind of Indians. They were wearing black Lycra biking shorts and thin breathable shirts in neon green, orange, and white. And cycling helmets. One looked like he was eating a power bar.

Frank waved both arms to them and called out. "Hey!" he shouted and took a few steps toward them. "Hey!" he yelled again.

The wilderness bikers looked at each other, then one of them started hoofing it down the hill while the others disappeared over the back side. The other four reappeared a moment later on the road riding mountain bikes with saddle bags, one of the riders was leading the empty fifth bike along. But the guy who had run down the hill was already out on the road, loping Frank's way.

Frank limped out to meet them.

The lead guy slowed to a walk when he was still a number of yards out. He was in his twenties. He looked at Frank's face with his tattoos, then back at the sheriff and the rifle. He got a wary look in his eyes. He said, "We heard shots."

He was a short, little guy, with dark, sun-freckled arms and hard-cut legs that looked liked they'd seen thousands of miles on bikes. He was wearing a CamelBak with a water hose.

Frank said, "That's the Kane County sheriff. We have apprehended two people with awful intent. The sheriff's been shot. We have some injuries. We need to get some help."

The man's friends rode up to him and braked. There were two girls and two other guys. They were all young. All a bit granola. One of the women had armpit hair that would make man's primate jungle cousins proud.

One of the guys spoke up, "That's the sheriff?"

"And today I'm her citizen deputy," Frank said.

A couple of them stole glances at each other, looked nervous.

Frank had smelled them coming. There was sweat, and sunscreen, and something sweeter. He saw the power bar package sticking out of the one guy's shirt pocket, and it confirmed Frank's nose. That wasn't a power bar. Not the regular kind. This was a consumable with a kick. Probably from Colorado. He said, "Relax, guys. Nobody's going to bust you for bud infractions. Not when we've got two terrorists in custody."

"Dude," the short one in front said in alarm.

Frank said, "You guys didn't by chance rent a satellite phone, did you?"

"We did," the blond pot-eater in the back said. He turned and fetched a phone out of his saddle bag and held it out. "We ran into trouble on our last bike trip out here. Didn't want that to happen again."

Frank took it and said, "You need to keep upwind of the field. From here north is contaminated with a biological agent."

Their eyebrows rose.

"Like pesticides?" one of the girls asked.

"He means like bacteria," the broad one said.

"Oh," she said.

Frank held up the phone. "I'm going to take this to the sheriff. In the meantime, I need you to help me with something else."

Frank limped back to the sheriff and handed her the phone.

"Thank the Lord," she said and took it.

"Yeah," Frank said. "Angel pot heads to the rescue."

"What?"

He waved the comment off. "Tell them they're going to need to bring in a hazmat crew. Maybe two-dozen pounds of anthrax. Tell them ten of us are exposed. For of us have had massive exposure. And don't forget to send someone for Sayyid." Then he turned and walked back.

The sheriff dialed. A moment later he heard her say, "Carol, I've got a code red."

Frank turned to the doughty band of pot heads before him. He said, "I need one of you to pedal me back up the road a bit. I'd walk, but my foot ain't doing so well."

The cyclists looked down.

"Whoa," one of the guys said.

"Bad bunion," Frank said. "So who will give me a lift?"

The bigger guy in the back raised his hand. "I'll do it."

"Thank you," Frank said.

The guy turned his bicycle out of the pack.

Frank limped up and seated himself on the cargo rack above the back wheel.

"You ready?" the guy asked.

Frank scooted back and grabbed onto the saddle post with one hand and the bike rack with the other. "Ready," he said.

The biker pushed off, then got his feet on the pedals and began to pump, good powerful strokes. The guy shifted up, and they were soon clipping down the road, Frank bouncing along.

When they got to the end of the flat part, the guy stood on his pedals to get a good run up the hill.

Frank said, "I need you to stop up there by those three big red boulders."

"Right," the guy said.

He pedaled Frank up and stopped. Frank hopped off. The dirt in the road was stained.

"What's that?" the guy asked.

"Blood," Frank said. It was from where the operator fell. But his neck must not have been snapped because a trail of blood spots led off the road. Frank didn't think the operator had gotten far. He said, "You wait here."

"Right," the guy said.

Frank limped his way off the road. He found the operator back in a little fold of ground behind some sage lying on his back, eyes staring straight into the sky, his hand covering the wound in his gut.

Frank reached down and felt for a pulse, but the operator had gone on to his reward.

With the area cleared, Frank limped back out to his bike taxi and said, "Let's go back down."

40
Bleach

THE BLACK HAWKS came flying in maybe fifteen minutes later, which meant they had already been in the air when the sheriff called, which meant Gary the trike pirate had either made good time on his three-speeder or flagged someone down and made the call. Either way, that soldier had done his duty.

The Black Hawks flew over the site maybe a thousand feet up to reconnoiter the situation, but the pilots did not set their birds down anywhere close to the meadow because their rotor wash would only kick up the anthrax. Instead, they landed back down the road, on the other side of the ridge where the bikers had come from.

A minute or so after landing, a number of military moon people came walking over the hill with all their decontamination equipment. Meanwhile other choppers arrived and began to work a pattern a few miles wide. Frank figured they were making a safety perimeter to keep folks out.

It took the moon men a few minutes to arrive. When they did, the lead said, "I'm Captain Richard Hellewell. Please give me a full report."

Frank reported what had happened at the site while a group of moon men went out into the sage meadow to clean the spill and another group set up a decontamination line.

The line consisted of a blue vinyl collection pool that was about a foot high, four feet wide, eight feet long, and was supported with a skeleton of aluminum poles. The pool was secured with stakes. Inside the pool went two black plastic elevation grids that were three feet square. The grids looked like large, flat plastic milk crates turned upside down.

If this decontamination line had been somewhere these folks could have run a garden hose, it would have had a shower at the far end. But this part of the desert was short on garden hoses, so two moon men stood to either side of the pool carrying handheld tanks and sprayers. They asked Frank to go first.

The process was simple. Frank stepped onto the first elevation grid in the pool. The moon man asked him to disrobe. Frank pulled everything off—boots, pants, shirt, undershirt, underpants, socks. He had to sit on the grid to get the lower items off because of his foot. When he was finished, he stood naked in the desert sun and breeze, and they asked him to step to the next elevation grid.

Behind him, the first moon man sprayed his clothes with a bleach solution. Another bagged them. The moon man with a sprayer at the second elevation grid asked Frank to hold his arms out. Frank did and shut his eyes. And then the man began to soak him, top to bottom, with a strong solution that smelled like a hundred-proof-chlorine indoor swimming pool. The bleach solution got into the wound on Frank's foot, which now really was roasting in Hell, but he didn't say a word. A minute or so later, the man finished, leaving Frank dripping in the breeze.

They then directed him off of the elevation grid and onto a piece of vinyl they'd laid down like a floor mat outside the pool.

Frank said, "I guess all this bleach means that when I grow my hair out, it will have that great frosted look."

The moon man was not amused. Instead, he pointed Frank to the moon man medic who examined his foot, wrapped it with sterile gauze, then gave Frank some fine army-green scrubs and booties to wear.

"I guess it's pajama day," Frank said.

"Sir, it's going to be pajama day for a while," the medic said and pointed him to yet another who motioned him forward. Frank complied.

"You ever been vaccinated for anthrax?" the medic asked.

"Yes," Frank said. "Back in the military, more than ten years ago."

"We're going to do it again. Three courses. You'll get one today. The next one is in two weeks. The final is two weeks after that."

Frank nodded.

The medic reached down to a little case open on a rock that

held a dozen little bottles of vaccination. He picked one up, poked a syringe into the neck of the little bottle, sucked the liquid out, held the syringe up straight, and pushed the air out with a little squirt. "Let me see your arm," he said.

Frank pulled up the sleeve of his PJs.

The medic poked him and pushed the vaccine in. "That's for the long haul. The spores can stick around for sometimes two months, and you want to be ready for the buggers. For the immediate-term, we're going to give you anti-microbials and anti-toxins."

"Thank you," Frank said.

The medic gave Frank three pills in a little paper cup and some water. Frank downed them, then was asked to stand aside.

Frank stepped to the side, then sat on the ground and elevated his foot. Weariness settled upon him, and he figured that since the action was over, his adrenaline had dropped, which meant he was going to have to deal with his foot without any of that super juice.

They helped the sheriff up and onto the first elevation grid in the pool. She stood there with help from one of the moon men, and began to take off her clothing.

Frank caught one of the pot heads waiting expectantly for the last articles of clothing to come off. But then the pot head saw Frank's death stare and suddenly decided the hills were incredibly interesting.

Maybe Frank was old-fashioned, but every woman deserved respect and privacy in a situation like this. And that one there deserved it in spades.

Frank himself looked out at the crew cleaning the spill as the moon men here sprayed and bagged her clothes, then sprayed her down. He heard her sucked in her breath once as the chemical burned in her wounds. After that the only sound she emitted was a few grunts of pain through gritted teeth.

When they finished, they put her on a combat litter, and the medic field dressed her wounds. He helped her get into her own pair of jammies, and then four guys carried her back down the road toward the choppers. The men were strong, capable, and didn't complain, the epitome of what soldiers should be.

They offered Frank a litter, but he climbed to his feet and said he could walk. But the man in charge said they didn't have time to wait for him to limp along, and so Frank put his arm around one man on either side, and he walked with his two new buddies behind the sheriff. Up the hill, past the blood on the road, over the top, and to a waiting Black Hawk with a red cross on a white field. As they made their way, more helicopters arrived. These were not military, but law enforcement and medical.

The soldiers secured the sheriff's litter inside and pointed Frank to a seat. He put on his safety harness and found he was close enough to reach out and grab her ankle. He gave her a squeeze as one of the medics checked her pulse. He said, "With those mad glider skills you could join up with James Bond or Batman."

She said, "Or the flying monkeys."

"What?"

"Didn't you say Bill was Almira Gulch?"

Ah, he thought. So she was coming around to his way of thinking. He said, "She's definitely somewhere in his family tree."

"I guess that makes you Dorothy," she said.

He said, "You're getting delirious. I don't look anything like Dorothy."

She said, "But you're going to Disneyland."

The female co-pilot overheard her and said. "Not quite. We're taking you to Vegas."

"Awesome," Frank said. "It's not every day you can get anthraxed, shaken down for your money, and then browse an all-you-can-eat buffet."

"We'll set you up at a bingo table," the co-pilot said.

Then the pilot flipped some switch, and she turned back to the controls.

Frank thought that Vegas was probably where these choppers had come from. More importantly, Vegas was probably the location of the nearest major hospital.

He looked at the sheriff. When the medic by the decontamination pool had asked if she'd ever been vaccinated for anthrax, she said no, which meant she was starting from scratch. And doing so with a lot of lost blood.

Not a good way to start.

The best an early treatment could do against anthrax was give a person fifty-fifty odds. He wondered how much her current blood loss would change that. Would it make it forty-sixty, thirty-seventy?

"You're going to be okay," Frank said and gave the sheriff's ankle another squeeze, but the sheriff was having a hard time keeping awake.

41

Coin Toss

THEY FLEW TO VEGAS, but it was not to the strip or a hospital in the city. It was to Nellis Air Force Base, home to more squadrons than any other air force base in the country.

They operated on the sheriff there and took care of Frank's foot. Then they were hustled onto a waiting transport plane that was the military's version of a Boeing 737. During the flight, they were asked to give their full report yet again to three individuals from Homeland, one from the FBI, and a third who Frank figured for CIA.

A few hours later, they touched down at Andrews Air Force Base in Maryland, just a few miles south-east of the nation's capitol. And then it was a ride in an ambulance to the Walter Reed National Military Medical Center in Bethesda, which was about thirty minutes north of the Capitol and about thirty minutes south of Fort Detrick, home of the United States Army Medical Research Institute of Infectious Diseases, otherwise known as USAMRIID, the Army's main facility for research into countermeasures against biological warfare.

There were other hospitals in the nation that were set up to handle anthrax cases. Almost all of them would have been closer. But Frank suspected they wanted to keep this quiet, which might be a sketchy proposition in a civilian hospital.

They were led up to a special unit where it appeared they were the only guests. Blood samples were withdrawn, temperatures and blood pressure taken, urine analyzed, chest cavities examined with x-rays. All to get a baseline. They were given more anti-microbials and anti-toxins.

When the medicine men and women finished, Frank and the

sheriff gave their report yet again to another batch of men and women in suits. And during all of this, Frank kept his eyes on the TVs. There were reports on some bizarre plot involving murder at the nation's largest turkey farm, and other reports on next year's summer Olympics, and more on the great weather the nation was going to have for the Fourth of July. But there were none about southern Utah, much less any terrorist cell with anthrax.

He asked a nurse if she would mind googling Utah on her smart phone and reading him the top headlines. She said the top news items were about a parade, quagga mussel legislation, and some old guy that got stranded with a bunch of buffalo on an island out in the middle of the Great Salt Lake.

It was a complete blackout. Which Frank figured was good.

That night the sheriff called her sister to tell her that she had an emergency meeting she had to attend in Washington and ask if she could watch Lily. Then she called Lily.

They let Frank call his sister Kim, but he was told to keep the whole thing under wraps. His cover story was that he was having to report on an old military matter. After the calls, the doctors and nurses poked and prodded and checked. They prodded and checked again during the night and again the next morning. More folks on the case returned with additional questions, which Frank and the sheriff answered.

The next day they took doses of anti-microbials and anti-toxins, and fought the little poison factories. On the third day the symptoms began. It didn't feel like death in the making. It felt like a cold. But on the next day the poison factories were in full swing, breeding in their tens of thousands, maybe their millions, and it became more than a cold.

On the Fourth, they were served Fourth of July cake, Fourth of July Jell-O, and Fourth of July ice cream. And Frank groggily tried to watch the news about the various celebrations and wondered if there were other cells out there.

It was also on Independence Day when the doctors found fluid building up in both of their lungs. The remedy was a long syringe and needle to suck the fluid and tens of thousands of the little poison factories away with it. But there were still many factories that had entered the blood stream—there were multitudes traveling around Frank's and the sheriff's bodies.

Over the next days, there was more fluid and its removal and pain and anti-microbials and anti-toxins and poking and prodding and oxygen masks, and still Frank's and the sheriff's chances were no better than the toss of a coin.

One evening, Frank was sitting with the sheriff when she called to talk to Lily on the phone and reiterate her cover story. She held the little rock sheriff in her hand and traced its contours as she told Lily what a grand time she was having and hid her labored breathing. And Lily said she loved staying with Aunt Marion, but really missed her mom.

After the call, two nurses came in, and the four of them tried to play a game of Bunco, but the sheriff didn't have the strength to do more than one hand.

A few days later, Frank began to feel better. He was by no means out of the woods, but it appeared his body had mounted its defense. However, the sheriff was still struggling.

Fifty-fifty, he thought. The toss of a coin. And all of that complicated by a massive exposure.

The sheriff was a fighter, one who managed her stress and worry by thinking one minute at a time. By looking forward. By laughing and being grateful despite the dark rings around her eyes and the drawn face and the difficulty breathing. And the whole time her little rock sheriff stood watch on the wheeled tray they kept next to her bed.

Anthrax incubated in one to six days. Frank watched the news, hoping not to hear of any outbreak. July seventh passed, then the eighth, then the ninth, and no reports of an influx of flu-like cases appeared anywhere.

Except Frank's came back. They said it was common, to experience a calm before the storm, and continued to pump him with anti-microbials and anti-toxins.

The sheriff, on the other hand, began to mend. Three weeks after they'd entered, she was looking hale and hearty. A few days later, she was cleared to go home, on an out-patient basis. But Frank was asleep when her ride came, and she left without saying good-bye.

A few days later, Frank's struggle turned a positive direction. A week after that, he was thinking he'd beaten the death factories. It was on that day, just after a lunch of chicken, rice, and green beans with a texture of Styrofoam, that a number of serious men in suits poured into the hospital wing. Two came into Frank's room and looked in the bathroom and closet. Two others stayed outside the door. They all were wearing shoulder holsters under their blazers.

And then another suit, a female this time, entered. She was followed by the President of the United States. The President was a big man, a former colonel in the Marines. On TV, you could feel the presence of the man. In person, it rolled off him in waves.

He smiled. "Soldier," he said.

Frank moved to get out of bed to salute, but the President waved him back down. "Do not stand up for me, sir. Good lord, do *not* stand up for me."

Frank remained where he was.

The President looked at the finished plate of food. "They feeding you steak?"

"Not quite, sir."

"You a steak man?"

"Medium rare."

"I've got a friend out west that raises Wagyu. It's an Angus-Kobe mix. You've got to mix those little Kobe buggers with something big like Angus to get a decent quantity of meat. And that meat—it melts on your fork before it gets to your mouth. Mr. Shaw, once you have a taste of that, you're ruined for regular beef."

"Sounds delicious," Frank said. And it did. Try as they might, hospital food just didn't have the power to make you stand up and shout.

"That settles it then. I'm going to have some sent over." He looked at the nurse. "We can do that, can't we?"

"I think so. We might have to check with the doctor."

"I would appreciate it if you would. We've got to get some blood in this boy's veins."

"Yes, Mr. President."

Frank said, "Thank you, sir."

"How much longer are they going to keep you here?"

"They tell me some spores can take up to sixty days to activate. So I'll be at risk for a while, but if the blood tests continue in the current direction, I might be out next week."

The President shook his head. "You survived some bad kitty litter."

"Sir?"

"Weaponized anthrax is often made with fine materials like talc or bentonite. This stuff happened to be made with bentonite, which is the type of clay used in all sorts of stuff, including some brands of kitty litter."

"We were going to be attacked with kitty litter?"

"You'll never look at it the same way."

"No sir," Frank said.

"I hear you were with the seventh Special Forces group."

"Yes sir."

"Honorable discharge."

"Yes sir."

"Ran into a little trouble after that."

"Yes sir."

"We all make mistakes, son. Every one of us. It's what you do afterwards that matters. And you've done a splendid job."

Frank's heart welled. The emotion shocked him, and he put it down to all the pills and poison factories.

He said, "The sheriff did most of the work."

The President smiled. "Strangely enough, that's what she said about you."

Frank said, "Did we get any intel out of this?"

The President sat on the corner of the bed. "A small mother lode," he said. Then he told Frank they traced the cell back to Germany, then Kuwait. The Lions of God were a new, well-funded group, with a lot of private Kuwaiti money.

"What about the women?" Frank asked.

"Interesting question. We don't know everything, but the one you fought in the field, she was a scientist. Trained at a German university.

Usually, these groups turn their women into suicide bombers. But this was something new."

Frank shook his head. "Is that where they got the anthrax?"

The President said, "They can tell bacteria family lines and trace most right back to the lab. Certain labs give birth to this or that family. This one wasn't one of ours. Not even one of the strains that we gave to Saddam Hussein decades ago. And it wasn't German, as far as we know."

"Russian?" Frank asked.

"We don't think so," the President said. "But don't you worry about that. We're going to bury these guys. We're going to find each one and bury them. And we won't be doing it alone. Our friends in the Middle East are just as determined as we are."

Frank thought of Sayyid and wondered how deeply the Saudis and others had penetrated that organization. He wanted to chat more about that, but the President steered the conversation to Frank's work and doughnuts. They briefly chatted about his plans and whether he had a wife or girlfriend waiting for him back home, and then the President said he would have loved to hear more about what Frank had done downrange, but he had some very important meetings about this matter to attend. He stood and offered his hand.

Frank shook it, and the President passed something circular into Frank's palm. He kept his grip and looked Frank in the eye. "The nation will never know about your excellent service. But I know." Then he got a little twinkle in his eye. "Even if you did choose the wrong branch of the military."

"Hooah," Frank said.

The President released his firm grip and said, "I can't wait for you to taste those steaks." And then he told Frank to get well soon, signaled his people, and left. The bustle of Secret Service agents followed him out and moved away down the hall.

When Frank was alone, he looked down at the large coin in his hand. It was a tradition in the military in some branches to have a special coin minted for a particular unit. They were thick and large and were given out as a gesture of gratitude, friendship, and respect.

They were made of silver, gold, brass, or bronze. He had no idea the President would have one. On one side of the bronze coin was minted the full-color seal of the President of the United States. On the other side was a circle cutout of the American flag bordered by a bronze ring. Around the arc at the top of the ring was written "For Courage Honor And Commitment." Around the bottom was the president's name.

Frank knew there were thousands of men and women, tens of thousands, who would have done exactly what he had done. But the coin still felt good and heavy in his hand, and he wondered just how many people had one of these coins from the President of the United States.

42

Fourth

THEY RELEASED FRANK on the twenty-fourth of July. He rode in a Hummer from Walter Reed back to Andrews Air Force Base, then flew in a transport back to Nellis with a handful of other passengers that looked at his tattoos but didn't ask questions. From there the military paid for him to take a little commercial flight from Vegas to St. George, Utah. When he walked out of the airport, he saw a taxi cab driver holding up a sheet of paper with "Frank Shaw" printed in big bold letters.

It appeared that Uncle Sam had decided to foot the bill to get him all the way back to Kanab. He rode in the taxi along the southern route that took him through Colorado City, a town of polygamists who had no relation to the one that had knocked him off the mountain, and past a range of towering orange, red, and white cliffs. He rode into Kanab without any fanfare.

The driver dropped him off in the parking lot of the Kane County Sheriff's office. In the parking lot sat his Nova. Across the way was the house with the chickens in the yard. Five of them were sitting on the decorative post fence watching Frank.

The day was a typical Utah summer day, full of sun and heat and a vibrant blue sky. A few blocks down, the light traffic motored by.

Frank walked over to the office, taking it nice and easy on his healing foot, opened the door, and walked inside. Carol, the same woman he'd seen here the first time he'd come to town, was sitting at the desk. She looked at him over the top of her reading glasses.

"Mr. Shaw?" she asked.

Frank said, "I was hoping you had my keys."

She smiled. "We've got keys and a few other things." She opened a filing cabinet and pulled out a clear Ziploc bag and put it on the desk. "You want to sign for it?"

"Sure," Frank said and took the clipboard and paper she handed him. He signed, and she handed his goods over.

She said, "We also have this." And she reached down and pulled out a wrapped gift. It was a small roll of something in bright pink wrapping paper and a bow on top.

He took it. "What's this?" he asked. The package was soft, like a roll of socks.

"Oh, a little something from all of us to you. Why don't you open it?"

Frank held his Ziploc under his arms, then found the seam on the wrapping paper, slipped his thumb in, and tore the paper off. Inside was a roll, but not of socks. It was a brand new six-pack of men's Hanes with a leopard print on them.

Carol said, "The sheriff said you might be needing a new pair."

Frank said, "I'm touched."

Carol shrugged. "We aim to please."

He said, "Is the sheriff in?"

"Not at this moment."

He felt a little disappointed, but figured she was probably spending quality time with Lily or out on patrol. "Well, tell her I said hello."

"I will do that," Carol said.

Frank turned and walked outside into the sun with his Ziploc and Hanes. He walked over to the Nova, slipped in the key, and unlocked the door. He looked around for any sign of the sheriff, but there was none, and he figured she would have known he was coming, and if she'd wanted to meet him, she would have been here. So he guessed he'd have to take a rain check on that lunch.

He got into the car and started her up. She roared to life, but not as loudly as she had before, and he realized someone must have fixed the busted muffler, and he wondered who the good Sam had been.

He backed out of the stall, then drove out of the parking lot and onto the road. He drove down to the main drag, signaled, then pulled out into traffic.

He didn't make it the full block before he heard a siren behind him. He looked in his rearview mirror and saw an SUV pulling up, its red and blue lights flashing.

His heart picked up a notch, and he looked down at his speedometer and saw he was over, and thought this was just his luck. He pulled to the side of the road, noting the fact that he'd just helped take down a terrorist cell, and yet the flashing lights still made him nervous.

The SUV pulled over behind him.

And then the door to the SUV opened, and Sheriff Hood got out.

His anxiety dropped, and a wave of happy expectation washed over him. He watched her walk to the driver's side door and thought he would have no problem at all having her pull him over more often.

She stopped outside his open window and said, "You in that big a hurry to get to Disneyland?"

He said, "I'm in no hurry at all."

"You were over the limit, Romeo."

"You can't trust those radars," he said.

"Spoken like a true ex-con," she said teasingly. "How you feeling?"

"Like a million bucks," he said.

"The plane flight was that good?"

"Any place that isn't a morgue is that good."

"Amen to that," she said.

He motioned at her leg and torso where she'd been shot. "What about you?"

"Better, but not quite a hundred percent yet."

He nodded, knowing not quite a hundred was a heck of a lot better than dead.

She said, "Have you eaten?"

"Oh, the lady wants to do lunch?"

"I hate having outstanding debts."

Frank smiled.

She said, "Why don't we go to Edna's. You can finally get your burger with a side of zesty garden tomatoes."

"Well, I won't say no to an officer of the law."

"Very wise."

Frank watched her walk all the way back to her SUV, enjoying the way she walked, enjoying more the knowledge that she'd made it back home to her little entrepreneur. She pulled out, and Frank followed her.

They sat at a booth in the back. When they opened their menus, Frank said, "I've got it. You're one of those soup and salad types, aren't you? You're going to order arugula and cucumbers."

She just smiled. The waitress came back. Frank ordered his Edna burger with the slices of garden tomato.

The sheriff looked up at the waitress.

Frank waited expectantly.

She said, "I'll have the beans."

"Beans?" Frank asked.

The sheriff smiled and handed her menu to the waitress who left to place their order with the cook.

"Beans?" Frank asked again. "When did beans ever make a top-ten food list?"

"You haven't had Edna's Bean Zing with zucchini."

"Really?" Frank said, not believing this.

"Really," she said.

"Beans," Frank said and realized this sheriff was full of surprises.

She took a sip of her cold water. Frank took a gulp of his. And then they compared notes about their time in Walter Reed. They chatted about the Fourth and crime in Kanab and Lily's rock business. She asked him about doughnuts, and he made her laugh with an anecdote about the time he'd delivered a doughnut singing gram and had the cops called on him. And then the waitress brought out their food.

The burger looked terrific. The beans looked liked beans.

But then the sheriff dipped her spoon in them and held out a bite for him to try.

Frank took it. Chewed. Felt his mouth celebrate in surprise.

"Leaping legumes," he said.

"Edna's a goddess," she said.

And Frank realized these beans might make a top-ten list after all.

They ate and chatted about her rugby days and where they both grew up which led to other topics. And then her cell phone rang.

She looked down at it and said, "I've got to go."

"You know, you've got deputies."

"Today's a big day," she said. "They're all on duty."

"What's so big about today?"

"It's the Twenty-fourth," she said.

He looked at her.

"July 24, 1847 is when the old Mormon pioneers arrived up by Salt Lake City, and Brigham Young declared 'this is the place.'"

"The place for what?"

"To put down roots and build their society. They were looking for freedom from oppression, and they figured they'd find it in the Great Basin desert, probably because nobody else would want to be there."

"Utah isn't so bad."

"Utah's great. But back then, coming from the lush valleys of Ohio, Missouri, and Illinois, the desert must have looked like a death sentence. But they gave it a go and made it blossom, and we now throw a big celebration with fireworks every year in honor of those old pioneers."

"Fireworks?"

"It's like having two Fourths of July." And then she pulled out her wallet and put two bills on the table that would cover the cost of the meal plus a good tip.

He said, "Hang on, Quick Draw. I still don't know your first name."

"It's on the city website."

She was going to make him google it? "Are you kidding me?"

But the twinkle in her eye revealed she was teasing. She enjoyed her joke a little longer then said, "Susan."

"Susan Hood," he said, getting used to the sound, and felt the man brain exerting itself. This time he didn't shut it down.

He said, "I don't know when I might be in Kanab again, but I've got this connection on Wagyu beef. I think it would be dynamite with Edna's beans."

"Wagyu?" she asked.

"It's an Angus-Kobe cross. It melts off your fork before it gets to your mouth. This is what I'm told."

"It sounds like a spectacular steak."

"It has to be tried. I just need your number to coordinate the event."

She tilted her head. "You're asking for my number?"

"I thought it would be a good idea."

She paused.

He said, "It's Wagyu steak. What have you got to lose?"

"I thought you and your buddies were on your way to pick up hot moms at the Bear Country Jamboree."

He said, "Maybe I already found one."

She looked at him, and he knew that her woman brain was factoring in at least a dozen things including his history and the tattoo on his face.

"I might have a boyfriend."

"You would have talked about him. So even if there is some guy, you're not fully committed."

She looked at him, ran two fingers across her bottom lip, thinking.

He said, "It's Wagyu beef. Nothing more."

The silence stretched long.

And then all of her dozen factors must have lined up because she nodded and said, "Okay. I can do Wagyu."

Frank grinned, then decided he really liked her eyes.

The sheriff pulled her law enforcement business card out of her pocket, took her pen and wrote a number on the back, then held the card out to him.

Frank took it, looked at the number that was written in a woman's clear, feminine script.

And then her cell phone rang again.

"You've got to go," he said.

"The sheriff's part of the parade," she said.

"There's a parade?"

"Like I said, it's a celebration."

Frank nodded, then motioned toward the front door and said, "We wouldn't want you to be late to the parade."

She smiled, turned, and waved to the waitress. Then Frank walked her to the door of the restaurant and out on the sidewalk.

She said, "So where you headed?"

"Disneyland," he said.

"That wasn't just a line?"

"My sister and nephew are still waiting. I missed celebrating the Fourth with them. I can't miss this."

"Enjoy the teacups."

"You'd better believe I will."

They bid each other farewell, and then the sheriff put on her sunglasses and walked to her sheriff SUV. Frank watched her start it up and pull out. And then he walked to the Nova parked in the sunshine. He started her up, pulled out into traffic, and headed down the main drag.

There were banners announcing Pioneer Day, and people were beginning to set up on the sidewalks and curbs with strollers and folding camp chairs. It had been weeks since the Fourth, but American flags still fluttered on every lamp post down both sides of the street.

They were seeking freedom, the sheriff had said.

Something shifted inside him.

He saw kids running around with snow cones. He saw two little girls being dragged along the sidewalk by Jack Russell terrier.

He thought of the kids in San Diego and Seattle and St. Louis and Nashville and Boston, and all the other cities on that map back at the ranch. He thought of their mothers and fathers.

And suddenly a number of holidays paraded before his eyes—Thanksgiving, Christmas, Hanukkah, Martin Luther's, Valentine's, Ramadan.

In America you could even celebrate things like April Fool's Day and that goofy Star Wars May the Fourth Be With You Day that Frank's neighbor Sam celebrated. All because of that one fourth of July so long ago.

The idea expanded, switching things around in his mind.

He gave the Nova some gas. The engine rumbled.

The flags and pioneer celebrators and storefronts rushed past.

The downtown gave way to a couple of subdivisions of homes which soon petered out, and then he was roaring along the desert highway, the sun shining, the wind blowing through his open windows, the radio blasting a great oldie. He began to hum along and tap the door frame.

He'd thought he'd missed the celebration. Heck, he hadn't even begun to celebrate.

The End

Dear Reader

I HOPE YOU enjoyed the ride. If you did, please consider leaving a review at your favorite bookseller's website, even if it's only a line or two. Leaving a review not only helps your fellow readers, it also helps me continue to bring you more books.

Your review means a lot.

And I'm sure it will also probably support a unicorn somewhere avoid extinction.

Author's Note

MUCH OF THE WORLD has given up on building empires of the sort that physically dominate other lands and peoples, although Russia under Putin seems to sometimes still long for the old days. However, the debates about how best to govern a people, state, or even the world continue. The Islamist view is that God has the best idea, and while he isn't here at the moment, he left enough instructions for us to run it on our own.

It sounds splendid, unless you don't think the instructions are really all that clear, or don't believe Muhammad talked to any sort of god, or run into those Islamists who feel God commanded them to implement this government by the sword or an AK-47, whichever is handiest.

Those who prefer a liberal democracy could easily ignore the Islamists if their numbers were few. But they are not. Furthermore, the Islamist ideology appears to be gaining adherents. And while it's true that folks like the Christian Dominionists seek a theocracy as well, none of them have tried to push it by cutting people's heads off.

If you are interested in learning more about Islam and the theocratic threat of Islamism, let me recommend three wonderful introductions by long-time journalists who write with clarity, wit, and a deep understanding of their subject, telling the story instead of laying out dry facts. These three volumes are: *Understanding Islam: An Introduction to the Islamic World*, 3rd ed, by Thomas W. Lippman, which will help you understand what the religion is all about; *The Crisis of Islam: Holy War and Unholy Terror* by Bernard Lewis, which explains the events of the twentieth century that have led to the rise of Islamism today; and *After the Prophet: The Epic Story of the Shia-Sunni Split in Islam* by Lesley Hazleton, which will help you understand the fundamental schism driving much of the conflict between Muslims in the Middle East.

After those introductions, you'll probably want to focus further on Islamism itself. Let me recommend you start with *Heretic: Why Islam*

Needs a Reformation Now by Ayaan Hirsi Ali, who herself was once a member of the Muslim Brotherhood and shares insights only someone who has lived it can. Next, I would read *The Looming Tower: Al-Qaeda and the Road to 9/11* by Lawrence Wright. It's is a fascinating narrative of the growth of Islamism (Wright calls it "Islamic fundamentalism") and the rise of al-Qaeda. Finally, I think you'll enjoy *A Battle for the Soul of Islam: An American Muslim Patriot's Fight to Save His Faith* by M. Zuhdi Jasser Ph.D., a practicing Muslim who is fed up with Islamism and the political correctness protecting it.

For those who want to know how to fight violent Islamists in the short term, I haven't found anything with more real-world insight than *Crush the Cell: How to Defeat Terrorism Without Terrorizing Ourselves* by Michael A. Sheehan who is arguably the one of the most authoritative front-line voices on counterterrorism, having worked as the Deputy Commissioner of Counter Terrorism for the New York City Police Department, Coordinator for Counterterrorism for the State Department, and as a Green Beret in the U.S. Army. For fighting Islamism in the long term, Thomas P.M. Barnett offers some interesting ideas in "The Pentagon's New Map" found in the January 29, 2007 issue of *Esquire* (google the article and the map).

Finally, some of you probably want more information on biological weapons. If you haven't read it yet, you'll love *Biohazard: The Chilling True Story of the Largest Covert Biological Weapons Program in the World – Told from Inside by the Man Who Ran It* by Ken Alibek with Steven Handleman. Not only does it have one of the longest subtitles known to man, it's a thrilling eye-opener.

After reading that, you may want to relax <grin> by googling "drones crop dusting" . . .

Acknowledgements

WHO HAS SOME of the best beta readers and experts around? Me.

A huge thanks goes to **Eric Allen** for a thoughtful first, then second reader response, and for saving me from humiliation by underwear; **Stephen Carlson** for not only demonstrating his drone on the BYU campus to me just before the Stadium of Fire celebrations (and giving me one of the key ideas of the book), but also for the many follow up discussions and passion for his tech; The team at **Damonza** for the cover art that just nailed it; **Devon Dorrity** for generously making time to put the cover together; **Kevin Evans** for the thoughtful reader response and the long conversation which confirmed he needs to be a character in his own novel; **Rick Hellewell** for his web mastery and his excellent and lightning-quick reader response; **Jared Johnson** for the read, multiple ride-alongs full of fascinating stories and insights, and for throwing in the helpful wrench at the very last moment about Kanab's tracking program (which actually led to a more delightful interaction between Frank and the sheriff); **Kip Motta** for the helpful read, expertise about flying, and enthusiastic support; **Edie Ogilvie** for sharp-eyed editing; **Gary Ogilvie** for taking time to read and bring his broad expertise in law enforcement; **David Rankin** for details and insights that only a real life flash flood chaser can provide; **Louise Speth** for the time spent reading and her surprising insights into both police work in general and female cops in particular; and **Anne Squire** for being such a fan. Thank you, all. Any errors in the text are, of course, mine.

Finally, my most supreme thanks goes to **Nellie Brown** who spent hours reading, copyediting, and listening to me tell her the funny parts and laugh at my own jokes.

By John D. Brown

Frank Shaw Thrillers

Bad Penny
Awful Intent

Epic Fantasies

Servant: The Dark God Book One
Curse: The Dark God Book Two
Raveler: The Dark God Book Three

Shorter Works

Bright Waters
Loose in the Wires
The Scent of Desire
From the Clay of His Heart

Don't Miss Out!

Join the many readers who have asked to be notified when the next book is out at by signing up at **johndbrown.com**.

About the Author

JOHN D. BROWN lives with his wife and four daughters in the hinterlands of Utah where one encounters much fresh air, many good-hearted ranchers, and the occasional wolf.

Feel free to drop by his website **johndbrown.com** to post comments or just say hello. He always enjoys hearing from readers.

76587742R00210

Made in the USA
San Bernardino, CA
13 May 2018